Losing Sight

Losing Sight

Tati Richardson

Generous Press

AN IMPRINT OF ROW HOUSE PUBLISHING
BELLINGHAM, WASHINGTON

Because we at Generous Press and Row House Publishing believe that the best stories are born in the margins, we proudly spotlight, amplify, and celebrate the voices of diverse, innovative creators. Through independent publishing, we strive to break free from the control of Big Publishing and oppressive systems, ensuring a more liberated future for us all.

Library of Congress Cataloging-in-Publication Data Available Upon Request

ISBN 9781955905817 (TP)
ISBN 9781955905824 (eBook)

Printed in the United States

Distributed by Simon & Schuster

Design by Neuwirth & Associates, Inc.
Cover design by Becca Fox
Cover illustration by Mlle Belamour
Chapter flourishes by Virgil A. Harker
Author photo by Lynda Louis Photography

First edition
10 9 8 7 6 5 4 3 2 1

Mama, thank you for seeing me for who I am.
Until the end. Always.

&

Dr. Gideon K. Mincey.
We miss you, Doc. Rest in Power.

DEAR READER

Losing Sight is a work of fiction that celebrates romance, healing, humor, sex, desire, friendship, sneakers, and magic. It also references topics that some may find difficult. These include:

Car accidents
Death (off-page), including cancer, loss of a spouse,
    and loss of a parent
Ghosts and supernatural occurrences
Miscarriage (mentioned briefly)
Parental abandonment
Sexual harassment/coercion

As always, proceed with love, caution, and care.

Love,
Tati

CHAPTER 1

"And that's it, folks. Derrick LaFleur has said goodbye to the game he loves one last time. And on his own terms, he will hang up his bowling shoes. Forever. Reporting for WWSN, I'm Nikki Ryan."

The sound of her own voice brought Tanika back to the present. She had been absently chewing on half a broken pencil as she reviewed segment footage with Danny Ramos, a network producer and one of her oldest friends. She stood and put a hand on his shoulder, squeezing gently.

"I think that's it, Danny. I think that's the final cut." Her voice was laced with exhaustion.

"Yeah, after I finally found a clip that I could use. You were squinting through every other take, Tanika. Like the sun was in your eyes. You alright?"

Tanika groaned, rubbing her forehead. "Well, blame that on the teleprompter. They made sure that thing was unreadable, just to make me look bad."

"Uh-huh." Having produced Tanika's segments for the last fifteen years, Danny was used to this attitude. Tanika was a perfectionist, and if anything was amiss, it was someone else's fault.

"I wouldn't put anything past them. Anything to get me outta here." Tanika slumped down in the chair next to Danny, tossing her pencil into a makeshift holder shaped like Tom Brady's butt—a gag from last Christmas's white elephant gift exchange.

"Don't I know it, kid," said Danny, smoothing down his sleek black ponytail. "I don't know what you did to piss off the big guys, but taking you off *Thursday Night Football* was the worst mistake ever. The new chick . . ."

Tanika held up her hand, which was enough of a signal to shut Danny up. The mere mention of Sara Taylor, her replacement for *Thursday Night Football*, made the cornrows under her wig itch. A former pageant queen, Sara was young and bright, with barely enough sports knowledge to qualify for the job. She didn't appear to be a "know-it-all," a complaint lodged against Tanika by viewers who preferred their female journalists to act a little less "uppity"—something Black women were called often. Most of all, Sara possessed the right amount of Meghan-Markle-racial-ambiguousness to resonate with middle American viewers. She was nonthreatening, unlike Tanika, whose dark brown skin, ample curves, and casual rapport with the athletes she interviewed weren't hitting the numbers with the target audience. Or so said Ross, the network president. Hence, Tanika had suddenly been relegated to sports purgatory, covering bowling in Reno.

On another monitor, Sara was interviewing Jaheim Covington, the wide receiver for New York. The perky brunette was smiling as if her teeth were insured by Colgate. Tanika's eyes twitched rapidly as she unwittingly snapped a pencil in half. It was her third broken pencil of the evening.

"Um, how about we take our anger out on these instead?" Danny passed Tanika a string of strawberry licorice. "Don't let the shiny new model bother you. You're the best to do it."

"Oh, you and I both know that." Tanika smiled and leaned back in the chair as she chewed. Danny was a good friend, but he wasn't exaggerating. She was damn good at her job.

"We also both know the network does what they want. They are putting me out to pasture. Like the heifer I am."

Of course, Tanika knew her demotion was about more than ageism. It was about colorism and ratings, but she wasn't about to divulge that to Danny. He wouldn't understand. It was easiest to point to the part of this that most folks could wrap their brains around—the problem of women aging.

Danny smiled, then quickly stopped. "Do you know your next assignment? G League? Minor League Baseball? Canadian League? Dear god, is it going to be the NHL? Seems like they're punishing you for more than just getting old."

Tanika shuddered. "I hope we're not going to Canada. I can't deal with the cold. Covering games in Buffalo was bad enough! But Danny, watch your mouth—I'm not old, just seasoned."

Danny shook his head, amused.

"You know how it is in this game. It's all about the visuals and what appeals to the viewers. These crow's feet do not." Tanika rubbed the lines around her eyes.

"Well, hey—maybe something better is coming around the bend? If you believe the rumors. I read the piece in *Sports Ragz*—"

"Those are just rumors, Danny." Tanika waved him off. "I'll believe they're naming me VP of Programming when I hear it from their mouths. Ross did call me in for a meeting tomorrow morning." In truth, she worried the rumors were the network's way of buying time until they could find someone who would fit in better with the executives upstairs. But honestly? The job should have been hers.

Vanity, thy name is Tanika.

Tanika was one of the best to cover professional sports, and she knew it. Throughout her twenty-plus years in sports journalism, the accolades were many. She had won an Emmy and a Peabody for her piece on eating disorders among jockeys. She had interviewed some of the biggest names in just about every major American sport, even Hall of Famers. Tanika didn't just cover stats and scores; she told stories that had heart, gravitas, and humanity. That's what had made her a favorite of the network.

That, and her slick public image. Just a touch over forty, Tanika had done everything the network had asked to make herself look "presentable." She got Botox, went on diets, wore waist trainers and hot, uncomfortable wigs in the heat of Florida spring training, and had even started going by "Nikki" because it tested better with audiences.

Tanika was at the top of her game. Yet, being at the top as a *reporter* wasn't sparking joy for her. She needed something more—something that could affect real change. She knew it and so did everyone else. The word on every gossip blog and entertainment news show was that veteran sports journalist Tanika "Nikki" Ryan would soon be promoted to VP of Programming of WWSN, a position that had been vacant for a few months. Despite sending numerous candidates through a rigorous interview and vetting process, they'd yet to find someone.

Tanika was trying not to be cocky, but she more than deserved the promotion. She had endured so much as a reporter. In the early days of her career, players, coaches, and GMs had sexually harassed her. If she had a dollar for every unwanted dick pic or invitation to a nearby hotel, she'd be a millionaire. Maybe billionaire. She had been passed over or ignored during post-game interviews. She had been mistaken for a player's girlfriend or mistress. But in the end, she'd survived and cut her teeth in the high-pressure environment. Her ratings had been consistently higher than those of her counterparts—and her prime-time specials had often produced so much social media engagement that they were discussed on talk shows the next day.

It had all been good, until it hadn't.

At first she couldn't read the font on her scripts, so she asked for a larger typeface. Then her eyes wouldn't adjust to the teleprompter, so she asked that they move it closer. No big deal. But then the dizzying headaches started. They got so bad that she couldn't think straight, having to do multiple takes of the same line. Tanika asked her assistant, Mya, to make an appointment with a neurologist. Clearly, something was going on with her brain if she couldn't understand words on a screen. When the neurology report and CAT scans came back spotless, Tanika deduced that it had to be her blood pressure. When her primary care physician ran every blood test known to humanity and they came back clean, too, Tanika grew nervous. Maybe it was stress. Maybe she'd made it all up in her mind.

The next time she sat in the exam room, her doctor patted her hand reassuringly. "Tanika, you're in perfect health, except I think you better go to an optometrist. Maybe you need glasses."

Glasses? Oh, hell no. She'd have preferred to hear that she had alien spores growing out of her ears. Age was and had always been a killer in journalism, especially sports journalism. She understood she couldn't look like a college coed forever, but a prescription for granny glasses felt like a step too far. Were her eyes really that bad?

Tanika should have known not to get too comfortable. She was an unapologetically Black woman on television. Any little thing—including flubbing a line or two—was grounds for being sacked. She always had to be perfect. Hell, she had seen worse happen to her colleagues over the years. Jemele Hill, at their rival network, had been silenced for expressing her political views. Tanika's idol and colleague Pam Oliver had been replaced by the very blonde, very young Erin Andrews and relegated to the occasional game. But Tanika had never expected the very serious suits of Worldwide Sports Network to replace her with an empty-headed debutante with no real journalism experience. She was too valuable—their highest rated and paid reporter. Besides, who else could they have gotten who was tough enough to put up with all the bullshit that came with this job?

Still, against all odds, they'd handed the *Thursday Night Football* slot to Sara. Now shit was becoming a little too real.

Watching as Danny made a few post-edit tweaks, Tanika thought of all the ways she could possibly stick it to the network. First, she could sue. For the last year or so, her segments had been getting shorter and shorter. Tanika had to fight for on-air time and practically barge her way into postgame press conferences or locker rooms. Second, she could ask to be reassigned to another division. Professional football was extremely lucrative. But with her vast knowledge of all major sports, Tanika could practically work in any division. She could even ask to be moved to their London office; it could be cool to cover the English Premier League. She'd already met Beckham a time or two. Yeah, she'd just ask for that if she had to. But she didn't really want any of that. She wanted to be VP of Network Programming. She had more than paid her dues.

If she got the promotion, Tanika would be the highest-ranking woman or Black person in all of network sports television. Tanika Ryan, Vice President of Worldwide Sports Network. She really liked the sound of that. That VP job was hers. She could taste it.

"Tanika? Nikki?" said Danny, trying to get Tanika's attention. "Where did you go?"

"Sorry, Danny. What's up?" She tried to focus on the screen, which was now blurry. She blinked a few times, adjusting her eyes to the lights.

"I asked you if you will take the VP job if it comes up."

Tanika feigned uninterest in the topic. "You know, I haven't thought too much about it. But it would be a great opportunity. Besides, I've been kind of bored lately. Reporting isn't fun anymore. I mean, this position could be historic, you know."

Danny smirked. "Uh-huh. But you hadn't thought about it, right?"

They both let out a laugh.

Just then, there was a knock at the door. A big ginger afro announced Mya's presence before she fully stepped inside the room.

"Well, if it isn't the world's greatest yet greediest assistant." Tanika waved Mya in. "Loving the hair color this week. Very fierce. Even better than the blonde," Tanika teased. Mya knew just how to tap-dance on Tanika's nerves, but they had a great working relationship. Tanika saw Mya as the little sister she never had.

"Thank you, girl," Mya said as she did a twirl. "As much as I love your compliments, I came to tell you that you have a call from Ross on line one. He says it's urgent. Want to take it in here or in your office?"

Tanika tried to temper her expression. Her meeting with Ross was scheduled for tomorrow, Monday morning. It was late Sunday night. This could be a good or bad sign.

"Thanks Mya. I'll take it in my office."

Danny gave Tanika a bump with his fist. "You got this."

Tanika hurriedly followed Mya down the hall to her office. "So, what did he say besides 'urgent,' girl? Did he sound happy? Upset? What?"

Mya walked briskly. "Girl, I don't know. He always sounds like an uptight white dude to me."

Tanika frowned. "That's not helping."

"Well, that's all I got," shrugged Mya, pushing open Tanika's office door.

Tanika's door was emblazoned with her name. Just *Nikki Ryan*, no title. Everyone knew what she did. She didn't feel the need to put anything else. She stepped inside and paused at her desk before picking up the phone. Ross Spiegelman, president of the network, was coming to her either with bad news or to substantiate the rumors. Bracing herself for either outcome, she asked Mya to come in and close the door behind her. She picked up the line.

"Ross, is everything okay? What can I do for you?" Tanika slipped into her plush leather chair and put her heels up on the desk.

"Nikki! How are you? How's the piece on LaFleur coming up?"

She focused her attention on her signed Kobe Bryant Lakers jersey on the wall. She wasn't Catholic, but she did the sign of the cross anyway. *Black Mamba, give me strength!*

"It's going well. Shame that LaFleur is retiring at the peak of his career. He still has a hell of an arm. Still throwing strikes."

"Yeah, well, when you're washed up, it's better you leave on your own terms than be sent out to pasture," chuckled Ross.

Tanika froze. Hadn't she just told Danny she was being treated like an old heifer? Ross's joke felt ominous. She reclined in her chair and watched as Mya paced the floor. There was no use in telling the girl to chill. Mya was always jittery. Not a good attribute in an assistant. But she loved her anyway.

"So, what is it, Ross? You never call this late."

Tanika could hear Ross on the other end, shuffling papers and making tapping noises—she imagined he was either typing on a laptop or using his stylus in an aggressive manner. She massaged her temples in annoyance. Maybe this aggravating man was the cause of all her headaches.

"Nikki, I can't begin to tell you what it means to me that you've been so flexible these past few months."

"Uh-huh, flexible," repeated Tanika, trying her darndest not to emit the sarcasm that was bubbling to the surface.

"Yes, ma'am. And you've been a real role model for Sara, easing her right into the Thursday Night team with ease. She really looks up to you, you know?"

Tanika rolled her eyes. "Anything for the team, Ross. 'Cause you know I'm a team player." Lies.

"Great, which brings me to this," said Ross.

"Hold on, Ross. Let me put you on speaker." Tanika signaled Mya to sit down before she wore her heels down to a nub. Mya slid into the seat in front of Tanika's desk and pulled out her tablet. Maybe this was it. Maybe this was the promotion she'd been hearing about.

"Well, here's the thing. You know that hotshot F1 driver, Colin Bello?"

Tanika's eyes grew wide. "Of course; I know Colin. He's a talented cat. Won three championships before the age of thirty. Also a little cocky, but he backs it up."

"Yeah, and word on the street is that the cocky son of a bitch is now setting his eyes on the US and stock cars. Says he's bored of Europe."

"Oh, really?" A scoop on Colin coming to the US would definitely put Tanika back on track and out of the hellscape of late-night, offseason sports reporting. "So, he really thinks he has a shot at the cup series here?"

"He sure does. But of course, you know how tough that's gonna be for him. Being . . . European and all."

Tanika frowned. She wished Ross would just say what he really meant. Colin Bello was a Black Brit, and he was about to enter a world where very few folks of his complexion had a shot, let alone won a cup. He was going into nearly uncharted waters. "Well, I'm sure he'll do great. When's the interview? I can do London on short notice."

Ross paused. "Ah, Nikki, I think you're jumping the gun. What I called to ask was if you'd maybe have a talk with Sara. Calm her nerves. This is going to be a big interview for her."

Tanika's ears began to ring, and her head joined in with a hammering drum solo. *Sara? Are they fucking kidding?* The girl was barely legal as a driver herself, let alone mature enough to interview one of motor sports' premier athletes. She took a deep breath. "Are you serious right now, Ross? Sara doesn't . . . what could she possibly know about Colin? She's not ready for that."

Ross sighed. "Nik, you know I'd love to send you over to London to talk to Colin, but it's truly out of my hands. The big dogs want Sara. You know, they're both young, fresh faces. And let's be honest, babe, you've been a little off your game lately. It'll be good for the network. You said yourself that you're a team player, Nikki. So, help us out!"

Young? Fresh faces? All code for Tanika and her style of journalism being played out. She began wriggling out of her Chanel jacket, suddenly burning with the rage of a thousand suns. Mya headed over to the mini fridge to get Tanika some ice for the whiskey she was surely going to down after this.

"Fine. I'll get Mya to schedule a lunch with her this week. Go over some talking points."

She could hear Ross clap his hands. "Fantastic! Try and do that by tomorrow. And Nikki, don't view this as a slight. We still need you.

You're valuable to WWSN. You're doing a bang-up job covering our other spots. We're looking into airing national lacrosse games, and I want to talk to you about that. Later."

Before Tanika could respond with a "Lacrosse? Hell no," Ross was gone.

"These funky bastards!" Tanika yelled, rubbing her head. "I can't believe this shit. Do you know how big a fish an interview with Bello would be? I mean, talk about catapulting me back to prime time! And they wanna give it to Sara?"

Mya poured a glass of Uncle Nearest and handed it to Tanika. "Funky bastards indeed. You sure you want me to make the lunch date? You can say I forgot. Just blame it on me."

Tanika rubbed her eyes. "No. Let's not get fired for playing games. Just schedule it. But nowhere nice or trendy. Somewhere basic. Hell, Cheesecake Factory for all I care."

Mya laughed. "I'm sorry, but those avocado rolls be banging! Don't hate on CCF!" Mya typed a few words on her tablet, then paused. "Um, speaking of appointments, anything else you want me to schedule?"

Tanika looked over her whiskey glass and rolled her eyes. "You ain't slick, Mya."

Mya threw up her hands. "C'mon, Nikki! It's been weeks since your doctor told you to go to the optometrist. You keep putting it off. I can do all the work to find someone, and you can just show up and get your eyes checked out. Maybe then you wouldn't be flubbing lines, having raging headaches, or squinting at players."

"I get headaches because this whole network works my nerves."

"Excuses. Tanika, there is no shame in needing help to see!"

"I don't need glasses," Tanika deadpanned. "Glasses do not vibe with me."

"Who said anything about glasses? They have these things called *contacts*! Ever heard of them?"

Tanika shuddered. "Nope! I hate anything getting close to my eye, let alone me sticking a finger in there. Not happening. Hell, I have to take a sedative before I go to the lash tech." And by sedative, she meant a shot of vodka.

Tanika's phobia of anything touching her eye could be traced back to middle school, when she'd reluctantly taken drops for a nasty case of pink eye. Her mother had bribed her with an unlimited supply of M&M's to get her to comply.

"What about Lasik? I heard it's simple and painless."

Tanika folded her arms. "Girl, if I don't want to stick a finger in my eye, I damn sure don't want a laser beam coming straight for them. Hell no." She'd seen that horrible scene in *Final Destination*. This conversation made her squirm.

Mya came around the desk and slid a comforting arm across Tanika's shoulders. "Listen, I get it. Image is a thing in this TV game. But I do not want the best boss I've ever had to lose her job or keep reporting about hog calling contests because she's too pigheaded—no pun intended—to get some help."

Tanika smiled, deciding the ignore the part where Mya had called her Miss Piggy. "Am I really the best boss you've ever had?"

Mya nodded. "Yep! You always approve my PTO. And you let me raid your closet for last season's clothes. Best boss ever. Now, want me to schedule that optometrist appointment?"

"Nice try, Slick Rick." Tanika laughed. "But you can look up some lacrosse stats and check Sara's schedule."

"Damn!" Mya snapped her fingers. "I thought buttering you up had worked."

Tanika playfully pushed Mya away from her side of the desk. "Hell no; now get back to your actual job."

Tanika felt her cellphone buzz in her pocket. She squinted at the text message, but the words were too damn tiny. Unable to make it out, she handed the phone over to Mya who declared that it was Ross. Again.

> ROSS: You're my fucking star, Nikki! Thanks for this.

Tanika groaned. She hated when Ross called her *his star*. It was as if she were his pet. Well, she was done being anyone's lapdog. She had to devise a plan. And this was the kind of plan that was going to take a village. Her boss chick village.

"Mya, after you make that meeting with Sara, text Jackie and Bronwyn for me. See how soon we can meet for lunch. It's your turn to pick this month's spot, remember?"

Mya did a fist pump. "I'm on it. And I promise that it won't have grass walls or neon signs."

Tanika laughed. Mya knew she hated Atlanta's faux trendy spots with a passion. "You know me so well."

CHAPTER 2

Gideon poured over the expense reports at his desk. After operating costs and paying Celeste—his sister-in-law and only employee, whom he had to beg to take a salary—it looked like he'd be in the black again. Barely.

He pulled off his glasses and sighed. Another late night. Since losing Lauren, things with his optometry practice had been tough. She had been the glue that kept everything together. She'd been an office manager, accountant, purchaser, and support system all in one. She'd put nervous first-time patients at ease, holding their hands or making jokes at Gideon's expense. She'd known every patient by name, remembering birthdays and graduations. She'd sent cards and even checked on the elderly patients when they forgot appointments. Lauren had made the office feel like a second home.

It wasn't until her death that Gideon had realized how much of the minute, day-to-day things she'd handled. From the sugar for the coffee to the files on her desktop, Lauren had kept a system, a rhythm for everything that she did. She'd been the beating heart and soul of Miles Optometry. And he'd taken it for granted.

Slowly, patients had started coming in less and less until he only had a small roster of faithful clients. Gideon initially blamed the drop on the new, cheaper big-box optometrist that had opened down the street. He wondered if his patients were opting for popular services he didn't offer—like Lasik—or the ease of online retailers who were affordable but often inaccurate with their work. Then, he'd found a spreadsheet on Lauren's computer labeled *Reminders and Follow-ups*, and he'd realized that his own neglect had hurt his business. He'd been so consumed with grief that he'd neglected to do the job of following up with patients, reminding them of their routine eye exams, or even sending out scheduled advertisements. There was no one to blame for this mess but him.

It was nearing 2:00 a.m. when he turned on the small television in his office. These days, the sounds of the TV were a substitute for companionship. He didn't have any pets because Lauren had been allergic to nearly everything. And he didn't have any kids, though Lord knows he and Lauren had tried. After the third miscarriage, they'd been resigned to being happy just with each other. And truly, they had been. But the reason for his happiness had since left this earth.

Gideon flipped through the channels, looking for something remotely interesting. A marathon of his favorite police procedural? Or his guilty pleasure—a thriller on the women's network. That could do the trick. When he got to the sports channel, he paused as a familiar face filled the screen.

"This is Nikki Ryan reporting from the National Lacrosse Eastern Conference Championships, where the Georgia Tornadoes go head-to-head with the Carolina Cardinals for what's sure to be a thrilling match. . . ."

Gideon turned up the volume and stared at the screen. He took in every inch of Nikki, who, if he was being honest, looked bored to death. Yet, even with a bored expression on her face, she was stunning. Just like he remembered from the cookout.

Gideon's cousin, Jackie, hosted a very famous end-of-summer cookout at her place every year. He and Lauren would go and have a good time, amazed at all the pro athletes that Jackie represented. Last year had been his first year attending solo. At that point, it had only been eight months since he'd lost Lauren, and he was still adjusting to life as a widower. Jackie had basically bribed him with her famous baked beans to get him out of the house. As he sipped a beer next to the buffet, Gideon watched as a curvaceous, brown-skinned beauty—dressed in denim shorts, fresh Dunks, and a low-cut tank top—swung her bob to the DJ's old-school mix. He was mesmerized. Her thighs glistened in the sun like chocolate diamonds. He could hear her laughter over the music and couldn't help but smile in response. Gideon must have been stupefied, totally in a daze, because he didn't notice Jackie pulling a very sweaty Nikki by the hand and making a beeline in his direction.

Out of breath, Jackie began, "Gid, this is my girl Nik. Nikki, this is my favorite cousin, Gideon. I don't know which one of y'all has the better sneaker collection. So, I figured you all should get to know each other and find out."

When he realized it wasn't a daydream, Gideon coughed, nearly choking on his beer. "Hey."

Nikki smiled wide, waving. "Hey. I like your throwback Hank Aaron jersey. That's fly!"

Gideon looked down at his jersey. "Um, thanks." He looked up into her eyes, which were the warm color of a cool Manhattan. Fatal mistake. She was waiting for him to say something else, but he was silent. When he forced himself to speak again, the only thing that came out was, "Sorry. I gotta run."

Gideon left without eating the plate of baked beans he was promised, and without getting to know Nikki.

In that moment, he'd felt guilty and embarrassed. It had only been a few short months since Lauren's death, and there he was, salivating over another woman and feeling things in his khaki shorts that he shouldn't. He wasn't ready. So, he'd bounced.

She must think I'm a weirdo. He stared at his screen, which had moved on to the actual lacrosse game. Since that ill-fated meeting, he'd thought about Nikki and debated asking Jackie to reintroduce them. He even thought about sending her flowers but talked himself out of it. She was a busy sports reporter, surrounded by athletes and big shots all day. He was an optometrist with a small office that was barely holding on. He couldn't possibly compete with the caliber of men in her circle.

Gideon returned his focus to the stack of paperwork in front of him, his eyes falling first on the small photo of his wife he kept framed on his desk. She was all smiles on their last vacation in Saint Lucia, holding up a conch shell to hear the ocean. He felt familiar tears welling up as he thought about the damage cancer had done to the life they had built together. Gideon folded his hands and bowed his head. He wasn't a religious man, but he thought he'd send a message to the one angel he hoped was still looking out for him.

Lauren, if you can hear me, give me a sign on what to do?

GIDEON STRODE BACK INTO THE OFFICE AT 10:00 A.M., MUCH TO Celeste's dismay. She looked up from her laptop and frowned as she stuck a pencil into her box-braided bun.

"Your excuse for coming in late better be that you got some ass last night and took the girl to breakfast."

Gideon paused. "Now you and I both know that's not true. Also, I feel really uncomfortable talking with the sister of my dear, departed wife about getting ass."

Celeste shrugged and smiled. "Sex is a basic human function, Gid. Everyone does it. Bees do it. Birds do it. Old people in nursing homes do it."

"Oh god, why did you plant that image in my head? All I can see is Poppa throwing back Viagra with an Ensure chaser."

Celeste pointed a finger in Gideon's direction. "That's ageist. One day, you are going to be old and hoping and wishing someone would snuggle up to your dilapidated equipment. So again, I ask. Why are you late?"

Gideon rubbed his eyes under his glasses. "If you must know Celeste, I did not have a date. I was up late last night reviewing the financials."

He had Celeste's attention now. She came around the desk and faced him. A little under six feet, she was nearly eye level to Gideon. "How did we do?"

Gideon turned toward a display of new prescription sunglasses, straightening out the frames. "Well, you were right. The back-to-school crowd did put us back in the black this month. It was enough but just barely. Maybe this month we can replace some inventory and donate the old frames to charity."

Celeste put a hand on Gideon's shoulder. "You know you don't have to pay me this month, right? That'll be some cushion."

Gideon frowned. "Celeste, I can't have you working here for free."

"Gideon, you are still my brother and my family. Family helps family. Besides, I don't need the money. I got my retirement and Stu's army pension. I'm good. I like helping you out."

"CeCe, I'm not a charity case. Lauren wouldn't have wanted that!"

"I know Lauren was your wife, but that was my sister for forty-two years of my life. I think I know her better than you. Trust me, that's what Lauren would have wanted. Let me go put on a pot of coffee." Celeste squeezed Gideon's arm, then turned, heading toward their small break room.

Gideon tilted his head up and closed his eyes, preparing himself to sit in his office for another grueling eight hours. He prayed today would be the day that things would turn around. He'd had this practice for nearly twenty years. He couldn't lose it. He couldn't ruin all of Lauren's hard work in getting things off the ground. He gripped the handle to his office door and let out a breath.

A miracle, L. You've gotta send me a miracle.

Something had to give.

CHAPTER 3

The ladies were meeting a little early for their monthly luncheon per Tanika's request. She needed to debrief, and the heated patio at Portico—Mya's pick for lunch—was the best place to do it. When Mya and Tanika arrived, Bronwyn was already seated, wearing her usual uniform of a flowy, brightly printed caftan and an assortment of gold bangles. They ordered a pitcher of sangria as they waited on Jackie, who rolled in fifteen minutes late as usual. Power walking in sky-high stilettos, designer shades, and a navy pantsuit that cost more than a mortgage, Jackie waved hello with her phone still glued to her ear.

"Sorry I'm late," Jackie apologized, sliding into her seat.

"We know," the table droned in unison.

After the waitress took their orders—and Bronwyn rolled her eyes at their meat-laden choices—the ladies played catch-up, filling each other in on the happenings of their lives. Once the drinks started flowing, so did the conversation.

"And then the girl said, 'I thought illegal motion in the backfield meant that you can't do the Wobble in the end zone.'"

Jackie, Bronwyn, and Mya howled with laughter as Tanika recalled her network-mandated lunch with her young replacement, Sara Taylor. Last week, Tanika had suffered through two hours with

Sara, who talked incessantly about her pageant days, asked basic questions about various sports that *any* reporter worth their salt should have known, and altered the Cheesecake Factory menu to her dietary restrictions because she had to *watch her macros*. At least there had been drinks—and plenty of them—a couple of limoncello martinis and several portions of avocado rolls to ease the pain. She had to hand it to Mya; those rolls were damn good.

"Well, did she at least know anything about Colin Bello? Do any homework on him?" asked Jackie in her soft, relaxed voice. Folks were always so amazed that Jacqueline "Jackie" Miles, sports agent to the stars, had a voice like Bambi's mother: calm, soothing, and sweet. It made it all the easier for her to disarm folks when she went in for the kill and garnered multimillion-dollar contracts.

Tanika huffed. "If doing your homework includes recalling vividly what he wore to the Met Gala and reciting his dating history, including that brief stint with that reggaeton star, then the answer is yes."

Bronwyn shook her head as she moved her vegan Cobb salad around her plate. "That blows, Tanika. This should be your interview. Not hers. I can tell from the television she has the wrong energy for reporting. Her vibes are off." That was a typical Bronwyn Carter answer. She was the crunchy granola one of their "Boss Chick Village," a name they'd given themselves back in their undergraduate days at Clark Atlanta University. With her husband, Kenny, Bronwyn had transformed her love of nature and the earth into a thriving chain of health food stores. She'd been trying to get Jackie and Tanika to go vegan since 1999. It hadn't worked.

Tanika took a healthy bite of her lamb chop. She chewed slowly, thinking of the right words to say. "The thing is, the poor girl thinks they hired her for her actual skill. Bless her heart. She has no idea it's because horny American men want to see something pretty relay stats to them so they can jerk off between commercials."

"And between quarters," interjected Jackie as she twirled her veal pappardelle around her fork. "Why do you think all major sports have cheerleaders?"

"Tasteless! Baseball doesn't have cheerleaders, right?" Despite her long friendship with Tanika and Jackie, Bronwyn was not a big sports person.

"Oh, trust me, it's coming," laughed Jackie. "MLB already has new rules. New jerseys. Might as well add bouncing boobs to the mix."

The waiter brought the bill. The friends playfully fought over it like they always did, until Tanika snatched it in victory. "I'm paying. I invited my girls out to lunch. My treat. Well, except Mya. She's a freeloader regardless." She opened the billfold and squinted at the check, moving it up and down, back and forth, until she could almost make out the total. No matter: she'd just overtip and add an extra zero, in case she was short.

She closed the billfold to find Bronwyn and Jackie staring at her curiously.

"Tanika? Do you need glasses, girl?" asked Bronwyn.

Before she could respond, Mya, with a mouthful of bread, responded. "Yep." Tanika shot daggers at her. "Well, maybe," Mya continued. "We don't know. She refuses to let me make an appointment with an optometrist. She's stubborn."

"Oh, so *that's* what's wrong?" asked Jackie. "No wonder you keep flubbing lines and stuff. You're never off your game. I thought it was maybe a new intern jacking up the teleprompter."

"It probably is!" declared Tanika, still telling herself that lie. "I don't need or want glasses. Glasses are going to make me look like an old lady."

"Not true! Oprah wears glasses," Jackie said. "And she looks fabulous. Matches them to every outfit."

"My auntie used to do that!" said Mya.

"Oprah also said she hates to be called *auntie*," Tanika scoffed, giving Mya a death stare.

"Honorifics aside," Bronwyn began. "Glasses can be very chic these days, Tanika. So many choices of frames and styles. I know you have that . . . that *thing*—" she softened her voice sympathetically, "—about not wanting anything to touch your eyes. So maybe contacts are out. But glasses are cool now. No one makes a big deal about glasses. This isn't high school."

Jackie and Mya nodded in agreement.

Tanika rolled her eyes, already growing tired of this conversation. "Of course *you'd* say that. *You* don't have to wear them! Neither one of you has something wrong with your eyes."

"Oh, I got Lasik like ten years ago," confessed Jackie. "Reading contracts all day jacked me up."

"And I wear readers sometimes," chimed in Bronwyn. "Kinda hard to read those nutrition labels these days."

Tanika sighed. "You all don't get it. I'm over forty. That's old in this industry. I'm already getting the Botox, covering my grays and natural hair with wigs, watching my carbs, all for the sake of looking good to the network and viewing audience." She shoved her credit card into the billfold, handing it back to the waiter. "Then again, look where all that has gotten me. Reporting in the informercial hour of sports viewing."

"You need to embrace this new phase of your life. Throw off the shackles of patriarchy and embrace your maturity. Let the hair go gray and natural. Stop wearing girdles and gadgets meant to constrict your womanly curves. Free the nipple! Liberate yourself from the male gaze." Bronwyn gestured wildly as she spoke, her icy gray locs swaying with every movement. If Freddie Brooks had a twin, it would certainly have been Bronwyn Carter.

"That's easy for you to say, Miss Au Naturel!" huffed Jackie, eying her friend up and down. "When's the last time you even wore a bra?"

"2002. Right after I gave birth to Tigerlily. And they are still perky!" Bronwyn, not one to shy away from displays of sexual freedom, bounced her boobs with her hands for greater emphasis.

"Girl, you are going to get us put out of this fine establishment!" Tanika laughed. "Put those milk factories away!"

"They haven't been milk factories in ten years, and you know it!" hissed Bronwyn, who folded her arms over her chest in protest. "But you know, sometimes, when Kenny and I want to role-play—"

"Oh, hell naw!" said Jackie. "I don't wanna hear what I think you are going to say!"

"Yeah, Bronwyn," groaned Tanika. "I'm not trying to picture Kenny in a diaper."

"Who said anything about a diaper?" frowned Bronwyn. "Now, a bib . . ."

The entire table protested and begged Bronwyn not to say another word, lest they all lose their lunch.

"Kink-shamers!" huffed Bronwyn as she drank the last of her prosecco.

"Anyway," Jackie declared, trying to get the conversation back on track. "Go to the optometrist, Tanika. As a matter of fact, you can visit my cousin Gideon's practice. He'll be private and totally discreet. He's not too far from you in East Lake."

"Gideon?" Tanika scowled as she recalled the last time she'd met Jackie's cousin. "Your weird cousin from the cookout last year, who ran off when I tried to carry on a conversation like a normal human being?"

Jackie bit her lip and sighed. "Yeah, that was unfortunate. But it was my fault. I didn't prepare either one of you, but especially Gid. He was still grieving the loss of Lauren."

Tanika raised a brow. "Who's Lauren? Ex-girlfriend? Or a dog that ran away?"

Jackie's eyes grew soft and sad. "No, his wife. She'd died of ovarian cancer not too long before you two met."

Tanika's hands flew up to her mouth, embarrassed at her caustic response. She had a habit of saying the wrong thing at the wrong time. "Oh, Jackie! I'm so sorry. I had no idea."

Jackie shrugged. "It's cool. Like I said, that was my fault. I should have told both of you before I tried hooking y'all up. I just wanted him to make a new friend at the very least, you know? Get out the house. Remind him that he has more life to live."

Now Tanika really felt like a jerk. From what she remembered, Gideon was cute. He was, she guessed, a little under six feet. Bald, with a beard. And of course, he wore glasses. He had a very chic but nerdy thing going on. At least, that's what she thought he had going on, based on very little data. Dude had taken off like Usain Bolt. But it didn't really matter, then or now. There was no time to date when WWSN consumed Tanika's life.

"Well, I appreciate the thought," started Tanika. "But you know me. Always on the go. No time for dating. No time to slow down."

"I wish you would!" said Bronwyn, reaching for Tanika's hand. "Maybe then you'd take care of yourself." Tanika appreciated the way her girls always looked out for each other, even if she wished they'd mind their own business.

"And here is his card," Jackie pulled out a cream business card with gold foil text. *Miles Optometry.* "I'll let his office manager, Celeste, know to expect your call."

"Now, hold on; I didn't say I'd go." Tanika twirled the card in her hand. "I'll think about it. Okay?"

"Fine," said Jackie. "But you better make an appointment soon, before flubbed lines become the least of your worries."

"Thanks, Ms. Jackie." Mya snatched the card out of Tanika's hand. "I'll hold on to this for safekeeping." Mya knew her all too well, predicting she was either going to lose the card or toss it.

This hussy, thought Tanika. Sometimes, Mya was too good of an assistant. She'd stay on her case until she called Gideon.

But she wasn't going to see him. No way. No how.

IN THE PARKING GARAGE OF WWSN, TANIKA SLUMPED IN THE SEAT of her Tesla. She was exhausted. Her eyes burned after hours of going over notes with Mya and piecing together footage with Danny—all for a fluff piece about a ninety-year-old sprinter. *Okay,* so maybe the real reason her eyes burned was because she'd been straining to see letters on her laptop and make out images on the screen. Tanika yawned. It was nothing that a little sleep couldn't fix. She'd be ready and bright-eyed in the morning.

She eased out of the parking garage and headed toward the highway. As she merged into the slow lane, her phone rang. It was nearly midnight. Who the hell was calling her that late? She glanced at the console and saw the caller's name flashing. Granted, she couldn't make out every letter in her current state of exhaustion, but she knew what it said: *Daddy.* She pressed to answer the call. Before she could say anything, her father's voice boomed.

"Why did I turn on my TV and see you talking about women's rugby? Why you ain't on *Thursday Night Football* anymore?"

Tanika sighed. "And hello to you, Walt. May I ask why you are calling me this late? It's almost midnight."

"No, you may not. Little girl, I'm grown and old. I ain't got nowhere to be. Now, answer my question. Why was this toothpick of a gal on my screen earlier this evening and not you?"

Here he goes, thought Tanika. She'd always had a strained relationship with her father. Growing up, her mother had been the buffer between them, shielding her from his wrath. A former corrections officer, Walt Ryan exuded no warmth. He didn't dote on Tanika like most fathers did with their daughters. He mostly criticized her, making her feel like a constant disappointment. Other than a love of sports, the two of them had nothing in common.

Tanika gripped the steering wheel, her knuckles cracking. "Well, WWSN wants to go in another direction. I can't fight management."

"What did you do? I noticed you been messing up lines here and there."

Of course he'd notice. "I didn't do anything, Dad. Like I said, they want to go in a different direction."

"I see." Walt coughed. She could hear the whir of the adjustable bed in his nursing home room. He was getting himself comfortable so he could make her uncomfortable. "You need to figure out how to get back on the sidelines in a real sport. That girl don't know football from a hole in the wall. She might be prettier and thinner, but she's got shit for brains when it comes to football."

Tanika gritted her teeth, unsure how to take his backhanded compliment. "Thanks, I guess." She wished she had the kind of relationship with her dad where she could tell him the truth. *I'm getting older, Daddy. I feel disregarded and disrespected. I'm scared this is the end of the line for me. Maybe I want something better for myself.*

He wouldn't get that. He'd just tell her she needed to work harder and smarter. It was times like this that Tanika really wished her mom was still alive. She had always known the right thing to say.

"Well, figure it out. I expect excellence from you, always. By the way, the next time you come to the nursing home, please make sure to bring wet wipes for me. This tissue is hard as hell." And with that, Walt hung up the phone.

Tanika rolled her eyes at the screen on the console. Typical. In her forty years of life, her father had never said goodbye when ending a call. The last time he'd said he loved Tanika was at her mother's funeral. His affection had been so infrequent in her life that when he'd uttered those three words, she'd thought maybe he'd been replaced by a body-snatching alien. But no, he had just been consumed by guilt and grief.

Tanika yawned again as she exited the highway in Sandy Springs and headed toward her condo. She had to get to bed soon; she feared she'd fall asleep at the wheel. The light, late-winter drizzle that had been blurring her windshield suddenly turned into a torrential downfall. Tanika panicked. She already hated night driving; she could barely make out the signs. And now, the floodgates had opened. She half expected Noah's Ark to come rolling down the street. *If Noah was a drunk, how'd he build the Ark anyway?* It was an inappropriate thought to have while operating a vehicle.

Tanika eased down the street and came to an intersection. She squinted at the streetlights. Through the rain—and with the glare on her window—it seemed as if the colors of the traffic lights were dancing nonstop. She honestly couldn't tell. Was it green?

Screw it. Tanika turned right through the intersection, saying a silent prayer to the rain gods for the weather to chill. It was all good, until she realized something was off. *Wait . . . are those headlights coming in my direction? Oh, god!*

Car horns blaring at her, she swerved, trying to get out of the way or find a street to turn around on. Her heart raced, her eyes unable to adjust to the blurring lights. She swerved again to the right, then to the left. She managed to prevent herself from hydroplaning, but her front end slammed into something, jerking her forward and deploying the airbags.

When the ringing in her ears subsided, Tanika lifted her head. Her face was sore from the airbag, and her shoulder ached like hell, but she was in one piece. She'd for sure have a black eye in the morning, but that was minor. Tanika opened her car door, wobbly, but able to stand. The front of her car was a freaking accordion, folded in on itself. She had hit a fire hydrant on the sidewalk. *Were there people on the sidewalk? Did I hit someone?* She dropped down on her knees and looked under the car, praying she hadn't killed a pedestrian. By the time she was satisfied that homicide wasn't going to be added to her record, two patrol cars were pulling over. *Fuck.* Tanika stood next to her car, getting soaked and praying her night wouldn't end in cuffs.

A flashlight blinded her eyes as the voice of the first officer boomed. "Ma'am. Do you need medical assistance?"

Tanika shook her head, the strands of her bob sticking to her face. "No. I'm fine. The rain was so bad, I couldn't see. And— "

Before she could say anything else, a female officer interrupted, stepping close to Tanika. She was tiny and white. "Ma'am, have you been drinking?"

Tanika's eyes widened. "No! Not at all. All I have in there is a cup of coffee. I can show you."

The officer put her hand on her gun. "Step away from the vehicle. Now."

Tanika instinctively held her hands up. "Okay." Her heart was beating rapidly, and at that point, getting soaked was the least of her worries.

The officer moved in closer. "Do you have identification? Insurance?"

Tanika nodded, hands still visible. "I do. But they are in my glove compartment." She watched as the other officer opened the passenger side and reached in, finding her insurance card, work badge, and license. "I don't own any weapons," Tanika added for good measure.

"Walk in a straight line, heel to toe," commanded the officer. Tanika sighed, hoping that her suede pumps could be salvaged after all this exposure to rain. But she did as she was told, then stood still once she was back within a few feet of the officer.

Clearly dissatisfied, the short female officer came closer. "Follow my finger." Tanika did so, even though her slender ivory finger was blurry as hell. "Are you willing to submit to a breathalyzer?" the officer continued.

Tanika frowned, getting annoyed. "I assure you; I'm not drunk."

"Then prove it." The officer held out the apparatus. "Blow."

As soon as Tanika blew into the breathalyzer, she heard the other officer yell, "Holy shit!" She wanted to turn her head but thought against it. This was already looking bad, and she didn't need it to escalate. She didn't need her dad planning her memorial.

The male officer—a tall, broad-shouldered Black man—approached now, all smiles. "You're Nikki Ryan! *The* Nikki Ryan!" He turned to the other officer, who held a blank expression as he tried to explain. "Peters. You have no idea who this is, do you? From *Thursday Night Football*! Or well, used to be. I'm a huge fan."

That *used to be* stung just as much as Officer Peters's nonchalant shrug at the mention of her name. When the breathalyzer came back as 0.0, Tanika took that as her sign to speak. "Thanks."

"You're good," said the officer. "No signs of intoxication."

"Good; can I go now? Take care of my car?" Tanika was cold, wet, and beyond embarrassed. She'd had enough for the night.

"What exactly happened, Ms. Ryan?" The male officer ran over with an umbrella, finally covering Tanika from the pelting rain.

Tanika sighed, noting that the lace front of her wig was so soaked it was lifting in the front. She patted it down with her fingers as best she could. "As I said, the rain was coming down so fast, and I couldn't see at all. I could have sworn I turned down the right street." She looked at the officers, both getting drenched in the downpour. The female officer seemed annoyed, while her partner listened intently, still holding the umbrella.

Tanika decided to turn on the charm. "I swear it's all been so much. My father called me from his nursing home. Maybe I got distracted. Plus, the sign was so small." With that, Tanika turned it up a notch with tears. "It's all been so stressful!"

The brother officer's last name was either Martin, Michael, or Mario; Tanika couldn't quite make it out from his name tag. He nodded sympathetically. "It's going to be okay, Ms. Ryan. It is true, those signs are hard to see when it rains. Right, Peters?"

Officer Peters said nothing, just grunted her dissatisfaction as she wrote furiously in her notepad.

Officer M lowered his voice. "Unfortunately, Ms. Ryan, we are going to have to issue you a ticket for going down the one-way street."

Tanika sighed. "I figured that. Can I get my phone and call a tow truck?"

"Sure thing," said the handsomer of the pair. "Actually, if you let me call it in, the truck will come faster. Oh, by the way, can I get your autograph? Can you make it out to Kyle?" He shoved a piece of paper and a pen in her direction.

Tanika smiled weakly. "Sure, it's the least I could do." She signed her name, making sure to add some flourish for Kyle.

Officer Peters handed Tanika the ticket, which she was sure would be a lofty fine. Tanika squinted, moving it farther from her face. She couldn't make out a damn thing. When she looked up, Officer Peters had her hand on her hip.

"Clearly, you need glasses. The next time you're out here without corrective lenses, I'm locking you up. Fancy reporter or not. Let's go, Marvin." She turned her back to Tanika and headed for the patrol car.

A few minutes later, the tow truck appeared. At least it was fast, as the officer had promised. Tanika's head throbbed. She was soaked, with a wrecked car and a busted pair of pumps. The night couldn't possibly get worse.

"You know," began Officer Marvin. "I loved you on *Thursday Night Football*, but that Sara Taylor. Whew. She's hot. Think you could pass her my number?"

Nope. This is worse.

Tanika slowly turned her head, plastering on a smile. "Well, sorry to disappoint you, but Sara is taken." She had no idea if Sara had a partner or not. Quite frankly, she didn't care. But Tanika damn sure wasn't about to play matchmaker for her network rival.

"That's too bad. Oh well. Keep the umbrella," said Officer Marvin with a smile and a tip of his hat. "Get home safe. Thanks for the autograph."

"Uh-huh," mumbled Tanika, not bothering to look in his direction as she made her way toward the tow truck, opening the passenger door to slide inside. In the smoky cab of the truck, Tanika started to type a text message but found her hands were slick and shaking, and her eyes were too strained to see her own words. She gave up and left a voice memo for Mya, who she knew would check her messages as soon as she woke up.

"Mya, make an appointment with Gideon Miles. ASAP."

CHAPTER 4

A singsong chime announced Tanika's entrance as she stepped into the waiting room of Miles Optometry. She took off her shades and looked around. It was a bright and airy space painted a sunny yellow, with cushy sofas, oversized tan chairs, and a few standard, poster-sized advertisements of folks smiling in designer glasses. Tanika was surprised that the office wasn't busy, given its plum location. But the light sheen of dust on a stack of months-old magazines told her that business must be slow.

"Ah! Ms. Ryan, you're here!" A tall, statuesque woman with braids rounded the corner, her voice boisterous. The purple in her top matched the random purple braids in her hair. Tanika rose to shake the woman's hand but found herself pulled in for a hug instead.

"I'm sorry. I'm a hugger. I'm Celeste. Office manager. You're a bit early, so Gideon—I mean, Dr. Miles, is wrapping up with another patient. He'll be with you shortly."

Tanika looked at her watch and nodded. "Sorry. I didn't realize how early I was. I guess my driver knew some shortcuts." In the days since the accident, Tanika hadn't trusted herself to drive. She'd hired a car service to take her around—a luxury that she'd long had access to but never utilized. Now, she really had no choice.

"Would you like a cup of coffee? When Jackie said you might be calling, and then I got word from your assistant, I couldn't believe it. Your exposé on corrupt judges and payola in the college cheerleading world? Riveting!"

Before Tanika could respond, Celeste was bringing her a small Styrofoam cup along with a pod of cream and packets of sugar.

"Thanks." Tanika took a seat by a small table. She added cream and sugar to the steaming cup, stirring slowly as Celeste watched her from her place at the front desk.

"You might be our first real-life celebrity client!" beamed Celeste as she typed away on her computer.

"Ah. I'm not a celebrity. I interview celebrities."

"And humble too! I could tell you were a sweetheart from TV! And you are way prettier. Camera doesn't do you any justice, Ms. Ryan."

Tanika smiled, sipping her coffee that was now entirely too sweet. "You're too kind, Celeste."

"I know they say the camera puts on fifteen pounds or whatever, but I can't tell with you."

"Um, is that a good thing or a bad thing, Celeste?"

Celeste laughed uncomfortably. "I'm just saying, you can't hide those hips if you tried. Here I go running my mouth. Dammit. I don't mean any disrespect, Ms. Ryan."

Tanika laughed. "It's fine. And call me Nikki."

"Okay. Nikki it is."

Just as Tanika was about to flip through a month-old *Newsweek*, the door to the examination room opened. Tanika looked up to find a man neatly dressed in a white doctor's coat, his arm locked with an elderly woman's.

"Mrs. Clark, make sure you use those eye drops every day, okay? And check your sugar levels too. Diabetes can do a number on your eyes. Celeste will check you out."

The woman nodded. "I will, Doc. And I'm going to send you some of my pound cake. I'll tell my grandson to run it up here to you."

Gideon laughed. "I don't need it and neither do you! Besides, can't you tell I'm getting chubby?"

Tanika gave Gideon a quick once-over. *He's exaggerating.* In fact, it looked like the man didn't skip the gym. Under that white coat was a fitted dress shirt tucked into slacks that hugged his thighs. She swore she could make out the imprint of some well-defined pecs. *Not that I'm looking.*

As her eyes met Gideon's, Tanika nervously smiled. He stood a little taller, straightened his tie, and pushed up his glasses.

"Oh, Ms. Ryan. I'm sorry for the delay. As you can see, I had a VIP client." He looked over to Mrs. Clark and winked. She waved her hand at him, dismissing his harmless flirtation with a giggle.

Tanika's smile brightened. "It's alright. I can see she was someone special."

"Come on in. Let's get started."

Tanika let out a breath and stood, making her way to the exam room. As she passed Gideon, who held the door open for her, she noticed that they were pretty much at eye level. She did the math. She was wearing heels, but still—this meant he wasn't super tall, maybe 5'9, 5'10 at most. Tanika didn't normally date men under 6'2. Not that it mattered. Gideon wasn't a potential date. He was her doctor. She watched as he wiped down the examination chair with care.

"Please, have a seat for me, Ms. Ryan."

Tanika slid into the chair, trying her best not to hit any equipment. "Call me Nikki. Or Tanika."

"Okay; which do you prefer?"

"Well, my friends call me Tanika." Tanika flashed Gideon a nervous smile. Why was she nervous? "Or Nik. Sometimes Tan. But most of the world knows me as Nikki, so . . ."

"Tanika it is," interrupted Gideon with a smile. *A really gorgeous smile.* "So, what brings you in today? I think your assistant mentioned something about headaches and blurry vision. Have you had a physical examination with your primary care doctor?"

Tanika nodded, watching Gideon with his profile to her, head down, taking notes. "Yes, and everything was all good. No diabetes. No high blood pressure or anything. I'm fit as a fiddle, Dr. Miles."

"Gideon."

"What?"

"My friends call me Gideon." Gideon turned on his stool to face her, a slight smile on his face.

Tanika smiled back, feeling a little more at ease. "Okay, Gideon. Did my assistant mention I ran into a fire hydrant?"

Gideon's eyes widened. "Ah, no she didn't. What happened?"

Tanika relayed the other night to Gideon, who nodded sympathetically. "I'm mortified. I could have killed someone. Or really been hurt."

Gideon rolled toward her. "Don't be embarrassed. You're here now to find out what's going on with your vision. I'm here to help. But tell me, how long have you had these issues with your vision? Because by what you're telling me, it doesn't sound like this happened overnight."

Tanika bit the inside of her lip, thinking. If she was honest with herself, the problems with her eyes had been happening well before she'd turned forty, but she'd ignored the symptoms. She'd ignored the whole thing because a dozen other things had seemed more important, and she hadn't had the time to address something as minor as her eyes. Now, she realized she shouldn't have taken such a cavalier attitude. She looked at Gideon, who was patiently awaiting an answer. "I don't know. Maybe about five or six years ago?"

"So, you've been straining to see since . . ." Gideon turned to flip through his charts. "Since you were thirty-six? Tanika, that's not good."

"I know. It's just . . ." Tanika sighed, fumbling for the words to say to this incredibly kind face. "My job is really demanding." *That's one way to explain my stubbornness.*

Gideon nodded. "Understandable. Well, Tanika. We are going to figure this out. Right now, I'm going to do a thorough exam to establish the health of your eyes and get a better sense of your vision issues. Read some letters, look through some lenses, look at your eyes via really bright lights. Think you can handle that?"

"Sure, bright lights in my eyes don't sound painful at all." Now she was making cornball jokes, a sure sign that the nerves were bubbling back up again.

Gideon laughed. "I promise you'll live. Can you follow this object for me?"

Gideon held up a tiny wand in front of Tanika's face. Her eyes followed the movement of the wand until Gideon was satisfied.

"Good. Now I'm going to ask you to read the letters up front in the mirror. Standard eye chart, okay? Read the first line."

Tanika read the letters as best she could. "Did I pass?"

Gideon gave a wry smile. "It isn't about passing or failing, Tanika. I'm going to cover one eye at a time and ask you to read the smallest line you can, okay?"

Tanika nodded. Gideon covered her right eye, and she blinked a few times, trying to adjust her focus and read. Gideon then covered her left eye and asked her to read an even smaller line.

"O-P-D-Z-E-8," said Tanika confidently. "Was I close?"

Gideon gave a low chuckle. "Not even close, Tanika. But you did as well as to be expected."

"Damn, I'm blind as a freaking bat," mumbled Tanika.

"I assure you, you're not blind," retorted Gideon. "Not quite. Though I have to say, it's a common misconception that bats are blind. They use echolocation."

"Oh, like *Daredevil*!"

Gideon gave Tanika a surprised expression. "You're a Marvel fan?"

"Not really," Tanika confessed. "But that was my only point of reference."

"Gotcha. But if you do decide to give *Daredevil* a try, I suggest the series, not the movie. It was terrible."

He's such a nerd. "I'll keep that in mind," Tanika smiled.

"Alright, let's get to the other portion of the exam."

Tanika watched as Gideon swiftly positioned a biomicroscope in front of her, explaining that he was looking at the pressure of her eyes as well as looking at her retina. That light was painfully bright, but she had been warned. Tanika appreciated how Gideon explained each step, putting her at ease. He even handled her nervous questions, laughing gently when she asked, "Are you going to touch my eyeball?" Not only that, but the man smelled so good. Gideon's cologne was subtle and not overbearing, not competing with whatever he used to freshen his breath. He literally smelled like a cinnamon factory, reminding her of cozy, fall days. She especially appreciated his fresh breath because their faces were so dangerously close. She instantly regretted accepting that coffee from Celeste.

"Tanika, you're going to look through a few lenses and read some letters for me so we can figure out your prescription. Can you move closer?"

Tanika slid her body to the edge of the seat, her nose fitting securely under the phoropter.

"Good girl."

Tanika swallowed. He had no business saying that in that way. *At least buy me dinner first, Doc, before you call me a good girl.* Her thighs clenched together in what was an attempt at telling her body to behave.

"Oh," Gideon coughed, clearing his throat. "Sorry, just a habit. I see a lot of, um, kids. Occupational hazard."

Did I say the dinner thing out loud?

"It's fine." It was *not* fine. She couldn't remember the last time she'd been alone in a room with a man. It had to have been before the playoffs. Tanika bit her bottom lip, trying hard not to moan.

She read a few more lines as Gideon circled through lenses, testing to see which level improved her vision.

"Which one is better?" Gideon asked. "One or two? Or maybe three or four?"

"Ugh, I'm not sure. Maybe one? Or was it four? Shit . . ."

"It's alright, Tanika." Gideon's tone was soft and reassuring. "We're going to find the right combination. No worries."

And he was right. Finally, Gideon found the right settings—the lenses that made the room magically come into focus for Tanika. He moved the phoropter away from her face.

"See, that was painless. No gorgeous brown eyes harmed in the process."

Tanika blushed, then rolled her eyes, trying her best not to smile at the compliment. "Yeah, painless for you. You're not the one getting light and air blown into your eyeballs."

"Are you always this snarky?"

"Always."

Gideon rolled back over to his desk and put a few things into the computer. He had a striking profile: a gorgeously broad nose, full lips, and a silver-gray beard that was perfectly manicured against his gingerbread-colored skin. Tanika waited, looking around the intimate exam room, trying to focus on anything other than Gideon.

"Well, the good news is you aren't going to need a super suit. But you do need corrective lenses. You have a severe astigmatism in your left eye and a condition called presbyopia in your right eye."

"So, what does that mean?"

"That means you have a really hard time focusing. You're a little nearsighted and a little farsighted. So, you need bifocals."

Tanika nearly fell off the chair. "Bifocals? Like a grandma? My grandmother had bifocals! I've got old-ass eyes."

Gideon raised a brow. "I wouldn't put it quite like that, but age does play a major factor. And I can tell you've been overcompensating one eye over the other."

"So, I have to get glasses."

Gideon tapped his pen against his palm. "You have options, Tanika. We can do contacts."

"No way! I cannot poke my eyes every day. And don't suggest Lasik. The idea of being wide awake and a laser coming straight at me? Terrifying. What if the beam goes a little to the left?"

"You watched *Final Destination*, didn't you?"

"Yes. Yes, I did."

Gideon threw up his hands, a small smile forming at the corners of his mouth. "My bad. Well, glasses it is. We can order progressive lenses or no-line bifocals. I'll show you how to look through them. You'll get used to it. And I've got some really dope frames in the gallery room. I'm sure a pair will call to you."

"Call to me?"

"My late wife used to say that glasses have a way of becoming part of you. Part of your personality. You have to find the pair that fits who you are. See what speaks to you."

"I see."

"Give it a try, okay?" Gideon placed a gentle hand on Tanika's folded ones. "Now, I have to do one more thing before you leave." He used his free hand to push up his own frames, a pair of simple round tortoiseshell glasses.

"What's that?"

"I need to dilate your eyes to make sure everything is healthy behind the scenes. Your eyes will be a little numb, maybe even sting, but it's harmless."

"So, I get to wear those big blue blocker shades? I don't know."

"I'll buy you an ice cream from next door if you let me."

"Let me guess, another occupational tactic learned from your kiddie patients?"

Gideon smiled wide, the corners of his eyes crinkling. "Hey, it works. So, whatcha say? I'll be waiting here after you pick out your frames. Celeste can show you to the gallery room."

Tanika stood and grabbed her purse. "Fine. But I want sprinkles and chocolate sauce. Extra if that junk hurts!"

Gideon opened the exam room door. "Only the best for WWSN's top anchor."

Tanika looked over her shoulder, giving a tight smile. Her heart ached a bit at Gideon's choice of words.

Celeste led her quickly to the glass-encased room, lined with walls and walls of frames. Someone had done an amazing job of arranging them all by shape and color.

"Now, feel free to try on as many as you like. If you find something you love, bring it out to me, and I'll get you squared away. If you need help, just shout." Celeste left Tanika to browse.

Tanika looked around. *What the hell, no use in delaying the inevitable.* She needed frames, and she needed them immediately. She picked up a pair of red frames. *Maybe I'll look like Sally Jessy Raphael.* But once she put them on, she quickly changed her tune. She looked like a ladybug. She moved on to a pair of wire-rimmed frames, which reminded her a little too much of her fourth-grade teacher, Ms. Betts, who had been mean as hell. Finally, she tried on a pair of high-end designer frames, a cat-eye shape with gold detailing on the temples. They were nice. On someone else, she would have loved these glasses. But Gideon's words played in her head. These weren't her. They didn't really fit who she was. Maybe she could ask Celeste for help. Just as she was about to turn and call for her, another woman appeared in the doorway.

"Oh!" Tanika flinched, her hand nearly knocking over the display case. "Have you been standing there the whole time?"

"Sorry. I didn't mean to scare you." The woman held up her hands. "But you looked like you could use some help."

The woman was dressed in a white coat similar to Gideon's, and her glorious puff of hair was adorned in a white headwrap. Her face was kind.

"Yeah. I'm a little overwhelmed. There are just a lot of choices."

"Then let's take a look, shall we?"

This woman had a calming presence, an effect that Tanika couldn't quite put her finger on. No wonder Gideon had hired this person. Something told Tanika to just let this stranger help.

The woman seemed to glide as she moved to stand in front of Tanika, staring directly into her eyes. "So, nothing here is speaking to you?"

"I guess not. Maybe Gideon's little theory is wrong."

"I assure you, it's not. Let me just look at you." The woman walked in a small circle around Tanika, who was taking in her own reflection in the mirror. "Something tells me you need a pair of frames that give you confidence."

Tanika scoffed. "I'm confident."

"Yes, usually. But not right now. There is a lot of uncertainty going on with you. You're blinded by the superficial. You can't see deeper than the surface of the present. But what you want, what you need, is right in front of you. You just need to see it clearly."

What kind of hocus-pocus shit . . . ?

"Um, I guess. But I don't think—"

The woman turned her back on Tanika mid-sentence. "I think I have the perfect pair for you. I've been saving them for just the right person." She opened a drawer at the bottom of the display case, reaching deep in the back, beyond where Tanika could see. She pulled out a black eyeglass case, carefully dusting it off with her fingers. Slowly, she rose, and as if she were carrying precious cargo, she gently placed the case in Tanika's hands.

"I think these would be perfect for you."

Tanika turned the case over in her hands, looking for a brand, logo, or price. "Are these a designer exclusive or something?"

"Something like that."

Tanika shrugged as she opened the case. Inside, she found a pair of matte black square frames. She held them up and squinted to see if she could make out a designer name on the temples. There was nothing there, just the midnight-black of the frames.

"Go on, try them on."

Tanika pulled out the frames, placed them on her face, and turned to look in the mirror. The square shape suited her bone structure, and with her current bob wig, she looked boardroom ready. She felt powerful. Dignified. And yes, confident. She turned her head from side to side, searching for flaws but coming up short. They were, in a word, perfect.

"Wow. I'll admit, they do speak to me."

"Just remember, the new vision you've gained will only work if you're willing to see the bigger picture."

"What does that mean?" *What is with these riddles?* Tanika appreciated the woman's help, but if this was some kind of sales tactic, it was annoying. She turned around, intending to say so.

But the woman was gone.

Celeste appeared at the doorway. "Ms. Ryan? Did you need some help? Oh! I see you've found a pair. These look *amazing* on you." She called across the hall to Gideon. "Gid, Ms. Ryan—I mean Nikki—has selected her frames. Come see!"

Gideon joined Tanika at the mirror, taking in her new look. "You look . . . fantastic. How do you feel?"

"Thanks. I think they really fit me."

"Yes. These are definitely all you."

Tanika turned toward Gideon. His eyes were focused so intensely on her, but she wasn't sure why.

Celeste interrupted the moment, approaching with her hand out for the frames. "I'll take these and hand them over to Tony. I'll put a rush on them; they should be ready in a day or so."

"Has Tony worked here long?" She wanted to put in a good word for Gideon's employee. Despite speaking in riddles, that woman had really helped Tanika find the right glasses.

"Tony is our lens cutter. The best. He's worked part-time for Gideon for many years. You can trust him to do a great job with your glasses. Don't worry about that."

He? So, Tony was not the lady in the white coat. *How many people work in this tiny office, anyway?*

"Tony will have these done no later than Friday. Your assistant can come and pick them up for you." Celeste looked between Gideon and Tanika. "Or you can always come and pick them up yourself. Make sure they fit."

Tanika carefully placed the frames back into the case and handed them to Celeste, who swiftly left the room, leaving Tanika and Gideon alone.

Tanika folded her arms. "You promised me ice cream."

"You haven't done your part of the bargain."

"This better not hurt."

Gideon put his hand over his heart. "I promise."

"You're a terrible liar." Tanika licked chocolate-macadamia-nut ice cream from a spoon. "That hurt like hell."

Gideon scooped up some of his strawberry-hazelnut swirl. "So, maybe I lied a little. I had to wrangle you to get those drops in. You were like a cat afraid of water—didn't want to get myself scratched. I did get you extra sprinkles."

The two of them were seated in a booth in the back of Creamy Dreamy, the ice cream shop next door to Gideon's practice. It was quaint and colorful, at least from what Tanika could make out in her hideous shades. The smell of warm waffle cones and other sugary delights helped Tanika relax and forget what she'd just been through. She could see why Gideon bribed his child patients with ice cream. It totally worked to ease nerves.

"Well, I'll make sure I leave an awesome review. You have a great bedside manner."

"More like chairside, but I'll take it."

They ate their ice cream in silence for a few beats, then Gideon cleared his throat. "Can I ask you something?"

Tanika, her mouth full of ice cream, nodded approvingly.

"Why were you so hesitant to get your eyes examined? Honestly?"

Tanika put down her spoon and wiped the corner of her lips. "Because—and this is going to sound vain as hell—I don't want to look old."

"Look old? What do you mean?"

"I work in sports journalism, Gideon. For a woman, it's all about looking good while giving out stats and interviewing players. WWSN keeps a close eye on superficial things they deem 'distracting' to their core audience, aka men. Things like wrinkles. A few gray hairs here or there. Glasses. Anything. I mean, my age and my looks are what got me booted off *Thursday Night Football*—"

"I'm sorry, what? Your looks got you booted off *Thursday Night Football*? But you look—"

Tanika waved off Gideon's compliment before he could finish it. "I promise you; my industry is that superficial. And it fucking sucks. I thought I could fake it until I made it. But running into a fire hydrant kind of nullified that."

She wasn't sure why she was telling him all of this. But the man had such an amiable face and gentle demeanor that it was easy for her to just spill her guts. She pushed her ice cream away, a little ashamed of her candor with a virtual stranger.

"Would it be bad if I said I'm glad you ran into a fire hydrant?" Gideon smirked into his ice cream.

"Yes, it would be. You think wrecking cars is funny?"

"I don't mean it like that. I'm just glad that it forced you to finally do something about your vision . . . and grateful that I got to see you again. A proper introduction this time."

Tanika swallowed a lump of ice cream, the iciness hitting her chest. "Oh."

Gideon scratched his beard. "Yeah, I've been meaning to ask Jackie for your number so I can apologize for how I behaved at her cookout."

Tanika waved her hand dismissively. "It's nothing. Hey, I've had my fair share of football players run the other direction too."

"I'm guessing Jackie told you that I lost my wife a few months before that." Gideon rubbed his bald head nervously.

"She did. And that's why I wasn't upset. I understand."

"Still, that was no way to behave. It was weird, running off like that. But I saw you, and I thought, 'Man, she's gorgeous.' And I felt a twinge of guilt, because . . ."

Tanika put her hand on top of Gideon's, noticing just then that he still wore his wedding band. "It's fine, Gideon. Really. No need for an explanation."

"Well, I'd love to make it up to you."

"But you already did! With extra sprinkles."

Gideon let out a booming laugh and shook his head. "No, I mean, I'd love to take you on a real date. One where I'm not peering down your eyeballs or bribing you with ice cream to get you to sit still."

"Oh." Tanika removed her hand. "Gideon, I'd love to, but with my schedule . . ."

"Oh, right." Gideon pushed up his glasses. "Yeah, I guess that was a silly thing to ask. With your schedule and all."

"It wasn't silly, it's just—"

If Tanika wanted to get back on *Thursday Night Football* or have a shot at VP of Programming, she would have to put in a lot of extra work repairing her relationship with the higher-ups. She knew this. It wasn't fair, but it was real life. She didn't say all of that aloud. She was going to try to keep this simple.

"My schedule is super unpredictable."

Gideon was shoving an enormous bite of ice cream into his mouth, nodding emphatically. "Hmm, I get it. Yeah, totally. It's cool."

Tanika was surprised by the swell of regret she felt at hearing Gideon's words. She'd used her job as an excuse once again. This was what she always did when someone wanted to take her out on a date. But Gideon was cute. And thoughtful. And adorably corny. She couldn't remember the last time she'd found someone remotely interesting.

Her phone buzzed, and she pulled it from her pocket. While she could barely make out the name flashing on the screen, she was sure it was Mya. "Hey, I think this is my assistant. I better let her call the car service so I can get back to the office."

Gideon picked up their empty containers to toss in the trash. "Well, Tanika, thanks for letting me check you out. Er, letting me check out your eyes, that is."

Tanika wiped her sticky fingers. "Thanks for the ice cream. Now that I have glasses, I'm sure I'll *see* you around."

"Was that an optometry joke? I'm the one that's supposed to do the jokes. You trying to take my job?" Gideon snorted.

"Never." Without thinking, Tanika took a clean napkin and gently wiped bits of strawberry-hazelnut swirl from his nearly white beard. Touching his beard made Tanika think of Christmas for some reason . . . and *sitting on laps.*

"You had a little ice cream in your beard."

"Thanks, Daredevil."

"Eh, your joke wasn't as good as mine, but I'll allow it."

"Your joke sucked too."

"True." She paused just inside the doorway of the ice cream shop, not wanting to leave just yet. "Hey, Gideon, will you tell your assistant I said thanks for the help with the glasses?"

Gideon's brow knit in confusion. "Assistant?"

"Well, your intern then? Colleague?"

Gideon shook his head. "You mean Celeste? It's just the two of us in the practice these days. And Tony cutting lenses. . . ."

"Huh." Before Tanika could solve the mystery of the woman in the white coat, her phone buzzed again. Her driver was letting her know he'd arrived. Gideon's Daredevil joke reminded her that she was still in those hideous blue blockers.

"When can I take off these shades? I want to be able to see the curb. Before I fall off it getting into the car."

"I should torture you longer, for fun, but I won't. You can take those shades off those pretty eyes now."

"Still using your kid-approved tactics on me?"

Gideon reached up, sliding the awkwardly large shades off Tanika's face. She froze, then flushed with heat, her eyes adjusting to Gideon's face under the fluorescent lights. If she were an ice cream cone, she would have melted instantly, leaving a puddle in the middle of Creamy Dreamy.

Gideon gently used a finger to move a strand of hair from her cheek. "Not this time." With that, he gave a nod to the cashier and walked out of the door.

Well, damn. Tanika blew out her breath.

Clean up on aisle twelve.

CHAPTER 5

Gideon was all smiles as he returned to the office. Sure, Tanika had turned him down. But flirting with her had felt good. And after seeing the reaction on her face, he realized he could still make a sister blush. That was reward enough.

Celeste was leaning over the front desk, her hand resting on her chin. "So, did you ask her out?"

Gideon sighed, taking out a cloth from his pocket to clean his glasses. "I did. And struck out."

"Aw, why! Wait . . . why are you smiling?"

"I put myself out there. I think I'm ready to date again, CeCe."

Celeste clapped her hands. "That is wonderful. But how could she turn you down?"

Gideon sat on the longest sofa in the waiting room. "She's Nikki Ryan, Celeste. She is a super busy woman. She doesn't have time to date."

"That's just a BS excuse. If you find someone interesting, you make time for them."

"And what makes you think you have her all figured out after one afternoon?"

Celeste sucked her teeth. "Oh, please. Women like her hide behind their jobs to avoid real intimacy. Trust me, I know. I used to be that girl."

"Is that right?"

"Yep. Then I met Stu, and I let my guard down. She just needs someone to shake her up a bit. Maybe that someone is you?"

Gideon leaned back against the sofa, scratching at his beard. Maybe Celeste was right, but convincing Tanika to let down her guard wouldn't be easy. None of it would be easy. How would dating one of the world's most recognizable sports reporters even work? This woman met rich, handsome athletes and TV stars all day. How could Gideon measure up?

"Celeste, I'm just—"

"Gideon, before you start putting yourself down, I need you to realize that you're an incredible guy. Just as you are. And if you could get a top-tier woman like my sister, one day you'll find another woman just as amazing."

"Thanks, sis. And thanks for helping Tanika pick out her frames today. Sounds like you took a page out of Lauren's book. She asked me to express her appreciation."

Celeste shook her head. "I didn't help her with the frames. I pretty much left her alone to browse while I did some paperwork in the back. I figured she wouldn't want me hovering over her."

"Did another patient stop by and help her browse?"

"Maybe someone came in while I was in the back. I didn't hear the front door chime. But that's odd that they wouldn't stay."

"Yeah." Gideon was perplexed. "Odd."

"Speaking of odd," continued Celeste as she turned toward her computer, "the frames that Nikki picked out. I've searched high and low for a SKU number, and I can't find it. There's no brand name. Nothing."

"Hmm. She must have found some old frames. Discontinued, maybe?" Gideon had to admit, this was unusual. Apart from the handful of new frames Celeste had begged him to order, everything on the floor had been purchased by Lauren. And Lauren had been meticulous when it came to inventory. There wasn't a frame she hadn't cataloged and accounted for. . . . Though maybe she'd just forgotten. When the cancer was in its later stages, there'd been plenty of times Lauren had forgotten things—sometimes even who Gideon was. These mystery glasses were just a reminder that she was human, and despite being perfect in his eyes, she'd made mistakes.

"Maybe," Celeste said with a shrug. "I'll just charge her a base price. I'll let insurance handle the rest."

"Cool. Whatever happened, Tanika sure did pick the right pair. She seemed almost amped about wearing glasses, which is a miracle for that woman. She had this sense of relief. Remember how my patients used to look after Lauren helped them find the *one* pair they liked—"

"Gid? Do you think maybe . . ."

Gideon turned to see Celeste looking at him with wide eyes. He rarely saw her flustered. "Do I think what?"

"Never mind. Nothing." Celeste blinked a few times, then turned back to the work on her desk.

Puzzled, Gideon retreated into his office.

CHAPTER 6

Tanika tried to focus on her notes, but it wasn't just her eyes tripping today—her mind could do nothing but replay scenes from her afternoon with Gideon. She could still taste the sugary sweet ice cream and feel the heat of Gideon's fingers on her cheek.

"Looks like you survived!" Mya entered Tanika's office without knocking, as usual.

"Of course, I survived. It was an eye exam, not brain surgery."

"So how was he?"

"Who?"

"Um, the doctor. Jackie's cousin?"

"He was nice. Really patient. Explained everything."

"Just nice? So why are you grinning like that?"

Tanika's hand instinctively went up to her cheek, feeling the distinct divots of her laugh lines. She hadn't realized she was smiling. *Embarrassing.*

Mya raised a brow. "Is he as fine as you remembered?"

Tanika's nose crinkled in mock disgust. "Why does it matter? He's alright." She didn't want to get into this with Mya. "I went there for an exam, not a date." *Although, there was ice cream. And those sweet smells. And soft touches. Lots of laughs. Cinnabon-scented breath that kissed my neck.*

Mya tapped on her tablet with a sly smile, looking like she could read Tanika's thoughts. "Uh-huh. Well then, let's talk about your interview with Sven Goransson, Canadian curling champion."

Tanika groaned, dropping her head to the table. "How much more of this can I take?"

Before Mya could respond, there was a heavy knock at the door, followed by a turn of the doorknob. Ross Spiegelman's robust frame filled the doorway.

"Nikki!" Ross stood with his arms outstretched. Tanika cut her eyes at Mya, who shrugged. Tanika rose and gave Ross the briefest hug possible.

"Ross! I'm not used to you hugging me." Tanika's cheeks burned from smiling in such an unnatural way.

"Well, I wanted to thank you for taking Sara to lunch. Although, I would have splurged a bit."

Mya snickered then covered her mouth, lowering her eyes back to her tablet.

"Regardless, Sara thought the lunch was very beneficial. She looks up to you as a mentor, you know."

"So you've said. Glad I could help."

"Her interview with Colin tomorrow will go well. But I'm little nervous there may be some key points she's missed. It might just be nerves. So, you think you can swing by her office and check on her?"

"Fine." Tanika broke the pencil in her hand in two. *Fuck.* Mya was going to kill her if she had to order another case of pencils so soon.

"You sure you're alright, Nikki? Something stressing you?"

"Not at all, just a lot on my plate right now. You know, gotta brush up on curling. Not to mention, Black History Month is coming up. . . ."

"Oh right. I was thinking Sara could do a special segment for you all's Black History celebration. Connect her to the Black demo a bit more."

You all's? Tanika felt molten-lava-level rage brewing not only at Ross's casual racism but the idea of Sara getting to do a special segment for Black History Month. It had been Tanika's idea to start doing special segments anyway, particularly when the network was getting heat from some of their POC viewers. She'd done some phenomenal interviews and investigative reporting. It was part of the reason why she knew that she was more than qualified to be VP of Programming. She'd had to practically beg the network to put some respect on Black History Month, and now they were willing to let the newest kid on the block do a segment.

Tanika smoothed out the lines on her skirt before speaking. "Well, I'm sure Sara will think of something great for her segment. In the meantime, I'll give her a shout about Colin."

"You're a doll, Nikki. I'm telling you—my star!" Ross rose from his chair and left Tanika's office as fast as he'd entered.

"*You're a doll,*" mocked Tanika in Ross's voice. "What an asshat." She rubbed her temples, feeling the beginning of another throbbing headache.

"So, are you going to talk to Sara?" asked Mya, who was bringing Tanika two ibuprofen and a glass of water.

"I'd rather get my coochie hairs pulled out one by one than to talk to her again." Tanika took the pills and downed them with the water, grateful for Mya's intuition. "But if I must."

"Well, if coochie is on your mind, . . . why don't you skip this and go back and see Dr. Miles?" Mya gave a knowing smirk.

Tanika frowned. "Given my situation at work, do you really think I have time to date? If it's not the traveling, it's the meetings. If it's not the meetings, it's the prep for the meetings. I just don't have the time for a man—even if he smells like apple pie and is fine as hell."

Mya pointed an accusatory finger. "Aha! So, he *was* fine!"

"Shut up, Mya." Tanika looked at her watch. It was nearing 3:00 p.m., and she knew Sara's segment on *Football Center*—which used to be her segment—would be over soon. "I'm going down the hall to be a 'team player,' yet again. In the meantime, can you do your job and stay out of my love life?"

"I make no promises."

· · ·

Tanika leaned against the door frame and watched Sara
Taylor powder her nose. She gazed intensely into her compact, only
pausing her touch-up to swipe at her phone. Tanika rolled her eyes
before knocking against the door to get her attention. Sara finally
looked up and gave Tanika the fakest of smiles.

"Hey Sara, can I come in?"

"Nikki! Hey girl! Come on in," Sara said brightly, waving her in.
"Not sure how you dealt with that rowdy crew over on *Football Center*."

"They take some getting used to." Tanika sat on the low futon
sofa that was directly behind Sara's vanity. She looked around. There
wasn't a laptop, a pen, or a notebook in sight. *Guess we're relying on
looks and vibes.* "So, Ross tells me that your interview with Colin
Bello is tomorrow. Are you ready?"

At the mention of Ross's name, Sara stiffened, hairbrush in hand.
"Of course I'm ready. Wh . . . why wouldn't I be?"

Tanika was surprised at the display of nervousness. Sara always
seemed ridiculously confident. *Looks like Barbie is human after all.*

"I know this is your first big interview. I'd love to look over the
questions you've prepared. Maybe give you some pointers on obvious
ones to skip, deeper ones to ask?"

"Why would I need you to go over my notes? Trust me, I'm fine.
Totally prepared."

Sara was brushing the life out of her hair. *Jeesh.* Tanika wouldn't
have been surprised if there was a single strand left. She leaned forward. "I think Ross is a little anxious. This is kind of a big fish for
the network. Colin's announcing his move to stock car and into the
American market. We have the scoop. No one else is breaking this
story."

Sara threw her silk-pressed strands over her shoulders. "Right.
You told me that. But like I told Ross, that's not the interesting part.
We want to know the real tea on Colin. The money, the dates, the
rumors—you know, stuff like that."

Tanika pinched the bridge of her nose. "Sara, we are a sports network. Not *TMZ* or that god-awful *Sports Ragz*." *Sports Ragz* was a gossip show and website dedicated to messy rumors involving athletes. It was trash journalism at its best.

"Of course, I'll throw a few sports questions in there. I just don't want to overwhelm the interview with gibberish about wheels and lug nuts."

Wheels and lug nuts? Gibberish? Tanika pressed her lips together and blew out a calming breath through her nostrils. "Sara, I'm just—"

"I got this," Sara interrupted, adjusting the hem of her pink slim-fit dress. "Nikki, I know you have your old-school way of doing things. But I have mine, okay? I thank you for offering to help me, but I don't need it."

"Old-school?" Tanika's voice rose about an octave, startling Sara. "I am a seasoned journalist. Some things are just standard practice."

"And how's that working out for you? I'm sure archery tournaments appreciate your type of journalism."

This bitch. Tanika dug her nails into her palms. She wanted to break something. Instead, she counted to five in her head to calm herself down. "Most sports fans appreciate a professional who comes prepared to interview athletes and has knowledge of the game, no matter how popular or obscure." Not someone who is going to ask about their dating lives, or social media followers, or what they're wearing to the awards this year!"

"Oh! That's a good question. I'll have to remember that one! *Awards shows . . .*" Sara typed in her phone. "See, you *are* helpful, Nikki."

At that backhanded insult, Tanika rose from the futon, her knees complaining on the way up. "Good luck, Sara."

"Thanks, girl! And can you close the door behind you? I need to get a power nap in. You know how it is before the game, right?"

Tanika closed the door. On the other side, she leaned against it and shook her head. A few of her colleagues smiled as they passed by, likely curious to see her standing outside of Sara's door. But they knew it was in their best interest to keep it moving.

Once she was VP of Programming, her first order of business would be to fire Sara. She wouldn't have WWSN reduced to gossip with a sprinkle of sports news. That was insulting. Damn near humiliating.

"Nikki? I got Sven's manager on line one," called Mya down the hall. "He wants to know if you're willing to be a sweeper as part of the segment."

Now *that* was humiliating. Tanika groaned, knocking the back of her head against Sara's door.

CHAPTER 7

When Celeste announced that Tanika's glasses were ready, Gideon offered to deliver them himself. Celeste raised a suspicious eyebrow, which he ignored. It was true; he never made house calls. He wasn't that kind of doctor. But he played it cool and asked Celeste to give Tanika's assistant a heads-up.

Armed with lens cleaner and tools to adjust her glasses, Gideon drove down to the WWSN building. As he parked the car in the deck, his stomach turned queasy. What the hell was he doing? This wasn't like him. He was behaving like an overeager puppy, doing anything to see this woman. But ever since their impromptu ice cream date, Gideon hadn't been able to stop thinking about Tanika. How she smelled like mangoes and leather: sweet and tough. How one of her brows lifted a little higher than the other when she smiled. He had debated getting her number from her patient file, but that was much too stalkery. No fine woman was worth losing his license over. No; bringing her glasses personally was the safest bet. He just wanted any excuse to see her again.

As soon as he exited the elevator from the parking deck, he was met by a woman with a reddish-orange afro, tapping on her tablet. As soon as she saw Gideon, she smiled.

"Well, well. I had no idea Miles Optometry provided this service. I'm Mya, Tanika's assistant." Mya grinned, her afro bouncing as she walked, gesturing for Gideon to follow her.

"Only for my VIP clients," Gideon lied. That felt silly to say. He didn't have VIP clients. Hell, he was barely holding on to his practice as it was.

They walked down a massive corridor of offices and cubicles until they got to an office with *Nikki Ryan* on the door. Gideon thought that was badass—she didn't need a title, just that name. Mya put her hand on the doorknob and turned to Gideon. "Just so you know, Nikki doesn't date. Ever."

Gideon hoped the defeated feeling in his chest hadn't shown on his face. "Oh, well, . . . it's not like that. I—"

"To be clear," Mya interrupted, "I damn sure hope you throw your hat in the ring. It would be entertaining to watch, at least." She winked as she finally opened the office door.

There was Tanika, dark brown skin glowing in a fitted ivory dress, a matching jacket slung over her chair. She was pacing her office, earbuds in, taking dictation on her phone as her wide hips swayed with the rhythm of her movement. Gideon's eyes traveled downward and noticed that she walked barefoot across the plush office carpet. She continued talking to herself even as he entered—from what he could catch, it was something about bass fishing.

"Nikki, Dr. Miles is here with your glasses!" Mya hollered, trying to get Tanika's attention.

"Oh! Hey." Tanika smiled as she put her phone down, giving Gideon her full attention.

"Hey. You look gorgeous." Gideon couldn't help but blurt it out. She *did* look good, and he found he could only be truthful around Tanika.

Mya glanced between the two of them, clearly a little more than amused at their awkwardness. "Imma leave you two to it. Nikki, if you need anything, I'll be in my office. Good luck, *Doc*," Mya whispered as she passed by Gideon.

After Mya left the room, Gideon turned to find Tanika with a frown on her face, arms folded across her chest.

"Were you flirting with my assistant, Dr. Miles?"

"She's not my type," Gideon replied easily, setting his doctor's bag down in the chair in front of Tanika.

"Oh yeah? What's your type?"

"Older. Overworked. Loves talking to herself while barefoot. And is in desperate need of bifocals."

Tanika let out a loud, boisterous laugh that made Gideon's heart thump wildly in his chest. He loved that laugh and wanted to make her do that repeatedly.

"You've got jokes. Well, since you brought up the bifocals, you might as well lay 'em on me, Doc."

Gideon pulled out the same plain case Tanika remembered from the shop. He opened the case, removed the glasses carefully, and gently cleaned them with a microfiber cloth. "Ready?"

Tanika nodded. "Yep."

Gideon moved closer to Tanika, inhaling that distinct scent of mangoes and spice. He willed himself to keep moving; otherwise he was going to stand there for way too long, sniffing her like a weirdo. He moved a strand of her hair out of the way and placed the glasses on her face. Once they were straight on, he stepped away.

"So how does that feel? Any blurriness? Tightness at the temple?"

She stood silent for several minutes, her eyes blinking. She was getting used to the lenses. Or that's what Gideon hoped.

"Everything okay, Tanika?"

"I . . . uh, okay. I think . . ."

"Are the lenses off-center? If something is wrong, I can help."

Tanika shook her head, but she didn't look sure. "Maybe it's just taking my eyes a minute to adjust."

Gideon nodded, reaching into his jacket pocket. "That's completely normal. Here's some info on no-line bifocals. Please try to wear them as much as possible. The more you wear them, the quicker you'll get used to them. Try not to look down when you're walking, as you might get dizzy. And, well, call me or have Mya call so we can fix anything for you."

Gideon paused. Tanika was quietly listening, looking stunning in her new glasses. *Damn. Is it my imagination, or do the glasses make her hotter?* He blinked. *Might as well go for it.* "Or maybe we can—"

Before he could finish his sentence, he heard a loud wailing sound coming from the office hallways. Mya came barreling in, out of breath yet amped beyond belief.

"Tanika, girl, all hell's broken loose."

"Girl, what is going on out there?" Tanika peered curiously at Mya. "And why are you smiling if hell is breaking loose?"

Mya glanced toward Gideon. "I'll fill you in after you wrap your current meeting."

The wailing continued, followed by what sounded like a door slam. Gideon had no idea that sports broadcasting was so emotional. "Maybe I should head out. Sounds like things are about to be off the hook."

Tanika gave a rueful smile. "Sorry Gideon. I think the glasses are fine. But thanks for stopping by. I'll give you a call if I need you."

Gideon nodded as Mya opened the door for him. Before he could say anything else, she'd shut the door in his face.

He sighed, shaking his head at the name emblazoned on the door. Striking out with Nikki Ryan was quickly becoming a habit.

CHAPTER 8

S omething strange was happening.

When Gideon moved to put her glasses on, the first thing Tanika noticed was his scent. She inhaled that familiar cinnamon smell, wishing she could bottle it up and keep it for herself. There was something soothing about it that made her feel comfortable. *What was it with this man?* But once the glasses were on, things got much weirder.

As her eyes adjusted to the lenses, the room around her became clear in a way it hadn't been in years. *Wow, these glasses make a huge difference.* Then she looked at Gideon and saw something entirely new: a bright halo of green, all around him. She blinked a few times to make sure she wasn't imagining things, but there it was, that glow. The sight of those various shades of green should have scared her, but instead it made her warm inside, and her heart beat double time as she looked at this man bathed in emerald light. It reminded her of that scene in *The Wiz.* She wanted to reach out and touch him, but as quickly as she had the thought, the light went away.

Gideon's face was tight with concern, so Tanika rushed to assure him that she was fine. The feeling—that warmth and blooming desire—lingered.

When Mya burst into her office, her ginger-colored afro was in focus for the first time in ages, but otherwise, she looked normal. It was around Gideon that the green halos flickered and shined. Tanika shook her head, then squeezed her eyes tightly. When she opened them, the halos were gone again. *Maybe I should tell Gideon.* No, she didn't want to sound entirely out of her mind.

"I think the glasses are fine."

She could hear what sounded like Sara losing it down the hall. She didn't need Gideon to be in the middle of whatever drama this was. So, she asked him to leave, even though part of her knew he wanted to ask her out, and part of her wanted to say *yes* this time. He had that look in his eye—the one guys had when they were just about to ask for your number. She felt it.

Once he was on the other side of the door, Tanika turned her attention back to Mya.

"What the hell is Sara yelling about?"

"Girl. Sara has fucked up. Royally." Mya's hands were rubbing together like Birdman's.

"How?"

"All I heard her say was she was never going back to London again. And something like, 'Dude's an asshole.' Ooh, your glasses look bomb, boss."

Colin Bello. That interview had only been a few days ago. What could have gone wrong?

"That's horrible, Mya. Was he harassing her?" She didn't want any fellow woman in this business being harassed. Especially not by some hotshot fuckboy like Colin Bello.

"Who knows. But do you realize what this means? A fuckup that bad can only mean that Sara will be gone from Thursday Night."

Tanika rolled her eyes. "You are far more optimistic than I am."

"Trust me, Tanika. If she was crying and yelling coming from Ross's office, it can't be good."

At that moment, the door flew open. There stood Ross, frazzled, his hands combing through his thinning white hair. There was a misty brown glare around his head that made Tanika feel a tumble of things at once—angry, defensive, a little uneasy. Her glasses were clearly playing tricks on her. These bifocals had to be defective.

Before she could say anything, Ross barked his orders. "Tanika. Pack your bags. You're heading to London tonight to interview Colin Bello." Ross promptly shut the door behind him.

Tanika and Mya looked at each other, wide-eyed.

"Told you. I'll get on the car service and make sure accommodations are straight."

Tanika nodded silently as she nibbled her bottom lip. "Okay. I guess I can do research on the flight over."

"You guess? You better take this for the blessing that it is!" Mya sucked her teeth as she headed out of the office.

Tanika didn't exactly feel good about capitalizing on another woman's mistake. Though she did appreciate that Ross thought she'd be able to save the network's ass. Even if WWSN's ass wasn't worth saving, especially after all the crap she'd been through.

And the crap she seemed to be going through now.

Tanika took off her glasses and looked at them. Nothing about them seemed out of the ordinary. And when she looked at herself in the mirror, she didn't see any colors or wild halos. She put the glasses back on and looked up Gideon's number; she knew Mya had added him to her contacts. *Praise the Lord!* Finally, she could read the names in her phone clearly. She could send a message without worrying that she was texting the wrong person.

TANIKA: Hi Gideon. Tanika here. Question? How long should it take for me to get used to these glasses?

GIDEON: Hi Tanika. It may take anywhere from a few hours to a couple weeks. Just be patient.

TANIKA: Is it normal to see lights?

GIDEON: Your eyes may be a little sensitive to
light. That's normal.

Tanika tapped her chin. That wasn't exactly what she'd asked, but
maybe that's all it was. Maybe she just had a weird sensitivity to light,
and it would pass once she got used to looking out of her glasses.

TANIKA: Thanks. :)

GIDEON: If you want, I can come back and take a
look. Just wrapping up in the office now.

TANIKA: I appreciate that but headed to London in
a couple of hours.

Tanika watched as a few bubbles appeared and disappeared until
finally she got a reply.

GIDEON: After you have your fill of fish and chips,
I'd love to take you out. If you have the time.

Tanika smiled as she quickly typed her reply.

TANIKA: For you, I'll make time.

CHAPTER 9

Tanika's legs bounced impatiently in a plush velvet chair at the Montcliff Hotel in West London. She squinted at her phone and then, inexplicably, her watch, as if she expected that time would be different. The makeup artist, selected by the network, was touching up Tanika's powder in a last-ditch effort to calm her down. She had been perspiring and sweating under the hotbox lights. She replaced her glasses and patted her forehead, making sure her lace front wig wasn't lifting.

"He's late!" Tanika yelled.

Mya was as red as the color of her afro and utterly flustered. She shuffled back and forth between the camera crew and Colin's agent, Rory Mitcham, who had a phone to his ear and held up the *one moment please* finger all the while.

"Nikki. I spoke to Colin's assistant. He had a meeting with his sponsors, and he is running a bit late in traffic."

Tanika rolled her eyes. "That's a lie, Mya. I just saw on Instagram; he was partying with some models last night. He's probably hungover."

"Yeah, I saw that too." Mya's full lips were tightly pursed. "I'll check back with his assistant. Maybe we can get his ETA."

He was already an hour late. Tanika was agitated. Her flight into Heathrow had been delayed. Due to rain, of course. She was operating on four hours of sleep. And now, this hotshot race car driver was late to their interview. *Isn't he the one who asked for a do-over? What a jerk.*

"He has twenty more minutes, or I'm out of here!" She wasn't yelling at anyone in particular, but when Nikki Ryan yelled, everyone stopped what they were doing and looked her way. Tanika was beyond agitated now; she was angry. Sure, many an arrogant and inconsiderate athlete had been late to an interview over the course of her career. Such was the way of superstars. But never in a situation like this—an athlete who had *personally* asked for her, demanding that she hop a transatlantic flight at a moment's notice.

Tanika looked down at her note cards. Despite her mood, she had to say *hallelujah*. Gideon was right; it hadn't taken too long to get used to the glasses. She could finally see her notes and the teleprompter—and she didn't look like a grandma while doing it. She flipped through, reviewing the questions she wanted to ask Colin. Standard stuff, plus a deeper dive on stock car versus F1. On the flight over, she'd brushed up on the differences and similarities between the two. Both had few minorities in the driver seat. Both had few all-Black pit crews or teams. But F1 was the only one receptive and embracing of its minority drivers. Colin Bello—along with others, such as Lewis Hamilton—were the darlings of the sport. Tanika thought it admirable that Colin would want to venture into stock car racing, which only had a handful of Black racers in its seventy-five-year history. American racing was extremely slow to embrace diversity behind the wheel.

On the plane, Tanika had been excited to talk to Colin—and just a touch guilty that Sara's screwup had been her blessing. She'd missed doing sit-down interviews. But now, she just wanted to leave.

She looked at her watch. Fifteen minutes had elapsed since her *twenty more minutes* announcement. Just as she was about to throw her note cards into her Neverfull bag, she heard applause. And then, a thunderous voice.

"Oh, enough with the bloody claps, now! It's showtime, babes!"

A slightly unsteady Colin, flanked by his small entourage who looked equally drunk, came strolling in. He had on skinny jeans cut at the knees, a white V-neck T-shirt that was surely worth more than Tanika's own purse, and a leather motor jacket along with a pair of trainers. To top it all off, he wore dark aviator shades—the regimental accessory of all Gen Z douchebags. His hair was messily brushed, or perhaps not brushed at all. Yet, he somehow still looked handsome. Amazingly handsome.

Around Colin was a bright yellow light, as if he had his own spotlight. Tanika rubbed her eyes under her glasses. *Oh no!* Her eyes were playing tricks on her again. There was no way this man was glowing. *I'm just sensitive to light*, she told herself. *Or tired. Or extremely damn horny. I just need to get some rest. Now, let's get this interview over with.*

Rory rushed over to Colin, whispering a few words. Colin looked at Tanika and smiled. This goddamn dude had the nerve to have a smile so perfect and blinding. It didn't mean she was charmed. She was far from charmed. She was pissed.

She started a slow clap. "Well, well, well. His highness, the crown prince of F1 has finally arrived. And it seems he also brought his court jesters." The entourage laughed uncomfortably as they hovered over the table of food provided by craft services. *Freeloaders.*

Colin walked over to Tanika. No, he *sauntered* over to Tanika with a walk that was pure sex. Tanika adjusted herself in her chair, uncomfortable. How old was this guy? Barely twenty-eight? Tanika was sure he must have watched old Denzel Washington movies or something to perfect that walk. She started to get up, but Colin put his hand on her shoulder.

"Tanika, darling. Please, do not get up. I want to apologize for losing track of time. Forgive me. Last night, my mates and I were tossed. And I'm totally knackered, eh." Colin sat in the chair across from Tanika as the hair and makeup team rushed to his side. "You look bloody fantastic, by the way. Quite fit. New specs?"

Tanika tried to mentally translate his words into American English. "Ah. So, you all were drunk? And you're tired? Well, that is absolutely no excuse to keep me waiting. I'm running on basically no sleep as well, so excuse me if I have very little sympathy. You requested me. Not the other way around, Mr. Bello."

Before she'd left for the airport, Ross had finally told Tanika the truth. Colin had initially requested Tanika to interview him, to break the news of his move to stock car. But the network had insisted on Sara, who had then insulted his taste in designers within the first five minutes of the interview. In return, Colin had apparently called Sara a *tart*. He'd said he'd do the interview again, but only if they sent Tanika.

Colin smiled. "Cheeky one, aren't you? And it's *Colin*, luv. Friends call me Ceezy. And I'd love for us to be friends, Tanika." Colin extended his hand to shake. Tanika looked down at his well-manicured hand for a moment, finally taking it.

"I'm never calling you 'Ceezy.' And those aren't possibly your friends, because that nickname makes you sound ridiculous."

Colin laughed. "You fancy me an arsehole, huh?"

"At this point, I don't fancy you at all," Tanika deadpanned. "Can we get on with this interview?

Colin bit his lip with his perfect teeth, pouting in jest. "Aw. We were just getting on. Fine, then. Let's get it going. I've got a feeling this is going to be fun."

Tanika nodded to Mya, who then turned to the visibly annoyed camera crew from the WWSN London bureau. They were tired, too, having set up hours ago. Tanika pulled the questions from her bag. Colin leaned over her and frowned.

"What is it now, Colin?"

"Let's just have a conversation. You know, let it flow naturally."

"That's not how I work. As someone who asked for me personally, I thought you'd know that."

Colin slowly removed his jacket, tossing it to the side. His biceps rippled, throwing Tanika off guard. She hadn't expected a race car driver to be so ripped. Then again, it was an endurance sport; you had to be in shape. She shook off the thought of Colin's body as one of the entourage appeared out of nowhere, picked up the jacket, and trotted back to the shadows.

Colin crossed his ankle over his knee and folded his hands. "You know why I asked for you, Tanika?"

"No, I don't. Why did you ask for me?"

"Because you're the best, Tanika. And the best requires the best to interview them. Don't you think?"

Not once had this man called her *Nikki*, the charming bastard. Tanika blinked a few times. The bright yellow glow had formed around Colin's head again. "Well, thanks for thinking I'm the best."

"Besides, I've seen you on the telly, standing there on the sidelines with that incredible arse. I wanted to see it in person."

Ugh. Well, there went the charm. "Do not mention my ass again, Mr. Bello."

"Oh, but it's such a fabulous arse, babes."

"My *arse* isn't the topic of conversation. Got it?"

"But it should be," Colin said with a devilish grin. If Tanika didn't need this interview, she would have gotten up and left. But so much was riding on this. She would grin and bear it. Besides, she had endured a lot worse over the years. She could handle one conceited English prick.

"Do you want to do this interview or not?"

"I thought this was part of the interview." Colin nodded toward the camera crew.

Shit! They were rolling. Tanika cleared her throat.

"At twenty-eight years old, Colin, you've won every major Grand Prix, and you won the F1 championship six times, three before the age of twenty-five. Now, you're walking away from it all to venture into stock car. Why?"

Colin took a deep breath. "Well, I feel like I've accomplished all I can in F1. And to be honest, Tanika, I'm bored."

"Boredom is leading you to stock car?" Tanika understood boredom and wanting to make a change. It was part of the reason she wanted the VP job.

"Of course, it's not just boredom. I love stock car racing. I grew up watching the races from America on your network, actually. I just want to leave a mark. I feel like I can make a difference."

"You do realize several Black racers over the years have said the same thing and failed. What makes you different?"

Colin sat straighter in his seat. "And I stand on their shoulders, truly. But I have the faith of my American sponsors. I'm coming into this with a well-financed team. Plus, I'm putting together a diverse and tight pit crew."

"And how exactly are you, an F1 Racer—excuse me, a Black former F1 racer—going to win over the overwhelmingly white, Southern race fans? It's not going to be easy."

Colin laughed. "Darling, I'm Colin Bello. I can charm anyone. Trust me. It's working on you, innit?"

Tanika bit the inside of her lip, trying not to recoil at his naivete. *God, he is young.*

"So, Colin, what will you do when fans aren't receptive to you? When you get called a slur? Or get spit on? Or see hateful, Confederate flags being waved in your face, even though the league banned them? Or when your fellow drivers won't respect you because you are a triple 'outsider'—foreign, Black, and from another racing league. Or god forbid, you find a noose in your garage? You do realize Black racers in America have faced these awful things. So, how will you hold onto your confidence, then? Or are you relying solely on your wonderful charm?"

Colin swallowed hard, looked at the camera, then looked back at Tanika. Tanika folded her hands, awaiting an answer. She had gone off script, just as Colin had asked, right? She almost felt bad for going at him so hard, but she had never apologized for tough questions, and she wasn't about to start today. Rory, Colin's agent, looked as if he was about to step in. But Colin nodded him away. There was an uncomfortable minute of silence before he spoke again.

"I'm not naive, Tanika. I know what I'm up against. Not only do I have to win over fans, but I also have to win the respect of a racing league that thinks F1 is a bunch of rich kids racing fancy cars. I respect stock car. I respect its history and traditions. I know it can get ugly. I know things have been ugly for someone who looks like me. Trust me, I've talked to some of the Black drivers who've broken through. But I just feel like I can make a difference. I mean, my work ethic in F1 should count for something. I'll outwork anyone. Everyone knows that. That's what makes me a winner."

Tanika leaned in, and her tone cooled to something sympathetic. "Colin, you're right about that. No one is disputing your work ethic. But these are the realities of the league."

Colin nodded. "I know."

His larger-than-life voice was small. Smaller than Tanika had ever heard. Through her glasses, the once bright yellow light that had surrounded him grew dimmer. Had she upset him? Frightened him? She momentarily felt terrible for pushing the interview in this direction, but these were questions that she was sure the audience back home would want answered.

Tanika moved on. "Work ethic aside, you also have a reputation for being a hothead and bad boy who parties late, not quite taking the business of racing seriously. Sometimes, you show up hours before a race after partying overseas. Do you intend on rehabilitating your image before or after you start racing in stock car?"

Colin's lips turned up into a sly smile. "What's wrong with a little fun every now and again?" His eyes trailed down the length of Tanika's body, focusing on her crossed legs. "You look like you like to have a good time, too, Tanika."

Tanika swallowed, giving herself a few seconds before responding. "My partying habits aside, Colin, good ol' boys don't take too kindly to wild party boys." She spoke this last phrase in an exaggerated Southern drawl.

"Maybe I can teach them to loosen up. Teach me new mates how to have a good time."

"Not sure they'll enjoy Monte Carlo and private jets over hunting and beer. But maybe you can change their minds, Colin."

Colin tilted his head and winked. Tanika shook her own head and laughed. Maybe this wild child *would* charm them. Whatever his magic touch was about, it was starting to work on Tanika; his yellow glow was back, too, beaming as if it were emitting sunshine into the room.

Tanika shook off the thought and blinked away the light show. "Aside from boredom, and already having won enough money to last a lifetime, what else is calling you toward a new life in stock car? Why not something close to what you know, like IndyCar?"

Colin rubbed his chin a bit, his five o'clock shadow visible. "My Dad. He inspired me to go into stock car."

Tanika raised a brow. "Your Caribbean engineer father, Joshua Bello, inspired you to go into stock car? How? Was he a fan?"

Colin smiled. "Well, my dad came to this country in the 1960s as a poor kid from Nevis. Windrush generation and all. He had not a penny to his name. But he got his degree, and then another advanced degree. Married my Jamaican mother, who became a doctor. Started his own firm. He was always building. Always learning, and now he's successful. He's my measure of success not only as a man, but also as a businessman. If he can conquer England, surely, I can conquer America."

Tanika nodded, admiring Colin's gumption. "But he wasn't on board with you being a race car driver at first, was he?"

"No. He thought I had lost my bloody marbles! But when he saw how passionate I was about it, how I just had a natural ability—and racing does involve a lot of engineering, by the way—he couldn't do anything but give his blessing."

"And your mom? I know she passed away about a year ago. I'm sorry for your loss."

Colin cleared his throat, clearly not expecting a question about his mother. "Mum was my biggest fan. She was. She never missed a race. Ever. That's another reason why I'm moving on to stock car. I don't have her in the stands anymore. So, what's the point?"

Tanika could see the sadness in Colin's eyes and swiftly changed the subject. She knew what it was like to lose a parent, specifically a mother. She thought it best to back off and pivot to something else. "So, the stock car season is around the corner. Are you still developing your plan of execution or—"

Colin cut her off. "I'll be starting the season in February."

"Colin. It's January! Preseason races have already started. Do you have a crew? Do you even have a car? What will you be racing?"

Colin smiled. "All of that is sorted out, luv. I know you think I'm mad. Everyone thinks I'm mad, jumping straight into the season and the points races. I assure you I'm not. I know what I'm doing. And yes, we do have a car fabricated already. I'll be racing a Ford, naturally."

Tanika briefly glanced down at her notes. "And for what team?"

Colin sat up. "Oh. I guess I should have said that earlier. I'll be racing for Lou Reddy Racing." He glanced at the camera. "They've been incredibly supportive and behind me one hundred percent."

Wait, what? Tanika worked on keeping her face neutral while she processed what Colin had just said. She hadn't come across that crucial bit of information in her notes. Colin's PR team had left it out on purpose.

Lou Reddy was known for his unscrupulous business practices. He'd made most of his fortune in the privatization of prisons. He was disreputable, smug, and quite frankly, an intolerable jerk. And when he didn't get his way, he fired drivers left and right. His team hadn't won a championship in nearly ten years. She couldn't believe Colin would want to race for someone like that. The utter hypocrisy of Reddy hiring a Black British driver was not lost on her.

"Lou Reddy? I'm surprised to hear that. He's staunchly conservative. He seems the antithesis of what you stand for."

Colin shrugged. "He also wants to win. And doesn't mind investing in a winner. We may have our philosophical differences, but winning is winning. And I hope to bring home the championship cup to his team."

Tanika couldn't hide her disbelief. "Colin, Reddy does not have the best reputation when it comes to social causes, especially those you support. Such as Black Lives Matter. He was quoted as calling BLM activists 'terrorists.'"

"Again, we have our differences." Colin's voice was sharp and annoyed.

Tanika went for it. "Colin, you could have raced for anyone. But Reddy? Do you even want Black fans? I mean they *are* out there, you know. Or are you just concerned with the money?"

Colin's lips tightened into a harsh line. "Of course, yes, I want Black fans. Again, it's nothing personal. Gosh, is everything about race to Black Americans? Bruv, it's just business."

"*Cut,*" Tanika yelled.

The camera crew grumbled in confusion. Tanika looked at Colin, covering her mic and whispering out of earshot of the crew. "Colin, look at me, *bruv.* Let's keep it one hundred. I'm speaking as Tanika. Not Nikki the reporter. Are you out of your goddamned mind?"

Colin's big brown eyes grew wide. "What's that about?"

"You want to win so badly, you so desperately want to 'leave your mark' in the league, in racing period, that you would sign a deal with the literal devil. Damn what Black people—your brothers and sisters in the States—think about the guy! Yes, to us, a lot *is* about race. So much of our existence comes down to that. But to you, it's just about money. You're pathetic."

"Wait, Tanika— "

"Colin, I wish you the absolute best. Good luck, but you probably won't last a full season."

Tanika shoved her cards into her bag and began to signal for a wrap-up, even as she heard Mya in the background whispering, "Nikki, no!"

Colin reached for Tanika's hand, but she pulled it away. "Tanika, seriously, luv. I didn't mean for this chat to go like that. I didn't. Your concerns are valid—but think! Like I said, I can make a difference!"

Tanika shook her head. "If some shit goes down on that track, trust me, Reddy isn't going to support you. You could die out there, and he'll just get another driver to replace you, with no time to mourn your loss. He is that heartless. Trust me. Lou Reddy has been Lou Reddy for all his life! A little Black British boy is just his newest plaything. You're not Rosa Parks, Colin. If you screw up, you are gone. Back to F1, where—despite your stellar record—you're going to be a laughingstock."

Colin sighed. "Tanika, I thought we could have a conversation without all of this! Bloody hell!"

"Colin, if you wanted a fluff interview, you should have stuck with Sara. But I forgot, you chose me based on how my ass looks on the sidelines."

"Clearly, I admire more than your arse. You're a brilliant reporter, Tanika."

"Thank you." Tanika felt heat rise in her cheeks, thrown off at the compliment. "Listen, let's just finish this out. I think we are ready."

She signaled to the cameraman to start again. "Now, back to your decision to partner with Lou Reddy—"

Colin cut her off. "I remember watching you report when I was younger. I didn't understand a thing about American football. Why call it *football*? No one uses their feet. But you on the sidelines amazed me. Really had me wrapped up in it."

When he was younger? Jesus, he made her sound like a dinosaur. She shifted in her seat and brought out her fakest smile.

"Well, I appreciate that and hope that I was able to explain that feet are indeed used in the sport. But, back to your decision to race for Reddy. Did you know he once said, on the record, that he didn't think Black drivers had the 'mental capacity' to succeed? What do you think changed his mind?"

"Tanika, I like to give people the benefit of the doubt. Surely his attitude has changed over the years. He hired me, didn't he?"

Tanika smirked. "So, you think that meeting you has changed his mind? Decades' worth of intolerance, gone . . . in a matter of, what, months?"

"People can change. This partnership isn't in the least dodgy. I swear it." He put his hand over his heart. Tanika couldn't tell if he earnestly believed the naive words he was speaking, or if he was just that good at bullshitting.

"Well, time will tell." Tanika glanced at the crew. "Thank you, Colin, for your time. On behalf of all of us at WWSN, we wish you much success."

Tanika relaxed her on-camera smile, let out a breath, and yanked off her microphone. Colin looked confused. Covering his mic, he asked, "Is the conversation over? I thought we could talk some more. I want to get to know you better. Maybe we could have dinner later. When does your flight leave? I know a great little spot that serves the best Persian dishes."

"I don't have time for dinner. And I don't mix business with pleasure. Have a good day, Colin. Hope you can finish sleeping off your hangover."

"So, you fancy me pleasurable?"

What a dick. A charming dick. Tanika grabbed her bag and made her way out of the hotel ballroom. Just as she was about to turn the corner, Colin's agent, Rory, appeared in front of Tanika.

"Excuse me?" Tanika attempted to move around Rory, who blocked her path.

"WWSN can't air this. Seriously. Tanika, this makes him look like a bloody selfish prick! And if Reddy gets word of this. . . ."

Tanika folded her arms. "Well, that isn't for me to decide." She kept walking, her shoulder pushing past Rory.

"Tanika! Wait! Wait!" Mya was out of breath, as usual.

Once they were a safe distance from Rory, Tanika stopped walking and turned to face Mya, shame making her face flush. She had lost herself in the interview. That wasn't her style.

"Mya, I know what you're going to say. I lost my cool. I wasn't a professional. I'm sorry. It's just when I heard him say 'Lou Reddy,' I couldn't let that slide."

Mya bit her lip. "No. I was going to ask if you wanted to get a drink at the pub. I saw a cute little one close by."

"Yes. After this, I could use a drink. And food. I'm starving."

"I got you, boo." Mya took Tanika by the arm as they walked out of the hotel and into the bitter, cold London rain.

TANIKA SLAMMED A SECOND EMPTY PINT ONTO THE BAR. "AND another thing, he was late!"

Tanika was—as the British liked to say—pissed. She was also simultaneously the American meaning of pissed. Drunk and angry. Her words began to slur in ways that Mya had never witnessed. Tanika signaled the barkeep for another pint. Mya, behind her back, shook her head at the barkeep and whispered, "It's okay. We're good."

Tanika put her hands in her hair. "I was sweating under those lights for hours. This wig is hot as fuck! I hate wigs. I want to wear my real hair on-air for a change. I mean, if I'm ever going to be on-air again. Once WWSN sees this interview, that's it. I'm fired. Forget about the VP job; I'd be lucky to report high school sports on the local news!"

Mya rubbed Tanika's shoulder. "It wasn't bad, Nikki. I mean, you asked great questions. You were really thrown for a loop with the whole Lou Reddy thing. Not to mention, Colin was . . ."

"A jerk!" Tanika thought about the feeling she'd gotten from first seeing him. That bright yellow glow had rattled her nerves. "As soon as he walked in. He gave me this weird feeling. He was so . . . I'm sorry. What were you going to say?"

"Um, I was going to say fine as hell," said Mya, biting the corner of her lip. "Did you see how his biceps flexed? And he was shamelessly flirting with you, honey. That makes for great TV."

Tanika rolled her eyes, sure that Colin flirted with anyone in a skirt. "I don't think being accosted by a man-child on TV is flattering. It has to be an all-time low."

"Tanika, he's like twenty-eight. Hardly a child."

"More like a man-baby."

"That body says otherwise!" Mya shook her head, amused.

Tanika belched, then raised her voice over the loud music. "I have shoes older than him, Mya. I know one thing: I have to get the hell outta London. What time is our flight out?"

Mya pulled up the itinerary on her phone. "We leave tomorrow at 10:00 a.m. The car service will be at the hotel at 6:00 a.m."

"Thank god. Tomorrow can't come soon enough." Tanika hated early morning flights, but this time, she'd make an exception.

"I think you need to soak up some of that beer," Mya said. "I ordered us a massive basket of fish and chips."

The food arrived like greasy, salty manna from heaven. Grateful, Tanika put her head on Mya's shoulder as Mya doused the fries with a generous amount of malt vinegar.

"What would I do without you, Mya? Huh, girl?"

"I'm guessing get totally wasted and fall flat on your ass in a pub in Chelsea. Clearly, I'm here to save you from yourself."

Groaning, Tanika popped a fry into her mouth. "Yeah, well, maybe another beer could help."

Mya shook her head. "You are cut off, ma'am."

"Maybe I should call Colin, 'cause you're no fun, Red! Ooh! I should call Colin *Goldy*!"

"What are you talking about?"

Tanika pointed at her with a limp fry. "The light! All around him I saw golden beams. You didn't see it?"

Mya blinked, concerned that her boss had lost a grip on reality. "Oh boy. Listen, I know today was a lot. Let's finish this food and get you to bed."

Tanika woke up later that evening with a raging hangover. *That was fast.* Mya had graciously ordered room service in anticipation of her headache: coffee, pastries, and a chicken salad. She devoured the meal in just a few bites, gaining the strength to do a little self-care.

Tanika took off the wig and washed her natural hair. She let her curls air-dry and wrapped herself in a fluffy robe. She put her glasses back on, grabbed her phone from the bathroom vanity, and sat on the closed toilet lid. There were a half dozen missed calls from Ross. Reluctantly, she listened to the voicemails.

"Nikki. Ross again. Listen, I know you are dodging my calls, and rightfully so. What happened today? It's all over the blogs that you and Colin had a heated interview. Now, I wasn't there, and I won't see it until we air it later in post. But I'm not pleased. Call me back."

"Nik . . . now I got Lou Reddy on the phone. Please tell me you didn't piss off the biggest name in stock car. Call me back. You know what? Don't call me back."

"Tanika, as soon as you land back in the States, I want you in my office. First thing. Don't even bother to drop off your luggage."

Well, fuck. The man had said *Tanika*. He was officially pissed off. There were three more voicemails. Tanika erased them without listening, sure of what they were about. So much for her great comeback.

Tanika scrolled further through her missed messages. There were a few texts from Jackie and Bronwyn, asking if she had landed safely. She shot them a quick reply, apologizing for not having done so earlier. Much to her surprise, there was also a text from Gideon. She closed her eyes for a moment—imagining his face—and was flooded with warmth. *Green. Lush. Verdant.* This man made her feel things she hadn't felt in a long time.

> **GIDEON:** Hope the interview went well. Hope the glasses are working out too. I also hope you consumed your weight in fish and chips. That's a lot of hope.

Tanika smiled and shot off her response.

> **TANIKA:** Still getting used to the glasses. I didn't eat that much, but I probably drank enough to be a

walking Guinness factory. Long story.

GIDEON: What happened? I mean, if you want to
tell me?

TANIKA: Let's just say I probably will be covering fly
fishing for the rest of my career.

GIDEON: Yikes. I'm sure it's not that bad.

TANIKA: Nope. It's worse.

Tanika looked at the time, realizing it was early evening in the
States.

TANIKA: Wait, are you busy? Are you heading out
tonight?

GIDEON: I'm in for the night. It's cool. So, want to
talk about it?

Tanika sat on the edge of the toilet lid, frozen, thinking about all
the choices she'd made. Her pride had led her to neglect her vision,
which, in turn, had led to a demotion. Of course, ageism and colorism *really* led to the demotion, but she had to admit, her failing
vision gave the network the excuse they'd surely been looking for. Her
choice to grill Colin the way that she had was also rooted in pride.
But she wanted the story, the real story. All the sacrifices she made in
the name of journalism didn't necessarily make her feel good. Maybe
she should have gone to law school? Or into law enforcement? Then
her daddy would have been proud of her. Maybe even prouder. God,
she couldn't bear to burden Gideon, a near stranger, with all of that.
She sent Gideon a quick text.

TANIKA: Not trying to bore you to death. Or to sleep. Speaking of which, I better get back to bed. But I'm looking forward to our date.

GIDEON: Me too. Night.

Just as she slipped the phone in her robe, Tanika heard a knock at the door of her suite. She figured it was Mya checking on her. Tanika looked out of the peephole. There stood a delivery man holding a large arrangement of flowers.

"Yes?"

"Yes. Delivery for Ms. Tanika Ryan, ma'am."

Tanika reluctantly opened the door, tightening the belt on her robe before removing the chain lock. "Yeah. I'm Tanika."

"Sign here, ma'am." He held out a tablet for Tanika to sign. She took the stylus and signed her name. The courier handed her the massive bouquet of flowers and nodded before heading back toward the elevator.

Tanika took a minute to take in the magnificence of the arrangement. It was a beautiful array of hydrangeas, roses, and birds of paradise. *Are these from Gideon?* She absolutely loved it, until she looked at the card.

Loved our banter, luv. Dinner when I get to the States?

Cheers,

C. B.

"Colin fucking Bello. You've got to be kidding me." She threw the card down on the table. She didn't want to be friends with Colin Bello. She had a strict policy on professional boundaries, not getting overly friendly with anyone she interviewed. And she certainly didn't want to be friends with a young, pompous, naive, and arrogant driver who had no idea what he was getting into. No matter how good-looking he was, with his bulging arms, dimples, and that charming little gap in his smile. Nope. She wasn't falling for it.

Tanika plopped down on the bed and stared at the ceiling. She had screwed up royally with Colin's interview. There was a chance that she wouldn't have a job to go back to once she returned stateside. Her phone, which was now on the nightstand, continued buzzing.

Tanika grabbed a fluffy feather pillow off the bed and screamed into it.

CHAPTER 10

Tanika could not stop pacing. Her Valentino pumps were making holes in Ross's fine Persian rug, no doubt. She was certain she was getting fired. So certain, in fact, that she'd asked Mya to brush up her résumé and edit a new reel just in case she needed to go back on the market. So long VP position, all because of that arrogant prick who thought he could smooth things over with a lovely huge bouquet and a smile. It was a nice smile—one that could melt the panties off any straight woman—but still. A smile attached to an arrogant prick.

Tanika was still pacing when Ross walked in. Chuckling as he approached, he placed both hands on her shoulders.

"Settle down, Nikki. I'm not here to sack you. You can stop wearing a hole into my very expensive rug."

Tanika's shoulders relaxed at his assurance, but only briefly. She slid into one of the buttery leather seats that flanked his desk. "Listen, Ross, I know the interview didn't go as planned, but . . ."

"Are you kidding me? Nikki, it was our highest rated interview in forever. It was a hit. The way you and Colin were going back and forth. Some real chemistry there."

Tanika wasn't sure if she believed Ross. That brown light was floating around his head again. Maybe her lenses were dirty? She removed her glasses and cleaned them with the small bit of cloth she kept in her pocket for this purpose. She replaced her glasses and tried to read Ross's face, a little unsure of what she had just heard. "And what about Lou Reddy? I mean, I kind of went hard on him."

Ross waved his hands. "Oh, please. The old man has heard worse. I'll hit a couple of rounds with him at the club. He'll be fine."

Ah. Of course, you will. As Tanika's nerves began to settle, she noticed that brown haze around Ross's head intensifying. *Murky. Queasy.*

"By the way, the viewers *love* your new glasses. Did you see the hashtag? #NiceSpecsNikki." Mya had sent Tanika a message about some trending hashtags, but she'd been too stressed to read them. She watched as Ross looked through his phone until he found whatever he was looking for.

"So. I was discussing it with the team, and we have an idea."

Tanika knew when Ross mentioned *the team*, his devoted group of brown-nosing producers, it wasn't going to be good. "And what would that be, Ross?"

A sinister smile flashed across Ross's face as he leaned against his desk. "What if you follow Colin for the entire race season? Get folks invested in his story. It would run sort of like a limited docuseries. Single camera. Up close and personal."

Tanika's mouth went dry. This was *not* what she'd expected when she'd walked into work this morning. "Why would I want to do that? What's in it for me? Because hanging around Colin Bello 24/7 isn't incentive enough."

"Listen. I know you are disappointed about being taken off Thursday Nights. I wasn't happy either. Trust me, I fought for you."

"Did you really, Ross? I'm having a hard time believing that. Rumor has it, you were the one advocating for a certain former beauty queen to replace me."

"Oh, Nikki! Those are just rumors!"

"Rumors that you are letting ruin my career." Tanika's voice shot up several octaves, approaching Mariah Carey levels. She took a deep breath to calm herself. "And now, you want me to do a whole season series with the guy, like I'm his personal Ken fucking Burns, to get all of America to fall in love with him. Or better yet, with Lou Reddy. Well guess what, no job is worth being around Colin Bello. Nor do I want to use him like that."

Ross pinched the bridge of his nose. "Why not, Nikki? You'll have free range here. Shoot this thing how you want. Bring in who you want. All we want from you is that same level of work we've grown to love."

Tanika sat up, tapping her fingers on the chair. "Give me a day to think about this."

"Deal. You've got twenty-four hours. Anything else?"

Now or never. "Speaking of rumors, if the VP of Programming job is still available, I want to be considered. Seriously considered."

"I mean, Nikki, like you said, *rumors.* I don't know anything concrete myself."

Tanika knew Ross was lying. She could feel it. "Ross, just promise me you'll go to bat for me when the time comes." She stood, extending her hand to Ross to shake.

Ross took her hand. "Of course, Nik. Scout's honor. In the meantime, let me know about the season series with Colin."

"I mean it, Ross. Don't bullshit me."

"I'd never do that to you, Nikki. You are my secret weapon. Remember? Invaluable! Priceless!" The faint brown glow hadn't dissipated once during their entire conversation.

He's definitely lying.

Tanika's nose wrinkled. "You don't need to kiss my ass. I told you I'd think about it."

Ross nodded, the look of consternation finally loosening its grip on his face.

Tanika smoothed down her crisp cream linen skirt and dug her heels into the carpet one more time for good measure. "Cool."

. . .

Mya stood just outside of Ross's office, chewing on a pen top, a look of panic on her face.

"Well?"

"On a positive note, we have our jobs."

Mya blew out a breath. "That's good. So, there's negative?"

"He wants me to follow Colin for the season. Like a docuseries."

"Ha! I told you that you and Colin had chemistry."

Tanika rolled her neck as she walked, stiffness setting in. "No, we don't."

Mya abruptly stood in front of Tanika, blocking the way into her office with a hand on the doorframe. "Yes. You do. The man sent you flowers and basically dry humped you with his words."

"Is that what you young folks call a dinner invitation? If so, I'll pass. And let me remind you that he's too young and clueless for me." Tanika ducked under Mya's arm and went into her office. "Give me some time to think. In the meantime, we still have a Black history program to prepare for. Are you all set?"

Mya did a salute. "I'm on it. Sara's doing a segment on the history of the Black Dallas Cowboys cheerleaders. She's gonna interview the girl from that show from back in the day . . . *Girlfriends*."

"Oh, how lovely." It was actually a good idea for a segment. One she might have thought of.

"Tanika, please! What is it with the pencils!"

Tanika looked down at her hand. Another pencil broken. "Order another box for me. Please."

"I'm getting mechanical ones next time."

"What's up . . . Nik . . . time's . . . money."

Even over FaceTime, Tanika could tell Jackie was out of breath, huffing and bouncing on what seemed to be an under-desk treadmill. "Jackie, I know you're a busy woman, but they have these things called gyms."

Jackie smirked and slowed down her pace. "Very funny, Nik. But I don't have time to go to the gym. I'm killing two birds with one stone."

"So, you're sweating in your good suit at your desk? I hope you have deodorant."

Jackie shook her head with a laugh. "Hussy, what do you want? You called *me*!"

Tanika had been pondering Ross's offer for the last nine hours, and she still didn't have an answer. So, she called the most rational person that she knew. Jackie was no nonsense and cut to the chase. She'd tell her the truth. No holds barred.

"So, Ross wants me to basically follow Colin Bello for his entire race season. Like a docuseries."

"Okay, and what's the problem? I saw the interview. Kid's a hot mess, but it could work."

Tanika kicked her shoes off and eased back into her chair. She had to get relaxed to tell her friend about the true shit show that was Colin Bello. "Jackie, he's wild and unpredictable. Did you know the flowers haven't stopped? My office is starting to look like FTD. Not to mention . . ." Tanika thought about the colors she saw swirling around Colin and how they made her feel. "I think he has a crush on me."

Abruptly, Jackie started to laugh *hard*, leaving Tanika to figure out what was so funny. Finally, Jackie got herself together, wiping the tears from her eyes.

"A crush? Tanika, I know you've been out the game for a minute but c'mon. This is beyond a crush. The man wants to jump your bones. Put you in traction for like a week."

"And I'm not trying to be in his presence long enough to let him get any of those ideas."

Jackie stopped her treadmill and got a bottle of water from her office fridge. "Then I got an idea. Tell Ross you'll cover his first race in Charlotte. Make sure WWSN gets the exclusive post-race interview for you. You won't follow him the entire season, just the major races. Daytona. Talladega. Darlington. You know?"

"That's cool. I can deal with that. And if push comes to shove, that won't interfere with football season. Especially preseason."

Jackie frowned. "You're still salty about that? You're thinking small, Ryan. I told you to let it go and focus on the VP gig. You need to be thinking big, bitch." Jackie said *bitch* a lot. But Tanika always knew she meant it with love.

Tanika nodded. "I told Ross to consider me. Keep me in the front of his mind."

"Speaking of men who have you on their minds," crooned Jackie. "You know where you and my cousin are heading for your date?" There was extra emphasis on the word *date*.

Tanika felt heat crawl up her neck, steaming up her glasses at the mention of Gideon. They'd been texting just about every night since she'd returned from London, but they still hadn't made concrete plans. She didn't want to rush it, but she was getting anxious. "Kinda waiting on him to let me know."

"Give him some time, Tanika. He's easing back into this dating thing. And to have you as his first date, talk about pressure!"

Tanika gasped, putting her hands over her chest. "What is that supposed to mean?"

"You're Nikki Ryan, the super famous, knockout-gorgeous journalist. Knows sports better than most dudes. I'm sure that intimidates most guys, but especially one who hasn't dated in years."

"I'm not sure if I should be offended or flattered, Jacqueline," Tanika said, purposely using her best friend's full name, which Jackie absolutely hated.

"Be flattered, chick. In the meantime, enjoy yourself. It's about time you went out with someone decent. And if you all hit it off, I promise to stay out of your business. I don't want it to be awkward."

Tanika laughed. "I hope you realize that was a lie before it left your mouth."

"It's true! I don't want to think about my bestie and my cousin bumping uglies."

"I think you're jumping the gun here. It's just going to be a casual date. Truthfully, you know my schedule is bananas. If anything, maybe we'll just have fun and end up being good friends."

"Uh-huh." Jackie looked down at her other cell phone. "Listen, I've got to go. Got a client I have to make sure doesn't screw up his brand-new two-hundred-million-dollar endorsement deal over a speeding ticket. Bye, boss babe!"

Jackie blew Tanika a kiss as the call ended. Covering Colin's major races wouldn't be bad. Tanika could deal with that. She looked at her last text from Gideon.

GIDEON: Looking forward to Sunday.

Tanika tapped her chin, looking at all the flowers on her desk. What she couldn't deal with was a relationship. No entanglements with Colin. And she'd keep things light and fun with Gideon.

That's all she had the bandwidth for.

CHAPTER 11

Gideon and Tanika had been texting for days since her trip to London. Gideon, honestly, was more of a traditional, phone-call kind of guy. But he learned quickly that Tanika loved texting because she'd been talking all day. Her voice often needed a break. On the nights either one of them had insomnia, they texted each other until the early morning hours. Gideon hadn't been up like that since he and Lauren were infatuated college kids. This time around, his forty-something-year-old bones were paying for it in the morning. Celeste never asked why he was so sleepy. She'd just add a double shot of espresso to his usual cup and keep it moving.

Gideon promised Tanika a memorable date. Yet here it was a few days before, and he had no idea what he was going to do or where he'd take her. Gideon hadn't been on a first date in nearly twenty years. Celeste had been absolutely no help in giving him ideas. And all his boys were married. Their idea of a good date was a movie and takeout. He knew he couldn't go out like that. So, he called the one person he knew had better intel on his date than anyone else.

Jackie answered FaceTime on the first ring with a smile. "Well, speak of the devil . . ."

"What do you mean?" questioned Gideon. "Uncle Roydell upset I'm not lending him money again?"

"Ha," Jackie laughed. "Unk hit me up last week, so he's straight. What I meant was I was just talking about you to my girl. So, what's up with the date? Where are you taking her?"

Gideon leaned back in his office chair. "That's the thing, Jack. I haven't been on a first date since 1999. I don't know where to start. She's *your* friend. Help me out."

"Haven't you been talking to Tanika? Texting or whatever? You still don't have a sense of who she is or what she likes? I'm her girl, but I wouldn't know what makes her tick date-wise."

Gideon sighed, fidgeting with the bonsai tree on his desk. "Our texting has been really surface-level stuff. Work-related conversations, usually. Or just asking how the day went. We talk about the latest sneaker drops . . . and, of course, sports."

Jackie laughed. "Tanika can talk sports all night long if you let her. I also know she doesn't open up easily. It takes time. But in general, Tanika is easygoing. Fun-loving. Loves to be active. She loves old school rap and probably knows all the lyrics to Lil' Kim's 'No Time.' I mean, don't get me wrong; you better not take her for burgers and shakes or want to Netflix and chill. Just do something fun, and you can't go wrong."

Gideon was taking notes in his notepad. "Anything else?"

Jackie rolled her eyes. "How about you stop taking notes and just try and go with the flow? This isn't some test you're being graded on, nerd. Something will come to you."

"Ha. Very funny from the girl who used to cheat off my geometry tests in ninth grade."

"That's because Ms. Shah hated my guts, and I didn't want to repeat the class with that witch again!" Jackie laughed. "But c'mon, Gid. You got this. Stop sweating it, okay?"

"Okay, cousin. Love you."

"You too, loser! You and Tanika are going to have a blast. I got a good feeling about it. So, chill out!"

Gideon shook his head as Jackie shot him the bird, and with a smile, disconnected their call.

*   *   *

GIDEON STOOD OUTSIDE OF CHEF'S WAREHOUSE, THE GOURMET market, pacing anxiously. Granted, he'd arrived a full twenty minutes earlier than expected, but he hadn't wanted anything to make him late, especially the notoriously unpredictable Atlanta traffic. Gideon really wished that Tanika had allowed him to pick her up, but she'd insisted on meeting him there. While he totally understood her reasons for doing so—safety being one of them—his ego was a bit bruised. He'd wanted to do the gentlemanly thing and pick her up, open the car door for her, and even let her pick the music for their ride. Gideon stopped pacing, the error of his ways dawning on him.

She's not Lauren.

Lauren had loved being a passenger princess. He couldn't expect Tanika or any woman to be just like his late wife.

At the allotted time, Tanika pulled up in her car and parked next to Gideon's SUV. When she got out, Gideon nearly lost his breath. Gone were the stuffy suits and bob haircut. Granted, Tanika could wear a paper bag and look great. But this was something else. Tanika's hair was loose and curly, with tiny silver strands here and there. Her new glasses looked incredible—the matte black was perfect, and the shape drew attention to her big brown eyes. Eyes that stopped Gideon in his tracks every time he looked at her. She wore a flowy, yellow-and-white-striped dress and accessorized her casual look with a worn leather jacket and light scarf. On her feet, she wore a pair of green, white, and yellow Nike Cortez. Gideon's heart skipped a beat. The Cortez was one of his favorite classic sneakers ever, next to the Stan Smiths he wore tonight.

"Am I late?" asked Tanika, looking at her watch. "Seems like you've been out here a minute."

"I'm ridiculously early to everything. You're good. And you look incredible, by the way. You are working those glasses. Love the Cortez."

"Thank you! Yeah, I figured since it was a cooking class and we'd be on our feet, I probably shouldn't wear heels." Tanika glanced down at her feet. "Honestly, when I'm not working, I rarely wear heels."

"You're perfect." Gideon immediately wished he could walk back the words. He was being too eager—or *thirsty*, as his nephew would say.

"I mean, you're good," he said in a more reserved tone. "Let's head in."

They walked into the tiny market, where a tall, lanky woman greeted them. She wore a beanie over shoulder-length locs, with a gleaming septum piercing and a dark green chef coat with what looked like a cannabis leaf embroidered on it. Classic seventies yacht rock was blasting through the speakers behind her.

"Hey y'all! Welcome to the Cooking with THC class! I'm your instructor, Chef TJ! Glad y'all could come out."

Gideon's eyes grew wide. What the entire hell. He'd totally misread the class description. He thought it had said cooking with TLC. Not THC. He looked over at Tanika, whose brow was raised sky-high.

"Tanika, I had no idea this was cooking with weed! I totally misread the description. We can cancel this and do something else."

But Tanika was already taking off her jacket and scarf. "Hold on now, Gideon. Let's not knock it before we try it. This could be fun. I take it you aren't a weed smoker."

Gideon took Tanika's jacket and scarf and draped them across the back of a chair. "The last time I smoked was probably ten years ago." In fact, he knew exactly where and when: in Jamaica, on vacation with Lauren. "But I'm certainly not opposed. I mean, I've seen the benefits of medical cannabis on my patients, especially those with glaucoma."

"Seriously? Ten years? Okay, what about college? Did you smoke much then?"

"Eh, maybe once."

Tanika gasped and playfully slapped his arm. "Wow. You went to A&T, home of the Greatest Homecoming on Earth, and didn't partake? Either you're a saint, or you're a square. God bless you, either way."

The chef's assistant came around to pass out aprons. Tanika slid Gideon's apron around his neck, her fingers slightly touching his skin, which made his pulse race. He could smell her scent, and when he looked down into her eyes, he was enraptured by the warmth he found there. She gently spun him around and tied the back of the apron, her hand settling on the small of his back. He couldn't remember the last time a woman had touched him like this. Actually, he could. Gideon swallowed the guilt he was feeling, taking a step back.

"You, okay? I can tie it a bit tighter."

"I'm fine."

"Cool." Tanika spun around, her back facing him. "Can you tie me up too?"

Gideon's hands were shaking as he pulled the apron strings around Tanika. Given the view, he took a few greedy glances. The curve of her behind, the wideness of her hips, her delicate neck that seemed to invite a nibble. He tied the apron and let his hands rest on Tanika's hips for a second too long.

He cleared his throat. "I think you're good."

Tanika looked over her glasses at him with a smile. "Yeah. I think I'm good."

Chef TJ went over a few sanitation rules before getting started, then explained the menu. "I'm sure some of you have never cooked with weed. Maybe you've picked up some goodies from Thyme in a Bottle or brought edibles from the dispensary. But cannabis has incredible flavors that you can infuse into any part of a meal. This is going to be a pretty basic menu. A green goddess dressing infused with THC oil for your avocado-tomato salad. A lamb ragu with tagliatelle pasta. And the grand finale, a CBD-infused peach crumble." The group—six couples gathered around the long chef's table—exchanged glances, collectively swooning at the ingredients before heading to their stations.

Tanika rubbed her hands together. "This should be fun. I don't cook much with my schedule. It's always takeout or delivery."

Gideon looked at the ingredients, taking stock of what seemed to be a minimal amount of weed and weed-infused supplies at their station. "It shouldn't be that bad. I mean, it's not that much weed. I doubt we'll be super high or anything."

By the time they finished the lamb ragu, Gideon and Tanika were high as two kites.

Gideon watched as Tanika used her finger to lick the rest of the ragu off her plate. The simple act shouldn't have made his dick as hard as it did. He blamed the weed.

"Oh my god. Either I'm high or that was literally the best pasta I've ever had. I'm losing my table manners over here."

"I think the Mango Haze–infused lemonade is probably what took us over the edge," laughed Gideon. "Just look at the Wilsons over there."

The couple to the right of them, Jake and Paul Wilson, were slumped over and laughing. Ragu was all over Jake's black beard, and Paul was feeding him the last of the tagliatelle. Gideon snorted. *Damn, I really am high.* The pasta really was good, though—the flavors warm, with the THC-infused olive oil providing an earthy note that added complexity to the dish. Gideon looked at Tanika, who was still giggling. *I could get used to cooking with this woman.*

Chef TJ floated by each station to give the couples tips on preparing their peach crumble. "Looks like you two had fun! Our dessert is going to be a peach crumble with a CBD-infused crust and bourbon sauce. The CBD should bring you guys down from the high."

Gideon watched Tanika gently combine the flour, pecans, and brown sugar, stirring them until they were mixed well with the butter.

In watching her move, he'd almost forgotten his job—the peaches. He quickly put them into a pan with the bourbon, cinnamon, and honey. *Oh, and the weed.* It all smelled so good and sweet. His eyes moved to Tanika's lips, plump and light brown. He guessed that nothing he'd eat that night would be sweeter than a kiss from those lips.

Thankfully, Chef TJ served coffee with the desserts to further mellow out the high. As she came around to Tanika and Gideon, her smile widened. "How long have you two been dating?"

Tanika laughed, a warm flush coming across her face. "Oh, this is our first date."

"Hmm," said Chef. "Really? He looks like he could eat you off the plate." Then she moved on, continuing to deliver coffee around the table.

She wasn't wrong. Gideon felt heat crawling up his neck. "Maybe I'm a little higher than I thought. Want to take a walk after this?"

"I'd love to."

THE STREETS NEAR PONCEY-HIGHLAND WERE EMPTY FOR A SUNDAY evening. Tanika and Gideon walked along the sidewalk, taking in the cool late-January air.

"I used to be a vegan back in optometry school," confessed Gideon. "J. Cole locs and everything." At this point he was rambling, but he would say just about anything to extend his night with Tanika. He was relaxed, albeit due to the weed. It was the most fun he'd had in forever.

"Really?" laughed Tanika. "I can't picture that. So, what made you stop being a vegan?"

"My Big Mama Bobbie Ann's fried chicken. There was no way you could head home to Goldsboro, North Carolina, and tell your very Southern family that you were a vegan."

"Hell no you couldn't! That's sacrilegious."

They laughed, pausing under the lights near the Majestic Diner. Tanika turned and adjusted the collar of Gideon's jacket. "Well, I like you bald, bearded, and a fan of fried chicken. It suits you much more."

Gideon blew out a breath. Slowly, he extended his hand toward Tanika, who threaded her fingers through his. Her palm was small in his hand, but the warmth that he felt was immense. "Tonight's been nice."

Tanika bit her lip. "I agree. Even if you low-key got me high on a first date."

Gideon's laugh boomed. "I swear I had no idea!"

"I didn't mind. Weed or no weed, I would have enjoyed it no matter what." Tanika smiled wide, and something inside Gideon's chest bloomed. He moved closer to her, and even in the cold, he could smell the spices of their meal mixed with her perfume. Just as he was angling to kiss her, he heard someone call out to them.

"*Psst!* Hey! You two!"

Tanika and Gideon turned in the direction of the voice and found themselves facing the storefront for Mother Mary's Tarot and Fortune Reading. A wild-haired woman—a dead ringer for Broadway legend Bernadette Peters—was leaning against the frame of the establishment, smoking a cigarette.

"You two lovebirds wanna get your fortunes read?"

Gideon frowned, waving this feral-looking lady off. "Nah, I think we're good."

Tanika shrugged. "What's the harm? It might be fun. Or are you like, saved, and don't dabble in the occult?"

Gideon laughed. "Jesus is my homeboy, but that's not the reason. I always think these folks are scammers."

"I can hear you," the woman said. "You coming in or not?" She put out her cigarette on the bottom of her combat boot and walked inside.

"What the hell. We're already high. Might as well," suggested Gideon.

Through the beaded curtain, the three of them sat at a dark, round wooden table, inhaling an overpowering amount of nag champa.

"Smells like a college dorm," whispered Tanika.

The woman poured herself a shot of something dusky and held out her hand toward Gideon. "Call me Mother Mary. You. Give me your hand, handsome."

Gideon held out his hand, and Mother Mary stared for a good five minutes. Sighing, Gideon rolled his eyes, becoming agitated at her setup, wishing she'd just get it over with.

"You've been in mourning too long," Mother Mary said. "It's time that you release the guilt and enjoy life. She wants you to be happy."

Gideon tried to snatch his hand away, as if he'd been burned by a hot stove. But Mother Mary held on tighter, continuing to talk. "You value sight but have been blind to your own grief. Release it. Now is the time to do that." Gideon shivered, his stomach squirming with a sense of unease. With a satisfied smirk, Mother Mary let his hand go.

"Next. Dollface, give me your hand."

"Do your thing, but I'm sure—"

"Shut it!" The woman scowled, staring down at Tanika's palm. Finally, she let go and stared at Tanika. She pointed her chin toward Tanika's eyes, which were wide behind her glasses. "The blinders are off for you now. What you've been seeing isn't a trick. It's the truth inside of people. The truth you need to know. Take it for what it is, and you'll be happier for it."

Tanika gasped, holding her palm to her chest. "What the hell!"

Mother Mary twirled her beads. "That'll be forty dollars. I do accept Venmo."

Tanika and Gideon walked out of Mother Mary's silently. They walked a few quiet blocks back to their parked cars.

"That was weird, right?" Gideon was rattled by the fortune teller's accuracy, at least about his own feelings.

"Yeah. I think maybe she knew we were high." Tanika laughed uneasily.

"Maybe." Something about the woman's words, as uncanny as they were, gave Gideon a boost of confidence. He moved closer to Tanika as she leaned up against her car. "But I hate that she interrupted what I was going to do."

"Which was?"

Gideon looked down at Tanika's lips, took off his glasses, and closed the space between them. When his lips touched hers, he let out a satisfied moan. He tasted a faint hint of the peaches from their dessert, mixed with her lip gloss. Tanika's lips parted, allowing Gideon to slip his tongue inside. His tongue danced with hers, painting his taste in her mouth. He pulled back, sucking her bottom lip, which he concluded was indeed sweeter than any dessert imaginable. It all felt like slow motion, as if time were reminding him to savor the moment. When he finally came up for air, his eyes met Tanika's, whose lids were low and hazy in the winter moonlight.

"Can you drive? Because last time, you ran into a hydrant and had to come see me."

"Very funny. I'm high but not that high. Plus, a very fine optometrist hooked me up with glasses. I can read signs and everything now." Tanika ran a hand through Gideon's salt-and-pepper beard. He shut his eyes tight, inhaling the scent on her wrist. "How far is your place from here?"

Gideon kissed the delicate skin of her wrist and felt Tanika shiver underneath his touch. "Maybe fifteen minutes, in Kirkwood."

"Text me your address."

CHAPTER 12

Tanika had barely parked her car before Gideon was dragging her by the hand into his large, craftsman-style home. She could blame the weed or even the fortune teller for her current state of horniness, but she'd be wrong in both instances. From the moment she'd seen Gideon standing in front of the market nervously pacing, he'd brought a smile to her face. Knowing he was just as nervous as she was had calmed her down. Wearing a classic peacoat, V-neck sweater, and a pair of custom Stan Smiths, he was even more handsome outside of his office. She'd known long before the date was over that she wanted to kiss him. Everywhere.

Gideon peeled her coat and scarf off and tossed them on a bench in the foyer, not once breaking their kiss. Her purse dropped to the floor next to the bench.

"Should I take my sneaks off?" asked Tanika breathlessly, leaning her head back as Gideon kissed along her neck.

"I don't care," he said, coming up for air. "Come here."

He maneuvered Tanika up against the wall, his knee gently parting her legs. She looked at him, her glasses slightly crooked and a little fogged up, but she could see that same green halo around him. That green, lush glow. She'd seen it all around him when she'd first shown up to the date today, and more than that, she'd *felt* it. It was like a flashing sign above his head. *Green-green-green. Go-go-go.* Maybe she should have asked Mother Mary if green meant *go give Gideon the drawers*, but she hadn't wanted to shell out more cash for that answer. Instead, she'd go on instinct. And instinct was telling her this man was the real deal.

Tanika stroked Gideon's back as he kissed her like a man desperate for resuscitation. When she cupped the back of his bald head, he moaned into her mouth, which made her nipples harden against his chest. She couldn't remember the last time a man had responded to her that way, but she loved it. Especially from Gideon.

"God, you taste better than I imagined," he whispered against her lips. He trailed his lips down her neck to the top of her dress. His tongue was warm and wet, dancing over her skin, raising her temperature like the steam of a sauna. She wanted—no, she *needed*—more than kisses from him. She needed to feel his hands touching her body. *Desperately.*

"Touch me, please." Tanika spoke in a voice so low she was sure that Gideon hadn't heard her. But he had. He took his hands and moved them from her waist to her breasts. He kneaded them gently, finding each nipple through her dress, rolling them between his fingers. Tanika let out a slight hiss, hoping that Gideon took that as a sign to explore further. When he began unbuttoning the top of her dress, she knew he was picking up on her cues. She loved a fast learner.

Tanika stood there, her chest heaving and breath ragged. The cool air of the house made her nipples painfully hard. She watched as Gideon took notice, moving his hands inside her bra to feel the taut, erect pebbles, which only stiffened more with his teasing, playful touch.

"You're so beautiful."

Pressed against Tanika, Gideon's erection was stiff against her thigh. She moved a hand between their bodies, finding her way inside the top of his pants. His hands stopped massaging her breasts. He froze.

"Gideon?" Tanika was worried she'd done something wrong.

"It's fine. It's just been a while since . . ."

"We'll go as slow or as fast as you want to."

Gideon gave a throaty chuckle. "I'm just trying not to come in those pretty hands of yours."

"I wouldn't care if you did." Tanika, with one hand, unbuttoned the top of Gideon's jeans, sliding into his boxers—where she found a very thick dick in her hands. She was pleasantly satisfied. Her thumb swirled around the top of his wet tip. That action made his hand slam against the wall next to her and his head fall onto her shoulder.

"Fuck, Tanika," Gideon hissed, his lips finding their way back to her neck, then across the shell of her ear. Wetness flooded her panties as she tried to press her thighs together. With Gideon's knee there, it was no use. The only relief she could get from the thrumming of her clit was rubbing her pussy against Gideon's thigh.

Much to her delight.

With her hand down his pants and her pussy grinding against his thigh, Tanika could tell that she was slowly sending Gideon into orbit. He looked down at her, finding her curls pressed against her face, her eyelids heavy with desire, and amusingly, her glasses crooked as all hell. Tanika knew she looked like a horny mess but didn't care.

"You've got my jeans soaked. Let me take care of that ache for you, princess." He held Tanika against the wall. She nodded yes, biting her lip. Gideon stepped back, slowly allowing Tanika to release her hands from his dick and her damp pussy from his jeans. He took off his glasses, placing them on a console table. She stroked his face, and he kissed the palm of her hand.

"You don't need to see right now," Gideon said as he slowly removed Tanika's glasses and placed them on the console table as well. "You just need to feel."

Yes, Doctor.

Gideon's hands fisted the sides of Tanika's dress, raising it to expose her thick, deep-brown thighs. When his fingers reached the seat of her panties, she marveled at just how wet and hot she was.

Tanika tried not to be impatient, but the slow movement of his fingers and the stimulation of the cloth against her clit was driving her insane. She needed him to touch her. To rub her aching pussy until she came all over his hand.

Apparently sensing her need, Gideon slowly moved her panties to the side, sliding his index finger up and down her hot, wet slit. "When's the last time someone made you come, Tanika?"

Once again, she felt compelled to tell this man the truth. "Two years."

Gideon paused his stroking and looked into her eyes.

"I think we were meant to stop that longing in each other." His fingers were paused just above her heated entrance. "I'm here to make you feel so good, Tanika."

With that, Gideon slid a finger inside of her. She bucked against his hand with a moan, her nails digging into his shoulders.

"Tanika, you're so tight." He carefully slid a second finger inside her. At first, his pace was agonizingly slow, but when she responded to a certain spot, he craned his fingers just right to reach that deep need, furiously increasing the pace while his thumb circled her clit.

"Oh god, Gideon!" Tanika's mouth formed a perfect O.

"Come for me, beautiful," Gideon begged, his fingers diving deep inside her pussy, which was making sounds so sopping that Tanika blushed, embarrassed. She peeked down to see his dick straining painfully against his jeans, begging to be inside her. God, she was trying her best to enjoy the moment. But as Gideon had reminded her, it had been ages since she'd had someone touch her. She didn't want to squander her opportunity.

Tanika threw her head back against the wall, one leg held up, supported by Gideon's tight grip on her thigh. She was close to coming; she could feel the buildup of electric tingles against her spine. Her essence was beginning to release all over his fingers, and Gideon was moaning louder and louder in response. She lapped and nipped at his bottom lip; her hands locked around his neck. It was the best ride ever, and she didn't want to let go.

As the pressure built, Tanika's body was losing control. She had to focus on something—anything—to sustain the high she was feeling. She looked over at the console and saw a photograph of Gideon and a woman in a wedding dress. A *familiar* woman. Tanika squeezed her eyes shut, sure that she was imagining things. She wasn't wearing her glasses, after all. She opened her eyes and tried to focus on something else. On the opposite wall were more photos of the same woman, with and without Gideon. Photo after photo.

He still had pictures up of his wife. He still wore his wedding band. He wasn't ready, and . . . maybe neither was she. *And why does that woman look just like the lady I saw at his office that first day, dressed in all white? No way. How?* Tanika shook her head. She couldn't do this.

Gideon was still working hard, intending to stroke her to climax, but Tanika was struggling to speak. "Gid, please. Can you . . . just hold on a second."

Gideon's eyes were heavy with lust. "Yes, baby. What is it?"

Tanika held his wrist, stopping his hand. Gideon pulled out his fingers, licking them with a smile that nearly unraveled Tanika. But she was determined to remain focused. She lowered her leg to the ground, pulled down her dress, and regained her balance. She had to get out of there.

"I think maybe we should slow down. I don't know if we should do this."

Gideon's brows knit. "Why? Did I do something?" He reached for Tanika's hip, but she moved away. She watched him search her face for an answer, and she wished she could fully articulate her hesitation without sounding like Mother Mary herself.

Tanika shook her head. "No. I mean, yes, it's just . . ." Before she could come up with the right words, her cell phone began to ring. Frantically, Tanika looked around for her purse before realizing it was still near the front door. "Sorry, I got to take it."

Gideon nodded, wiping his hand down his face. "Sure."

It was Mya calling. Late, so it had to be an emergency.

"Hey, Mya. What's up?" She tried to sound as normal and non-finger-fucked as possible.

"Tanika, you're never going to believe this, but Sara is in the hospital."

Tanika froze. She'd wished for a lot of things, but she'd never wished bodily harm on Sara. "What happened?"

"Girl, it's nothing. Well, it's something. She's in the hospital with a serious case of food poisoning. She ate some bad sushi at Nobu or something. Ross wanted me to contact you as soon as possible. With the big game coverage coming up soon, they're going to need you back on *Football Center* to fill in for Sara."

"Seriously?" Tanika's eyes went back over to Gideon, who was adjusting himself and putting his glasses back on. He grabbed Tanika's glasses and handed them to her; she nodded thank-you. She could tell he was a little dejected—the green glow was a little dimmer. Still warm but flickering a bit. She shook her head.

"Well, Mya, tell them I'll do it. I gotta go." She tucked her phone back in her purse. "Hey, that was work. I've got to fill in for Sara on *Football Center*. She's sick."

"Oh," Gideon raised a brow. "That's great. I mean, not Sara getting sick, but it's great that you'll be back on a program that you loved."

Tanika reached for her coat and scarf. "Yeah. Listen, I had a great time. I'll text you later, okay?"

Gideon shook his head. "Damn. It's like that? Alright, but . . ."

Tanika gave Gideon a swift kiss on the lips and didn't wait to hear him say goodbye before she was out the door and headed to her car. As she pulled out of the driveway, she looked up to see Gideon standing on the porch, leaning against a brick column. He gave a quick wave before turning around and heading back inside.

No matter what she was feeling, or what any fortune teller was saying, it was clear that she wasn't ready to deal with a relationship. Or maybe it was just that she wasn't willing to live in the shadows of a woman that Gideon was clearly still in love with. Wouldn't she always be playing second fiddle to a ghost? She'd seen how coming second had destroyed her parents' relationship, leaving her mother feeling unloved and Tanika feeling unwanted. She didn't want to feel that way again.

Tanika pulled out of the driveway and put her Pandora on shuffle. The first few chords of Curtis Mayfield's "The Makings of You" flooded her speakers as she headed down the highway. Instead of going home, Tanika headed toward the one person she knew could help her make sense of all this.

CHAPTER 13

Tanika rang the doorbell of Bronwyn's East Atlanta bungalow, the sound of Tibetan singing bowls announcing her arrival. It was late, and she hadn't really expected Bronwyn to open the door. But after bouncing impatiently in the cold for a few minutes, the door swung open in front of Tanika. Bronwyn wore a loose green caftan, and her locs were up in a wrap. There was a shimmer of indigo light around Bronwyn's head, making her look like an actual goddess. Tanika blinked until she realized that it was just the entryway light.

"Hey girl! What are you doing here? I thought you were on a date?"

"I saw a ghost." Tanika blurted out. "I mean, I think I did. Shit."

Bronwyn stared at Tanika. "Your eyes are a little red. Have you been smoking? I've told you time and time again, if you're going to do weed, it is best to brew it in a tea!"

"Bronwyn!" hissed Tanika. "Are you going to let me in or not?"

"Oh! Yeah, come on in." Bronwyn moved aside, allowing Tanika to step into the foyer, gesturing for her to lead the way to the sitting room.

Tanika headed down the hall and nearly screamed when she reached the living room and found a man butt naked in downward dog. "Oh my god, Kenny!"

Tanika turned her head, facing the wall. It wasn't the first or last time she'd seen Kenny naked. He and Bronwyn were ultra free-spirited. Tanika was sure she'd seen him fully naked, balls to the wall, at least four hundred times in twenty-plus years. It never got less shocking. *But I can see why Bronwyn has so many damn kids.*

"You caught us during our couple's yoga session," Bronwyn said to Tanika when they finally made it to her sitting room, Kenny's behind safely out of sight. "It really helps us to connect, you know?"

Tanika nodded, noticing that it was unusually quiet in the Carter house. "Um, where are the kids?" Bronwyn and Kenny didn't just have children; they had a brood. They had started making babies as soon as they got together. They called their parenting style "gentle and noncombative." In all honesty, the kids were basically free-range like chickens, clucking around wildly and making noise.

"Well," sighed Bronwyn. "Tigerlily is staying over at her girl-friend's house. Or is it her boyfriend's this week? Thyme is at the library studying for his homeopathic exam. Honeysuckle and Briarwood are at a mindfulness retreat. Golden is probably up planning his next rally. Plum and Periwinkle are asleep, finally. I had to threaten them with no Nintendo for a week!" Bronwyn tucked her feet underneath her and turned toward Tanika. "You didn't come to talk about the kids. You mentioned a ghost."

"Right." Tanika nodded. "So, I was at Gideon's house, and we were getting kind of hot and heavy. And I was trying to focus on something to, you know . . ."

"Sustain your orgasm." Bronwyn drummed her fingers on her chin. "Despite the red eyes, I can tell you have a post-orgasmic glow. Go on."

"Right. That's when I saw his wife. His *dead* wife. I mean, I didn't actually see her; I saw photos of her. All over the place. But the thing is, I'd seen her before."

"Slow down," Bronwyn held up her hand. "You'd seen who before? His actual wife? Or her ghost?"

"Hell, I don't know. After my exam at Gideon's practice, a woman who looked just like his dead wife helped me find these glasses." She gestured to her face. "When I asked Gideon to thank his assistant for me, he seemed totally confused. Fast forward to tonight, and I see photos of this beautiful woman in his foyer. I am telling you, it's the same woman! It felt like she was there! Watching us. I couldn't even see the photos clearly, Bronwyn. I wasn't wearing my glasses. But she had the same *glow* about her. The same exact brightness."

Bronwyn stood. "Come with me. Take your shoes off."

Tanika frowned but followed Bronwyn's instructions, kicking her sneakers off and leaving them in the sitting room. She trailed behind her friend, down the hall, past the sunroom, and down another small, dark hallway. Bronwyn stood outside a closed door at the end of the hall, dramatically turning to Tanika. "I think there is something you need to do."

Bronwyn opened the door to a small room. Inside were a few mismatched, colorful floor pillows, a brown-and-rust-colored Turkish rug, and an altar. On the altar were old pictures and an assortment of fruit, nuts, flowers, various liquors, Florida water, and a lot of other stuff Tanika didn't quite recognize. She watched as Bronwyn lit candles, one by one, until the tiny space was bathed in light.

Tanika sat on the floor, looking around. "What is this place, Bron?"

"It's my ancestral altar. A place to venerate the dead and speak to them."

Tanika's eyes widened. "Bitch, I am not trying to have a séance."

"You need more than two people for that," Bronwyn corrected as she sat down next to Tanika, spreading out her caftan with a flourish. "No, we are going to ask your ghost for protection and permission. Let them know you mean no harm."

"Permission for what?"

Bronwyn gave a slight smile. "To let Gideon love you and for you to love Gideon."

"Love?" Tanika nearly shouted. "It was *one* date, Bronwyn!"

"Fine," Bronwyn sighed. "Maybe not love, but permission to get close. Tell me, when you met the ghost, what did you feel? Hostility? Anger?"

"Not at all. She was kind. Helpful. She told me what I wanted was *right in front of me*. Said I just needed to see it clearly. And she was saving these glasses for the right person."

"Wow." Bronwyn was blinking back tears. "I think we better get started. It won't take long." She reached over to a small table in the corner, grabbing a pen and small notepad. She handed them to Tanika. "I want you to tell . . . what's her name?"

"Lauren Miles."

"Yes. Tell Lauren your intentions with Gideon. And anything else that comes to you. Ask for her permission to be in his life. Stuff like that. Got it?"

"I think so. What if she gets upset?"

"Oh, trust me! We'll know. Start writing."

Tanika let out a deep breath and wrote.

Lauren,

Hello. I am Tanika. I think we've met. Thanks for help with the glasses. They are fly.

I want to tell you that I like Gideon. A lot. I am a good person, and I think Gideon is amazing. I just want to get to know him. Please allow me to be in his life. I could never take your place. If I could give him a fraction of the happiness that you gave him, and vice versa, that would be wonderful.

PS: Sorry we were dry humping in front of your photos. That was mad disrespectful. Won't happen again.

Tanika looked up from the pad and shrugged. "I guess I'm done. Now what?"

Bronwyn nodded. "Good. Now we go to the altar. Say a few words. Light your note on fire in the bowl. And hope that Lauren hears you."

Tanika couldn't believe she was going through with this. But if anyone knew anything about communing with ghosts, it was her very own self-proclaimed medium bestie, Bronwyn.

The two women approached the ancestral altar. Tanika watched as Bronwyn lit a stick of palo santo and a bundle of sage. She waved them around the altar and Tanika seven times, then pulled out a chime and played three notes.

"Ancestors, we welcome you to this space. We come with full hearts and open minds. Sister Tanika is here to communicate with one Lauren Miles. Please allow her message to get through."

Bronwyn signaled for the piece of paper from Tanika. Tanika ripped it off the pad. She watched as Bronwyn folded it as small as she could before placing it into the bowl. She handed Tanika a long matchstick. "Okay, now light the note, sis."

With shaky hands, Tanika struck the matchstick and lit the paper. They both watched as the flame grew and the paper eventually turned into ash.

Tanika waited a few beats before turning to Bronwyn. "Am I supposed to get an answer now or later?"

"I mean, I highly doubt that you'll get an immediate response. But in time, you'll know."

Just then, the door of the room flew open, bringing with it a gust of wind that extinguished every candle in the room. Tanika shrieked, grabbing Bronwyn's hand. If this was Lauren, she sure knew how to make an entrance.

"It's okay! Total coincidence," Bronwyn said, trying to calm a very terrified Tanika. "I mean, probably. This room is drafty sometimes. Let me get the light."

Once Bronwyn switched on the light and came back to the altar, she froze, still as a statue, her eyes transfixed.

"Bronwyn, what's wrong?"

Bronwyn slowly turned. "I think you've got your answer, Tanika. Come look."

Tanika rolled her eyes. Bronwyn had lost her marbles. But she lowered herself back down to the altar. And when she looked in the bowl, she saw it for herself.

In the ashes of her burned note, three handwritten fragments of her letter remained, clear as day.

Y-E-S

CHAPTER 14

"Gideon, you've been fixing those magazines for the last half hour since Mr. Douglass left. What's going on with you?"

Celeste folded her arms, staring at him as if he'd lost his mind. And maybe he had. It had been a few days since his date with Tanika, and they had only sporadically texted. He knew she'd be busy covering Sara's spot on *Football Center*, so he didn't want to bother her. He could admit he was out of it.

Celeste took the stack of magazines out of his hands, motioning for him to sit down. Reluctantly, he did.

"You never told me how your date with Tanika went. From the way you're moping around here like you lost your puppy, I'd guess not so good."

Gideon sighed. "It was going great. Until it wasn't. We had a great time at the cooking class. We took a walk. Then . . ." Gideon stopped. He didn't feel entirely comfortable telling his dead wife's sister that he'd been making out with a woman inside the home they once shared. "Then, it sort of went south."

After Tanika ran off that night, Gideon had headed back inside. When he went to look for his phone, which had fallen behind the console, he realized what could have scared Tanika off. Right there on the console—in Tanika's direct line of sight—was his wedding photo.

He'd never moved it. It was sitting there collecting dust as Lauren's visage stared out, bright-eyed and smiling, frozen in time. Taking in the whole space, Gideon saw what Tanika must have seen—photo after photo of his wife, still hanging on the walls. Gideon's heart ached inexplicably, pulled in multiple directions: both missing Lauren and missing Tanika. It was confusing as hell. Although that fortune teller had been scarily accurate, none of her intrusive statements had given him an answer for the one question he'd kept asking himself since Lauren's death: *How can my heart release the grief it holds for one love to make room for a new one?*

That night, Gideon had tried to take his mind off it all. He'd grabbed a beer and tried to watch *Rush Hour*, one of his favorite movies. Chris Tucker always made him laugh. When that didn't help, he started cleaning the kitchen floor. By the time he made it upstairs, he was exhausted. Without thinking, he opened the door to the master bedroom.

The master bedroom had been untouched since Lauren's death. Bottles of perfume collected dust on the dresser. Her photo was still on his nightstand, the one of her blowing out her thirty-fifth birthday candles. He could even see a slight indentation from her head in the pillow on her side of the bed. As his eyes moved across the room, he swore he could still see Lauren sitting at her vanity, fixing her lipstick. He stared at her reflection in the mirror, and she winked back. He could smell her. He could hear her laughing.

Oh my god! Don't look at me like that, Gideon! You'll make us late.

Gideon closed his eyes, trying to block what was clearly a hallucination. He shut the door again and headed for one of the spare bedrooms, where he slept the nights he didn't crash on the sofa downstairs.

He tossed and turned in bed for hours. Unable to sleep, he ran a semi-cold shower, his dick still throbbing. He leaned a hand against the slick bathroom tiles and pumped a soapy hand over his hardness. His mind flitted between images of Lauren and images of Tanika, both in states of lust. When he focused on Tanika, her pussy wet and gripping his fingers as she rode them, moaning and saying his name, Gideon released with a primal wail that reverberated through the bathroom.

Celeste snapped her fingers. "Hello! Where did you go, Gid? I asked you if you're going to see her again."

Gideon shook his head, embarrassed by the memory he'd just been lost in. He forced his thoughts to come to the present. "I doubt it'll be anytime soon. She's busy. The date ended because she got a call from work. She's filling in her old slot on *Football Center*, and then she's headed to travel for work. Something about stock car and a rodeo."

"Like I always say, that type—women like Tanika and me—likes to hide behind the job. Listen, if it's meant to be, it's meant to be. You'll know."

Gideon picked a piece of nonexistent lint off his white coat, avoiding Celeste's eyes.

Suddenly, breaking the awkward silence between them, the television in the lobby came on. Gideon and Celeste looked at each other.

"Did you do that?" Gideon asked.

Celeste shook her head. "Lost the remote to that TV a while ago. How the hell did it just turn on?"

Gideon looked up at the television, which was somehow on WWSN. On the screen, in living color, was none other than Tanika Ryan. "Well, I'll be damned," Gideon whispered.

"Well, fellas," said Tanika to her fellow anchors on *Football Center*, "Los Angeles actually has a shot to bring home another championship as long as Smith's ACL holds up. I think it will."

"I don't know," countered her ever-disagreeable colleague, Jacob Goldstein. "He's been a bit shaky on it during practice."

"I think he can turn it up during the game," said league Hall-of-Famer Key-Juan Washington. "In the words of Iverson, 'You talking about practice!'" All three of them laughed, and Tanika looked like she was actually having fun for a change. She was in her element, and it showed. Gideon smiled up at the television.

"Well, Nikki," said Jacob, "I guess you got a look into the future since you got new glasses. Are they made of crystal balls or something?"

Tanika laughed. "Let's just say I have better insight than the two of you, but it has nothing to do with glasses." Tanika paused and cleared her throat. "But I do want to thank Dr. Gideon Miles over at Miles Optometry in East Lake for the new specs. I'm sure some of you all noticed a few months ago I was flubbing a bit. Well, I was in denial that I needed glasses. This isn't sponsored, but you all go see him. Tell them Nikki sent you."

"Well, I'm going to have to go see this Dr. Miles if he's got you *seeing* LA in the big game," laughed Key-Juan, before the show cut to commercial.

Gideon and Celeste gaped at each other.

"Did she just shout you out on national TV? Oh my god! You must have blown her back out!"

"What? Celeste! I swear I didn't ask her to do that! I'd never use our relationship for free promo. Also, there was no sex!"

"Fine then." Celeste reached up to put her hands on Gideon's shoulders. "But don't you think that was a little strange that the TV, which has been off for months because we lost the remote, just happened to come on showing WWSN with your girlfriend anchoring? And that girlfriend shouts out your practice?"

"She's not my girlfriend, CeCe."

"Boy, after that, she better be; I got a feeling she just gave you the boost you needed. I know you aren't super religious, but baby boy, I think we'd call that a miracle. And I can only guess who orchestrated that."

Gideon looked at Celeste like she had two heads. "You're not saying what I think you're saying, are you? Because that is kind of creepy." Especially given the fact that Lauren's picture had gotten a full view of him and Tanika getting frisky.

"I'm not saying anything. Just count your blessings, that's all." Celeste headed toward the front desk, and as if on cue, the phone started ringing. And it didn't stop, all afternoon long.

Gideon leaned against the back of the chair and felt a pinch in his back. When he reached behind him, he found . . . the remote. Gideon scratched his head. Maybe he'd sat on it and turned on the TV. That was plausible, right? Gideon held up the remote and showed it to Celeste, who was still on the phone.

She mouthed the word *miracle* at him and continued scheduling appointments.

ONCE CELESTE LEFT FOR THE EVENING, GIDEON WENT INTO HIS office to decompress. He looked at the picture of Lauren holding the conch and decided to put it in his desk drawer for now. He pulled out his cell phone and scrolled to find his last message to Tanika.

> **GIDEON:** I saw what you did on Football Center. Thanks. You didn't have to, really.

> **TANIKA:** No problem. I had to shout out the man who saved me from a life of blurriness.

Gideon smiled as he thought about Tanika squinting at everything when they'd first met. Her stubbornness was actually adorable.

> **GIDEON:** We haven't talked since the other night.

> **TANIKA:** Yeah. Sorry. Still filling in for Sara.

Gideon let out a sigh and tapped the end of the phone against his chin. He might as well rip the Band-Aid off.

> **GIDEON:** I know why you left. At least I think I do.

> **GIDEON:** Lauren and me. In the wedding photo.

Gideon watched as the bubbles appeared and disappeared. It seemed like ages before Tanika finally replied.

> **TANIKA:** I know we haven't talked a lot about her. Actually, we hadn't talked about her at all. Lauren was a big part of your life. I should have asked more questions. About your loss. But I guess in that moment I felt like maybe I was a substitute for her.

Gideon's heart squeezed against his chest as he stared at her words. *A substitute?* Gideon had hoped in all their conversations that he'd never given Tanika that impression.

> **GIDEON:** Never. In that moment, all I could think about was you, Tanika. How you smelled. How you tasted. How you said my name when I touched a certain spot. My focus was on you. I'm not filling an empty space.

The video call app began to ring, and Gideon answered. There on the screen was Tanika, who looked to be in a janitor's closet with brooms and mops. The glasses with the red lip made his heart flutter. She was stunning.

"I think that last line deserves a face-to-face answer," said Tanika with a smile. "Excuse the mops. It's the quietest place on set."

"I meant what I said, Tanika. You aren't some placeholder."

"I believe you."

"So, when can I see you again? Or do I have to bribe you with ice cream to make that happen?"

Tanika let out a laugh and covered her mouth to muffle it. "Ice cream will make me say yes to anything, but you don't need to do that. I'd love to see you again. It's at the top of my list. But after this last hour, I head to Houston for the rodeo coverage for Black History

Month. And then I'm covering Colin Bello's races. That's an entire production. I won't be back home for a couple of weeks."

"Oh." Gideon tried hard to hide his disappointment, but he was failing miserably. "We'll get together when you have the time."

"I know it seems like I'm using work as an excuse. But the stakes are high for me right now. I can't afford to say no to anything. I need to be focused if I want to get back on top."

"I understand. Will you at least call me on the road? I don't care what time. I'm sure I'll be up."

Gideon heard a loud buzz on Tanika's end and then a knock. "Tanika, you in here? We need you back on set."

Tanika looked at Gideon, lowering her voice to a whisper. "Of course, I'll call you. I promise." She held up her fingers in a *V* shape. "Scout's honor."

Gideon snorted. "That's a Vulcan salute."

"Oh! Is that what that is? Anyway! Gotta go."

"Be safe, and good luck, sweetheart." *Sweetheart?* Gideon hadn't meant to say that, but it flowed out so naturally.

Tanika pushed up her glasses, winked at him, and signed off. Gideon wished he could bottle the feeling that that wink gave him.

Meeting Tanika. The fortune teller. The television. All of it. Maybe Celeste was right. Maybe it was some kind of miracle orchestrated by an angel.

An angel that he knew all too well.

CHAPTER 15

"**M**an, Tanika, it's been a blast having you on these past few days." Key-Juan gave Tanika a brotherly grin.

Jacob nodded. "Yeah. Sara is cool and all, but she doesn't vibe with us the way you do. Shit just feels awkward."

Tanika looked up from her notes. "Thanks guys. I missed you too."

"Think they gonna bring you back to Thursday Night when the regular season starts?" Key-Juan was multitasking, no doubt scrolling Instagram looking at the latest baddies. It was his thing to do between takes.

"I don't know, y'all. I'm just here doing my part." Tanika turned her face to the makeup artist, who'd come over to touch her up.

The truth was that the big game was in a few weeks, and Sara had already declared she'd be just fine to cover it. As a matter of fact, getting sick had apparently made Sara drop the five pounds she'd been struggling to lose, so she was "pumped."

Tanika knew she was doing a great job. Ross had even admitted the ratings were higher this week when Tanika was on *Football Center* with Key-Juan and Jacob, compared to Sara's recent numbers. Still, that didn't mean she'd be right back where she belonged.

Before she had a chance to catch her breath in prep for the next segment, Mya was by Tanika's side with her tablet in hand, ready to run down her day.

In one breath, without looking up, Mya said, "So, we leave out of here to Houston in about three hours. Your bags are already packed. Bronwyn called to confirm our monthly lunch at Wild Seed. Your dad called. And um, who were you laughing with in the janitor's closet?"

Tanika breezed past her question, fixated on the mention of her dad. "Make sure my blue and red blazers are packed. Tell Bronwyn and Jackie we'll be there. I'll call my dad from the car heading to the airport."

Mya tapped her stylus against her tablet case. "And who were you on the phone with? You came out grinning like a fool!"

"I was talking to Gideon, if you must know."

"Ooh, Dr. Miles. Did you tell him why you ran out on him the other night after he fingerbanged you in the hallway?"

"Mya!" Tanika looked around, making sure no one heard. "Seriously!"

"So, are you going to see him again? Before things get hectic?" Mya changed her tone, asking with all the earnestness she could muster, red afro bobbing as she spoke.

Tanika adjusted her lapel mic. "Maybe. Depends on our schedules."

"Shit." Mya looked down at her phone. "Now your daddy is calling *my* phone! What the hell!"

Tanika motioned for Mya to hand over her phone. With all the enthusiasm she could muster, which was a thimbleful, Tanika answered the phone. "Hello Daddy, I told you to call Mya if there was an emergency. Is there an emergency?"

"Well, you weren't answering your phone, so I called that assistant of yours. Now when did you start wearing glasses?"

At the mention, Tanika took off her glasses, stuck them in her jacket pocket, and rubbed her tired eyes. "Weeks ago, Walt."

"Don't sass-mouth me, girl. Good for you. Well, maybe you'll stop screwing up your lines now. So, I see you're back on *Football Center*? That's good. I guess."

"Daddy, why did you call me?" She pulled her glasses out of her pocket, checking for smudges before putting them back on.

Walt coughed and then spoke. "I called because I need to remind you not to settle for being a coanchor with those two half-wits. Or interviewing spoiled little European boys who race toy cars."

Tanika was surprised but shouldn't have been. "You watched my interview with Colin?"

"Yeah, that soft little boy is sweet on you, but stay focused. Eyes on the prize, baby girl. It's either VP or nothing."

"Ugh, I'm *not* interested in Colin Bello." Tanika's eyes widened. "Wait, how do you know about the VP job?"

"Unlike you, my eyes work just fine, so I can read this thing called the internet. Rumors are that you're up for the job. Or heading back to *Thursday Night Football*."

The bell rang to signal the end of the commercial break. "Daddy, I've gotta go. I gotta finish this segment, and then I'm heading to Houston. I'll call you when I land. And don't call Mya unless it's a real emergency. Like you're dying or something."

"We dying a little every day, girl. I'll see what I can do to not disappoint you." Walt hung up the phone without a goodbye, per usual.

"HELLO EVERYONE! I'M NIKKI RYAN, AND WELCOME TO A SPECIAL night presented by WWSN's Black History Month programming. It is Black Heritage Night here at the Houston Rodeo. And . . . wait y'all. Can we start over?"

Tanika paused, taking in the sights and sounds of the rodeo. She took a deep breath . . . then coughed. The one thing she hated about the rodeo was the smell of horse and bull poop. But the thing she loved most was this night. It was full of heritage and pride in a sport that had been defined by Black cowboys, Indigenous riders, and Hispanic vaqueros. Aside from football, this had to be one of Tanika's favorite events. She looked at the gorgeous crowd of Black and brown faces adorned in Western attire. If this arena full of people could be proud of who they were and what they came from, surely she could be too. Tanika motioned for the crew to start again, and Danny gave her an enthusiastic thumbs-up.

"Hello everyone. I'm *Tanika* Ryan, and welcome to a special broadcast tonight, part of WWSN's Black History Programming. It's Black Heritage Night here at the Houston Rodeo, and for the first time in history, we will be live-televising the Rodeo Series competition, including bull riding champion and star Ray-Lee McQueen. . . ."

Tanika finished her intro, then shot some B-roll footage with the crew before they all took a break. She stood near the bull pens, away from the crowds, going over her notes on her phone.

"Wow, Tanika, is it?" Mya handed her a bottle of water, grinning. "About time you started using your full first name."

"It just felt right, you know? I don't know."

"You know what would feel right to me? Laying up under one of these cowboys! Girl, these men are fine!"

Tanika laughed. "Yeah, I can't lie. Cowboys are pretty damn hot. It's the thighs."

Mya pointed. "Yep. Definitely the thighs in those tight-ass jeans."

Danny came over and gave Tanika a fist bump. "Nik—excuse me, *Tanika*. That was great. Think we can get some footage of you over by the ring?"

"Sure. No problem."

Tanika stood ready as the crew adjusted her mic pack. But before she could relax, loud screams broke out all around her, and all kinds of people went running. Tanika didn't see anything out of the ordinary—she was utterly confused by the pandemonium.

"He's loose! Big John is loose!"

Tanika turned around and saw an enormous bull charging straight for her. She let out a scream and closed her eyes. *Am I going to die? Thank god I have on new underwear.* Suddenly, she felt herself being lifted high off the ground. She opened her eyes just a crack, enough to see that she was being carried by a pair of strong, sturdy shoulders, with the wide brim of a cowboy hat shielding her from the glare of the sun.

"You alright, miss?" said the voice attached to the shoulders. "Can I put you down now?"

"Yes." Tanika's voice came out in a squeak, even as the sound of her racing heart thundered in her ears. "I'm good."

Slowly, the scenery changed. Tanika was lowered to the ground so gently, it was as if she were floating down on a cloud. Once she felt her feet beneath her, she focused on the stranger's plaid torso, which was adorned with a bright buckle. On it, encrusted in rhinestones, were six letters: *RAY-LEE*. When she looked up, she was staring into the face of Ray-Lee McQueen.

Tanika swallowed roughly, her throat like sandpaper. She adjusted her crooked glasses. "Thanks. Oh my god, was that bull really headed my direction?"

"Big John sure was. He's a mighty temperamental bull. But it also didn't help that you had on a red blazer, ma'am."

Ma'am? I'm not that old, but he's fine. So, I'll allow it.

Tanika looked down at her outfit. "I guess that's what I get for dressing like I'm taunting a wild beast. But bulls can't see colors, right? Regardless, that's what I get for trying to be stylish with a cape blazer. Is Big John Spanish? Or does he just hate my fashion sense?"

"No ma'am. He's from Texas," said Ray-Lee seriously, missing her joke entirely.

Mya and Danny came running. "Oh my god! Are you alright?" Mya was immediately patting Tanika down. "Are you in one piece?"

"Stop fussing over me! I'm fine! Thanks to Ray-Lee here." Ray-Lee just nodded and tipped his hat.

Danny was out of shape and out of breath. It took a few seconds for him to speak. "We caught the entire thing on camera! It was incredible!"

Tanika's eyes widened. "Danny, don't . . ."

"Sorry Tanika, you know we gotta use this. You were literally saved by a cowboy. This is some good stuff!"

Tanika felt the heat rise from her chest to her face. She looked at her friends, then back up at Ray-Lee. If you looked up tall, dark, and handsome, his face and body would have been the first search result. *How tall is he? Like 6'5? And that skin?* He looked like polished onyx with his lush, curly beard and pearly white smile. And of course, the lights were playing tricks with her again, because around him was a sparkly pink light. It felt like cotton candy and rosé—sweet, sticky, and too bubbly. She felt her knees buckle.

"Steady, now," said Ray-Lee in a heavy baritone that stimulated every part of Tanika. "Why don't you sit and take a load off?" He pulled up a stool from a nearby trailer and eased Tanika by the elbow, as if she were as light as a feather.

"Th . . . thanks. I'm Tanika Ryan, by the way." Tanika held out her hand for a shake.

Ray-Lee smiled and tipped his Stetson before shaking her hand. "Oh, I know who you are Ms. Ryan. I watch you all the time on *Thursday Night Football* and *Football Center.*"

"I appreciate that. And good luck to you out there!"

"See you around, Ms. Ryan. Maybe wear a different color blazer next time?" Ray-Lee winked and strode back to his camp to prepare for his event.

Mya was fanning herself. "My god, that man is sex on two legs!"

They watched as Ray-Lee walked over to his team, the jeans on him cupping his ass in the most disrespectful way.

"I'm straight, and he could get it," Danny concurred.

"He's hot, that is for damn sure," agreed Tanika.

"And if I'm not mistaken, this man was flirting with you. Girl, what is it with the dudes these days? You've got them eating out the palm of your hand," Maya said.

Tanika shrugged as she stood from the stool, trying to get her bearings. "Girl, I have no idea. But it's strange." Yes, plenty of athletes had hit on Tanika, especially early in her career when she was young, new, and had boobs that sat up to her chin. But now? She wouldn't have expected that—with her softer body, older face, and bold demeanor—any of these hotshot dudes would be into her. So, what had changed? She had a theory, but it was too preposterous to even think, let alone say out loud.

"Come on, you two," Tanika said. "Let's go. I've got to join Tank Ballard in the announcing booth in like five minutes. I'm sure he's waiting on me."

Tanika was grateful to be paired with Tank, an announcing legend on the PBR circuit. While Tanika had studied up on the stats and key riders in each event, Tank knew how to add nuance and heart to each person's story. He was a wealth of knowledge when it came to rodeo, especially the Black cowboys and cowgirls involved in the sport. With his brown weathered face and gravelly voice, he looked and sounded like a seasoned cowboy himself, totally in his element.

"Up next, we have the bull riding competition. The guy to beat tonight is Ray-Lee McQueen, one of the few Black professional bull riders in the country. It's gonna be a real treat to see him in action, Tanika."

"Yes, he's been pulling in some hefty purses lately. With scores topping out at ninety-two in some competitions."

"Yeah, he's real talented. I heard you got to see his agility up close and personal." Tank nudged Tanika's shoulder.

Tanika looked at Tank, working to contain her horror. *Going there on-air, are we?*

"Well, Tank, let's just say Big John the bull is no friend of mine. But Mr. McQueen was there to get me out of harm's way. So yes, I must say I'm a little biased in his favor."

Tank laughed. "Well, I would be too. Let's watch now."

Tanika turned her attention to Ray-Lee, who was straddling Big John in the bucking chute. He looked powerful and in total control even just sitting there. He adjusted his hat a couple of times before gripping the bull rope, then nodded to indicate he was ready. The bucking chute opened, and the cheering grew louder. Tanika winced as she watched Ray-Lee get thrashed around on the animal. Yet, somehow, he made it look so graceful—as if he and the bull were just dancing. Tanika took a look at the clock and then at Ray-Lee, who was still holding on well past the allotted eight seconds.

"Looks like he's going to beat his own personal best!"

Tank was on his feet, hat in hand. "Well, I'll be damned! He's gone and done it! Ray-Lee McQueen has not only set a personal record, but also a circuit record!"

Finally, Ray-Lee dismounted the bull, and the arena went nuts, cheering wildly and giving him a standing ovation. That included Tanika and Tank, who clapped and cheered in their booth. Ray-Lee took off his hat and waved to the crowd. Tanika even thought she saw him point to her in the booth. *Surely, I'm imagining things.*

"Well folks, you all at home just watched history live in the making, as Ray-Lee McQueen has won the Houston Rodeo bull riding finals. This was a wonderful conclusion to Black Heritage Night here. For WWSN, I'm Tanika Ryan with Mr. Tank Ballard, signing off."

Tank gave Tanika a hearty handshake. "I think you got a future in PBR announcing, young lady."

Tanika laughed. "I don't know about that, but this was the most fun I've ever had in the booth for any sport."

There was a knock at their door as Mya entered. She held out a note to Tanika, barely suppressing a squeal. "For you. From Mr. McQueen."

Tanika opened the note.

Would love if you joined me at our team campfire tonight. Leave the red blazer.

—Ray-Lee.

Tank peered over her shoulder. "Looks like Ray-Lee trying to rope more than a bull tonight. He's trying to get him a stallion." Tanika raised her eyebrows at the old man. Did he really just declare she was a thick, fine woman? *Well, he's certainly not lying.* She looked at the note and pondered. *What the hell.* When would she ever get the opportunity to chill with a real-life cowboy?

CHAPTER 16

anika freshened up at the hotel, changing into a pair of jeans, a V-neck t-shirt, and a pair of black cowboy boots. She would much rather have been wearing a pair of Jordan 11 retros, but as the saying goes, *when in Rome.* Technically, Ray-Lee didn't count as a person she wouldn't see outside of work; she hadn't interviewed him, and bull riding wouldn't be one of the sports she would cover regularly. At least, she hoped it wouldn't be. Besides, the man saved her life. The least she could do was respond to his invitation to join him at the campfire.

As she made her way past rows of trailers and campers behind the arena, Tanika wondered how she was supposed to find this gathering. But she stopped in her tracks when she heard an acoustic guitar paired with a silky, baritone voice. When she rounded the corner, she saw Ray-Lee sitting on a lawn chair, strumming a guitar and singing an old George Strait tune around a gas fire pit. The fire made his pink glow even brighter, as if it were a homing beacon for horny women.

A singing, bull-riding, fine-as-hell cowboy . . . and he lands in your lap. Or rather, you land in his. She was amused by the whole scene. *What are the odds?*

Ray-Lee looked up from his strumming and smiled. "Miss Ryan. You made it. Say, Willie, pull up a chair for Miss Ryan."

"Of course, I had to come. You saved my life," Tanika said, sitting in the chair positioned closest to Ray-Lee. "And please, call me Tanika."

"Well, Tanika. It was mighty fine of you to join us. We got beer and well . . . beer."

"I'll take a beer. It's all good." Tanika rarely drank cheap beer, but again, when in Rome. *Or should it be, "when in rodeo"?*

The campfire was packed with Ray-Lee's fellow riders, and of course, a slew of *buckle bunnies*, groupies who followed the rodeo riders. Someone threw Ray-Lee a beer, and he caught it with one hand, carefully wiping the top of it before handing it to Tanika. She popped the top and drank, thankful that the beer was ice-cold.

"This is nice. Do you all do this after every event?"

"Just about. Lets us clear our heads before we head out to the next competition or head home."

"So, where is home?" Tanika watched as Ray-Lee leaned back in the chair, his legs spreading wide across the fabric. Tanika had to swallow hard and look elsewhere, lest she be caught looking at this man's thighs. Black men were fine, but a Black cowboy was an *aphrodisiac*.

"Home is a two-hundred-acre sheep ranch outside of Austin," said Ray-Lee. "I'm also into solar wind power and alternative fuels."

"Really? Wow."

Ray-Lee laughed. "I know I look like I can't string together a proper sentence. And sometimes, I can't. But I'm a little smart, Miss Tanika. Graduated with honors from Prairie View with a degree in agriculture."

Tanika was truly impressed. "So, with everything you have going on, why are you bull riding?"

"I like the thrill, I suppose. The way I can make a bull submit and bend to my will. I feel powerful. Been riding since I was a boy. And plus, I'm damn good at it."

Tanika's mind lingered on the words *bend* and *submit* a little too long. She swallowed and fanned herself, her glasses fogged with steam. "Boy, that fire sure is hot."

Ray-Lee looked at the fire, then back to Tanika. "I can get you some ice, Tanika. Would you like that?"

She shook her head. "I'm fine. Probably a hot flash." *Now why the hell would I bring up menopause in front of this man?* She dropped her head between her hands and groaned.

Seconds later, she felt a strong finger lift her chin. "Nothing wrong with a little sweat sometimes."

Tanika, for the first time in her career, was speechless. She swallowed as she felt a bead of sweat roll down her neck, then her back. She shivered.

"I tell you what," said Ray-Lee, picking up his guitar. "Why don't I sing you a song? Any requests, Tanika?"

Tanika loved country music. It was one of her guilty pleasures— and one she wouldn't dare share with anyone. She tapped her chin. "Do you know any Breland?"

"He's one of my favorites." Ray-Lee struck up the first few chords of *For What It's Worth*, and the circle around the fire began to sway to the song, with Ray-Lee delivering gorgeous vocals. All the while, his eyes were aimed right at Tanika. She was mesmerized. The whole day had felt like a movie. She'd been rescued by an actual singing cowboy who was now shamelessly flirting with her. *Couldn't pay Shonda Rhimes enough money to write a fairy tale this good.*

When the song ended, the crowd dispersed to grab some barbecue that Ray-Lee had catered.

"What? You sing. You farm. You bull ride. But you cater your barbecue? Seems very anti-cowboy."

"Nah. They don't let us do any real pit smoking out here. So, catered it is. Are you hungry?"

Tanika's stomach was doing flips, full of the fizzy pink feeling she got from this man. There was no way she could eat. "No thanks. I ate before I came," she lied. She'd just eat something from the mini bar when she got back.

"You mean to tell me you came to Texas and won't even partake in any real barbecue? It's a crime and a shame, I tell you."

"Fine. I'll have a small bite."

Ray-Lee piled a plate full of meat, picked up his fork, and stabbed a piece of brisket. "Open up, buttercup."

Was she really about to eat food off this man's fork? Tanika didn't know him from Adam. But he also didn't seem like he'd take no for an answer. Before she knew it, she had opened her mouth wide, and the brisket landed on her tongue. It was heavenly. "Hmm! This is delicious."

"It's alright. I do make better brisket though. You'll just have to come out to my ranch and have some."

Tanika raised a brow as she slowly chewed. "Are you inviting me to your ranch, Mr. McQueen?"

"Why yes I am, Miss Ryan." Ray-Lee took a napkin and delicately wiped the corners of Tanika's mouth. Tanika swallowed, overwhelmed by his rugged smell of sweat, aftershave, and smoke. Ray-Lee was smooth. "The question is, will those pretty lips of yours say yes?"

Tanika looked into Ray-Lee's eyes as he moved closer. His eyes, however, were laser-focused on her lips. She had to look away as she answered. "I have a really busy schedule." Something was bothering her, but she couldn't quite figure out what. She replayed Ray-Lee's words. Her mind flashed back to Bronwyn's altar and the message in the ashes.

Say yes. Yes. Y-E-S—

To Ray-Lee? Tanika wasn't sure about that. Even if she was to believe Bronwyn, Lauren surely wouldn't be leading her into the arms of another man.

Ray-Lee was just a few inches from her face. "I could show you around my town. Cook you a fine brisket dinner. Let you ride my favorite horse, Shadow. And I don't let just anyone ride her. Most of all, I'd make you eggs any damn way you want for breakfast. Because you *would* be staying over for breakfast, Tanika."

"Why . . . why would I be staying over for breakfast?" Tanika's brain had officially turned to vapor, all rational thought out of reach. This was a real-life fantasy. She blamed this short circuit on reading too much Beverly Jenkins and Brenda Jackson as a teen. They had built her expectations up way too high.

"Because," Ray-Lee leaned forward, his lips so close to hers she could feel the heat of his breath. "When I picked you up and carried you, I didn't want that to be the last time I got to feel that gorgeous body of yours." Then, without warning, he pressed his lips to hers.

Tanika closed her eyes and leaned into the kiss, searching, trying to keep up with Ray-Lee's movements. She tried to get a feel of his full lips, but he overpowered her. His forehead knocked her glasses to the side. His beard looked so soft from afar, but in reality, it was scratchy and rough. When his tongue made its way inside her lips, it felt like an intrusion. The whole thing was off. It didn't feel warm. It felt foreign. Detached and routine. Like he pulled this move on a lot of women. *It feels nothing like . . .*

Tanika pushed away, touching her lips. "I'm sorry, but I'm seeing someone." *Where the hell did that come from?*

Ray-Lee frowned. "Really?"

"I'm sorry. It's new. You seem like a good dude, and I'm not trying to lead anyone on."

"So, he's not your man, really? Just a guy you're seeing. So, you're technically single." Ray-Lee gave Tanika a devilish smirk.

"Yes . . . well. No. Yes and no. It's complicated." What the hell was she saying? She and Gideon hadn't solidified anything. Hell, they'd only been on one official date. Under any other circumstance, Tanika would have done a reverse-cowgirl on Ray-Lee's dick by now and not thought twice. But the thought made her feel queasy. As soon as the queasiness set in, Ray-Lee's sparkling pink aura burst like soda bubbles.

Ray-Lee leaned back in his chair. "I see." He reached into Tanika's back jeans pocket for her phone. He grabbed her thumb delicately to unlock it—definitely a move he'd practiced once or twice—added his number to her contacts and handed the phone back to her.

"Well, if that *situation* don't work out, you know where I'll be, Miss Ryan. The invitation is open for you."

Nikki would have been turned on. Nikki would have fucked this guy in his trailer and called it a day. But Tanika felt a little sick at his obvious moves. She was too old for that.

"I think I'm going to head back to my hotel. Thanks for tonight."

Ignoring Tanika, Ray-Lee snapped his fingers in the direction of a petite buckle bunny standing nearby. She wore a blonde weave and Daisy Dukes with a flannel shirt tied up to expose her taut, bronze stomach and boobs. She bounced over, and Ray-Lee sat her on his lap, putting his hat on her head. Before Tanika even had time to leave the scene, his fingers were skirting over those young, cellulite-free thighs. Whatever he was saying had the young woman giggling and blushing.

A cowboy and a gentleman. Tanika scoffed, shaking her head as she watched the entire thing. So much for her cowboy fantasy.

AFTER KICKING OFF THOSE DAMNED UNCOMFORTABLE COWBOY boots, Tanika threw herself across the bed. What had she been thinking, taking that man up on his invitation to hang out? She'd been so enthralled; she didn't know what had come over her. Ray-Lee had clearly just been looking for someone to warm his bed for the night. She took her phone out of her back pocket and checked her messages.

| **MYA:** Did you ride the pony or nah?

She erased that one.

She had a string of group messages from Jackie and Bronwyn:

| **JACKIE:** What's this I hear—you almost got killed
| by a bull? That's no way to go out!

| **BRONWYN:** Oh my god! Maybe he could sense
| that you ate beef or something.

> **JACKIE:** Bronwyn, you sound ridiculous. It was obviously the red jacket she had on.

> **BRONWYN:** I still say he could sense the meat emitting from your pores.

Tanika shook her head. She'd text those two fools in the morning. There was a voicemail from her father, but there was no way she'd answer that. She was sure he wasn't calling with concern about her safety—probably asking what she was doing at a rodeo in the first place. Finally, there was a text from Gideon.

> **GIDEON:** So I'm watching WWSN, and I see you almost get attacked by a bull! Do I need to fly to Houston?

Tanika looked at the clock. It was nearing 2 a.m. in Atlanta, but she took a chance and responded.

> **TANIKA:** Almost is the key word. I'm fine. I'll just remember not to wear stylish capes near bulls in the future.

Before she could send a second message, chat bubbles began to appear on the phone.

> **GIDEON:** Thank god you're okay. Trust me, I was looking at red eye tickets. Glad I waited up.

He waited up for me? Tanika's heart squeezed hard in her chest.

> **TANIKA:** Please don't worry. I was saved by one of the bull riders there, LOL.

GIDEON: Good. (Pretending not to be jealous that an actual cowboy rescued you.)

Tanika snorted with laughter, hoping Mya didn't hear her in the adjoining suite.

TANIKA: No worries. Me and Mr. Bull Rider didn't have a connection.

GIDEON: Great, because I can't compete with a bull-riding cowboy.

TANIKA: Who also sings while playing guitar . . . by the campfire.

GIDEON: A singing, guitar-playing, bull-riding cowboy? What the fuck? Yeah, I give up. Can't compete with that.

TANIKA: There's no competition when it comes to you.

Maybe that sounded a bit heavy-handed, but she truly meant it. Gideon wouldn't have pulled the fake smooth act that Ray-Lee did. He didn't need to. Gideon was naturally charming.

GIDEON: I can say the same when it comes to you.

FaceTime began to ring, and Tanika answered.

"I just wanted to see your face." Gideon had perched the phone up next to his bed. A stack of papers was next to him. He was shirtless, and dear god, the muscles. His six-pack had a six-pack. Tanika's initial assumption was totally correct. Apparently, this man lived in the gym in his spare time. Doctor by day, gym rat by night.

"And you're half naked."

Gideon looked down. "Want me to put on a shirt?"

Tanika bit her lip, trying her best not to salivate. "Never. Actually, new rule. All FaceTime calls should be shirtless from now on."

"I'm glad you like what you see." Gideon was blushing, his skin flushed to a golden caramel. Shirtless, with the graying beard and bald head, Gideon looked like an older male model. Tanika could have looked at him all night, but she was getting tired.

"I do, trust me. But before you get totally freaky, I'm warning you, I'm sleepy." She stifled a yawn.

"You're lucky you're sleepy. Otherwise, I was going to hit you with some of my nastiest phone sex."

"What if you say nasty stuff to me until I fall asleep?"

"Bet," said Gideon, clearing his throat. "Conjunctivitis. Blepharitis. Endophthalmitis."

"Are you listing eye diseases right now?"

Gideon licked his lips in mock seduction. "Yes. Some real nasty shit. . . ."

Tanika's shoulders were shaking with laughter. "This is so hot! Ooh . . . keep going, Dr. Miles!"

Gideon kept Tanika laughing until she fell asleep with a smile on her face.

CHAPTER 17

Tanika and Mya met Bronwyn and Jackie at Wild Seed for their monthly Boss Chick Village luncheon. Wild Seed was Bronwyn's vegetarian restaurant. It was connected to her flagship health food store, Thyme in a Bottle, named after her oldest son. Tanika wasn't thrilled about most of the selections at the restaurant, but she did love the vegetarian lasagna and salad bar. Besides, the boss chicks always ate for free, so there was absolutely no complaining there.

"Try our new strawberry-basil lemonade spritzer." Bronwyn brought glasses on a tray. "It's all freshly pressed in-house, of course." Bronwyn loved to experiment with vegan offerings, and she always used the girls as taste testers for the restaurant's newest experiments. Some experiments were better than others.

Jackie took a glass and sipped. "Hmm. This is yummy. It sure would be better if it had some tequila in it. Bronwyn, when is this place going to get a bar?"

Mya nodded, taking a sip. "I gotta agree. A bar in here would be fire!"

"Now, I've told you I won't put a bar in here unless all the liquor I procure is ethically sourced, organic, and vegan," chided Bronwyn. "That takes a whole lot of research."

"Well, call me when you need taste testers for the liquor part," said Tanika. "Because I sure could use it."

"What's going on, girl? Network still bugging about the Colin Bello thing?" Jackie put a forkful of black bean taco salad into her mouth.

"No, that's not it. They went for your idea—I'm just covering his major races. I appreciate the suggestion."

Jackie raised her glass. "You're welcome. Happy to help you negotiate."

"So, what's the issue, my love?" said Bronwyn, her jade bangles jingling as she took Tanika's hand. "You look so stressed. You've barely touched your lasagna."

Tanika looked at her friends. She was sure Mya and Jackie would think she'd lost her mind. But after the ancestral altar thing, Tanika knew at least Bronwyn would believe her. She took a deep breath. "Well, I know this is going to sound ridiculous, but something weird is going on with me, . . . and I think my glasses have something to do with it."

"Your glasses? Is the prescription messing with you? I know my cousin is good at what he does, but maybe he was a little distracted by your fine self during your exam," Jackie teased.

"No, the prescription is perfect. Maybe a little too perfect."

"Then what the hell does a pair of glasses have to do with anything other than giving you sight and making you look fabulous? I noticed you're back on *Football Center*. Where's Sara?"

"That's it!" Tanika raised her hands. "It's the glasses, I'm telling you. Making things happen. It's just been a snowball of weird occurrences ever since these glasses came into my life."

She looked directly at Bronwyn, who was so surprised to hear her friend speak openly that she froze with her spritzer midway to her mouth.

"Hold on." Mya broke off a piece of warm naan from the basket on their table. "You're going to have to start from the beginning. What weird occurrences?"

Tanika leaned closer to her friends, speaking almost in a whisper. "When I got my glasses, I started seeing and feeling everything a little differently. Let me break it down. The first day, when Gideon delivered the glasses to my office, I saw this bright blast of green light all around him. And that green light made me feel . . . I don't know. Safe? At peace?" After a pause, Tanika confessed, "Maybe a little aroused."

"Ew!" said Mya. "Girl, you getting moist at work? You freaky!"

"Ugh, I don't know if I want to hear you talking about being *aroused* by my cousin." Jackie held her hands to her ears like a child. "*Ouch!*" Jackie yelped as Bronwyn pinched her.

"Grow up, both of you! Let's listen to Tanika. Like *really listen*. Tanika, continue, please. Tell us more about this green light?"

Tanika took a sip of her spritzer. "It's not just green—I'm seeing other colors too. Around other people. When I had my interview with Colin, he had a bright golden-yellow light around him. I figured I was jet-lagged or getting used to my glasses. Nope. It kept showing up while I interviewed him—it seemed to get stronger when his answers were confident and faded to a flicker when he was on the defensive. And when I saw Ross with my glasses on, the light around him was brown, and it made me angry."

"I see." Bronwyn narrowed her eyes, as if making mental notes. "That's interesting."

Jackie looked confused. "I don't get it."

"Neither do I," Tanika sighed. "But I know one thing. As soon as I got these glasses, my luck at work changed too. Sara pissed off Colin, and I got to do the interview. Sara got sick; I filled in for her at *Football Center*."

"Don't forget you got saved by a fine-ass cowboy," said Mya. "Talk about good luck!"

Tanika frowned. "Yeah but, as fine as he was, I got a creepy feeling from him. I saw this pink fizzy light around him that made me feel a little drunk. Or high. And then it went away, and I got an intense, uneasy feeling."

"Girl I was wondering why you didn't jump his bones! I saw the video. The man was an Adonis." Jackie deferred to humor when she was uncomfortable. And she was clearly a little uncomfortable.

Tanika bit her tongue, not wanting to tell Jackie too much. She'd told Ray-Lee she had a man. And that man was Gideon.

"Does this just happen when you look at men? What about women?" asked Bronwyn. "Do any of us have lights around us?" Bronwyn waved her hands around Jackie's head, Mya's, and then her own.

Tanika thought about it. "Funny you should mention that. Up until recently, I'd only seen these glows around men, specifically men that I felt unsure about. In situations I needed clarity to understand. But the other day, I saw Sara coming out of Ross's office. She looked panicked. Maybe a little nervous. It was unlike her. And all around her was this glowing violet light. It made me feel a little sad. No . . . *melancholy*. I think I freaked her out by staring, so she bolted the other way. I'm telling you, none of this happened before I got glasses."

Bronwyn nodded. "I think there is a perfectly logical explanation for this."

"There is?" Jackie and Tanika asked, almost in unison.

"Yes. You're seeing auras."

"Like chakra auras?" asked Tanika.

"Something like that! Hold on a second." Bronwyn walked over to a tall rack near the to-go counter where a variety of new and used books were displayed. She peered at the shelves until, looking pleased with herself, she found what she was looking for. She brought a thickish brown book with ornate gold foil to the table. "This is a guide about the twenty-two possible auras and what they mean. And why you feel certain things around people." Bronwyn flipped through the guide. "Ah, it says a muddy brown aura could mean that the person is greedy and self-absorbed. And probably blocked in some way."

"That sounds like Ross for damn sure."

"And yellow means high self-esteem and playfulness."

"Everyone can't pull off yellow!" said Mya. "But Colin's fine ass could pull off anything."

Tanika thought about Colin. "High self-esteem seems pretty accurate for Colin too. He definitely is feeling himself. But when I asked him tough questions, personal questions, his golden aura faded to barely a glimmer."

"And pink," continued Bronwyn. "It usually means gentle and harmonious. But sometimes it can be angry or primal, as it's a lighter shade of red. You said that in the case of the cowboy, it sort of . . . switched off, right?"

"It did. Fizzled out like carbonation in a flat soda."

"That means it wasn't in harmony with your own aura."

"Man, guess that means y'all couldn't bump auras," laughed Jackie. "Sorry. But this stuff can't be real."

Bronwyn gasped. "So, you're doubting Tanika's experience, Jackie? I believe her."

"Of course *you* would. This is very on-brand for you, Bronwyn! But Tanika, this isn't like you. You're usually so pragmatic."

Ignoring Jackie, Bronwyn continued to thumb through the guide. "And you said Gideon had a green aura, right?"

"Yes. Bright green and warm." Just the thought of it pulled at something deep inside Tanika. "It felt so . . . *luxurious*. I can't explain it."

Jackie raised a brow. "Is this gonna be more about their sacred sexual connection, Bronwyn? Because again, this is my cousin you're talking about."

Bronwyn closed the guide. "I don't think Tanika is ready to hear that part anyway. Not yet."

"That bad?" asked Tanika. "You have me worried."

Bronwyn smiled gently. "Only time will tell."

"Okay Miss Cleo, you ain't gotta be all mysterious and shit." Mya was suddenly invested in this. "You can't just come out with it? What does the green mean?"

"I don't think it's time."

"Want to hear something odd?" Tanika looked over at Jackie. "This *is* about your cousin, but I'll keep it PG. Mostly. Can you handle that?"

Jackie nodded.

"After our date, which was amazing by the way, we ran into a fortune teller. She told me some really wild stuff about not having blinders on, and *what I seek was in front of me.* I wanted to think it was just her hustling us, but it was similar to something I'd heard just weeks before. It was, almost verbatim, what a woman in Gideon's office told me when she helped me pick out these glasses."

"Celeste told you all that? Unlike me, she's not one to give unsolicited advice."

"That's just it, Jackie. It wasn't Celeste. It was a different woman, a woman in a white coat. When Gideon told me he didn't have an assistant, I was so confused. So, I didn't think too much about it. But the night after my date with Gideon, when we were getting kind of hot and heavy, I looked at a photo on his console. And I swear, right there in the photo was the lady from the office! It was his wife!"

"Hold on!" Jackie threw up her hands like a referee calling a time-out. "Are you telling me that Lauren's ghost led you to these glasses that are making you see auras? And bringing you good luck?"

"No," Tanika shrugged. "Well. Maybe. I don't know."

Bronwyn smiled widely. "It all makes sense to me. Lauren's spirit led you to Gideon. That's why you saw her at the practice! And that's why you're seeing green auras all around him. Especially when you two are intimate."

Mya nearly choked on her kale salad. "You saw a ghost while you were fucking?"

"I'm not sure Lauren's ghost visited at *that* moment," assured Bronwyn. "She, did, however, visit us at my house at the altar. I think she gave Tanika her blessing."

"Bron! We said we'd keep that on the low."

"We don't keep secrets around this table! Besides, this is wonderful news."

"Now y'all dialing up the dead? This is getting too freaky, even for me." The scowl on Mya's face looked as if she'd ingested an entire bag of sour patch candies.

"So, what do green auras mean according to your little guidebook, Bronwyn?" Tanika tried to redirect the conversation.

"I don't know if I should say."

This time it was Jackie who pinched Bronwyn.

"Ouch! Fine. I'll tell you. Green corresponds with the heart chakra, the center of love, compassion, and forgiveness. It indicates a person with a loving, kind heart. A person who is open to change and growth. Who is healed or on a journey of healing. And here's the most interesting part: *perceiving* a strong green aura, and finding a sense of safety there, might just mean—" she opened the guidebook and read directly from the page, "—*you are in love with an individual who brings you into harmony and peace.* In other words, Gideon balances you out."

"Whoa." Jackie and Mya exchanged glances.

"No way. No way, Bronwyn. I hardly know the man!"

"Well, how do you feel when you're with him?"

Tanika bit the corner of her lip. "I feel great around him. Comfortable, secure, adored. Maybe a little warm and fuzzy. But we've only been on one official date. I mean, two if you count him bribing me with ice cream. We talk all the time on FaceTime or text. I . . ."

This can't be possible. It's only been a couple of weeks.

Bronwyn grabbed Tanika's hand again, her locs swinging onto the table. "I know that face. Stop overthinking it. I knew I loved Kenny after the second date. And we got married three months later. We are still incredibly happy. It's possible, love."

"Who said anything about marriage?" squealed Tanika. "Who said anything about love?"

Jackie shook her head. "When I tried to introduce the two of you, Gid ran off. It wasn't time. Listen, I don't always agree with Bronwyn and her hippy-dippy shit, but I think she's right. So, maybe now is the time for you two to be together. Just because I don't want to hear about y'all bumping uglies doesn't mean I can't see how right this is."

"Speaking of—you can tell me." Bronwyn winked. "He is a gorgeous man. Is he well-endowed? Does he know your tantric levels?"

"I bet it's heavy," Mya agreed. "He walks like it's heavy."

Jackie pushed her chair back, the legs scraping the floor. "And that's my cue to get my lemon bars to go! Kenny, pack me up, babe! I'm out!"

Tanika, Mya, and Bronwyn broke into riotous laughter as Jackie shot them the middle finger on her way out the door, grabbing a bag of lemon bars from Kenny.

"So," Bronwyn continued as if the conversation had never been interrupted. "You're in love with Gideon, huh?"

Tanika moved her lasagna around her plate. "I don't know, Bron. I feel all gushy and giddy around him. We talk a lot. Underneath the glasses and white coat, he's fine as hell. He makes me laugh, and I feel like I can really be myself. But part of me thinks he's not ready. He still has pics of his wife up, for goodness' sake. I'm afraid I'd feel like filler. Like a poor man's Lauren. And anyway, I'm not ready. I'm basically married to my job."

"I get it. But you cannot ignore what your heart is telling you. Hell, what *Lauren* is telling you. You aren't experiencing all these things for no reason, Tanika. The auras. The opportunities at work. Your boost in confidence. That clear-as-day message on the altar. And anyway, have you asked *him* if he's ready?"

"No. I haven't brought it up. But he's not ready, Bronwyn. He can't be."

"You all need to have the conversation. Ask him about where he is in his grieving of Lauren instead of making assumptions. Like I said, either he's healed or on his way to healing. You can grieve someone you loved and make room to love someone new too. And when it comes to you and your job, I've seen you change lately. Like you said yourself, you're seeing things differently. The heart is a complicated, wondrous thing, my love. I think you both need to learn to make space for each other."

Tanika recalled what Gideon said to her that night at his house. *We're meant to stop that longing in each other.* Her chest ached. She swallowed the last of her spritzer.

"I think Jackie is right, this needs tequila."

Bronwyn laughed, then leaned closer to whisper. "Kenny has a flask in the office. Given the circumstances, I think you could use a shot."

CHAPTER 18

Gideon walked into Miles Optometry to find a waiting room full of patients. He smiled. It had been this way for weeks, ever since Tanika had mentioned his practice on *Football Center*. He was overwhelmed but grateful for the business. Things were going in the right direction, and he had Tanika to thank for it.

"And we are booked well into next month!" Celeste ducked into his office to give an update between patients. "Everyone is coming in asking for 'the Nikki Ryan glasses.' I lie and tell them that Tanika had custom frames. But I had to scour several catalogs to order pairs that were close matches for customers who want Nikki's look."

"'The Nikki Ryan glasses?' Wow, maybe Tanika should think about getting a brand deal for specs."

"You joke, but I already got some calls from manufactures asking me if I think she would be interested and who her agent is. I sent them Jackie's info."

"Jackie is a shark. She'll get Tanika a deal whether she wants one or not."

"So, what are you going to do to thank Tanika for this business? Might I suggest jewelry? Something big and shiny."

Gideon rubbed his beard. "Jewelry? Are we there yet?" *Is this woman off her rocker?*

"Oh, Gid," sighed Celeste. "I'm not asking you to propose to the girl. I'm saying, get a bracelet or a necklace. Something sparkly."

Gideon's heartbeat slowed. "I was about to say, we should have a second date before making lifelong commitments."

"But when you know, you know, right?" Celeste was beaming.

Gideon folded his arms and leaned back in his chair, feeling protective of his private life. "Celeste, isn't it strange for you to talk about me dating again? Or to imagine me marrying again? You're rooting for my new relationship, but I was married to your sister for almost fifteen years."

"Gideon, you are my brother and my family forever." She reached across the desk, offering her hand to Gideon. "I want nothing more than for you to find happiness. My sister is gone, sweetie. Life goes on. You are *alive*, so have a life. If Tanika makes you happy, I'm all for it. She's wonderful."

Gideon squeezed Celeste's hand. "Thanks Cee. And she does make me happy. I haven't laughed this much in ages. I feel like she gets me."

"So, when do you see her again?"

"I don't know. Her work schedule really *is* a beast. She's in Charlotte now, getting ready to cover another of Colin Bello's races."

"Colin Bello? That cute little English thing that used to race in Europe?"

Gideon raised a brow. "You watch F1 racing, Celeste?"

"Oh no, *I* don't watch, but Stu does. For whatever reason, he likes for me to sit there with him while he watches. So, I crochet, and he watches racing. I guess I've learned a few names and faces along the way."

Gideon thought about his life with Lauren. He used to do the same thing; while Lauren watched her *Housewives* reality TV shows, he'd do a crossword puzzle or browse the sneaker catalogs. Just to be near her. He missed the beauty of the mundane, everyday things they'd shared. "I get that," he finally said.

"Hey." Celeste gave Gideon a soft smile, getting to her feet. "You'll have those days again. Who knows, maybe with Tanika. In the meantime, I'll brew more coffee because your afternoon is packed." As she left the room, she called over her shoulder, "I still say get her a sparkly bracelet."

Gideon's phone buzzed in his pocket.

> **ERIC:** Hey G. You coming thru to Sneaker Con, right? Tickets are going fast. The TSs are going to be the hottest thing going but you gotta come thru early. There's going to be a raffle for those.

"Shit." Eric was Gideon's friend and sneaker plug. Thank god he had texted, because Gideon had almost forgotten about Sneaker Con. It was the premiere showcase of sneakers in the country, and this year, it was coming to Atlanta. Eric had a booth, and Gideon was hoping to have a shot at the exclusive Travis Scott Nikes. *Hottest sneakers on the planet.* Gideon wanted them. Badly. But he also thought about Tanika. Sneaker Con could be the perfect date for when she got back from Charlotte.

> **GIDEON:** Yeah, I'll be there. Could I get two tickets? Is the event sold out yet?

> **ERIC:** Almost. But I can cop an extra ticket. No problem. Just tell me who it's for.

> **GIDEON:** Her name is Nikki.

> **ERIC:** Nikki. You got a new woman? That's cap!

Gideon was a lot older than Eric. He wasn't one hundred percent sure what *cap* meant.

GIDEON: No lie. I mean, she's a good friend. Hold a ticket for her, okay?

ERIC: I got you, bro. It'll be waiting for you at will call. And your pockets better be heavy cause it's about to be a fiyah con this year. Trust me.

GIDEON: I'll be ready for sure.

Gideon sent Tanika a text.

GIDEON: I know you're busy, but when you get back, that Saturday is all mine. Taking you somewhere special.

TANIKA: Ooh is it a secret?

GIDEON: Maybe. But you'll have a good time.

TANIKA: Count me in. I'm looking forward to seeing you.

GIDEON: Cool.

As he was slipping his phone into his pocket, it buzzed again, and then again.

TANIKA: I miss you.

TANIKA: I sound silly, right? Shit. Never mind.

Gideon smiled. And he thought she never sweat under pressure.

GIDEON: I miss you too, Tanika.

TANIKA: 😄 Gotta do some interview prep. I'll call you tonight.

GIDEON: Looking forward to it.

When Gideon looked up, Celeste was right in front of him, holding a cup of coffee.

"Mm-hmm. Not your girlfriend, my left foot! You're sitting here smiling like a pure fool at that phone."

Gideon took the cup and shook his head. He felt heat creeping up his neck, his collar suddenly feeling tight. "Leave me alone, CeCe."

Celeste hummed "Love and Happiness" all the way back to the front desk.

Gideon sipped the coffee. *Am I in love? Is it too soon for that? Does Tanika even have time for me in her life?* Too many questions swirled around in his head. Gideon blew out a breath.

He would take it one day at a time.

CHAPTER 19

Even though this was mid-March just outside of Charlotte—not August at the equator—Tanika was sweating buckets. Heat rose from the practice track and made the press lanyard around her neck feel like a branding iron. Even in a sleeveless top and khaki capris, perspiration rolled down the back of her neck, loosening the hairs of her bun at the nape, tickling her endlessly. At this moment, she was grateful she'd ditched the wig. Mya trotted over with a cold bottle of water, and Tanika downed it in seconds.

"Fuck, it is hot as hell out here. Want another one?"

"Yes. Please. And if we're hot, just imagine what Colin is feeling in that suit and helmet in his car. Temps get dangerously hot out there. It can get up to 120 degrees."

Colin rounded the track and pulled into the pit, where Carl Morgan, Colin's crew chief, stood waiting. "Still about five seconds off! Dammit." Carl could barely get the words out, his cheeks were so stuffed with chewing tobacco. Tanika watched him spit an ample amount of juice. The juice dribbled down his chin as he wiped it with the back of his hand.

Not the most refined guy on the planet, but Carl Morgan knows his shit. As if realizing women were present, Carl stopped, shoved his hand into his pocket, and turned to talk with Colin's assistant, Errol.

"I know nothing about racing," Mya admitted. "What's so bad about five seconds?"

Tanika pointed to Colin's crew, moving quickly to change the tires. "It's a closely choreographed dance. Five seconds off messes up the rhythm with the race, the crew, and the pit. Everyone has a specific role. If any one thing is off, the whole thing is off. Five seconds could be the difference between winning the race or losing it. It's the kind of discrepancy that could get you seriously injured or killed." Tanika turned to face Mya but was startled to find her producer Danny directing a camerawoman to get a close-up of her face.

"Really, Danny? Can't I just say stuff off-the-record for once?"

"Hey, that was some good shit you said. It's a *dance*. If you don't like the shot, maybe we use this as a voice-over paired with some B-reel for the promo?"

"Danny! Seriously, just a little heads-up when we're rolling, okay?"

Danny laughed. "My bad. You just shouldn't be so casually good."

Since arriving in Charlotte, Tanika, Danny, and Mya had been attached at the hip. For days, they'd been following Colin Bello around like puppies. Tanika had barely gotten any interview time with him, as he was being carted around for press junkets, team meetings, and sponsor dinners—the newest darling of the American race world. He was being presented as an English gentleman who planned to lend some refinement to this sport. The thought made Tanika snicker. *Colin Bello is more rowdy rascal than gentleman.* She listened during the pressers as Lou Reddy proclaimed that Colin would bring some of the "class" from F1 over to stock car, for "a new generation of race fans," all the while slapping Colin on the back heartily as if they were best friends. Colin did his press rounds dressed in a sparkling clean racing suit emblazoned with sponsors and backers. But in the after hours, Colin dressed in James Bond–like suits that fit him like a glove—unlike most racers, who looked like farmers off the track. *So much damn denim and flannel.* Tanika hated to admit it, but Colin had a body made for bespoke.

Tanika was already thirsty, but her mouth went completely dry as she watched Colin exit his car after a final lap. He held his helmet under his arm, cradling it like a baby, sweat dripping profusely down his face. Between his tailored suits and racing gear, Tanika couldn't choose which one he looked better in. His faux-hawk was tightly curled, his beard slick with perspiration. He walked upright, proud, as if he had just dismounted a sleek black steed, showing no evidence of having just been spun madly around by g-forces in a tiny car. He tossed his helmet to Errol, unzipped his suit, and peeled his arms out of the sleeves, revealing nothing but a white tank underneath. White tank. Rippling brown skin. Veiny, tight biceps. Golden aura bright as the sun. *Well, damn.* Tanika blinked, trying to focus on something, anything other than Colin. He looked directly at Tanika, winked, then continued debating the logistics of his ride with his crew chief.

"I heard racers wear diapers," whispered Mya, gripping her tablet to her chest in horror. "You think he peed in that suit?"

Tanika was glad for the distraction. "Mya, seriously? Racers do not wear diapers. Well, actually, some do. Depending on the kind of race. They just don't drink a ton of liquid beforehand. Some take meds to hydrate without drinking water."

"Fascinating." Mya tapped furiously on her tablet, and Tanika winced, hoping her assistant didn't slip a question about *peeing* or *diapers* into her interview notes for Colin.

Speak of the devil. As Colin sauntered toward her, Tanika stood tall, trying to focus on his face and not his body.

"Were you watching me, luv? How'd I do?" He pulled off his gloves and stuck them in his pocket.

"Quite frankly, Mr. Bello, you were slow around lap ten. That west bank corner was getting you every time."

"Oh, now I'm Mr. Bello?" Colin's eyes sparkled. Tanika was grateful when he threw on a pair of shades, shielding her from his intense goldenness. "Right, well, I've got to just get used to handling the car."

"Darlington is next week. Are you sure you're ready?"

Colin smirked, aware of the camera crew and entourage that had gathered around them. "Wanna tour of the garage, Tanika?"

"Sure, but you didn't answer my—" Before Tanika could finish, Colin was reaching for her hand. It was surprisingly soft. "Come along, Tanika. It's blazing out here. And you're too beautiful to sweat, babe."

Tanika responded more quietly than she meant to, well aware that she was still holding his hand. "Okay."

"Good."

As they walked toward the garage, Colin leaned in. "You won't accept my flowers. You ignore my calls. Do I need to buy you an island to get your attention, Tanika?"

"Absolutely not."

"Then come to dinner with me."

"Once again," Tanika turned to Colin. "Absolutely not." She could only hope their exchange was not being caught on camera.

Tanika followed Colin and his entourage into the Lou Reddy Racing garage. Tanika looked around, genuinely awestruck. It was like a museum. Classic race cars lined the entrance. A display of racing awards filled a massive wall; although it had been a while since one of Reddy's drivers had held the cup in the winner's circle, the team's history was damn impressive. There was not one or two but *three* cars at Colin's disposal, all of them emblazoned with the various sponsors of the team. It was an active garage; the massive crew created a cacophony of noise, riveting and banging. And of course, Lou Reddy's office sat above it all, as if he were The Big Man himself.

Tanika watched as Colin removed his sunglasses and accepted a fresh T-shirt from his assistant. He slipped it on, the lower half of his racing suit still slung low around his hips. *Too sexy. Colin Bello is not supposed to be sexy.* Colin was a subject, part of the job. *Jobs aren't supposed to be sexy. Subjects aren't supposed to be sexy.* Colin was sexy.

"So, Colin. You have qualifiers on Friday. Preseason got off to a rocky start. I know previous races this season have been tough. Think you'll get a better start position or possibly the pole?" Tanika asked, refocusing. Danny was close, and the camera was rolling, trying to get every word.

Colin turned. "I hope so. Tanika, I'd be lying if I said I'm not nervous. This isn't F1. Back there, I knew every course. Every turn. Now, I gotta learn these new tracks, you know."

"I see. And your crew chief is saying you're slow."

"I felt that. Coming around the left bank, as you said. I need to get to know this baby." Colin reached out his hand and slowly caressed the body of his car, without breaking eye contact with Tanika. "A car is like a woman. You gotta learn every curve, every inch of her. It takes time. You can't rush the process. Especially if you want to win."

Tanika swallowed. "An . . . and—yes," she stuttered. "And is winning important to you?"

"Of course, winning is important. But it isn't everything. You learn more from losing, I suppose." Colin leaned against the car.

"But you're not used to losing?"

"Hell no, I'm not." He held Tanika's gaze a moment longer, then rephrased for the camera. "Absolutely not."

Tanika shook her head. Just as she was about to ask her next question, a loud voice rose over the noise of the garage. Approaching quickly was Lou Reddy, accompanied by a tall, dark drink of a man whom Tanika didn't recognize.

"And there he is! There's my golden boy," laughed Lou as he slapped Colin hard on the shoulder. "How we looking for Darlington?"

"Going to do my best, Lou!" Colin smiled, lips tight.

Tanika watched as Colin's golden aura dimmed and flickered in Lou's presence. *He has no idea how* golden *Colin truly is.*

Lou leered at Tanika. "And here's the gal who decided to go for my throat on national television. You better feel lucky that Ross and I are friends. Otherwise, you'd be out of a job."

Tanika was unintimidated by Lou's empty threat. She was almost *amused.* The light around Lou's head was a murky black and brown, like muddy clouds getting ready to rain crap down onto the room.

"Well, if you didn't have such a track record, Mr. Reddy, maybe I wouldn't have had to bring it up."

"You think you got balls, huh, little lady?" Lou practically snarled, then seemed to take notice of the camera and mic. "Well, I'll have you know I'm actively engaging with the Black community. See." He patted the back of the other man and pushed him forward as he nodded. "This here is Fredrick Livingston, my diversity and inclusion director, also in charge of PR. I ain't even know we had one of those, but apparently now we do. Fred, this is—"

"Everyone knows Nikki Ryan." Fred Livingston extended his hand toward Tanika. Tanika took the man in: tall, dark, with a perfect goatee, a dimple in his chin that couldn't be hidden, and a suit so slim it looked like it had been sewn on him. His aura was a mustard-yellow all around. It reeked of pretentiousness, just like his outfit. She had taken Bronwyn's advice and studied up on auras. If she recalled correctly, this corroded yellow meant he was naturally deceitful, possibly with ulterior motives.

Tanika shook hands and forced a smile. "Mr. Livingston. I've heard good things about you. The initiatives to get more minorities in the pit and in corporate offices are commendable."

"Thank you. And your work speaks for itself. I hate that you aren't on *Thursday Night Football* anymore, but hey, football's loss is our gain it seems. Maybe I can persuade you to reconsider and stay on to cover the entire racing season. I know I'd love to see you in the booth."

Tanika folded her arms across her chest. "I'm only here for a few races, Mr. Livingston. Just to cover the major ones that Colin qualifies for."

"That's too bad," Fred came closer, putting his hand gently on her shoulder. "Please, it's Fred. And if there is anything I can do for you, let me know. Or, maybe, I can show you around Charlotte. We can talk more about our diversity initiatives over dinner."

Mya raised her brows and pushed her sunglasses up, whistling and looking down at her tablet. Tanika took a step back, releasing her shoulder from Fred's grasp. "Thanks, but I'm really here to cover Colin."

Well, it looks like my intuition was spot-on. Tanika said a silent thank-you as she pushed up her glasses, grateful that she was able to see a man like Livingston coming a mile away. She may not have had a code name or cape, but Tanika was making good use of her new superpowers all the same. *Take that, Daredevil.*

"Yeah, she's here for me, mate. Don't you want the new poster boy to look good?"

"Of course, we do, Colin." Even as Fred addressed Colin, he continued to look at Tanika. "Ms. Ryan, I look forward to hearing from you."

He turned to follow Lou Reddy who was crossing the garage to chastise an employee.

"You done flirting with that geezer? Don't you have a story to get at?" asked Colin. "That story being me."

"Geezer?" Tanika rolled her eyes. "Chill out, baby face. Also, I was not flirting. I don't even know the man."

"Fred Livingston is fifty-one. Divorced. One teenage son," Mya chimed in. "I mean, in case you wanted to know."

"Thanks Mya. You're quick with the tea, as always."

Colin continued his rant. "Like I said: *geezer.* And you can do better, Tanika, than some suit worried about whether we get enough black jellybeans in the jar."

If not for her fresh manicure, Tanika would have rung Colin's neck. She didn't appreciate Mr. Livingston's energy, but she did appreciate the importance of his role. "His job is to make sure you aren't the *last* black jellybean in this jar, especially in the event your experiment goes belly-up and costs Lou a ton of money. Remember, you aren't the first Black racer. And hopefully, you won't be the last. Have some respect for Livingston!"

"Tanika. I'm not some baby-faced bloke, as *you* call me. You don't have to speak to me that way," Colin huffed. "I'm heading to the back to get out the rest of this suit."

"I'll be here," Tanika said, giving him the captain's salute. *What a prick.*

Danny signaled his team to turn off the camera and take a break. "You know something, Tanika? If I didn't know better, I'd say Colin was jealous." Mya nodded to Danny, humming her agreement.

"Jealous? Of what? Certainly not Livingston?"

Mya laughed. "For months, Colin has been trying to get you to notice him. The flowers. The snarky retorts in interviews. He's got it bad for you, but you won't pay him any attention. And now some guy more your speed shows interest? He's trying to mark his territory."

Tanika watched as Colin headed toward the locker room, sauntering confidently on his bowlegs. *Why on Earth is he so interested in me? Is it some spell the glasses put on him?* She dismissed the thought. "Colin can get any woman he wants. I'm just one of the few women in this world who has turned him down. That makes me a challenge. I hate to tell him that he's running a race he can't win."

Danny threaded his sleek black ponytail through the back of his WWSN baseball cap. "You need to put the boy out of his misery. Why not go on one date with him?"

Tanika snapped her head so fast, she nearly put her neck in traction. "When did you start giving me romance advice, Danny Ramos?"

"My bad. But anyone can see the kid has a thing for you. It's clear from a mile away."

Tanika sighed. A little crush was one thing, but this kind of workplace infatuation was another. She had to nip it in the bud before things got out of hand.

"I'M HERE IN THE WINNER'S CIRCLE AT DARLINGTON RACEWAY WITH Colin Bello, who—despite starting tenth in the field overall—came out the victor over race favorite Duke Johnson. Colin, how does it feel to win your first major race in stock car?" Tanika held the WWSN microphone in Colin's direction as they both faced the camera.

"Tanika, it feels bloody fantastic." Colin placed a champagne-soaked arm around Tanika's shoulders, yelling to be heard over the cheering crowd. "I had a bit of a rocky start earlier in the season, but my hard work has paid off. I want to thank my team at Lou Reddy Racing, including Fred Livingston in corporate, for their support. My agent Rory Mitcham, and my best mate and assistant Errol. Look, a boy from South London did it, yeah? And I'm going to try and do it again in Talladega in a couple of weeks. We're coming for the cup, baby!"

"Congratulations Colin. Back to you all in the studio."

Tanika took off her headset. "Well, damn. You did it Colin."

Colin finished signing an autograph and turned to her. "I told you I would. And if the cameras weren't on, I would have kissed you. I think you're my good luck charm."

"I'm glad you didn't."

"Why not? I'm a decent bloke. You're absolutely gorgeous. Love the hair, by the way. With the black specs, it's very sexy." It was impossible for Colin to turn off the charm.

Tanika reached up and touched her twist-out curls. "Thanks. It's too damn hot out here to be in a weave or a wig."

"Imagine how I feel. I'm sweating me bollocks off in this suit. You could have warned me it was so bloody humid in the South."

"My bad. You had to find out for yourself."

The crowd hushed as a large entourage approached Colin and his team. Tanika recognized the lumbering figure coming down the middle—Duke Jack Johnson. Now two sets of men faced each other like cowboys preparing for a duel at sunset. Tanika looked between the two camps, and her stomach roiled. This wasn't going to be good. She spotted Danny and the crew, who nodded to her, letting her know that the cameras were rolling.

"Just wanted to congratulate you, Colin. Though you got a lucky break in lap twenty when Teddy blew out his front. Otherwise, I would have beaten you for sure."

Colin frowned. "No luck about it, mate. I'm a damn good driver. And you wouldn't have beaten me anyway. Not with that shitty car you've got."

Duke stepped to Colin, getting right in his face. "You only been in this league five minutes, boy. Show some fucking respect." He had about five inches on Colin, but Colin didn't back down.

"Oh shit," said Mya, pulling Tanika by the shoulder. "We need to get the hell out of here."

"Boy? I'm not your fucking *boy*, mate. You need to give respect to earn respect, bruv." Colin was flanked by Errol and his boys, who could have doubled as extras in a BBC show about East London drug dealers. Duke didn't know who he was messing with.

"I ain't your *bruv*, so fuck you!" Duke pushed Colin. Colin, without a word, threw a left hook, which connected with Duke's jaw. The entire crowd began to push and shove each other. Without thinking, Tanika ducked in between the men and pulled Colin out of the melee.

"Are you out of your mind? Don't blow it on your first shot, Colin," Tanika hissed. Danny and the crew were still filming. If this brawl made the top of the WWSN news hour, it could spell disaster for his career. She put her hand on his chin, his face angry and sweaty. "Colin, look at me! Do you want your career in the States to end before it begins? The cameras are rolling! Walk away, Colin!"

Colin jerked his head out of Tanika's hands and looked around, his expression going from anger to terror as the cameras flashed and folks began to murmur. His hand slid from his forehead down his face. Without a word, he walked away from the maddening noise of the crowd.

"Is he okay? Shit, are *you* okay?" Mya was out of breath, red afro bouncing as she shouldered her way through the horde of onlookers to Tanika.

Tanika nodded. "I'm fine. Though I'm not sure that Colin will be. I hope so."

She watched Colin's broad back get smaller and smaller in the distance.

CHAPTER 20

Back in her hotel suite in Charlotte, Tanika took a long shower. Today had to have been one of the most bizarre days in her long career. After the two-hour ride from South Carolina, Tanika desperately needed to decompress. She wrapped herself in a towel and flopped on the bed to watch television. Every sports network and news desk ran the story of Colin and Duke's altercation, including a shot of Tanika pulling Colin out of the crowd. *So much for hoping it wouldn't air.* Tanika let out a sigh. She wasn't sure why her first instinct had been to pull Colin out of the melee. Part of her—the soft part—felt protective of Colin, like he was a snarky little brother. The other part of her, the hardened sports journalist, didn't want to see him fail. Often, the one shot was the only shot. Tanika rolled over and pulled out her phone, wanting to text the only person that could get her mind off it all.

TANIKA: Today was a trip. I guess I can add referee to my résumé.

GIDEON: Oh, you mean the fact that you pulled that young brother Colin out of the fight? Yeah, I'd say you were a superhero. You need a cape.

Tanika stared at the screen. Was he reading her mind? She'd just had that thought.

>TANIKA: Wait, you watched the race?

>GIDEON: Confession. I watch just about every sport you report on.

>TANIKA: Table tennis?

>GIDEON: Lee Wong is a bad man!

>TANIKA: Ballroom dancing?

>GIDEON: I like to cha-cha.

>TANIKA: Lacrosse? Bowling? Speed skating?

>GIDEON: If you're there. I'm watching.

Tanika stared at the phone, mystified. In past relationships, men would be interested in her career as long as it gave them access. She could introduce them to major athletes or get them tickets to prime sporting events. They were never particularly interested in her interviews or the more niche sports she covered. She couldn't recall a man paying much attention to what really made her passionate. It was all about what she could do for them. Gideon, on the other hand, seemed truly interested in *her*.

>GIDEON: Can you promise me not to jump into any more fights between two dudes? I don't want to see you hurt before I get a chance to take you out.

TANIKA: Still not going to tell me where we are going?

GIDEON: Nope.

TANIKA: How am I supposed to dress? What if I show up naked?

GIDEON: Although what I've seen of your body is banging, I really don't want anyone else to see you naked. So clothing is not optional.

Tanika looked down at her towel and bit her lip, debating what to say next. *What the hell.* She was an adult, and she couldn't remember the last time she had phone sex. And she was so damn horny, she could explode.

TANIKA: What if I told you I was naked right now?

Before she knew it, Gideon was calling her on FaceTime. She sat up on her elbows, propping the phone up on the lamp next to the bed. Gideon was in his white coat, at what seemed to be his office. "Prove it."

"Wait, are you at work? It's Saturday."

Gideon leaned back in his chair. "Yes. Thanks to a certain someone's shout-out, I've been busier than ever. Just saw my last patient for the day. And before you ask, my door is locked, and I'm alone in the building. So, like I said . . . prove it, baby girl."

Tanika moved the phone down the length of her body, then back to her face. "See?"

"Tsk," Gideon sucked his teeth. "A towel isn't naked, Tanika."

With one hand, Tanika opened the top of her towel and let it fall to her sides. All her typical insecurities—her stretch marks, flabby middle-age-spread stomach, and cellulite-y thighs—also fell away. She lifted the phone until it was at arm's length and slowly panned the camera down the length of her body, then back up.

Gideon's face was strained, as if he was concentrating on remembering what he'd just seen. "Damn." His teeth bit into his full bottom lip. "Such a beautiful body, Tanika. I can't wait to touch you again. Matter of fact, why don't you touch yourself for me and tell me what I'm missing."

Tanika felt heat flowing from the pit of her stomach down to her pussy. Her fingers moved languidly down her body, drawing a line from her clavicle, to between her breasts, then over her belly. She rested her hand at the juncture of her pelvis and stomach.

"Move the camera so I can see, Tanika." Gideon's voice was gruff.

Tanika moved the camera away from her face, angling it down the rest of her body.

"Touch your pussy," breathed Gideon, hoarse with need. "Slowly. I want to watch you part those wet lips and slide a finger in between."

"Yes, Dr. Miles," she purred.

Tanika did as she was asked and parted her folds *so slowly*. Once exposed, she found her clit already pulsating, her pussy soaked. She slid an index finger inside and arched her back. "Fuck, Gideon."

"Move those fingers." While she couldn't see his whole body, Gideon clearly had a hand down his pants. "Move your fingers in and out of that pretty pussy, baby. Rub your thumb against your clit. With the other hand, pinch those deep, perfect nipples for me."

"Oh god." Tanika threw her head back on the pillow, then frantically propped her phone on the table at an angle where she hoped he could see the show. This freed her left hand to fondle her breasts, which overflowed in her palm as she tweaked one nipple and then the other between her fingers. The other hand followed Gideon's instructions to the letter, making her come so close to where she needed to be. She pushed her fingers in deeper, trying to reach a place only Gideon had.

"Damn, Tanika. Open your eyes and look at me, princess." Tanika met his gaze, then took in the whole picture. Gideon had shifted his camera slightly downward. The sight of him stroking himself against his crisp white doctor's jacket nearly made her come right then and there.

"Hmm. If I was there, I'd slide a wet finger out your pussy and play with that sweet, tight ass, Tanika."

"Oh my fucking god!" Tanika was so close to coming, her thighs shook. And then she saw a burst of light: first the warm green glow of Gideon, then a full rainbow explosion behind her eyes. She came fast as lightning. "I'm coming, I'm . . ."

Once it was over, she didn't move, letting her hand stay inside of her, her walls pulsating all around her fingers.

She looked at the screen. Gideon had taken off his glasses and was still pumping away.

"I want to see you come, Gid. Please." Tanika exhaled slowly as she spoke.

"Anything for you." Gideon flipped the camera away from selfie view, and now Tanika could clearly see his hand fisting his dick, which was glistening with pre-cum. She couldn't wait to feel that very thick and capable dick again. The thought made her mouth water, and she found herself wishing she was there to wrap her lips around it. She watched as he moved his hand up and down, moaning with every stroke. She loved when men moaned. Gideon's moan was rough and commanding, completely uninhibited for a man who seemed so reserved.

"Fuck, I'm about to—" With two quick jerks, Gideon was coming all over his white coat, his hand totally covered.

They were quiet for a moment. Tanika reached for the towel to clean herself up, while Gideon set his phone back up on his desk, wiping his hands with antibacterial wipes and peeling off his soiled coat.

"I have never jerked off in my office. You got me doing things I said I'd never do."

"Are you saying I'm a bad influence?"

Gideon gave a low chuckle. "Never that. I think you're good for me."

Tanika smiled. "I think you're good for me too."

"Since we're already being bad," Gideon raised a brow. "Want to go for another round?"

Before Tanika could answer, there was a knock at her door. "Hold on, Gideon." She threw on a robe and looked out the peephole. There was a man holding an enormous bouquet of flowers. *This again?* Tanika opened the door.

"Ms. Ryan? These flowers are for you."

Tanika took the heavy vase from the courier and placed it on the table next to the door. "Thank you." But before she could close the door, a woman appeared, holding a small red box, a police escort trailing behind her.

"Um, am I being arrested?" asked Tanika.

"No ma'am," smiled the woman holding the red box. "This delivery requires extra security and a signature. Please sign here."

Tanika took the iPad the woman presented. She was hesitant to sign without understanding why this gift came with its own uniformed cop, but she wanted to get this over with. Squinting, she scribbled a signature, and the courier handed her the box. There was one word printed in gold cursive on the box: *Cartier*. She didn't need her glasses to recognize the iconic logo.

She lifted the lid on the box just enough to see inside . . . and nearly passed out. She steadied herself with a hand on the doorway. Someone had sent her a diamond eternity necklace set in platinum.

"Have a good day, ma'am."

"Hey, wait! I can't accept this necklace!" It was too late. The flower courier, woman from Cartier, and officer escort had disappeared into the elevator together.

Stunned, Tanika brought the bouquet and jewelry box into the bedroom. She searched the flowers for a card and finally found it.

Picking up her glasses from the nightstand, she put them on and read the card.

Thank you for saving me from myself. Dinner tonight? As friends.

—CB

Tanika smiled at the note from Colin. The gift was over-the-top, but he'd gotten the *friends* part right. She'd have to let Mya know she would finally accept his dinner plans.

"Um," a voice said from her phone, "that bouquet is massive."

"Oh shit." Tanika had almost forgotten that Gideon was waiting. She picked up the phone from the bedside table and turned it to face her. "Sorry. Those are from Colin, thanking me for saving his butt today."

"And the necklace too?" Gideon lifted his chin to point behind her, where the Cartier box sat on the table. "I overheard; your gift had an officer escort. That's an expensive thank-you."

"I can't accept that. I won't. Even if we are cool, I don't want him getting the wrong idea."

"Good. Because if anyone is going to be lacing you in diamonds, it's me."

"I know you aren't jealous," Tanika laughed. "Besides, I'm not really a jewelry kind of girl. Now, if you gift me a pair of dope-ass kicks, then I'll really know that you love me."

Tanika swallowed that last part, embarrassed she'd said any of that out loud. *Talking about love this soon? I'm ridiculous. Letting Bronwyn and these damned auras get to me.*

But Gideon was completely unfazed. "I'll keep that in mind."

THE CHAMPAGNE WAS FLOWING AS TANIKA AND MYA JOINED COLIN and his entourage in the VIP section at the hottest club in uptown

Charlotte. After getting stuffed at The Palm, Colin had insisted that they all go dancing and have a good time. As a rule, Tanika didn't club with athletes, but she made an exception for Colin. He was growing on her.

The rest of the party was off grabbing drinks or dancing, leaving Colin and Tanika alone in their section. Tanika had never seen Mya let loose like this on the dance floor, sweating out her afro as she grinded on Errol.

Colin was watching Mya too. Tanika couldn't blame him; Mya was working it. "She's really cutting shapes, ain't she?"

"If that is English for throwing that ass, then absolutely."

"The girl got nyash, for sure." He took sip of his champagne before turning his attention back to Tanika. "You don't want to dance? I can take you for a spin on the floor, yeah? I got moves." He did a little breakdancing shoulder. Tanika giggled.

"No thanks. I'm already out in an extremely uncomfortable pair of heels. I'd much rather sit." Tanika poured herself another glass of champagne, moving her shoulders to the newest banger from Megan Thee Stallion.

Colin looked appreciatively over his glass at Tanika's chair dancing moves, then down at her feet, crossed at the ankles. "Want me to rub your feet?"

"Oh, heck no. I only let my podiatrist, my pedicurist, or my man touch my feet."

"Your man? You got a man, huh?"

"It's new." Tanika felt the heat rising to her cheeks.

"Ah, so that's why you been playing me to the left with all the flowers and cards. Cartier ain't good enough for you, innit? What do you want? Tiffany? Harry Winston?"

"Jesus, Colin," Tanika laughed, putting her hand on his arm. "You don't need to buy people's affections. That certainly doesn't work for me. Regardless, I'm not interested. I'm older than you. I'm in a different place in life that requires something more than what you can give me. I would never be able to keep up with your lifestyle, and you'd get bored of mine very quickly."

"I see." Colin's face was serious. "But I really like you, Tanika."

"I like you too, Colin. As a friend. Can you be cool with that?"

He nodded. "I'm down with that."

"So, no more flowers. Or expensive necklaces, or whatever else you buy to seduce women these days."

"Got it. Message received." Colin chuckled dryly, looking a bit sheepish.

Tanika smiled. "And I'm telling you, as a friend, don't blow your shot here in stock car. You raced your heart out today and proved you got the stuff. And you aren't scared to stand up to these good ol' boys."

"You mean that?"

"Of course I do! You got it, kid. Dudes like DJ are threatened. But you cannot stoop to their bigoted levels. Seriously, let the racing speak for itself."

"Thanks, Tanika." Colin outstretched his arms and pulled her in for a hug. When they pulled away from each other, she looked at him carefully. Gone was the bright, bold yellow light around Colin. But unlike Ray-Lee's pink glow, which had fizzled out suddenly and left Tanika feeling ill, Colin's aura had just sort of . . . evaporated. Things felt good between the two of them. Friendly. Content. Tanika smiled.

"Okay Bello. Let's stop being mushy and kill this champagne. I heard a rumor that you bathe in it."

"I do. Why do you think my skin is so flawless? It's the bubbles."

At this, they both laughed so loudly that the people around them paused what they were doing to look.

Colin held up his champagne flute. "Cheers, friend! And seriously, thank you. Without you, today could have been much worse."

"No problem." Tanika clinked the rim of her glass with his. "Anytime, friend."

CHAPTER 21

Gideon was proud of himself for keeping the date a secret. He insisted on picking up Tanika from her condo; the only thing he told her to do was dress comfortably. When she texted to ask if sneakers were cool, he laughed to himself, then texted back: *Sneakers are preferred, actually.*

When Tanika opened her door, Gideon's mouth nearly watered. She wore the tightest high-waisted jeans he'd ever seen, which put her gorgeous hips and ass on full display. She paired the jeans with a simple white V-neck shirt, and on her feet were a pair of pristine Air Max 95s colored in cool gray, blue, and white. Gideon had inadvertently matched her sneaker color palette with his own pair of suede Chanel sneakers. Tanika's hair was pushed back with a hairband, framing her face like a silver-streaked black cloud. His eyes took it all in, then went straight to her glossy pink lips, which he desperately wanted to kiss.

"I'd kiss you, but I don't want to mess up your gloss." Gideon pushed his specs further up his nose, a nervous habit of his that had nothing to do with the fit of the glasses.

"Well," Tanika said, smiling, "I have a full tube and can reapply at any time."

Gideon took that as an invitation. He gave her a tame peck on the lips, not sure what she was up for. But when she pulled at the hem of his shirt to deepen the kiss, he let go, held on to her hips, and savored the berry taste of her lip gloss.

"I missed you," Tanika groaned into Gideon's lips. "I'm so tired of being on the road."

"I've missed you too," said Gideon. "Although I did watch you on TV, . . . and I had a special FaceTime or two."

"You know, I'm not really one for talking on the phone, or video chatting for that matter. But your voice is so sexy. And your face is too handsome to not want to look at every day."

Gideon felt his cheeks flush. "You trying to make a brother blush, huh?"

"Is it working? I can't quite tell, with the beard."

Gideon laughed. "Speaking of which, should I dye my beard? Since we're getting more patients—thanks to you—Celeste seems to think I need new advertisement photos. She says coloring the beard will make me look younger."

"Are you serious?" Tanika gasped, both hands flying to Gideon's face. "I love your salt-and-pepper beard. It's distinguished. Besides, I'm sick and tired of trying to hide aging. It happens. We need to embrace it."

"I see you've started wearing your hair out on-air now." Gideon took a twisted curl between his fingers. "I really like it."

"Thank you! Together, we can be two hot silver foxes, embracing our forties and aging gracefully like the Gen Xers we are."

"Is that right?" Gideon took Tanika's hand. "Well, come on, with your fine foxy self. I don't want to be late for the surprise."

WHEN TANIKA REALIZED THAT GIDEON WAS TAKING HER TO Sneaker Con, the happy scream that escaped her mouth was totally worth his temporary hearing loss.

"You have no idea how many times I've wanted to go, but my schedule was always too packed!" Tanika squealed again, taking in the convention center around her.

"Well, I bought the tickets on a whim, but I did contact Mya to double-check that you were free this weekend."

"You did all of that?"

Gideon nodded proudly, tucking his hands into the pockets of his sweats. "Yep. How'd I do? Pretty good?"

Tanika grabbed Gideon by the bottom of his shirt, fisting it to bring him closer. She kissed him in the middle of the aisle, apparently forgetting where she was. Gideon knew PDA wasn't normally her thing; he was flattered. When she finally released him, a small crowd had gathered, watching them go at it. Tanika was clearly embarrassed, her cheeks hot and her hands sweaty.

"Damn." Gideon wiped his lip with his thumb. "I'll take that as a yes."

They walked around the convention, debating which shoe was hotter or uglier, which was their favorite of all time (they both loved the classic Jordan 1s), and which shoe had the best comeback (the classic Penny Hardaway). A few people stopped Tanika, asking for a photo or autograph. She was gracious with her fans. Finally, they made it to Eric's booth, DunkMasters. He was busier than ever. After a few minutes of browsing and waiting for the crowd to thin, Gideon got Eric's attention. Eric made his way over, giving him a handshake and a hug.

"Hey E, I wanted to introduce you to . . ."

"Oh snap! Tanika," Eric interrupted, engulfing her in a big hug. "Man, I haven't seen you in a minute. You haven't called me about any new drops."

"I know! I've been meaning to tell Keke that I wanted to holler at you. I so want you to get those CAU dunks for me. In my right size. Last time, you got me an 8. Too big, dude."

Gideon was completely surprised, looking back and forth between the two. "Wait, how do you two know each other?"

Tanika grinned. "Eric is my shoe broker!"

Gideon laughed. "Hold up! Eric is *my* shoe broker!"

Tanika shook her head. "This is wild. E has been my friend for years. His wife Keke does my hair."

Eric threw up his hands. "Hey, what can I say? I'm the shoe plug for everyone. But I had no idea when you put Nikki on the list, she was *this* Nikki. Tanika is like family, man."

As if by magic, Keke rounded the corner carrying a stack of boxes, setting them down on the display counter. "Tanika! Is that you, girl?" The two hugged. "Girl, I'm so happy to see you. And look at your hair. Loving that you're finally taking my advice and wearing it natural. I was getting sick of laying down lace fronts on you!"

Tanika twirled, showing off her cute twist-out. "I know. I feel like a new woman thanks to you!"

"So, Gideon and Tanika, are y'all going to enter the raffle for those Travis Scott Reverse Mochas?" asked Eric. "Only a few sizes left. And folks are buying up the tickets."

Gideon looked at Tanika. "Are we seriously going to bid against each other?" He had purchased twenty tickets ahead of time.

"Looks that way. Or are you afraid of some competition?" Tanika put her hands on her hips. She was cute, but he wanted that damn shoe.

He stuck out his hand for a fist bump. "Well, baby, may the best man or woman win."

Tanika bumped his fist. "Oh, it's on, Dr. Miles."

CHAPTER 22

Tanika left Sneaker Con with Gideon by her side and bags of sneakers in her hands—but without the elusive Travis Scotts. They'd both been outhustled by a celebrity, rumored to be a rapper of Canadian origin, who had purchased a ridiculous amount of raffle tickets. There was no way they could have competed with that price tag.

They decided to drown their sorrows in beer from the gas station and barbecue from JJ's Rib Shack. In the parking lot of a QuikTrip, they sat in Gideon's Audi SUV, listening to the best of UGK. They held their brown bags of beer with sticky fingers, surrounded by piles of messy napkins. Tanika thought it was the perfect ending to a nearly perfect day.

"I haven't had JJ's in forever." Gideon wiped his hands.

Tanika rubbed her full belly. "Yeah, it was so good!" She looked at Gideon, wanting to ask him if he liked Eric's booth setup at Sneaker Con. But he had a faraway look, as if he wasn't with her in the car anymore. Even before she asked, Tanika knew it was a memory connected to his past. To Lauren. She could feel it.

"She loved barbecue, huh?" Tanika took the last sip of her beer, giving him space to answer.

He gave a slight smile. "Lauren loved to eat everything. Especially barbeque because she was from Texas. She would and could eat me out of house and home. And she was a tiny thing. Like barely 5'2 and could pack it away."

Tanika put her hand on her chin. "What else do you miss about her?"

Gideon's eyes were soft in the streetlights. "I may hear a song. Go to a restaurant. Watch a show. A corny commercial. Anything can trigger a memory. It'll take me back to the good times. When she was healthy. When we were joking together, having impromptu rap battles, getting annoyed with each other, or arguing about the direction of the toilet paper. Before the cancer took everything. Then, I just get angry that our life together was cut short. We still had a lot on our bucket list to do."

"Oh yeah? Like what?"

"We wanted to travel the world." He took a swig of his beer. "We talked about it all the time—we wanted to close the practice for a year or so and do outreach with Vision Without Borders. It provides people in developing countries with vision healthcare. Service was really important to Lauren. To both of us. I don't know, maybe one day I'll do it. Right now, I don't think I could."

"That's beautiful. I am sure one day you'll get to travel the world and help people the way you want to. The way Lauren wanted to. Life's not over for you."

"I've been getting that message lately." Gideon intertwined his fingers with Tanika's. "I miss Lauren. I'll always miss her. She was the glue that kept the office together. Shit, she kept my life together. Before she died, I took that for granted. Spending nearly twenty years with someone is a long time. But you're right—I'm here. I have a life to live, and I don't plan on living it alone. Lauren wouldn't want that."

Tanika lowered her eyes. She cared for this man, and it was time to be completely honest with him. "We haven't known each other long. I want to trust you when you say you're ready to move on.

But—the pictures on the wall. In your home. In the office. Lauren is still very *present*." She paused, considering the part Lauren had already played in their relationship, whether Gideon knew it or not. "Sometimes, I fear I'm in competition with a ghost." She tried to untangle her fingers from Gideon's, feeling a bit ashamed that she centered herself in the conversation. But Gideon would not let her go. He held on tighter. And for the first time that day, Tanika realized that Gideon wasn't wearing his wedding band.

"Tanika," Gideon said softly, moving closer to her over the console. "Hear me when I say that you are not in competition with Lauren. The heart is an enormous organ. I do hold her memory sacred. But there is space for me to do that and to love again." He took her left hand and pressed it to his chest. "My heart is open and ready to love you."

Tanika's own chest felt tight. She thought about Bronwyn's words at lunch, about love, compassion, and healing. Now Gideon was telling her something similar, assuring her he was ready to open his heart to her. So, why couldn't she reciprocate? *How did this wonderful man end up in my world? I truly don't deserve him.* Her lips quivered, tears forming in her eyes.

"What is it?" Gideon covered her whole hand with his so that her palm pushed against his pec. She could feel his heartbeat.

"I don't want to hurt you, Gideon."

"Then don't hurt me, princess. Simple as that."

Gideon wiped the lone tear rolling down her cheek that had managed to escape from Tanika's eye. "Tanika, baby, please don't cry over me. Or are you crying about those Travis Scotts we lost out on?"

Tanika burst into laughter. "Damn. That did hurt." She removed her glasses to wipe her tears.

Gideon pressed his lips against Tanika's. She reveled in the taste of him. Barbecue, spice, and hops mingled with every kiss. And then there was his smell—like all the best parts of Christmas. Her tongue searched desperately for his, again and again, greedy for sensation. His hands moved under her shirt, gripping her at the fold of her waist, his fingers kneading the fleshiest part of her. The feel of his hands, coupled with the cold from the air conditioning, sent a spark that zipped straight to Tanika's pussy.

"Let's go back to my place," she breathed. "I can't fuck you for the first time in a QT parking lot."

"Alright, let's go." Gideon pressed one last kiss to Tanika's lips before pulling out of the brightly lit parking lot. They were only a few miles from her condo, and as luck would have it, every single traffic light was green.

Definitely a good sign.

CHAPTER 23

Gideon pounced on Tanika the second she'd dropped her bags at the front door and kicked off her sneakers. He kissed her until he was breathless, moving his hands under her shirt and finding her nipples hard, straining through the fabric of her mesh bra.

"I've been dreaming about your body for weeks," he whispered, his tongue gliding along the shell of her ear. "Ever since that night on FaceTime." He felt her shiver under his touch, and his body responded in turn, dick aching with the need to be inside her.

He had to tell himself, *Take it slow. Savor this woman.* This was the woman whose curves had been driving him wild for much longer than a few weeks. He'd been wanting her since that day he first saw her in person, so long ago at Jackie's barbecue. And her ass in those tight, high-waisted jeans had already had his dick hard for most of the day.

Gideon traced paths with his tongue between Tanika's ear, jaw-line, and neck, noting that his movements affected Tanika in the most delicious way. He watched her throat pulse as she leaned back, enjoying the sensation. He kept his hands steady, applying all the right pressure, rubbing her nipples to what he hoped was a delight-fully painful point.

"I've been dreaming of you too." Tanika's hands moved to the front of Gideon's fitted polo shirt, stroking his abs. "I can't believe you hide this body under that white doctor's coat."

"Thanks." Gideon smiled shyly and felt a hint of a blush rise just above his beard.

"The sexiest part about you—besides this body—is that you're as humble as you are fine."

"Oh yeah?"

"Absolutely. After spending decades of my life surrounded by athletes, cocky businessmen, and egos galore, you're a breath of fresh air." Tanika stared up at him. "And I want to breathe in every part of you."

Gideon could tell that Tanika wanted to say more, but she held back. She let her hands do the talking for her, moving under Gideon's shirt as she stroked his back, her nails running up and down his spine. Gideon moaned in response, moving his kisses from her neck back to her lips, giving extra attention to her full bottom lip, which he sucked and rolled between his teeth.

She reached up and pulled his shirt over his head, his glasses snagging on the fabric for just a second. She tossed his shirt to the floor impatiently. He kicked off his sneakers and stood in front of her. His camo cargo joggers were housing a nice, thick erection—an erection that was begging to be touched.

She eased closer, moving her hands down Gideon's abs and into the waistband of his pants. "And I can't believe you're blessed with all of this." His breathing was ragged as her nails grazed the top of his pelvis, coiling through his nest of hair, until her fingers reached his dick. At the first stroke, her thumb swirled his head. It was already wet with pre-cum. Gideon's eyes rolled into the back of his head, his legs feeling like jelly. This is what Tanika Ryan did to him. If she stroked him one more time, he was going to lose it.

"Baby, we need to move, otherwise I'm going to lose it right here." He didn't recognize his own voice, which came out hoarse and rough.

Tanika took his hand and led him to her sofa. It was large and long enough for them to be comfortable. *Thank god.* Gideon wasn't sure he could make it to the bedroom. Tanika pushed him down on the sofa.

He bit his lip, his eyes roaming all over her. "You've been teasing me all day with that ass in those jeans." He took off his glasses and reached for the top of her jeans, slowly unbuttoning them, then pulled them down over her ass and thighs. Tanika stepped out of them and stood above him in black panties, a swirling tattoo of flowers running from her hip to the middle of her thigh. Gideon moved to the edge of the sofa. He gripped the back of her thighs, pulling her body closer. He traced the tattoo with his finger. "Beautiful. What kind of flowers are these?"

"Magnolias. Magnolia is my middle name. It was my mom's favorite flower."

"Magnolia? Can I call you Maggie? Magpie?" Gideon asked, smiling as he licked the soft edges of the artwork.

"Magpie? Absolutely not."

His lips still tracing the tattoo, Gideon asked, "You sure? Because I like Magpie." He caught her gaze and held it, even as his tongue moved to the inside of her thigh. He hummed "Maggie May" by Rod Stewart.

"What do you know about Rod Stewart?" Tanika giggled.

"Rod is a blue-eyed soul legend. I like legendary."

"Is tonight about to be legendary?"

Gideon looked up to see Tanika biting that juicy lip of hers. His tongue hit a sensitive spot. *Guess you got your answer*, he thought.

"Shit, you can call me whatever you want. Just keep doing that." Tanika's hands found Gideon's beard, slowly caressing it. "I love the way your beard feels against my thighs," she moaned, nearly breathless.

"I need to taste you," breathed Gideon against the seat of her damp panties, taking a moment to inhale her scent. "I need a full drink of you. Not the tease I got before." He pulled Tanika's panties down, exposing her pussy to the cool air.

Gideon placed a chaste kiss at the top of her pelvis. "Look at this pretty pussy. I know you taste as good as you look." Gideon lowered himself to the floor, lifting Tanika's right leg over his shoulder, her foot resting on the couch. He pulled her to him and parted the lips of her pussy with his stiff, hot tongue.

"Shit, Gid." Tanika gripped the back of the sofa with one hand and adjusted her leg, supported by Gideon's strong shoulder. Though they were a week away from spring and the condo was air-conditioned, Tanika was sweating. His eyes darted up to see her watching him. *If she wants to watch, I'll give her a show.* He reached behind her to cup her ass as he plunged his tongue deeper into her wetness. When his tongue slid upward toward her clit, Tanika let out a guttural moan. Gideon took the hint, sucking and licking the sensitive nub harder and further. He satisfied her until her juices coated his beard and face.

Tanika had his dick harder than it had ever been, but he wanted to make sure she got hers before he got his. He inhaled her, tasted her, licked her, until she was losing all sense of balance, her leg slipping off his shoulder as she writhed and fell further into him. When she came, Tanika screamed his name, the sound echoing off the walls.

After it seemed like Tanika had come down from her high, Gideon took a seat on the sofa, leaned back, and guided her on top of him. He took off her glasses, placing them next to his on the end table near the sofa. He motioned for Tanika to lift her arms, removing her T-shirt. Her breasts spilled over her bra as her nipples, hard and dark brown, strained against the mesh cups. He squeezed one gently through the bra and heard Tanika let out a satisfied hiss. He unhooked the bra, finally letting her breasts free.

"God, you're beautiful." Gideon's thumbs circled her nipples. "I could look at you all day. And night." His hands glided up and down her torso, feeling all the delicious parts of her—the soft folds of her waist and belly, the hard of her rib cage, the dips in her hips. He had the urge to sink his teeth into her, as if she were a ripe fruit. She looked down at him, her curls flopping into her face, the streaks of gray at her temples shining like bright beams of moonlight.

"I need you inside me. Please."

That *please* did him in.

Gideon rubbed his clothed erection against Tanika's bare pussy. "It's yours, princess. Take it."

Tanika ground against him, leaving a damp trail where she rubbed his pants again and again. Gideon could only imagine how her pussy was humming with need. She slipped her hands inside Gideon's pants, removing his dick, which jerked against his stomach.

"There's a condom in my pocket." Gideon nodded toward his left pocket. Tanika reached inside, then put the packet between her teeth. He lifted his hips underneath Tanika and slid his pants and boxers down.

Tanika moved from Gideon's lap, and he immediately missed the weight of her. She bent down, licking a bead of wetness from his dick. He felt himself seize up, pressure in his balls building to dangerous levels. She straddled him again, stroking his length a few times before she tore open the condom and slid it on his fully erect dick. She took hold of him and guided him inside of her. As their bodies met, they both moaned their satisfaction. The look on Tanika's face said she reveled in the pleasure of being stretched to capacity. Gideon enjoyed being the one to do it.

He gripped her ass as she rode him at a slow, agonizing pace, grinding her pussy on him until every bit of willpower was shattered inside of him. He looked up at this gorgeous woman—her head thrown back, her hands resting on his thighs—and swore she was a vision of pure ecstasy. He lifted his hips a little, angling himself into her deeper, until he reached the spot that had her clawing at him to hold on. Perspiration trickled down his brow as he hungrily watched Tanika's breasts bounce. He lifted up, putting a perfect, teardrop-shaped nipple in his mouth. She gasped as he rolled his tongue around one nipple, then the other, his teeth grazing them in a way he knew drove her wild. She dug her acrylic nails into his shoulders, sending sparks all the way down to the base of his dick. *Enough of this.* His body couldn't handle it anymore. He had to take over.

Gideon cupped his hands underneath Tanika's ass, and in one confident, swift move, he had her on her back. Despite his modest height, Gideon was deceptively strong, flipping all nearly two hundred pounds of her like she was a sack of sugar. Throwing her around as he liked. The sensation of Tanika's walls pulsing around him was almost too much.

"Look at me, baby. I want to see your face while you take this dick," Gideon commanded. Tanika slowly opened her eyes and looked at him. His bottom lip tucked between his teeth in concentration, his eyes laser-focused on her. "That's a good girl," he growled as he moved faster. She reached up and stroked his beard, tugging it a bit, which only made him drive into her harder.

They tried to catch their breath, to say words that made some type of sense, but nothing came out of their mouths but groans, screams, and expletives as the sound of his dick entering her pussy again and again made them lose all sense of control. Her pussy squeezed around him, milking him for everything that he had.

Gideon shook his head slightly. He wasn't ready to come. "Get on your knees," he said roughly. He pulled out, and he instantly felt the absence of her possession. But once she was on her knees with Gideon behind her, he rewarded her obedience, his tongue dipping into her, fucking and sucking her clit from the back. She dropped her head onto the sofa arm and screamed into it. Just as his ears were ringing with pleasure, Gideon thrust his dick into her pussy, jolting her forward. He increased his pace, moving furiously as her ass slapped against his pelvis.

"Gideon, shit. Oh god!" When she tried to put her hands back to slow him down, he pinned both of her wrists with one hand.

"Don't run from the dick, baby. Let me give it to you like I know you want it."

Gideon panted his words as he shifted his body weight, putting a foot up on the couch to aim his dick at the sweet spot in Tanika's pussy. Somehow, he knew her body, knew how to find her secret places and press himself *right there*. Watching his hard, thick dick go in and out of Tanika was the most satisfying thing Gideon had ever seen.

"Fuck, I want it."

"I'm almost there, baby." Gideon felt his body on the precipice of orbit, a low hum building inside of him. He let go of Tanika's hands and gripped her ass to steady himself as he jerked, releasing every ounce of himself inside of her.

He couldn't move. He had to allow his heartbeat to steady a minute. *What has this woman done to me?*

Once he was able to breathe, Gideon kissed Tanika down the length of her back and eased out of her. He found the kitchen wastebasket and threw away the condom, then returned to the couch and pulled Tanika onto his lap. "That was . . . amazing."

"Otherworldly." Tanika wrapped her arms around his neck.

He kissed Tanika's clavicle and shoulders, tasting the salty sweat from her skin. "I knew we'd be good together, but damn."

"That's a confident statement. What if we were whack?"

"Us? Whack?" Gideon kissed Tanika's chin, then her cheek, then the tip of her nose. "Baby, chemistry like ours doesn't produce whack sex. Besides, we have years of pent-up sexual frustration to get out. It wasn't going to be whack." He put his hands over his head and readied himself to settle into the warmth of the sofa.

"Oh, you think we're done? We haven't finished making up for lost time. Like you said, two years is a long time." Tanika waggled her brows, and Gideon playfully smacked her ass.

"I didn't say we were done, princess. We're just getting started. Next round is in your bedroom." Gideon lifted Tanika over his shoulder with ease, loving how she felt in his arms. "I presume it's down this hallway, right?"

"Yes, caveman, it is." Tanika pointed in the direction of her bedroom, laughing until they reached the bed.

For hours, Gideon tended to Tanika's body, making love to her in every way imaginable. He left no part unkissed, unlicked, or untouched. She took him into her mouth, hot and wet, that look of ravenous hunger on her face, and he saw an explosion of light as he came. He knew he didn't want to let Tanika go. Ever.

I am so far gone.

For the second time in his life, Gideon was in love. *Ruined* by Tanika Magnolia Ryan, forever.

They pleased each other until the sun rose through her bedroom window, signaling a new day and endless possibilities.

CHAPTER 24

"I'm sure mine is bigger. Way bigger. Deeper too."

"Oh yeah? I don't believe you. Show me."

Tanika stood with Gideon in front of the door to her sneaker closet, which was actually a spare bedroom that she'd turned into storage space for her collection. It had gotten to the point where her regular walk-in closet couldn't contain it anymore. When she opened the door, Gideon gasped.

"You've got to be kidding me." Gideon walked into the space slowly. He pointed toward the left wall. "I know those aren't the Nike SB Concept Lobsters? And then you have the LV dunks! You know what? I must admit your collection is hot. But . . ."

Tanika raised a brow. "But what? My collection is dope, and you know it, Doc."

Gideon put his hands on Tanika's waist, pulling her closer as he whispered in her ear, his lips grazing her sensitive lobe. "My collection is still bigger."

In her weeks off between travel assignments, Tanika had been spending more and more time with Gideon. The more time she spent with him, the more she realized Jackie was right. They had a lot in common. Aside from a love of sneakers, they loved Southern rap classics and hole-in-the-wall restaurants. They both had families that got on their nerves. Tanika told Gideon about her dad, who always wanted her to be perfect, and about her mother, who had felt helpless to intervene. Gideon told Tanika about his parents, who had been teens when they'd had him and had acted more like siblings than parents, dropping him off with whatever relative was available at the time. Eventually, Gideon opened up about Lauren and the toll her cancer had had on him and the practice. Both Gideon and Tanika were passionate about their careers, having known what they wanted to do at a young age. Tanika had played sideline reporter at her cousin's Pop Warner football games; Gideon had pretended to give eye exams to the neighborhood kids using a broken mirror and a flashlight.

Tanika talked about all the cities and countries that her career had taken her to. Gideon talked more about Vision Without Borders and all the places that he and Lauren had wanted to visit. They decided it was time to make a new bucket list, together.

CHAPTER 25

"**B**abe, you're going to make me late to get to the studio. I have some video I want to review with Danny on my piece with Colin."

"So, still following his races, huh?" Gideon sat on a small vanity chair, watching Tanika get ready. She scowled at a row of what she called her *straitjackets*, in other words, work clothes. One of the first things Gideon learned about Tanika, once they got close, was that she would rather wear jeans and sneakers than tight skirt suits and heels any day.

She slid into a mauve pencil skirt. "If I didn't know any better, I would think you sounded jealous, Dr. Miles." Gideon turned her around so he could zip up the back of her skirt. She kissed his bald head before returning to her closet to find a shirt. He loved when she did that.

"I'm not jealous. But after all the shenanigans you told me about, and the flowers and jewelry, it's clear he has more than a crush."

Tanika waved her arms. "I'm not worried about that. I told him we are friends. I don't get involved with people I have to work closely with. Trust me, I learned the hard way in my younger days. Plus, he's a kid. And *you* are not." Tanika threw on a sleeveless white button down, tucking it into her skirt. She slipped on a pair of Adidas flip flops and tossed her pumps into her handbag.

Gideon rose, putting his hands around Tanika's waist. "Alright. I trust you." And he did. He lifted her hair and kissed the nape of her neck. "How about after you finish work this week, I take you away for the weekend? Maybe down to Hilton Head? Or maybe a quick flight to Miami?"

Tanika sighed, leaning into his kiss. "Babe, I wish I could, but I have to be back in Charlotte to interview Colin as he prepares for his race at Daytona the following week. Then, I'll be in Daytona covering that race."

"I could come with you to Charlotte. And when you have some downtime, we can drive over to Asheville for the day. I can even show you my little hometown. Goldsboro isn't much, but it does have some of the best barbeque in eastern North Carolina and some dope breweries." He was getting excited about the possibility of a road trip with the woman he adored.

Tanika turned to face Gideon. He could read the rejection in her eyes before she even spoke. "Gid, I really wish we could, but when I'm at work, I rarely have any downtime. And usually, I just want to crash at the end of the day. You understand, right?"

"Yeah, I get it." Gideon swallowed his disappointment.

"Once I'm off the road for a while, we can plan to get away. I promise. I think we both could use the break. But for now, to thank you for your stellar performance last night, the break I can promise you is *breakfast*. Want to get peach cobbler French toast from Breakfast Club before we both head to work? My treat."

"Stellar, huh?" Gideon kissed Tanika on the nose. "I suppose I'll accept the French toast." He sneaked his hand under Tanika's skirt, stroking the delicate skin behind her knee. "But what I really want is a repeat of last night. Since it was stellar and all . . ."

"Hmmm," Tanika groaned, turned on by the wicked smile Gideon was giving her. "Please behave, Dr. Miles. Or I'll have to report you to the board of ethics."

"Tanika," Gideon growled, his tongue sweeping across her neck. "You know when we play doctor it just turns me on more."

"I know. But we've got to get to work."

Gideon held up his fingers in a *V.* "I promise we won't be late. Scout's honor."

"You're the worst." Tanika let out a laugh. And before she knew it, her skirt was around her ankles.

CHAPTER 26

Tanika had to admit, having a steady lover greatly improved her mood at work. She bounced around the halls, saying hello to everyone. She passed the sugar in the break room. Even Sara got a genuine "Good morning!" out of her. She was happy for the first time in a very long time.

"There you are. I was looking for you." Mya met her as she rounded the corner toward her office. "Well, look at you all bright-eyed and bushy-tailed. Or should I say, well-fucked. Even your skin is glowing."

"Is it?" Tanika put her hand up to her face, feeling hotter than usual. "It's just a new skincare routine."

"Don't bullshit me, Tanika. I know your skincare routine well. And ain't nothing changed except you getting some dick."

Tanika smirked. "Well, thank Dr. Miles for that. And what's so urgent that it couldn't wait for our morning meeting?"

Mya pulled Tanika to the side of the hallway. "Girl, have you read the *Sports Ragz* page today?"

Tanika frowned. "I don't read that filth. What did they say?"

"Remember your boy Ray-Lee McQueen? From the Houston Rodeo?"

Tanika stilled, remembering her last unsettling interaction with Ray-Lee. "Yeah, what about him?"

"Well, come to find out, they are stripping him of his titles. He's been using steroids—on himself *and* his bull. And they only found out about it because Ray-Lee went on some steroid-induced rage fest at another contest. Like, throwing stuff and whatnot. He may lose some endorsements too."

"That's horrible." Tanika's stomach roiled. She knew she hadn't had a good feeling about Ray-Lee, but at the time, she'd thought it was because she was stuck on Gideon. No, what she'd felt was her intuition on high alert—those auras giving her a clear sign. *Good looking out.* She was thankful she hadn't given that brother the time of day beyond a campfire song, subpar domestic beer, and bad first kiss. She'd dodged a bullet.

Mya and Tanika kept walking. Just as they passed by Ross's office, Sara Taylor exited. She looked furious; her usually violet aura now had splotches of red gathered around her head. Tanika was about to ask if she was alright, when Sara stopped and pointed a finger in her direction, a snarl overtaking her expression.

"You!" Sara fumed, moving closer. "I don't know what you did, but you're a backstabber. I've only tried to be a friend to you."

"First off, you need to calm down." Tanika moved Sara's finger out of her face. "Second, I wouldn't say we are friends. Finally, I have no idea what you're talking about."

No sooner than the words had left her mouth, Ross was calling Tanika into his office.

"Nik—I mean, *Tanika*. Can I speak to you for a moment? In private?"

Sara dropped her voice to a whisper. "This isn't over, Ryan."

"What did you do to the bootleg duchess?" Mya watched Sara as she clicked down the hall in her overpriced Manolo Blahniks, glowering at everyone she passed.

Tanika shrugged and waved off Mya before entering Ross's office. If Sara was blaming her for something, it couldn't be good.

"Would you like a drink, Tanika?" Ross motioned for her to sit on the leather lounger nearest to the window. "I got bourbon.

Vodka." He didn't wait for a response before fixing a bourbon neat for himself.

"No, Ross. I'm good. What's going on? Why is Sara throwing another full-blown tantrum in the hallways?"

Ross took a sip as he sat across from her. "Tanika, first I want to say you've been doing an amazing job. That rodeo segment with Ray-Lee has been on a loop on social media for weeks now. And your series following Colin Bello? Some great stuff."

Tanika gave a tight smile. "Thanks. I appreciate that."

"Here's the deal." Ross gave Tanika his serious *cutting to the chase* look. She wondered how often he practiced that look in the mirror—brows pinched, lips pursed. "I think we got some things wrong here. Sara is just not working out for us."

Tanika felt a flood of emotions. Surprise, irritation, glee. She tempered her response. "Oh, really? That's too bad, Ross. She's . . ." Tanika searched for a genuine compliment. "She's eager to put her spin on the job."

"A little too eager." Ross finished his drink and set the glass down a little too hard, slamming it against the wood of his desk. "I know you've tried to mentor her and guide her in the right direction, but there've been too many mistakes. First, screwing up the Colin Bello interview, and then failing to engage our audience on *Football Center*. She doesn't listen. She wants to do things her way. Thank god you were there to pick up the pieces."

Tanika's jaw was as tight as a wound clock. She didn't want to be the savior who stepped in for the network anytime someone screwed up. She wanted to be valued for her own unique talent and abilities. Ross's aura was mucky-brown as ever, reminding Tanika who she was speaking with. She knew she needed to be cautious but speak clearly.

"Ross, I don't want to be called in just because someone messes up."

"I hear you," said Ross, sounding actually sincere. "Which is why we want you to come back to *Football Center* and *Thursday Night Football* when the preseason starts up."

Tanika couldn't believe what she heard. She waited a beat to see if Ross would explain himself.

"I'm going to be honest, Tanika. We hired Sara because we thought we could get a younger demo with her. She's pretty and young. And when you started flubbing your lines and squinting at the teleprompter, it seemed like the right time to make a move. But Sara doesn't know jack shit about sports, and it turns out that's a problem with most viewers. We saw an uptick in engagement when you were back on-air and Sara was gone. Folks appreciate your insight and knowledge. You 'keep it real' with them, as the people say."

No shit. Tanika bit the inside of her cheek. She had the urge to *do* something—to spew expletives at Ross or do an "I told you so" dance right on top of his desk. Instead, she stared him down.

"I see."

Ross smiled wide. "So, what do you say, Tanika? Want to come back to covering football?"

Tanika thought about how angry Sara had looked, leaving Ross's office. She also thought about that unsettling aura she'd seen around her. Maybe she shouldn't care, but it was still another woman of color out on her ass. "What about Sara?"

"Pfft!" Ross blew out a sour breath, throwing up his hands. "We'll move her elsewhere. Put her on the minor sports you were covering, like lacrosse. Maybe competitive cheerleading since she seems more suited for that. So? Will you come back? I know Jacob and Key-Juan would love to have you back too."

After all this drama, do I even want to go back? Tanika knew this was the moment to ask. "So, what's going on with the VP position?"

Ross looked a bit startled. "Oh. Well, that's still up in the air. The board isn't sure what direction they are going in, but trust me, I threw your hat in the ring."

Tanika wasn't sure if she should believe him or not, but what else did she have to go on? "Well, I'll go back to covering football for now, but—"

Ross shook Tanika's hand, cutting her off before she could finish. "Oh, thank goodness! Tanika, you are a star! *My* star, you know that!" He circled his desk and picked up the phone as if to make a call. Tanika knew that was her signal to leave. She took in Ross's familiar brownish aura one more time and made her way toward the door, a touch of suspicion rising.

"Hey Tanika!" Ross called out, phone cradled between chin and neck. "One more thing."

"Yes?"

"This new look." He gestured toward her. "The hair. The glasses. I love it. Seems to be resonating with our Black and female demos. But just don't go a step too far, okay? We don't need you looking like Whoopi Goldberg. This isn't *The View*, you know." He chuckled dryly, then returned to his call.

And there it was.

Tanika shook her head and walked out the door. *Fucking asshole.*

When she got back to her office, Mya was pacing. "So, what's the deal?"

Tanika shrugged out of her blazer and draped it across the back of her chair. "You can stop pacing, dear. I'm not fired. Matter of fact, it's good news. I'm back on *TNF* and *Football Center*."

Mya rolled her big hazel eyes, but she looked relieved. "Seriously? Is that what Sara was mad about? Did she forget that she stole your spot to begin with?"

"It's not even about that for me." Tanika frowned. "Yeah, I was mad with Sara, but the bigger issue isn't Sara. The issue is the network thinking they can move Black women around like pawns. Like there can't be more than one of us who can bring something different to the network. I don't feel good about that. Hell, I don't even know if I want to go back on-air anymore."

Tanika looked at the clock. It was nearing lunchtime. She hadn't been at work for long, but it had already been a lot. She had to get out of there and take a breather. Plus, she didn't need any more run-ins with Sara.

"Mya, tell Danny I'll be back for edits on that latest Colin piece. I just need to get out of here."

Mya smiled. "Don't be slick. You're heading to see your Dr. Feelgood."

Tanika gave a wink, grabbed her bag, and headed out of the building.

CHAPTER 27

"**G**ood morning, my dear sister!" Gideon placed a kiss on Celeste's forehead as he balanced a box of Krispy Kreme donuts in one hand and a tray of coffees in the other.

Celeste narrowed her eyes. "Why the hell are you so happy, Gid?"

"No reason. Can't I be happy? Business is going well. We are in the black. My stress level is down. . . ."

"And you got some," interrupted Celeste. "God, why didn't I notice before? Not only did you get some, but you are also getting it on the *regular*. This is the demeanor of a man regularly getting fucked."

Gideon nearly spit out his coffee. "Jesus, Celeste. Boundaries."

"Well, it's the truth, ain't it? I know when a man is happy because of a woman, and you have that look. So, you and Tanika getting along well, huh?"

Gideon smiled in spite of himself. "Yeah, it's only been a few weeks, but it's going great. When she's on the road, we talk every night. When she's in town, we make time for each other. She's incredible."

"Sex must be good too. I can tell Tanika got some pent-up freak energy in her."

Gideon shook his head. "I'll neither confirm nor deny. I'll say I'm happy. That's all." He placed a donut on a napkin and slid it toward Celeste. "And I don't want to talk about it with my sister."

"Fine." Celeste took the donut and bit into it. "I'm just glad you ain't walking around here all sad and serious like before. I'm happy to see you smile, Gideon. I mean that."

"Thanks." Gideon kissed Celeste again on the forehead before grabbing a stack of patient files. "But no more questions about my sex life, please."

"Doc, you're such a prude." Celeste stuck out her tongue.

AFTER SEEING PATIENTS BACK-TO-BACK ALL MORNING, GIDEON finally had a moment to breathe. He felt the familiar rumble of his stomach, rubbed his tired eyes under his glasses, and called out, "Hey Celeste, what are we ordering for lunch?"

"No worries. I got it, babe."

Gideon looked up to see Tanika standing in the doorway, holding drinks and bags from Zunzi's, a South African sandwich shop in West Midtown. The smell of sausage rolls and grilled onions filled the air. Gideon hurried to kiss Tanika, taking the bags from her hands.

"What brings you by? Not that I'm complaining!" asked Gideon, as he watched Tanika saunter over to his desk in her Louboutins, mauve pencil skirt, and vest. He knew that she hated wearing heels, but if she knew how good her legs looked, maybe she'd reconsider.

"Well." Tanika sat in the chair across from him opening the bags to lay out their lunch. There were sandwiches, chips, and rooibos peach tea. "One, I needed a break because shit is getting stressful at work, and two, I wanted to tell you the good news."

Gideon picked up his sausage roll and took a bite. It was absolute heaven. With a full mouth, he asked, "What good news?"

Gideon watched Tanika take a few bites of her salmon sandwich and swallow slowly. She wiped her pretty mouth before responding.

"I'm back on *Thursday Night Football* and *Football Center* when the preseason starts."

"That's amazing, babe!" Gideon put down his sandwich and leaned over, planting a kiss on her lips, tasting a hint of peach. When he pulled back, Gideon noticed a slight frown on her face. "Is my onion breath that bad?"

Tanika smiled softly. "No, not at all. It's just . . . I wanted to be back covering football so badly. I missed it. But now that I got it back, it feels wrong."

"Why?"

"Maybe part of me thinks I need to move on from this. Maybe my dad and Jackie are right. I'm thinking small."

Gideon pushed his sandwich away. "What's going to truly make you happy?"

"Maybe the VP role. Heck, I don't know." She picked up a fork to get a few pieces of salmon that had fallen onto the wax paper. "Even though Sara basically ousted me from my old job, I don't feel good about getting it back either."

"I see. Not as cold-blooded as you thought you could be."

Tanika looked sad. "I guess not. It just doesn't feel as good as I thought it would to get rid of her from my spot. Plus, I have this feeling that something is going on with Sara. I don't know."

"Baby, you just have a heart and don't want folks to know."

Tanika laughed, a sound that made Gideon melt. "I'm a *G*. I can't show weakness. Especially not at my job."

"If by *G* you mean gorgeous as hell, or better yet, *Gideon's*, then that's true."

Tanika's cheeks reddened. "Just eat your damn sandwich, Gideon!"

After lunch, they compared their schedules and began planning their next date. Gideon had always thought of himself as more spontaneous, but he understood that with Tanika's schedule, they had to plan way ahead of time. For this woman, he could be patient.

"Sure you don't want to extend this lunch? I could lock my office door for a minute." Gideon nuzzled his nose against Tanika's neck.

She smelled like mango, woodiness, and all the delicious things he loved about her.

Tanika gave a throaty moan. "Gideon, I'm telling you once again I can't be late, babe. I've got to get back to work."

"Damn, you won't even let me seduce you properly." He nipped at her earlobe.

"You're great at seduction—the best—but not right now!" Tanika playfully pushed him off. Gideon pulled her back to him, kissing her soft and deep. She whimpered into his lips. "Hmmm, why do you always kiss me like it's your last time?"

"I don't know," said Gideon between quick, soft pecks. "Maybe because I know life is short. We have to seize every moment."

"Well," Tanika's eyes went soft with understanding, making Gideon smile, "How about on my next free weekend we take that little trip you were talking about? Drive back up to your hometown? I'd be down for that. No distractions. No interruptions. Plenty of barbeque."

"Sounds like a plan. It's a small town, so don't expect glitz and glamour. I can introduce you to my Uncle Roydell. He may ask you for two bucks, but he's harmless."

Tanika gave him one last kiss. "Perfect. I'll have my two bucks ready just in case."

Gideon leaned against his doorframe, watching Tanika leave. He hated to see her go, but watching that ass in that skirt? Worth the temporary pain.

"Mm-hmm," said Celeste from her perch at the front desk. "If I didn't know better, Gid, I'd say you were in love."

Startled, Gideon turned. "Jeesh, have you been sitting there the entire time?"

"Yep, watching the two of you act like teenagers. You can't keep your hands off that girl. Gideon, you've got it bad."

Gideon felt heat creep up his collar. "Let's get back to work, Celeste."

CHAPTER 28

"Y ou never called me, Ms. Ryan."

Tanika looked up from her phone to find Fred Livingston in front of her. Again. She was making her way from the press box and back to WWSN's trailer when he stopped her in her tracks. "I'm sorry. Was I supposed to call you for something? I think we got all that we need from you for our profile on Colin."

Fred leaned against a pole, looking casually cool in his league polo, khakis, and aviator glasses. If Tanika hadn't gotten a douchey vibe from the guy the first time, maybe she would have considered him handsome, a little debonair—the kind of guy she would have considered dating, in a past life. Now, though, all their interactions felt beyond creepy.

"I thought maybe we could have had dinner when you were in Charlotte."

Tanika shook her head. "Sorry, I just don't have time for that right now."

"Seems to me you have all the time in the world for Colin." Fred frowned. "Going to private dinners with him. Going out to the club. Thought you didn't date athletes, Ms. Ryan?"

Tanika took a step back. How did he know all that? Was Fred spying on them? "Colin and our respective *teams* went to the club to let off some steam. That's it. I don't know if you've noticed, but he's a little young for me."

Fred shrugged. "When has that ever stopped two attractive people, especially a fine-ass cougar such as yourself?"

The way he said *cougar*—as if it were a slur—made Tanika's skin crawl. "Again, I do not mix business with pleasure, Mr. Livingston."

"Really?" Fred asked, all slick smiles and overpowering cologne, his tepid yellow aura blaring like a caution light. "So, what brings you pleasure these days, Tanika?

"Certainly not conversations like this."

Fred nodded curtly. "I see." He put his aviators back on. "I was going to ask Ross to have you cover stock car permanently. But it seems that might not be a good fit. Once you're done with Colin, I guess it's back to football?"

"Yes, it is." He was getting on her last nerve. Tanika straightened her back, reminding herself that this man could not shake her confidence, no matter how hard he tried. "I've certainly enjoyed *most* of my time here. Now if you'll excuse me, I have a job to do."

TANIKA MADE HER WAY BACK TO THE WWSN TRAILER AND slammed the door. Mya and Danny both jumped at the noise.

"That dude is awful!" exploded Tanika. "He's the absolute worst."

Mya frowned. "Who?"

"Fred Livingston. It's like he has eyes on me. Since meeting him in Charlotte, dude just pops up everywhere. It makes me uncomfortable. He is either asking me out or implying that Colin and I have a thing. Or both at once. Which is so odd."

Mya offered her a water bottle. "He's just a creep. Let it go."

Danny scratched his head. "Isn't he the DEI and PR dude? What does your relationship with Colin have to do with him?"

"Not a damn thing." Tanika folded her arms, a prickly feeling crawling up her spine. "I can't shake it, but something feels off about Fred. I don't know—"

Just then, Mya's phone beeped an alert, followed by Tanika's and Danny's. They reached for their phones.

"Oh my god!" said Mya, covering her mouth. "You've got to be kidding."

"Oh shit!" Danny froze, staring at his phone.

Tanika read the alert from the network aloud. "'Effective immediately, Ross Spiegelman, President of WWSN, is on leave from the network pending an internal investigation. In the meantime, Tanner Dobbs will be interim President.' What the hell is this about?"

"I'm going to *Sports Ragz* for the real tea." Mya scrolled until she found the article, and her mouth formed an *O* as she skimmed. "They are saying that Ross is—allegedly—being investigated for sexual harassment claims brought by Sara Taylor. More to come."

"Seriously?" Tanika was floored. Sure, Ross said some racially insensitive shit sometimes. But sexual harassment? That was new. New, yet certainly believable. Poor Sara. She recalled the woman's aura the last time she'd run into her—violet with splotches of red. The anger she'd shown Tanika hadn't actually been about her. Sara had likely been feeling traumatized and emotionally overwhelmed, all while trying her best to hide it.

"Damn." Danny read from the same article. "They are saying that Sara and Ross had been involved for *years*. Speculation is, it's part of the reason she got the job. Said the suit may result in millions lost for the network."

Tanika leaned against a chair, taking it all in. Sara wasn't well-versed in sports, and it had always been a mystery why or how she—of all people—had gotten this job. Now that Sara was out of favor, she was pissed, but also free. She didn't have much to lose, so she could call Ross out publicly. Tanika's mind was swirling fast as her phone began to ring. It was a number she didn't recognize, but she thought it best to answer anyway.

"Hello?"

"Hey Tanika, it's Tanner." Tanner Dobbs, Ross's second-in-command, was a mild-mannered and soft-spoken guy. Tanika had always liked him. "I know you've seen the email from the company."

"Yeah, I have. Gosh, this is a mess."

"I know. I just called to assure you I'm here for you. Whatever you need. And there will be no immediate changes. I know you'll be wrapping up your interview series on Colin Bello soon and returning to football. I support that wholeheartedly. To be honest, you never should have been pulled." He sighed, the exhaustion apparent in his voice. "That was Ross's idea."

Tanika sat down. "Ross's idea? But he said the board 'wanted to go in another direction.'"

"I'm sorry, Tanika. That wasn't entirely true. It was Ross basically strong-arming the board into giving Sara a shot. I voted against it. You're amazing at what you do."

Tanika felt like smoke must have been coming out her ears. All those months of being relegated to the informercial hours of sports coverage. All those concessions she'd made. Tanika felt used. Being ousted from her position had really been about Ross and his wayward dick, nothing more. Not to mention, she'd wasted so much time hating Sara for something that Ross had orchestrated. Ross had lied to her constantly, leading Tanika to think things were beyond his control, even implying that *she* was the problem. Had the VP job been a lie too?

Tanika had to ask. "Tanner? Did Ross mention me for the VP of Programming job?"

"No, I don't believe he did. But you'd be perfect for it. Some of our best new programs in recent years have been your ideas, your initiative. I can tell you've been getting a little restless. I am sure these past months haven't helped. If you're ready to leave reporting, I'll put in a word with the board. You have my word."

She believed him. "Thanks, Tanner."

"Sure. And call me anytime. This is my direct number. I gotta run."

With that, Tanner ended the call, leaving Tanika completely dumbfounded. Mya and Danny watched as she stared up at the ceiling of the trailer.

"Are you okay?" Mya put a cautious hand on her shoulder.

Tanika shook her head. "I'm fine. Just realized I've been lied to for almost a year. Probably longer than that. Ross is the one who wanted me replaced on football, not the board. And he never mentioned me for the VP job."

"*Pendejo!*" declared Danny. "I never liked him."

"I need some air." Tanika opened the trailer door and stepped out, not bothering to wait on an objection from Danny or Mya.

Unsure of where to go or what to do, she stood leaning her head against the outside of the trailer. She closed her eyes and took a few deep breaths, smelling a mix of smoke and rubber as the faint sound of car engines swirled around her. The heat in Daytona wasn't totally unbearable. Tanika allowed the sun to warm her face.

"You meditating or something, luv?" said a familiar, unmistakably British voice.

Colin was wearing his racing jumpsuit and a durag, his smile wide and a little mischievous. Tanika blinked at him. "Dude, what are you doing here? Why aren't you doing practice laps?"

"I'm done, actually." He leaned against the trailer next to Tanika. "Came to see you."

"Your speed and time getting any better? How'd you do?"

Colin gave Tanika a big smile. "Second."

"And Duke?"

"Duke came in fifth. He's bloody narked."

"Does that mean *pissed off*?" She raised a brow.

"Exactly."

Tanika let out a laugh. "God, Colin, you don't have to show up the guy so bad."

"It's not my fault; I'm just that good."

"Well, I'm glad you're getting your sea legs here in stock car."

"Yeah. And I remembered what you said." Colin sighed. "About someone like me not getting many chances. I can't screw it up. And I get it, Lou is not the ideal person to race for, but I'm doing it for the other little Colins who are going to come up behind me, yeah?"

Tanika nudged him gently. "I'm glad you get it."

"Now, why are you out here looking completely gutted?"

She took another deep breath and let it out. "I don't want to burden you with that."

"We're friends, right? So, talk." Colin nudged Tanika back, encouraging her.

"I just realized that someone wasn't who they said they were, putting me in a really fucked-up position."

"I see. I say fuck 'em and do you. Who gives a shit?"

"It's not that easy, Colin."

"Yes, it bloody is." Colin pulled out a vape, taking a drag before handing it to Tanika. "Want a smoke?"

Tanika shook her head. "Should you be smoking around all this gasoline and flammable shit?"

"Only thing hot right now is me. So, it's cool."

Tanika fell out laughing. It felt good. "Why are you so cocky, Colin?"

"Not cocky, luv. Confident," Colin said with a wink. "Let some of that confidence rub off on you, eh?"

Tanika nodded. "You're right."

Colin took a hit from his vape. "I'm always right."

Mya opened the door to the trailer. "Oh, hey Colin. Tanika, you ready to go over some of the footage?"

"Yeah, I'm cool." She turned to Colin, giving him a fist bump. "Kick butt out there, brother."

"You be a confident boss, alright?" said Colin.

Tanika gave a smile and headed back into the trailer.

CHAPTER 29

Gideon made it to the gym for the first time in three weeks. He was grateful for the break—he'd been swamped with patients and could use the release. Especially since he hadn't seen Tanika in a couple of weeks. Her assignments had taken her from one side of the country to the other, delaying their getaway trip. Gideon was disappointed, but he totally understood. From what he'd read, WWSN was having a major leadership shake-up—and thus doing everything under the sun to keep ratings as high as possible. Tanika was certainly part of that. Besides, part of him was a little nervous to be spending time on a romantic trip with a woman. The last time he'd taken a trip like that was when they'd thought Lauren's cancer was in remission. They'd made love from sunup to sundown, hardly leaving their room in Saint Lucia. It had been their last trip together.

Gideon ran on the treadmill, glancing up at the wall of televisions. The TV directly in front of him was tuned to *Sports Ragz*, the show that dug into the personal lives of athletes. Gideon wasn't into gossip television, but at that time of day, it was mindless noise to keep him focused on getting his five miles in. He put his earbuds in and waited for the Bluetooth to connect, then started jogging again.

"And in other news," said the reporter. "Rumors are flying that former F1 turned stock car racer Colin Bello has a new love. And it'll surprise you all."

Gideon looked up at the television as it flashed a montage of Colin with a variety of famous and beautiful women. He had to give it to the brother; he had great taste. He'd managed to snag and bag some of the baddest women in the world.

"Yeah," said the other reporter. "Really surprising, since his love interest is no other than Tanika Ryan of WWSN."

Gideon nearly tripped when he heard Tanika's name. He paused the treadmill and stood, staring at the images on the screen.

"We are guessing the pair have gotten close these past months, with Tanika doing a series of interviews profiling Colin's first year in stock car."

"Tanika, who is about fifteen years older than Colin, is a veteran sports reporter and notoriously private, but our sources say the two have been seen out and about outside of the track."

The television showed what looked like a photo of Colin and Tanika outside of the WWSN trailer, with Tanika shoulder to shoulder with the guy, laughing. Gideon fumed, his chest getting tight with anger. *Bullshit.* This was a rumor. Obviously, a totally unfounded rumor. Tanika had told him herself; she and Colin had become friends. So, why was he so angry? Gideon wiped his face with a towel. He knew he should turn the channel, but he couldn't.

"Well, we will see if this relationship lasts. As you all know, Colin is known to love them and leave them."

"But Tanika could be the cougar to put him in his place." One reporter made a claw with her hand and mouthed *rawr.* The other reporter laughed as they shot to commercial break.

Tanika wouldn't date someone like Colin. She was his. *We are together. Aren't we?* Granted, they hadn't exactly defined the relationship. He hadn't thought he'd needed to spell it out. They were adults, for god's sake.

Gideon started up the treadmill again, increasing the incline and pace until it hurt. His face began to sweat, lightly at first and then profusely, until his beard was soaked. He yanked off his tank and threw it on the floor beside his machine. He ran faster and longer than he ever had, anger and disgust pulsing in his veins.

CHAPTER 30

Tanika knocked on Sara's door, waited, then knocked again. When Sara finally opened the door, she stared at Tanika for a few beats, then turned her back. Tanika took that as an invitation to follow her inside.

"Hey, Sara. I just came to see how you're doing," Tanika said. It had been about a week since the news broke—first the sexual harassment claim, then details of Sara's relationship with Ross, complete with photos and actual receipts from hotels and restaurants. WWSN was turning into a shit show, and the board was losing its mind.

"I'm fine." Sara reapplied her foundation at her vanity.

Tanika leaned against the other end of the vanity. "I had no idea you and Ross were . . . you know. And I want you to know, I believe you—"

Sara cut her off. "I shouldn't be speaking to you without a lawyer. You may have to be subpoenaed, you know."

Tanika threw up hands. "Fine. I was just trying to be nice. One sister to another."

"Sister?" Sara scoffed. "Girl, cut the shit. You haven't liked me since day one."

"I'm not going to lie. You took my job, Sara. I've been covering football for nearly twenty years. And here you come, with no experience, and scoop me. How do you think that made me feel? So no, I didn't instantly warm to the woman who stole my job."

"You're right." Sara put down her makeup sponge and sighed, facing Tanika. "I know. To be honest, I wouldn't like me either. But after Ross finally wore me down and convinced me to sleep with him the first time, he—" she paused, tears welling up in her eyes, "—he assured me I'd have a prime position when I got here. You know Ross. Whatever he wants, he gets. Promises were made."

"I don't envy what you've been through, Sara. But you made decisions at the expense of another woman," said Tanika. "Other *women*." She thought about Ross's wife too. So many people had been impacted by Ross's abuse of power. "You didn't have to sleep with him to get to the top. Sara, I mean it. With a little time and dedication, I think you could be really good."

Sara folded her arms, her aura flitting between indigo and violet. She was hurt and embarrassed. "Isn't that rich of you to say? Given that you're sleeping with Colin Bello. So much for journalistic integrity."

"That's bullshit and you know it!" Tanika was upset, but she knew that Sara's ego was bruised. Lashing out was understandable. And given the rumor mill that was swirling around her, Tanika was an easy target.

Ever since the rumors about her and Colin had broken, there'd been one story or another in the gossip rags or circulating on social media daily, each one more outlandish than the last. Someone had even leaked a photo from their night at the club. It was total hogwash. She'd had her attorneys put out a statement saying there was no truth to the rumor and threatening *Sports Ragz* with a defamation lawsuit. That hadn't seemed to put the fire out, though. Worst of all, Gideon had seen all of this. Tanika continually assured him that they were fine, that it was just a harmless rumor. She hoped she'd done enough to put Gideon's mind at ease, but she wasn't sure. Things had felt off between them ever since.

"So, what's the truth?" Sara looked skeptical.

"Truth is, Colin and I are friends. That's it. He's like an annoying little brother. Besides, I'm seeing someone."

"Oh really? Another baller? Team owner?"

Tanika shook her head. "Nope, I don't date athletes. Or anyone in the industry. If you must know, he's an optometrist."

"Sounds . . . boring."

Tanika laughed. "He's wonderful, actually. I provide enough excitement for the both of us."

"Good for you." Sara spoke dryly, turning back toward the mirror. "Well, if you'll excuse me. I need to go over my notes on Ray-Lee's bull steroid scandal."

"Fine. I'll leave you alone."

As Tanika walked to her office, her phone chimed. It was her group text notification.

> **JACKIE:** I'm going to ask one last time, are you cheating on my cousin? I'll beat your ass. Friend or not.

> **TANIKA:** Jack, calm down. Of course not!

> **BRONWYN:** I can't lie; the pictures look really cozy. You do look good in every single pic, so props to the paparazzi for capturing your good side.

> **JACKIE:** 🥊

> **TANIKA:** Put the gloves away, Tyson. Pictures do not tell the entire story, and you both know that.

> **JACKIE:** You've got to squash this. I can do it for you. Maybe have my PR connects figure out something. Gideon isn't built for drama like this.

He's so low-key. I can't imagine what he's thinking.

> **TANIKA:** Listen, I'm seeing him later tonight. Everything will be fine.

> **BRONWYN:** Keep us posted. Gideon is a great guy.

> **JACKIE:** The best guy.

> **TANIKA:** Of course.

Two minutes pass, and the group chat buzzes again.

> **JACKIE:** 👊 I love you. But I'll fuck you up.

Tanika had to laugh. She was grateful that both she and Gideon had people in their corner. Beyond grateful. But this ridiculous story had to die, quickly.

TANIKA WATCHED AS GIDEON MOVED HIS FOOD AROUND ON HIS plate. In the dim lighting of the beautiful Yalda restaurant, Gideon was gorgeous. His beard was shimmery with beard oil, and he was perfectly dressed in a cardigan over a crisp powder blue dress shirt. After weeks of missing each other due to her hectic schedule, she'd picked this spot for their date night because they had both been eager to try it. It wasn't going as planned. The evening felt tense. Tanika had hoped that the romantic atmosphere of the restaurant would set the mood for them, putting Gideon at ease, but her hope was waning. And it was just the appetizer.

"Not a fan of tabouli?" Tanika asked, eager to break the silence.

"Guess not." Gideon pushed his plate back, staring at Tanika. His eyes were sad. Tanika felt a thud in her chest, hating that she was inadvertently responsible for making this beautiful man feel anything other than good. Gideon rubbed his forehead. "Please explain to me again why the paparazzi are so sure that you and Colin are a couple. How?"

Tanika sighed. "I told you. I have no clue. There must be someone in their camp leaking this 'story,' if you can even call it that. For what reason? I'm not sure. Colin is an amazing driver, and his antics generate enough buzz as it is. He doesn't need the gossip."

"He's amazing, huh?" Gideon's tone was beyond sarcastic. More like venomous.

"Why are you acting like this, Gid?"

"Acting like what?" Gideon looked over his glasses at Tanika.

"Angry with me! I didn't set this up! I don't need this kind of heat on me either. Rumors like this can kill my career."

Gideon leaned across the table, his voice in a pointed whisper. "What am I supposed to think when you brush me off again and again, telling me about scheduling issues, yet there are pictures of you with Colin having a grand ol' time all over the place?"

"I was working!" Attempting to calm her rage, Tanika focused on Gideon's twinkling green aura. It was fading into the floral background of the restaurant. "I'm always working. I'm not brushing you off. Be for real."

Gideon rubbed his hand over his bald head. His voice softened. "I knew when we started dating that you were a busy woman. But paparazzi? I just didn't know it would be like that. That's next-level."

Gideon nodded toward the window. Just outside the restaurant, a guy with a camera was obviously filming in their direction. It was unnerving.

"Trust me, this is new for me too. The paparazzi part, that is. But my schedule has always been a killer in my relationships. It's why I've never succeeded in that department. After a while, no matter how much a guy said he liked me, he would get frustrated and think the worst. Just like you are now."

Gideon tucked in his bottom lip, looking sheepish. "I'm sorry. I'm not trying to make you feel guilty for being great at your job. I'm just . . . still new to all this."

Tanika reached across the table for Gideon's fingers, intertwining hers with his. His hands were always so soft, his nails perfectly buffed. She loved a man that took care of himself. She rubbed the top of his knuckles and was relieved to see a slight smile forming at the corners of his lips.

"I know, babe. But you have to believe me. I'd never, under any circumstances, mislead you. I don't date multiple men at a time. I don't date at work. And I certainly don't date immature men like Colin." Tanika shuddered. "He is young enough to be my child."

Gideon let out a laugh and squeezed Tanika's fingers. She felt a rush of relief.

"Are we good?" Tanika asked. "Because I really don't want to end this date before I get my kebobs."

"God, you're greedy." Gideon lifted Tanika's hand, pressing a kiss to the back of it. Tanika secretly hoped the paps got a shot of that. "We're good. Just remember what I said."

"What's that?"

"Just don't hurt me. Simple as that."

"I'd never. But you also need to trust me."

"I trust you." Gideon removed his fingers. For a split second, Tanika wanted to pull them right back to her, to keep him close, to give him assurance that she was here. For him. *For as long as you'll have me.* Instead, she watched him across the table.

Gideon finished the last of his red wine. "And another thing. I've had you, and I damn sure will not share you."

His authoritative tone made Tanika's nipples stiffen. *Okay, Daddy.* In another world, she'd have been disgusted by a guy coming at her like that, like she was his possession. But she knew the real Gideon. The real Gideon was respectful, kind, and warm. This was foreplay. And she *loved* Foreplay Gideon.

"Is that right?" Tanika asked, trying hard not to smile. She pressed her thighs together.

Gideon looked up from the drink menu. "Absolutely, baby. And if all goes well, I'm going to have you tonight too."

"I hope that's a promise, Dr. Miles."

He looked around the restaurant, as if taking in the decor for the first time all evening. "You look more beautiful than all the flowers in this building. And I have suffered through weeks of pent-up frustration. I'm absolutely taking you home tonight."

CHAPTER 31

After skipping dessert, Gideon and Tanika barely made it across the threshold of Gideon's house before they were kicking off sneakers and tearing off clothes. Tanika wore an A-line halter tied at the neck that she knew Gideon had been itching to untie for hours. He grabbed her gently by the back of the neck, and she gasped—just the sound she knew he wanted to hear. His tongue traced her jawline to her ear.

"I missed you," he growled, nipping at her nape, his hands now in her hair.

Her breath quickened as his grip tightened on her curls. "Then show me."

Gideon hoisted Tanika, pressing her back against the door. As if he were a well-trained waiter balancing a stack of porcelain plates, he carefully maneuvered both of her legs onto his shoulders, pushing up her dress in the process.

"I can smell you. You're making my mouth water."

Under Tanika's dress, he left a trail of kisses along her thighs, nuzzling her with his beard because he knew it drove her wild. He moaned into her panties.

That moan reverberated all around Tanika's clit.

"Fuck, wet already, baby doll?" Gideon pulled Tanika's panties to the side, teasing her wet folds with his tongue. "Hmm, so sweet."

"Yes," Tanika cried, holding on to Gideon's strong-as-fuck shoulders, her back pressed hard against the cold wooden door. She was dizzy with lust. Staring down from her position midair, this man between her legs was a sight to behold. She palmed his bald head.

He continued his assault on her pussy, lapping at her, darting his tongue in and out of her heated center. Finally, his lips wrapped around her hardened, sensitive nub. *Is he trying to suck my soul out through my clit?* Tanika's eyes were rolling to the back of her head. Her knees shook with every wave of orgasm that crashed down on her.

"Fuck! I'm coming!" Tanika clutched her thighs against Gideon's head, so tight she feared she'd cut off oxygen to his brain. She felt his hands grip her knees and push them open gently as he came up for air. Gideon's face and beard were entirely wet from her. He gently lowered her to the ground.

"You good?"

Tanika nodded.

"Good, because we aren't done." Gideon led her by the hand through a set of barn doors, up a set of stairs, and into a narrow hallway. Tanika's legs were wobbly beneath her as she followed behind. Gideon stopped for a moment at the first of three doors, then seemed to change his mind, leading her further down the hallway. He opened the door to the room, whose centerpiece was a gray upholstered queen-sized bed, and ushered her in.

Gideon stood behind Tanika. She inhaled their commingled scents—sweet and spicy— filling the room all around them.

"Let me finally take this off you." He pulled at the top of her halter dress. With a gentle tug, the bow came apart, and the dress fell to her waist. Tanika watched as his eyes drank in her exposed breasts. Her nipples were so perfectly hard under his gaze, two polished stones of onyx.

"No bra today?" He swallowed like his mouth was watering.

"No bra. I tied my halter tight enough. Or I thought I did."

"They are—you are—gorgeous." Gideon pulled Tanika closer, lowering his head to her breasts. He pushed them together, sucking both nipples at the same time. "And delicious."

Tanika hissed. Gideon's mouth was sending conga drumbeats from her nipples to her clitoris. "Gid, you've got to fuck me. Please."

She felt Gideon smile against her breasts. He released her nipples from his lips one at a time, with one wet pop, then another. "Whatever my lady wants." *My lady?* The sentiment pulled at something in Tanika. She leaned into Gideon as he helped her step out of her dress. Her blue panties were drenched, and the sudden contact with cool air made her even wetter.

Gideon's eyes moved over her body, from her head to her pussy to her toes. "God, you're so fucking beautiful. And you're mine."

Tanika felt the hairs stand up on the back of her neck. "Yours?"

"Don't play with me. I said mine, princess." Gideon couldn't hide the erection in his slacks. Tanika swallowed.

"Yes, okay. . . .*Yours.*"

Gideon captured Tanika's mouth, parting her lips with his tongue. She tasted the faint hint of her pussy on his lips. The two of them tasted so good together. She deepened the kiss, wanting to taste more. She fisted his button-down, desperate to see him naked, then lost her mind. Without thinking, she ripped his shirt apart, sending buttons spilling onto the floor.

Gideon paused, pulling back from Tanika. The look in his eyes said, *Girl, you don't know what you just did.*

"Get your ass on the bed." Gideon smacked Tanika's ass, sending a jolt through her body.

She gave him a wicked smile, "Yes sir, Dr. Miles."

She crawled to the center of the bed, slowly removing her panties, tossing them on the floor. Gideon stood in front of her, unhurried, removing his slacks and boxers. Once naked, he slowly closed a fist around his erection, moving it up and down. Tanika was salivating.

She was no size queen, but Gideon was thicker than he was long. And Tanika loved a thick dick, one that stretched her walls, gave her a sense of fullness beyond capacity. Gideon hit her G-spot every time.

"Play with yourself," Gideon commanded. He got on his knees on the bed and stared down at Tanika. She moved a finger inside of herself, her juices pooling with each stroke. She arched her back and inserted another finger, reaching and pumping. With her thumb, she circled her clit.

"Oh, god." Her eyes were heavy as she peered up through her lashes at Gideon, who was still stroking himself. A slick moisture appeared at his tip, and Tanika wanted to lap it up. She got to her knees, inching herself closer.

"Did I say stop?" Gideon's hand was sticky with his own desire.

"No," Tanika whined. She looked hungrily at his dick. "But you look so good right now. I need to have a taste."

With his thumb, Gideon parted Tanika's mouth, opening it so wide that the muscle in her jaw was straining. When Tanika felt him slide his dick onto her tongue and let go, she allowed her lips to wrap around him, devouring his length. Gideon threw his head back, relishing the pressure and suction that only her lips could provide. It was only when Gideon grabbed the sides of her face that Tanika realized she still had her glasses on—a fact that seemed to make Gideon's dick even harder.

"Harder, princess."

Tanika followed his instruction, sucking harder and faster, circling the top and clamping down on him with the force of suction. Gideon wobbled slightly, and Tanika feared that he was about to black out.

"Nik. Slow down now, baby. I don't want to come like this."

Tanika gave a few slow licks before responding. "Maybe I want you to."

Gideon would have none of that. He pulled out of Tanika's mouth and eased back. He smirked as she gave him a pout.

"No worries. I'm going to reward you, princess."

He reached into the nightstand, pulling out a condom and sliding it on in record time. Gideon grabbed Tanika by the ankles and pulled her closer to the edge of the bed. Through her glasses, Tanika saw Gideon enveloped in that rainbow of light that she only saw when it was the two of them, together. That light felt like pleasure. Pure, intense pleasure.

She squealed with delight. Gideon removed his glasses and then Tanika's, putting them on the nightstand.

"You aren't going to be laughing in a minute." Gideon playfully pinched her nipple, and she moaned. He held her legs apart spread-eagle and thrust inside her.

"Oh, *fuck!*"

Gideon pumped furiously, and she arched up and met him there. They slammed against each other again and again with reckless abandon.

"Tell me it's mine." Gideon said through clenched teeth. When Tanika didn't respond right away, he pulled out.

"Nooo . . ." she whined, pulling at his waist, feeling the absence of him.

Gideon looked down at her, eyes heavy with something that could only be defined as covetousness. "Say it."

Tanika swallowed, her breathing erratic. Her heart refused to slow. "Yes. This pussy is yours." She pulled him closer, grabbing on to his thighs, close to begging. "Let me give it to you."

Satisfied with her answer, Gideon moved back inside Tanika. This time, his strokes were slower, methodical. He moved his hips in search of that spot he knew got Tanika off. And when he found it, Tanika cried out, squeezing him further inside of her than she'd thought possible. Gideon hit the spot repeatedly until tears of joy rolled down Tanika's face.

"So, is this dick mine?" Tanika asked softly, turning the tables on Gideon. Her eyes closed tightly as she relished the weight of his body on top of hers, declaring ownership of her with every stroke.

Gideon bent down, licking the tear from her cheek, placing a gentle hand on her throat as he turned her head to face him. "Look at me, princess."

Tanika opened her eyes and looked up at Gideon, who was sweating, all golden-brown muscle. The lush green heat he emitted was splitting into red, orange, yellow—she was seeing every single color of the rainbow as an orgasm threatened to crash down on her. As Tanika started to come, the colors burst open and ran together like crayons melting. It felt like a sunset was enveloping them. It was the most beautiful thing she'd ever seen.

Gideon smiled down at her, his stroke slowing. "Not just the dick. *I'm* yours." He lowered himself into Tanika one more time and then exploded, growling.

Exhausted, he collapsed next to her, his dick still surprisingly hard.

Tanika laughed. "Down boy, give me a second to recuperate."

"He's recuperating too. Just still excited." Gideon lifted up to remove the condom and drop it in the waste basket. He pulled up a duvet from the foot of the bed and tossed it across their bodies. She snuggled up to Gideon, who placed a kiss on her forehead.

Now that she could breathe, Tanika took in her surroundings, looking around the room. It was awfully bare for a bedroom. There was just a bed, a nightstand, and a lamp. No artwork, TV, or anything colorful. She might have expected that in a bachelor pad, but it was unlike the rest of the house, which was warm and thoughtfully designed. Some of which had to have been Lauren's touch. This room felt so cold. So sterile.

"Is this the guest room?"

"Yeah." Gideon yawned, at the edge of sleep. "It's the guest room."

"Do you not sleep in your room?"

"Sometimes."

Tanika rolled her eyes. "So, we couldn't have fucked in your bed?"

Gideon's body stilled next to Tanika's. "I . . . I didn't think that would be appropriate. I sleep here most nights."

Tanika sat up on her elbows, facing Gideon. "Why?"

Gideon propped himself up, too, reaching for his glasses on the nightstand. "There are just too many memories in the other bedroom. Hell, I can count the number of times I've slept in there since Lauren died on one hand."

Tanika remembered the way Gideon had hesitated at the door when they came upstairs. She nodded. "So, let's make new memories. Remember, you said you have more life to live. I don't want to have sex in the guest room every time I'm over here. Or am I a *guest*?"

"Tanika," Gideon let out a sigh. "Do you really want to have sex in the bed where my wife died? Where we made love for fifteen years of marriage? That is so . . . *weird*."

"And fucking me in the guest room isn't weird?"

"So, what do you want me to do, Tanika?" Gideon sat all the way up. "Move? Get a new house? I mean, the market isn't really prime for that. Or you want me to move in with you, since you don't like the setup at my place? Are you ready for that?"

"Before we talk cohabitation, can we at least start with getting a new mattress?" She laughed wryly.

Gideon didn't crack a smile as he threw off the covers. "I'm going to take a shower." He walked out of the bedroom, slamming the door behind him.

Tanika pulled the duvet up to her neck and shook her head. It was so clear: Gideon wasn't truly ready to start over. He was still holding on to his life with Lauren.

Tanika had been so scared to hurt Gideon, she hadn't considered the real possibility of Gideon hurting her. Now that possibility was staring her in the face.

CHAPTER 32

Gideon stood in the shower, scalding-hot water drenching his body. He wasn't sure how long he'd been standing there, just letting the water run. He'd lost all track of time. He was so angry he was shaking. He had to calm down before he went back into the room and faced Tanika—if she was still there.

He couldn't believe Tanika had made a joke out of his loss and pain, reducing them to simply replacing a mattress. It wasn't just about the mattress. It wasn't just about sex. In the room he'd shared with Lauren, his life had forever changed. Clearly, Tanika had no idea how hard it was to move on. She'd lost her own mother. He would have thought she understood that grief doesn't have an expiration date.

Of *course* he wanted to be able to make love to Tanika in his own bedroom, on a plush new mattress and fresh linens. He wanted to make new memories in his space. But he didn't want to bring her into a room that was filled with the lingering smell of perfume and sparkling trinkets, the possessions of another woman—one who had profoundly shaped his life. However, the more he thought about it, the more he realized it wasn't just the bedroom that was filled with Lauren. Pictures hung on the wall in almost every room. There was still a random pair of ballet flats in the hallway, a cardigan hanging on the coat rack, things he couldn't quite bear to put away. Lauren was everywhere. Gideon was surprised Tanika had even made it past the front door.

He turned off the shower and wrapped a towel around his waist. He walked down the hallway back to the guest room. Quietly, he opened the door. Tanika was fast asleep, curled up under the duvet. Her hair was all over the pillowcase. He watched her breathing, her chest slowly rising and softly falling. Gideon took a step inside the door and paused. He couldn't sleep there tonight.

He crept into the master bedroom and lay on the bed, still wrapped in a towel. He flexed his fingers across the floral comforter, stroking the empty space next to him. He could still smell the faint scent of the bodywash the hospice nurse had bathed Lauren in for the last time. After she died, he'd removed the medical gear and anything that reminded him of the cancer, of the pain that Lauren had been in. But he'd never washed the comforter, never moved Lauren's pillow from her side of the bed, never bothered to make the room his own, alone. He closed his eyes, feeling a tear roll down his cheek.

Gideon realized he wasn't angry at Tanika because he was still mourning. He was angry because she'd called him on his shit. Although he'd said he wanted to be with her, he still had his walls up. He'd turned his house into a tomb enshrined to Lauren, and with each day that passed, he was withering away too.

"Hey handsome, why so sad?"

Gideon turned to see Lauren next to him, her chin propped up on her hand. She was glowing, dressed in white. He took a sharp breath. "What is happening?"

She smiled, her large puff of hair like a halo above her head. *"Gideon, you're crying. Why?"*

The tears spilled hot and fast down Gideon's face. "Because I miss you, L. I need you. I can't do this."

Lauren shook her head, her face tilted just so, a slight teasing smile on her lips. *"No, you don't need me, my love. Not now. You're ready."*

"I thought I could do this, Lauren. But all I'm going to do is hurt her. Or be hurt."

"You need to release me, Gid. Be happy."

"I . . . can't." Gideon's breathing sped up, but the air was sharp, as if sand was filling his lungs. "I won't. I can't lose you again." He knew he wasn't making sense. But if anyone could understand him, it was Lauren.

"Release me," Lauren repeated. *"It's been too long."*

"How?" Gideon closed his eyes. The air in the bedroom was cool, but he felt a warm sensation. It felt like a hand, stroking his cheeks, moving down into his neck and onto his chest, easing his breathing. The warmth spread through his body, down his spine, to his toes, until he was cradled in its embrace.

"I love you." Lauren's voice sounded different now, uneven and far away. She whispered something he couldn't quite hear. And then as suddenly as it came, the warmth left Gideon's body.

Gideon shivered, his eyes jerking open. The alarm clock on the nightstand read 6:00 a.m. He felt Lauren's side of the bed and remnants of warmth were still there. Had it been a dream?

"Tanika. Shit!" He threw on a pair of sweatpants and went down the hallway to the guest bedroom, where he found the door open and the bed haphazardly made up. He leaned against the doorframe. He didn't bother to look around the house or wonder if Tanika was in the kitchen making coffee.

He already knew she was gone.

CHAPTER 33

"Tanika? Did you hear me?"

Tanika turned her attention from the enormous window of Jackie's sprawling Buckhead mansion, where she'd been watching the rain beat down. Jackie was doing her best impression of a cater waiter, placing a well-prepared charcuterie board filled with meats, cheeses, fruit, nuts, and spreads on the ottoman in front of Tanika. Mya brought over a cold bottle of champagne and three flutes. Bronwyn was at an organic products convention, so she was missing out on their impromptu girls' night in.

"Sorry, Jack. I was in another world." Tanika took a handful of almonds, popping one into her mouth.

"Did you at least clear up the entire Colin situation?" Jackie slid next to Tanika on the couch.

"I thought I had. At least I think Gideon is cool about it. But the pictures the gossip sites put out looked *sketchy*."

Mya nodded. "It isn't a good look, but I think the network is loving the free publicity."

"This is my life Mya, not a publicity stunt. I'm trying to kill this rumor before it grows. But every time I shut it down, it just takes off somewhere else. Like a weed." Tanika groaned. "But the conflict with Gid isn't just about the rumor. He's pissed at me about the whole guest room comment."

"What guest room comment?" Jackie looked confused. "If you said something to piss off my cousin, beating your ass is still on the table."

Mya laughed. "For someone with such a delicate voice and tiny stature, you sure are a pit bull in a skirt."

"Speaking of which—" Jackie whistled and her French bulldog came running into the room, climbing onto her lap. "—can't leave PeeWee out of a girls' night in."

Tanika frowned. "Isn't PeeWee a boy?"

"PeeWee adheres to no gender norms," Jackie said with a straight face. "Also, you're deflecting." She rubbed PeeWee's belly, waiting on Tanika to answer.

"You sure you want to hear this? It involves us, um . . . being naked."

"Hold please." Jackie poured a generous glass of champagne and downed it in two gulps. "Now, I'm ready."

Tanika fidgeted with the edges of her sleeves. "We were making love. And lord, it was good. Sorry Jackie. And I noticed the room we were in was kind of bare. It was the guest room. So, I asked him, why is he sleeping with me in the guest room? And he said it was because the master bedroom had too many memories. So, I made a joke and said, 'Can't we just get a new mattress?'"

Jackie winced. Mya shook her head. Even PeeWee looked judgmental. Tanika felt herself heat up; she hadn't expected this reaction from her friends. This was nuclear-level embarrassment.

"No, you didn't, Tanika!" said Mya. "That's so cringe."

Tanika grabbed the bottle of champagne, poured until her flute was almost overflowing, and drank until the bubbles burned her throat. She looked at Jackie, who was clearly fuming. "So, are you going to beat my ass?"

"No, but I should tell PeeWee to bite your ashy ankles." Jackie rolled her eyes. "How could you say that, Tanika? People mourn in unusual ways for as long as they need to. His wife *died* in that bed. This is all new for him. You of all people should understand that."

"I know. I miss my mom all the time. But I felt like he was treating me like an afterthought. Like a booty call in his own home, sexing me in his guest room."

Jackie pinched the bridge of her nose. "Tanika! Just because he doesn't want to screw you in the same room—hell in the same bed—that he shared with his wife doesn't mean he thinks of you as an afterthought. If anything, it seems like he respects the hell out of you, even while he respects Lauren's memory. You ever think about it like that?"

"Nope." Tanika shook her head stubbornly. "At that moment, I felt like I wasn't worthy, wasn't important. And maybe I never will be. Lauren will always be there."

"I know you've said you've gone to therapy to work out the issues with your dad, but every now and then they show up." Jackie tore off a piece of prosciutto and chewed it viciously.

Tanika's eyes grew wide, more than offended that Jackie would bring her father into this. "What the hell does Walt have to do with anything?"

Jackie pointed a tiny, fierce finger in her direction. "Face it, girlie. Because your dad cheated on your mama repeatedly and treated her like a stranger in your own home, flaunting the infidelity in her face, you fear you'll never be first in any man's life. You use perfection as a coping mechanism. As long as you're stuck in that story, you'll always come second."

Mya nodded. "And you feel second at work too. As soon as Sara was hired, the rage just grew. I'm tired of ordering pencils, girl."

Tanika gulped. Why did these women have to know her so well? Their words stung, but they were only being honest. Since graduating as her high school's valedictorian, she'd felt that overachieving was the only way she could shield herself from being hurt. From her career to her appearance, she was determined to be perfect in every aspect of her life. She put up walls to prevent anyone from

LOSING SIGHT | 229

treating her the way her father had treated her mother. Now, she realized that her need to be flawless was the reason relationships never worked out for her. And she was over it. Belonging to the cult of perfection was exhausting, and Tanika was ready to release herself from the obsession. The facade she'd created for decades was crumbling. Professionally, she'd been demoted. Physically, she had wrinkles and gray hair, and wore glasses now. Yet, her world hadn't totally fallen apart. Through magic or miracles, Tanika and Gideon had found each other.

Jackie was right. Gideon wasn't her father. He'd accepted all of her and still valued her. Flaws and all. Why couldn't she do the same for him?

Jackie reached out to hold Tanika's hand. "My cousin isn't your dad, boo. He is kind, gentle, and sweet as can be. He would never intentionally hurt you. You can't be looking for the next shoe to drop. You can't be in a rush to hurt him first just to, I don't know, get it over with. I wouldn't have tried to set the two of you up if I hadn't seen the potential for something good between y'all."

Tanika felt her shoulders drop, relaxing for the first time since her fight with Gideon. She smirked, one brow raised. "Is that right? Don't tell me you've become a romantic, Jacqueline Miles."

"Never," said Jackie quickly. "I'm a shark. An agent. I make deals. Broker relationships. And the two of you, I feel, could be one of the best relationships that I've negotiated. *If* you do your part to work this out." Jackie said the last part with a smile, but Tanika shook her head.

"I appreciate that, Jackie. I do. But despite me really liking Gideon, I think I fucked up. And I really don't believe he's ready. Timing has a lot to do with a relationship's success. Now isn't the time for us, I guess."

"You don't have to cut it short before it begins. Maybe this connection is like a good wine. You have to let it breathe before you can really appreciate it. So just take your time."

Thunder rocked the house, and the lights flickered. PeeWee jumped out of Jackie's lap and into his plush doggie bed just near the fireplace. Their phones dinged in chorus, alerting them to a tornado watch in the area.

"Well, ladies," Jackie declared. "A tornado ain't nothing to play with. So, I guess you all are sleeping over. I have seven bedrooms, so do not argue with me. Just pick one and get comfortable."

Mya grabbed the bottle of sparkling rosé. "You ain't gotta tell me twice. This place is like a palace. Or a fancy hotel."

"Listen, Red! If you spill a drop on my cashmere blankets, I'll sue you." It was an idle threat despite the look on Jackie's face. Tanika knew Jackie was super proud of her house and loved to show it off. She also hated being alone during storms.

Tanika laughed. "Mya, if I were you, I'd put the bottle back and back away, slowly."

"Damn, Jackie's a mean little elf!" Mya reluctantly set the bottle of rosé down. "I'm still taking home these cute slippers you make us put on. And I'm taking a bubble bath too."

Jackie rolled her eyes, turning back toward Tanika. "Anyway, let Gideon cool off, and y'all will get back on track. If you don't want that, then don't drag it out. He doesn't need another crack in his fragile heart. And you know I'll break out the brass knuckles."

Tanika reached for Jackie to give her a side hug. "I won't make you get out the brass knuckles. Trust me. But Jack?"

"What's up?"

"I'm going to need you to go to anger management. With that calm, soft voice of yours, you are deceptively volatile."

"Please," Jackie said, sucking her teeth, then popping a grape into her mouth. "I've tried it. They kicked me out."

Tanika gave her best friend a kiss on her forehead. "You're hopeless, Jackie Miles."

Jackie looked up at Tanika. "And I need you to realize that things may *seem* hopeless, but they aren't."

Tanika wished she had an ounce of the optimism that Jackie had. "What if you're wrong?"

Jackie ran a hand through her pixie cut. "Listen, you know I don't believe in all that mumbo jumbo that Bronwyn was talking about—your glasses and auras or whatever. But you said it yourself, everything changed after you went to Gideon to get your eyes checked. You're not having these visions or whatever for nothing. It's a sign, babe."

Tanika laughed. "Which is it, you believe in these things, or you don't? Next thing you know, you're going to tell me the ghost of Lauren is going to send me another sign to remind me I've got her blessing."

The thunder roared again, this time shaking the house with force as the chandelier flickered again, then went dark. Jackie and Tanika looked at each other in the dim light.

"There's a flashlight in the drawer. You grab that, I'll get the champagne and the glasses," said Jackie, jumping up from the couch.

"I'm opening up the Bible app!" Mya touched her phone screen frantically until she found the King James Version and began reciting Psalms 121 as she opened the drawer for the flashlight.

"I'll grab PeeWee!" Tanika hoisted up the hefty hound and glanced up at the chandelier, mouthing a quiet *Okay girl, I get it!*

Then they all ran from the room, not daring to look back.

TANIKA TWIRLED AN UNBROKEN PENCIL BETWEEN HER FINGERS AS she pretended to listen to Mya run down her schedule. She'd tried hard to concentrate, but her mind was on what Jackie said the other night. *Jack was right.* If Tanika didn't process her anger about her father, she'd always be stuck feeling second place with Gideon.

She and Gid had spoken sporadically since that night in the guest room. Things were cordial, but that was it. It felt like they were back in the friend zone. Now she was staring down at her phone, waiting for some kind of response from him.

". . . and we have to wrap up the profile on Colin with the race in Bristol," Mya tapped her iPad as she continued. "Finally, I've squared away all your football preseason interviews. Network is also asking you to do a profile on the training camp with Atlanta's new QB. And . . ." Mya stared at Tanika, annoyed. "Are you listening to me?"

Tanika stopped twirling her pencil and removed her bare feet from her desk. "I'm listening. Bristol with Colin. Atlanta QB. Got it."

"Your inability to focus is getting on my damn nerves. Just text him."

"I did!" Tanika tossed the pencil back into the holder. "I just don't want to seem desperate.

"But did you apologize?"

Tanika rolled her eyes. She wasn't that cold. "Of course, I did, Mya." She pulled up the text thread on her phone. "'I'm sorry for making it about me and not your feelings.' He just replied, 'We're cool.' That is it. Like we're back to being homies. Talking about generic shit like weather and tourney brackets."

"People still say *homies*? God, you Gen Xers are so ol—" Mya stopped abruptly when she saw Tanika staring daggers at her. "My bad."

There was a knock at Tanika's door. Before she could call "come in," Tanner Dobbs appeared. He reminded Tanika of a more coiffed Jack Black, with a sweet round face and beard. But unlike Jack Black, he definitely wasn't a comedian. Kind as he was, Tanika didn't think she had ever heard him laugh. "Hey Tanner, how can I help you?"

"I come bearing good news, Tanika!" Tanner walked in, nodding toward Mya who moved to sit on the sofa, motioning for Tanner to take a seat at Tanika's desk.

Tanika looked at Tanner and for the first time, she noticed the soft orange light that crowned his head. *Orange.* If she was remembering what the aura book said about orange, it meant that Tanner was all about business and goals, action-oriented. He wasn't about to waste Tanika's time, and she appreciated that. It was a huge change from Ross, the consummate bullshitter.

"What's the good news, Tanner? Is it the VP job?"

"No word on that yet. But the good news is, you're nominated for a Sporty Award."

Tanika's jaw hit the floor. "Are you serious?" In her twenty-plus-year career, somehow Tanika had never won a Sporty, the sports world's equivalent to an Emmy. Sure, she'd won a lot of awards, including an *actual* Emmy, but a Sporty nomination was an honor bestowed by her peers, to be voted on by athletes and others working directly in sports. She leaned across the desk. "For the pieces I've done on Colin? They've been getting a lot of buzz. That's great."

Tanner shook his head. "Um. No. It's Best Viral Moment . . . with you, Ray-Lee McQueen, and the bull."

"Dear god. My first Sporty nomination, and it's for me basically antagonizing a bull? That isn't going to garner me an ounce of respect among my peers." Tanika dropped her head in her hands.

Tanner chuckled. "I get it. Not ideal, but it did push traffic up to record numbers on our website."

"Is Ray-Lee going to be there?" Tanika remembered their last interaction and the unsettled feeling she'd got around him. And the steroid scandal certainly did him no favors in her eyes. She trusted her intuition now, which was hard at work even when she couldn't see Ray-Lee's pink, fizzy aura. It felt natural for her to be cautious around him.

"I think so. I know he's had some issues, so this may be good for his image. I spoke with his agent, who seems to think he's turned a new leaf, for what it's worth. Another bonus—the Sporties are in Vegas. I love a good buffet."

"Same," Mya chimed in. "The buffets are popping!"

"That they are," Tanika chuckled. "I guess I'll go. Not what I expected to be nominated for, but I'll take it."

Tanner rose from his seat. "Good. We need all the good press we can get. I'm sure you've seen Sara's latest exposé on Ross."

"Unfortunately, I did."

In the month since leaving WWSN, Sara had gone on an interview tour, speaking to several rival networks about how Ross had promised to advance her career in exchange for a sexual relationship. She even had audio recordings of Ross telling Sara he'd do everything in his power to get her a prime spot at WWSN. Some of the conversations were so sexually graphic it would make porn stars blush. Ross had denied all allegations, but it certainly wasn't looking good. Tanika couldn't be angry at Sara. She hoped Sara got whatever sense of justice she needed, and Ross could go to hell for all she cared. But she did hope the network wouldn't go down with him. The board was bracing itself for a multimillion-dollar lawsuit from Sara, which—according to rumors—was just a few weeks away.

Tanner extended his hand for a shake. "Thanks for keeping the ship afloat here, Tanika. I mean that." He left the room, his soft, peachy aura lingering just the slightest bit behind him. Tanika appreciated Tanner. He was a no-nonsense type of guy, a straight shooter. Unlike Ross, who had apparently been lying for years and doing damage to everyone in his path, especially Sara.

"Hey Mya, can you set up a lunch date for me and Sara when we get back from Vegas?

Mya's red afro bobbed in surprise. "Um. Okay. Should I book CCF again?"

Tanika sighed. Not her proudest moment there, relegating her first formal meeting with Sara to a basic chain restaurant. *I can be petty sometimes.* "No. Get me a reservation at Marcus Samuelsson's new spot. See if we can get something private. I think we deserve a do-over."

"Oh snap! Can I come? I've always wanted to check it out. I've heard it's as good as Red Rooster in Harlem."

"Sorry, Mya. Gotta talk about some confidential stuff with Sara. Reporter to reporter. You understand?"

"Hmph. Imma remember that!" Mya scowled into her iPad.

"Says the woman who has yet to pay for a single meal in ten years. I mean, I can change all of that."

Mya looked up, abruptly stopping her typing. "You're right, Ms. Ryan. Let me shut up and do my job."

"Thank you, *Ms. Forbes*," Tanika laughed. Mya truly was the best assistant she'd ever had. Ten years had seen their relationship morph from strictly professional to deeply personal. Technically, Tanika was Mya's boss, but in reality, Mya was as much a part of the Boss Chick Village as Jackie or Bronwyn. Even if she was their annoying little sister. Every day, Tanika felt blessed that Mya was in her life.

Tanika glanced back down at her phone. Although she'd been the last to text Gideon, she didn't want to play childish games. They were adults. They should be able to resume dating—or whatever this was they were doing—after a spat. Well, it had been a spat to Tanika. Maybe it was something worse for Gideon. She didn't want to speak for him or assume she knew his feelings.

> **TANIKA:** Hi.

> **GIDEON:** Hey.

> **TANIKA:** I'm heading to Vegas for the Sporty awards. I was nominated. If I win, it'll be my first.

> **GIDEON:** Congrats to you. Enjoy Vegas. Wear some shade coverings for your glasses.

Tanika paused. Was he seriously trying to give medical advice here? How low had she sunk in his eyes? She pressed on.

> **TANIKA:** Wild thought but why don't you come with me to Vegas? It'll be pretty cool. Meet athletes from across a lot of sports. Chow down on a gourmet buffet. Sleep in luxury bedding.

Tanika hoped, more than anything, that the last part would entice Gideon.

GIDEON: When is it?

TANIKA: In two weeks.

GIDEON: Sorry. I have a Black optometrists conference in Dallas to attend. I'm a keynote speaker.

Tanika felt hurt. He hadn't shared that he'd be speaking in Dallas. Honestly, she would have loved to support him instead of going to Vegas for a stupid viral video. She got it: Gideon was back to compartmentalizing his life, and she was back in the patient/homie/friend zone.

TANIKA: Okay. Well, enjoy.

GIDEON: You too. I hope you win.

I don't. Tanika didn't type that part; she just thought it. And then she wondered what the hell she meant by that. Probably because winning the award would mean having to be in Ray-Lee McQueen's presence. She wasn't sure if she could stomach that. Then again, why *shouldn't* she win this award, silly as it was? She was Tanika "All I Do Is Win" Ryan, dammit. She refocused her attention back to her text conversation.

TANIKA: Thanks. Hope your speech goes well.

Tanika waited a few moments for Gideon to respond. She watched bubbles appear in the text box, then disappear, and then appear again, but no words came through. Eventually, the bubbles disappeared completely, and so did Tanika's hope that things between them would get better.

So much for winning.

CHAPTER 34

Tanika stood on stage, squeezed to death in silver LaQuan Smith *haute couture*. Ray-Lee stood next to her at the mic, dressed in a white Stetson and classic tuxedo—looking finer than ever. Tanika adjusted her glasses, looking past the glare of the stage lights to smile at the audience. She moved closer to the microphone.

"Um, thank you for this award. I never thought in twenty years of covering sports I'd be awarded this honor for a viral moment brought to you by a temperamental bull and the wrong color blazer."

The audience laughed and clapped. Tanika knew most of the audience had no idea bulls were colorblind and thus guessed the self-deprecating bit would land well. She gave a tight smile as she continued. "But I truly appreciate the honor. More than anything, I appreciate Ray-Lee McQueen for saving me from becoming literal bull crap."

Before Tanika could take a step back from the podium, Ray-Lee stepped in and wrapped his arm around her waist. She froze, startled at the intrusion of space. They were on live television. If this were any other setting, she'd have elbowed him in the ribs. Instead, she plastered on a fake grin as Ray-Lee began speaking.

"I didn't expect to go viral for just being there for Ms. Ryan. But I certainly would do it all again for this beauty of a woman. And I'm just glad Big John wasn't put out to pasture for his actions."

The crowd applauded. Tanika tried to move out of Ray-Lee's vice grip, but he held on, his thumb stroking her side as he kept on with his speech.

"It's been a rough year for me. But I thank you all for your support. I truly appreciate this honor. Thank you."

The music began to play them off as they were escorted to the back of the stage. As soon as they were out of the sight of cameras, Tanika laid into Ray-Lee.

"What the hell is wrong with you? Grabbing me around the waist like that!"

Ray-Lee tipped his Stetson and gave an infuriatingly charming smile. "Listen, just trying to give the people more of what they wanted. That's all." He held his hands up. "Didn't mean no harm."

Tanika looked Ray-Lee up and down. The fizzle of pink around him told her all she needed to know. "Listen, I know that sweet cowboy thing is all an act. Deep inside is a guy who does anything to win, including doping that poor bull. We had a viral moment, but that's it. I don't want to be linked to *you*—" she gestured to his aura, not caring that he didn't know what she was pointing to, "any further."

Ray-Lee stepped toward Tanika, his tall, massive body dwarfing her. He leaned down, turning his hat so that only she could see his face, his lip twisted into a snarl. "Why don't you calm down and enjoy the night? I knew you were feisty, and I thought it was right cute at first. But now it's chafing my hide. I would have had my way with you back in Houston if you weren't such an uptight bitch."

Tanika's blood ran cold as she stepped away from him. "Don't ever talk to me again."

Ray-Lee tipped his hat, giving her that lie of a smile. "Gladly. See you around, Ms. Ryan."

Tanika watched as Ray-Lee was congratulated by several people, including a few of her own network execs. She shook her head, thinking of that kiss at the campfire and feeling grateful that she hadn't taken it any further with Ray-Lee. A gorgeous man with a terrible personality, he was the epitome of an adage her mother loved to say: *Don't covet your neighbor's yard; it might be fertilized with shit.*

Danny and Mya came around the corner with outstretched arms, all smiles and cheer. Danny had traded in his usual baseball cap and plaid for the night, wearing a gorgeous custom tuxedo with his long black hair loose around his shoulders. Mya's afro was braided up into an intricate mohawk style, and she wore a gorgeous sky blue Christian Siriano dress, reminiscent of '90s Brandy in *Cinderella*. She hugged Tanika. "Oh my god, you won! Wait, why don't you look excited? You look like you want to throw up."

"Or punch somebody," Danny suspected.

Tanika pushed a curl out of her face and attempted to look happy. She didn't want to bring Danny and Mya's joy down with the nasty truth. "Yeah, I just need to get out of this dress, y'all. I can't breathe. I just want to get to my room."

Mya nodded. "Sure thing. We can go. I'll send the car around."

"And you need some In-N-Out." Danny put a comforting arm around Tanika's shoulder. "There is nothing that a burger and shake can't fix."

BACK IN HER SUITE, DANNY DELIVERED TANIKA A DOUBLE-DOUBLE, fries, and chocolate shake from In-N-Out before letting her relax for the evening. After wiggling out of her evening dress and kicking off the world's most uncomfortable heels, Tanika scarfed down her food and headed to the shower. She unpinned her hair and stepped in, not caring that she was washing away a very expensive hairstyle. She was over the entire night. Her face hurt from the performative smiling.

She'd hated being on stage, accepting an award for something so unserious. Under the warm water, she closed her eyes, letting the shower rain down on her. She wanted to wash away the makeup, the germs from the constant barrage of hugs, and the soreness of her muscles after being stuffed into evening clothes and paraded around in stilettos. Most of all, Tanika wanted to wash away the feel of Ray-Lee touching her. She shuddered. *Dude is such a creep.* It was upsetting to think she'd be tied to that fool by a viral video clip for the rest of her career.

Tanika wrapped herself in a fluffy robe and slippers. She sat on the sofa and flipped on the TV, searching for a romantic comedy to get lost in. Finding nothing, she pulled out her phone and searched her messages. There was a string of congrats messages from her friends, including Jackie and Bronwyn. Nothing from Gideon. She was tempted to call him and ask how his speech went at the conference but decided against it. *I should give the man his space.*

Just as she settled had on another watch of *Deliver Us from Eva*, there was banging at her door. She frowned, hoping that it wasn't Mya back so soon. Tanika had sent Mya away to go have fun on the Strip with some of the younger members of the network. She took her glasses off and placed them in the pocket of her robe, rubbing her temples, hoping the person at the door would go away. She just wanted to be left alone for a while.

After a moment of silence, whoever it was knocked again, more softly this time. Tanika shuffled to the door and peeked out of the peephole. There stood Colin, his tuxedo bowtie slung haphazardly around his neck as he leaned against the door.

"Colin?"

"*Taniiiika*, darling," Colin slurred. "Up for a little company, luv?"

Tanika folded her arms, a little more than pissed that Colin would show up at her door drunk and unannounced. *And how the hell did he know where I was staying?* Given the circumstances, this was inappropriate. She didn't need to add any more fuel to the Tanika–Colin rumor mill. She blew out a breath and spoke through the door.

"Colin, I don't think that's a good idea."

"Really? I wanted to talk to you. As a friend. No funny business, yeah?"

"Go back to your suite, Colin."

"It's important! I wouldn't be here if it wasn't."

Tanika opened the door slowly, and Colin peered around it. She moved to the side, allowing him to enter her room.

Colin slumped in, turning to Tanika. "You ready for bed already? Or something else?"

Tanika had forgotten she was only wearing a robe. She tightened it around her ample waist. "I'm in for the night. It's been a long day."

Colin plopped down on the sofa, leaning on the arm. "But the night's still young. We could hit the casinos. A couple of clubs. We should celebrate our wins. Me for Rookie of the Year. You for your viral thing. You looked beautiful up there, by the way. Didn't really care for the bloke next to you."

Tanika huffed. "Neither did I. But I'm cool, Colin. I just want to sleep."

"Fine. Then let's just talk a bit, take it easy, yeah?" Colin patted the empty space next to him. "You look stressed, luv. Is it about the job?"

Tanika moved to the sofa. She leaned back into the cushions, closing her eyes and taking a deep breath. "No."

Colin gave her a wicked smile. "Is it a man? Still seeing the bloke you mentioned awhile back?"

Tanika turned to Colin, her eyes filled with fury. "I'm not talking with you about this, especially since the rumors about us—*you and me*—are part of the reason me and him are all out of whack."

Colin frowned, fiddling with his loose tie. "I'm sorry. But . . ." he paused, rubbing his hands against his pants. Tanika raised a brow. It was unusual to see Colin acting nervous. She was curious about where this conversation was going. He leaned in closer, a hand on Tanika's shoulder. "Hear me out. Our rumored love affair is doing wonders for me here in the States. Why don't we just pretend to date? You know? Get photographed at a few more places. Go to some tropical locales. You know, a Kardashian-style PR assault."

Tanika couldn't believe what she was hearing. "Colin, are you out of your damn mind? This is my life! Not some damn rom-com!"

"I mean, the public love us! We have good banter, Tanika. You said it yourself: we are friends."

"Yes, I did. And that's why—"

"That's why we need to strike while the iron is hot! Get us some brand deals and boss up! We could take this thing to the next level!" he interrupted. "I mean, Fred was looking over the numbers and—"

"Hold up." Tanika held up her hand and squeezed her eyes shut, her head thumping like an EDM concert on full blast. "So, all of this is Fred's idea?"

"Yeah. I mean it's great PR for the brand. And since I'm new and *winning*," he winked, "Fred thinks this'll push me to the forefront of the league."

Tanika was fuming. She felt steam rising from her head, making it impossible to sit still. She rose quickly from the sofa and started pacing the room, her heels lifting from her slippers with every step. "Colin, I knew Fred was a lot, but I had no idea he'd stoop this low." She paused as a realization dawned on her. "He's the one who released the pics of us at the club and on the track, isn't he?" *What an asshole. Anything to give Lou Reddy and his team good PR.*

Colin shrugged. "Perhaps. But regardless, those photos have generated incredibly positive PR."

"For you!" yelled Tanika. "It is great PR for *you* because you're young, hot, and male. I'm an older professional woman. I've been in the sports game for over twenty years. Never once have I dated an athlete, especially not anyone I've ever worked closely with. Don't you think there's a reason for that? People think I've lost my mind dating you, like some reckless cougar!"

Colin gave her a seductive grin. "I've never been with a cougar. So, consider yourself the first to pop that cherry, luv."

Tanika pointed to the door. "Colin, get out! Seriously. Before I lose my shit!" *Correction, I have already lost my shit.*

"Oh, come on, Tanika," Colin whined, sprawling across the sofa, clearly in no rush to leave. "Just think about it, luv. We could be the next Bennifer. Maybe Colika? Tanlin? We'll workshop the name."

There was another knock at the door. Tanika blew out a breath, grateful that Mya would be back to save her, just in time for Colin's departure. Tanika walked to the door, flinging it open without a word.

She froze.

Standing there—looking perfectly handsome in his light gray tee, dark jeans, and navy Dunks—was Gideon.

Holy fuck.

CHAPTER 35

Gideon eyed Tanika. He couldn't tell if she was surprised to see him there at her hotel suite or mortified.

Tanika pulled her robe tightly. "Gid . . . what the hell are you doing here?" She leaned in and gave him a quick peck on the cheek. Gideon inhaled Tanika's scent, her usual mango and spice mixed with something else he couldn't pinpoint. Something foreign.

"I gave it some thought. You're right, Tanika. I need to start over. I can't keep living in the past. I can't treat you like a guest in my bed. I just wanted to tell you that in person."

"But . . . but how did you know where I was staying?" Tanika fidgeted with the tie of her robe.

Gideon smiled. It was cute to see Tanika nervous for once. "I asked Jackie, who got in touch with Mya. She gave me the details. I left right after my speech at the conference. I know it's late, but do you want to hit a buffet?" He took her in, giving her a devilish smile, and reached for her waist. "Then again, you are dressed for bed. Let's test out those sheets."

Just as he was about to move forward, Tanika pressed a hand against his chest. "Gideon, wait. I need to tell you something. I—" Before Tanika could finish her sentence, a man wearing a half-buttoned tuxedo shirt and undone tie appeared at the door.

Gideon took a shocked step back, staring at the guy. At first, he didn't recognize who he was looking at. But as he stepped closer, the reality of the situation dawned on Gideon.

Colin Bello.

"So, who's this?" slurred Colin, his arm wrapped around Tanika. "If it's room service, we got all we need, mate." Colin gave a wink that made Gideon want to punch him in the face.

Gideon looked between Colin and Tanika. He blinked a few times. *Am I seeing what I think I'm seeing?* "What the fuck is going on?"

Tanika closed her eyes, took a deep breath, and shoved Colin off her. "This isn't what it looks like."

"The hell it isn't!" yelled Gideon. "You had me convinced it was just a rumor, just gossip, but . . . you're fucking Colin, aren't you?"

Tanika's eyes widened. "Trust me, I'm not!"

"Trust you? You are standing there in a hotel robe. This dude's tux is half off. You expect me to believe you?"

"Yes! I do!" Tanika's nostrils were flaring. Gideon wished she wasn't so beautiful when she was upset. It would have made this situation a lot easier.

"Hey bruv," interjected Colin. "Why don't we pipe down, yeah?"

"Yo dawg, chill with all that *bruv* shit!" Gideon shook with anger as he gripped the handle of his suitcase. He felt like a fool. He looked back at Tanika. "I should have known you were lying."

"I'm not lying to you! Nothing is going on. Please come in and talk about this. You're making a scene."

Tanika tried to reach for his hand, but Gideon jerked back, disgusted. Horrible thoughts ran through his mind as he tried to collect himself. He couldn't touch her, knowing her hands had been on another man. He didn't want to be there. He didn't want to be near her. He should have known—there was always at least a little truth to rumors.

"I only asked you to do one thing," said Gideon, his voice cracking on the last syllable. He willed his tears not to drop. He wouldn't dare give her or this man the satisfaction of seeing him cry. "You couldn't even do that."

"You asked me not to hurt you. And I'm telling you I'd never hurt you this way." Tanika bit her lip, tears welling up in her eyes.

As Gideon turned to leave, a flash hit his eyes, and the sound of rapid clicks filled his ears. He squinted in the direction of the light and saw a photographer dressed in black emerging from behind the row of plants near the elevator bank. There was another man too, clearly recording video with an iPhone. *Paparazzi.*

"Tanika, is this a love triangle?"

"Who is the new man?"

"Are you cheating on Colin?"

Gideon felt Tanika's hand on his arm.

"Please, let's talk about this," she begged, wincing as the camera flashed again, pulling him closer to her. "Come inside, please."

Gideon couldn't believe it. He was in the middle of a goddamn circus. He pulled his arm away. "I'm going back to the airport and taking the next flight back to Atlanta."

He turned his back on Tanika and Colin, pushing past the cameras, letting the flashes, clicks, and shouting voices fade into the distance.

CHAPTER 36

Tanika watched as Gideon headed toward the elevators. She called out to him, but he wouldn't turn around. She yelled at the paparazzi, disgusted that they'd followed Colin to her room. The man with the camera was almost at her doorway now, right where Gideon had once stood.

"Get out! Leave! Now!" Tears fell down her cheek as she yelled. As she took a step forward to force the door closed, Tanika felt her foot crunch down on something and heard a snapping sound. She felt the pockets of her robe and gasped. She looked down, lifting her foot. *My glasses.* Tanika dropped to her knees.

"Oh fuck," she wept, picking up the pieces of her broken glasses. She held them close to her chest, heaving with sobs, and rocked. "GET OUT!" she yelled until the paparazzi finally retreated.

Colin knelt down, joining Tanika. "Tanika, I'm sorry. I didn't think . . ."

Tanika shook her head, peering up at Colin through heavy, wet lashes. "That's the problem. You don't think. Please, just go. You've done enough damage for the night. But you got the story you wanted, right? The PR will be going hot for days. You just brought a good man into your insane web of lies."

Colin stood, looking sober and stunned. "I'm sorry. Truly. I'll see what I can do to mitigate the backlash. I didn't mean for any of this to happen, luv."

Tanika sniffed, putting the broken glasses into her pocket. "Please leave." Tanika pointed down the hallway and saw hotel guests close their doors, having gotten their fill of the drama.

Colin pushed past the last paparazzo loitering in the hallway, cursing as he entered the elevators.

Tanika slammed the door and headed straight to the minibar, pouring herself a Johnnie Walker Red on the rocks. She drank it fast, letting the hot, spicy liquor burn her chest before the ice could settle and cool the glass. She poured herself another drink. And then another, until she couldn't see straight, the room totally blurry around her.

Eventually, she passed out on the sofa, her broken glasses cradled in her hand.

The buzzing of her phone on the coffee table woke Tanika up. She squinted at the time on the phone screen, which she could hardly see without her glasses. It was 5:00 a.m., and it was her father calling. She had a few hours to get herself together before her flight. She didn't want to waste time she could be sleeping talking to her father, but she answered anyway. Otherwise, he'd just keep calling.

"Walt?" said Tanika, her voice groggy. She could feel bile rising in her throat from all the liquor she drank the night before.

"It's damn near 8:00 a.m. Why aren't you up?"

"Because I'm in Vegas, and it is 5:00 a.m."

Walt cleared his throat. "Well, no matter. What's this I hear, you won an award for having a virus?"

Tanika snorted. "A viral clip, Daddy. Like on the internet."

"So, it wasn't for real work?"

Tanika sat up on the sofa, rubbing her throbbing head. "Believe it or not, Walter Ryan, it was for real work. I was on an interview and then got charged by a bull. Did you even watch it?"

"Naw, Nurse Nancy told me. I don't need to watch to know you probably was up there looking a fool. Tanika, you don't have to debase yourself for this job. Have standards."

Tanika rubbed her tired eyes. She was hungover, emotionally exhausted, and in no mood to hear her father berate her. She felt a trickle of heat move down her spine. "Listen, Walt. If you aren't going to call me to congratulate me, or ask how I'm doing, or to say hello like a normal fucking father, then I'm hanging up. You can call one of your other kids for this shit. Not me."

"Now, you hold on a second! Show me some damn respect. Who the hell do you think you are talking to?"

"I'm talking to the man who never told me I did a good job. Who, when I became a reporter, asked me why I couldn't aim higher. Who apparently still believes I am wasting my time. Who made me feel like I was second-best at everything, when in fact I was damn near perfect at everything. So let me remind you who *you're* talking to, sir."

Tanika was fired up now, releasing nearly twenty years of anger that she'd only ever shared with a therapist. She stood and paced, trying not to stumble as she let her words fly. "You're talking to the woman who pays your medical bills. The person who sends you money every goddamn month, who pays for that fancy nursing home. The only one of your kids who still calls you, because you abandoned them all. So, I suggest you respect *me*, old man."

Several beats of silence stretched between them before Walt answered. "I just see so much potential in you, Tanika. You can be better. There is always better."

Tanika felt tears coming on fast and strong. "But even if I reach better, it's not going to be good enough for you. It never is. If I make VP, then you'll ask why I'm not President. If I make a billion dollars, you'll ask why I didn't make two. You've always done this to me. You did it to Mama. . . ."

"Hey!" Walt's voice cracked. "Don't bring your mama into this. I loved your mama."

"Did you?" Tanika sniffed, wiping her tears with the sleeve of her robe. "There was always your job. There was always another woman. You never made Mama a priority until it was too late. And even then, you were upset that her being sick inconvenienced you. If it doesn't serve you, then it's not important to you."

Walter coughed, then took an audible gulp of something, possibly water, but more than likely Jack Daniel's. He cleared his throat before coming back to the phone. "Are you done, Tanika? Feel better about saying what you had to say? Do you feel like a grown woman?"

Tanika shook her head. She was over forty years old, and he still didn't get it. He still didn't get *her*. "I will continue to pay for the nursing home and your bills. But in the meantime, don't call me. Don't call my assistant. I will call you if I need you. Goodbye, Walt."

As she hung up the phone, Tanika heard the door of the adjoining suite open. Mya walked in, looking as if she'd had more than enough fun last night.

Tanika smiled through her tears. "Wow, I'm surprised you didn't get married to a stranger last night. Or did you? You look a mess."

Mya shuffled toward the sofa, plopping down. "What happens in Vegas stays here, right? I partied too hard. Somehow, I ended up at an Usher after-party. It was litty. But I'm so ready to leave." Mya looked around the room, her eyes landing on the broken glasses on the coffee table, then on Tanika's tear-streaked face. "I take it your night didn't go exactly as planned either. Where's Gideon?"

Tanika thought about the events of the past few days. Ray-Lee. Colin. Fred. Gideon. The paparazzi. Now, Walt. "Long story . . . let's go home."

CHAPTER 37

U *nbelievable.*

Gideon sat in his SUV, unable to move. Photographers with cameras were outside of Miles Optometry, waiting on him to arrive. He was grateful his car windows were tinted. The tabloids had been running the story nonstop: the Tanika Ryan love triangle. Now, it was more than just *Sports Ragz* hounding them; the story had made its way onto morning talk show TV and *People.* The headlines were shameless and ridiculous. By far, his favorite one asked, "Is Tanika Cheating on Colin with a Low-Wage Doctor?"

Low-wage doctor? He hadn't spent four years in optometry school to be called low-wage. What an insult.

He couldn't stay in his car all day. Glancing in his rearview mirror, he saw the sign for Creamy Dreamy. He thought of his first unofficial date with Tanika. The colorful sprinkles. Her laugh. The way he'd felt when she touched his beard. How ridiculous she'd looked in those shades after her glaucoma test. *No. I can't think about her anymore.* She'd made him feel like a fucking fool. But he did have an idea. He put on a pair of sunglasses and a low brimmed Aggies baseball cap, walked right into Creamy Dreamy, and out their back door. Sight unseen.

He nearly gave Celeste a heart attack when he came through the back door of Miles Optometry, rattling a trash can as he entered.

"Jesus, Gid! You scared the shit out of me." She clutched her chest. "I thought someone was trying to break in. Those fools are relentless."

"Sorry. I had to evade the cameras somehow." Gideon took off his hat and sunglasses, placing them on the front desk. "How long have they been out there?"

Celeste shrugged. "I don't know. Long before I opened this morning. I cursed them out and told them to leave, but they were going on about the right to free press or something. I'd like to press something alright. But I did close the blinds so they can't peer inside."

Gideon slumped down in a chair in the lobby. "This is embarrassing. How are any of my patients going to take me seriously now?"

Celeste chuckled. "You know something, Gid. I got a feeling business is about to boom even more. Folks want to check out the hot doc that Tanika Ryan is in a so-called love triangle with. Even though we all know that's some made-up nonsense. Right?"

"Doesn't feel like nonsense when you catch her in a robe with *him* in her hotel suite." Gideon looked at the floor, avoiding Celeste's eyes.

Celeste gasped. "Are you serious, G? You sure it wasn't a misunderstanding?"

"CeCe, she was half-dressed, and he was drunk. Obviously, something was going on."

"Well, what did she say? Did you hear her out?"

"I didn't have to! I didn't want to stay there and listen to her lie to me, Cee. I'm too old for games. And so is she, quite frankly. If she wants to mess around with a dude half her age, let her. I knew it was a bad idea to date her. I can't compete with some young, hot, rich racer."

Celeste threw a wadded-up piece of paper at Gideon, bonking him right on the head. "Do you hear yourself? No one talks about my brother that way! You are just as wonderful and deserving as anyone, including that hotshot Colin. I just think *maybe* you jumped to conclusions. I find it hard to believe Tanika would cheat on you."

"She wasn't happy with me, CeCe. She was uneasy with the idea of me still holding on to parts of my past with Lauren." Gideon didn't want to go into great detail with Celeste. No mention of the bed required—she got the picture.

Celeste folded her arms, leaning over the front desk. "Well, can you blame the girl? You're still holding on to *objects* when memories should be good enough. Sure, treasure a few special things. But you can't make your whole house a museum to Lauren. That's not right. Especially when you're in love with someone else."

"I never said I was in love with Tanika," Gideon scoffed, pushing up his glasses.

"Oh baby, you didn't have to. I've seen a change in you these past few months. I know Tanika did that. You were getting back to your old self again. Glowing and laughing and talking about the future. That was love."

Gideon rose from his seat. It didn't matter if it was love or not. There was absolutely no turning back. *Whatever we had is over.*

"I'll be in my office. Let me know when my first patient arrives." Gideon went into his office and closed the door.

"AND IF ONE OF YOU SPINELESS ASSHOLES PUBLISHES MY PHOTO, I will sue the living shit out of you!"

Gideon's office door was closed, but the high-pitched voice of his cousin Jackie was unmistakable. She said a brief hello to Celeste and opened Gideon's door without a knock or warning.

"Please tell me you aren't holed up in your office trying to avoid those fools outside." Jackie strode across the office floor, shrugging off her designer coat and taking a seat in front of his desk.

"And hello to you, too, cousin. No, not avoiding them. My last patient just left."

"I hope you're in here thinking about how to apologize to Tanika."
Gideon's eyes twitched. "Me? Apologize? What the hell for?
I'm not the one who answered the door to their hotel room in a
skimpy-ass robe with a dude on the other side!"

"First of all, I know for a fact the robes at the MGM Grand are
not skimpy. They are quite luxurious," admonished Jackie. "Secondly,
you jumped to conclusions. You didn't even give Tanika a chance
to explain."

"What on earth kind of explanation could she have given me?"

"Nik told me that Colin just showed up at her room, drunk,
blabbing about some scheme. He was trying to convince her they
should pretend to be an item for PR, continuing with this farce of a
story started by the tabloids—and his team, it seems. She told him
no way, and that he was out of his mind. She was trying to get him
out of her room when you showed up. Unannounced, by the way. It
was hella romantic, but hey, you were unannounced. How was she
supposed to know you'd appear right at that moment?"

Gideon ran a tired hand down his face. Maybe Jackie and Celeste
were right. Maybe this was all a misunderstanding. But did that really
change anything? "Does it matter what's the truth or not? Do you not
see that circus outside my office door? If I knew this would happen,
I never would have pursued her. Hell, I ought to blame you. You're
the one who wanted to set us up in the first place."

"Really!" Jackie's eyes narrowed. "You blame me for wanting you
to meet an incredible, smart, and sexy woman? A woman who I
thought—no, I *knew*—would mesh well with you? Who, up until a
few days ago, you were having a great time with? You, the man she
was falling for."

Gideon looked up from the patient notes he'd been pretending
to study. "Falling for me?"

Jackie shook her head. "Nope. I've said enough. You need to talk
to her."

"No the hell I *don't*." Stubbornness took hold of Gideon and
wouldn't let him go. He was always one to admit when he was wrong,

but now, he'd rather have been wrong than a heartbroken fool. He put down his pen and crossed his arms tightly across his chest, locked in a stare down with his cousin.

"I know exactly what this is about, Gideon *Joseph* Miles."

When Jackie pulled out his middle name, he knew she was about to give it to him straight, no chaser.

"What, *Jacqueline?*"

"Everyone you have loved has left you. Your parents basically threw you on Big Mama's doorstep and never looked back. Lauren, God rest her soul, was taken away by a vicious disease. All these situations were something you couldn't control. You don't want to be hurt. You want to be in control of your pain. Control the narrative. So now, you're ready to dip on Tanika because you *think* she's cheating. I get it. Sometimes, that's how I roll too. But this time, Gid, you're wrong. You're running for no reason!"

Well damn. Gideon ran a hand through his beard. He'd paid therapists tons of cash for years, and none of them had ever described his issues with abandonment so succinctly as Jackie. But he wasn't going to give her the satisfaction. She'd hold it over his head for eternity. By the slight smirk on her face, she already knew she was right too.

"Gid, you're hardheaded as fuck! Please call her. Seriously, before you ruin a good thing. She's too afraid to call you. Every time I bring it up, Nik starts crying. And I'm no damn good with tears. I'm an agent, not a therapist."

For a millisecond, Gideon's heart ached at the thought of Tanika in tears. He tried to push the feeling away, but he didn't want her to be crying about this. Okay, so maybe this mess wasn't her fault. Maybe she didn't cheat. Regardless, he didn't think he was capable of being with a public figure. He'd tried, and it hadn't worked. "I'm not made for this," he whispered.

"No, you're made to love and forgive." Jackie reached over the desk and grabbed her cousin's hand. "This rumor will pass. Soon, some celebrity of note will do something ridiculous, and your fifteen minutes of infamy will be gone. Trust me, I see it with my clients all the time. And some of them are a hot mess."

"I hope it does pass. But, Jack, I need a break. This situation taught me that maybe I'm not ready to date someone like Tanika. Maybe I'm not ready for a lot of things."

Jackie slapped Gideon's hand and sucked her teeth. "You're tripping, and you know it." Jackie's phone began to ring, but she silenced it. "Look, I have to go. I have PJ Dawson's shoe contract to negotiate, and he's asking for a ridiculous percentage of sales. If I don't land this, that snake in the grass Antonio Steele is going to try and backdoor me." Antonio was Jackie's rival at another firm; she hated the guy with every fiber of her being. Gideon was pretty sure Jackie was the only person he knew with a real-life archnemesis.

"Will you get me a pair when they come out?" Gideon was happy to change the subject for a moment, even though sneakers made him think of Tanika.

"Maybe. I'll see what I can do." Jackie winked. As she reached for the office door, she stopped. "Think about what I said, okay?"

Gideon nodded. "Will do, cuz. Love you."

Jackie blew a kiss and headed toward the front door. He could hear her cursing out the remaining paparazzi, threatening each one of them on the way to her car.

Gideon sighed as he leaned back, rubbing his tired eyes under his glasses. He stared at his phone, scrolling to Tanika's name, then scrolling away again. He needed a sign. He pulled the photo of Lauren from his desk drawer and sighed.

Lauren, honey. I know you want me to be happy, but at this point I don't know what that means. I wish you could tell me what to do. What's the move?

He looked at the time and remembered that his next patient was Brandon, a precocious five-year-old with pediatric cataracts who loved Spiderman and comic books. Brandon was a nervous wreck when it came to eye exams, so Gideon kept stickers on hand just for him. He opened the bottom drawer of his desk, moving old optometry magazines out of the way as he searched for the last booklet of Spiderman stickers. *I swear they're in here somewhere.* Instead of stickers, he found an old brochure for Vision Without Borders.

He picked up the brochure and thumbed through it. *Is this what I'm supposed to do?* The brochure's appearance couldn't have been a coincidence.

A service-based sabbatical would be the perfect escape from the storm that was now his life. Although, with the practice booming right now, there was a lot to consider. He'd take a few days to think about it. He flipped to the last page of the brochure, looking for contact information, and a small booklet of Spiderman stickers fell out and onto his desk. One of the stickers, in big red comic-book letters, read: *Release it.*

He smiled, looking up to the heavens. "Message received, Lauren."

Gideon slid the stickers into the bottom pocket of his lab coat and tucked the brochure into the top pocket, closest to his heart.

CHAPTER 38

Tanika was seated at a corner table at Marcus Bar and Grille in Edgewood, waiting on Sara. Mya had confirmed that Sara had accepted the invitation, but it had been nearly twenty minutes, and Tanika was still waiting. It was the height of happy hour, and the place was packed. Tanika feared that maybe Sara didn't see her; Mya had requested a semiprivate spot when she made the reservation, so she was seated in the corner near the back. Maybe Sara had decided the crowd was too much to deal with, especially given the recent media frenzy around her lawsuit.

Tanika was finishing a lovely whiskey cocktail and about to ask for the check when Sara finally arrived. She was dressed down in a basic navy tee, jeans, and heels, but somehow, she made it all look chic. She carried her Chanel handbag and wore matching oversized sunglasses, no doubt trying to avoid being recognized.

Sara slowly removed her sunglasses as she sat across from Tanika. "What is it, Tanika? I haven't got all evening. Don't tell me WWSN sent you here to beg me to drop the lawsuit against them. I won't." She didn't bother to offer an apology for being late, but Tanika hadn't expected that.

"Ah, no." Tanika pursed her lips, trying her best not to snap back at Sara. "I just wanted to talk to you. No hidden agenda. I just want to see how you're doing."

Sara signaled the server over, ordering the same cocktail that Tanika was drinking. "You have until the time my drink arrives to tell me whatever it is you want to tell me."

Tanika nodded. She actually admired the fact that Sara wasn't going to take any shit from her. "First, I wanted to tell you I'm sorry."

Sara knit her brow. "For what?"

"For not being there for you. I sensed that something was off, but I felt threatened. I saw a young, pretty woman who was ambitious and just wanted a shot. I should have really been a friend. A *real* mentor. For that, I'm sorry."

The server brought over Sara's drink. She took a long sip before responding. "Wow. I wasn't expecting this. Especially since I basically took your job."

Tanika shrugged. "That wasn't all you. Well, some of it was on you. But most of it was Ross and his personal agenda."

Sara gave Tanika a shy smile. "Yeah, but I was kind of a bitch to you. I wouldn't like me either."

The two women laughed, and for the first time since they'd met, Tanika and Sara both relaxed. They ordered their food—Tanika squinting at the menu without her glasses—and eased into casual conversation.

While she waited on another drink, Tanika wiped the corners of her mouth and leaned in closer.

"I have to ask, Sara. Why didn't you tell anyone what Ross was doing? HR? The board? I mean, I understand he was harassing you, wearing you down. Lord knows I get how men in his position can be. You feel backed into a corner with no escape. That can mess with a person. But—did you want this job that badly? He's a creep. And old enough to be your dad!"

"I was scared." Sara put down her fork. "After my time as Miss United America, I was lost. I wanted to prove I wasn't just some pretty face or airhead beauty queen. I'd always been interested in journalism but didn't have a degree or background in that area besides a few red-carpet hosting stints. Then Ross came into my life, like a knight in shining armor. He was all about me at first, pretending to be a friend. Made me feel like I had potential. Most of all, he told me that I was smart. For me, that meant a lot. I was glad someone could see past the superficial. He made all these promises that he could get me a prime spot on WWSN. I told him I didn't know that much about sports. Well, except gymnastics. I know everything about gymnastics because I competed in college. Division II. I could have gone to the Olympics if I didn't have those ankle injuries."

"Wow, I didn't know you were a gymnast. Did you tell Ross that?"

Sara rolled her eyes. "Yeah, but he didn't care. He said the network wasn't interested in tapping into the college gymnastics market because it wasn't lucrative. He didn't give a damn about my ideas. After the first few months, all he seemed to care about were my looks. He said I had a pretty face for football and that I needed to focus on that. He stopped telling me I was smart and started telling me to shut up if I knew what was best for me. Ross had all the power and wasn't afraid to use it. So, I did what he told me to do. Among other things." Sara lowered her eyes and pushed her tomato and burrata salad around her plate with a fork.

"Sara, you are more than how you look," Tanika said. "You *are* smart and ambitious. That piece you did on the Black Dallas Cowboys cheerleaders was great. With a little media training and some research, I think you can be an amazing reporter. If that's what you really want to do."

Sara nodded, tears in her eyes. "I want to be a good reporter, I really do. Thanks for seeing that in me."

"All it takes is one person to believe in you." Tanika smiled. She couldn't see Sara's aura now, without her glasses, but she could feel the shift in energy. The woman in front of her looked more confident and hopeful. Sara seemed grateful to have someone in her corner.

Sara leaned back in her chair, looking thoughtful. "I never thanked you for bailing me out on the Colin piece."

"Well, I wish I'd never taken it. Look where it's landed me."

Sara laughed. "I mean, being tied to Colin isn't such a bad thing, is it? He's hot. And rich."

"Not only is Colin immature, but he's not the man I'm in love with," Tanika blurted, surprised by her own candor. She gulped her water, eyeing Sara over the rim of her glass. She had no idea why she was telling her formal rival about her love life.

"The optometrist? The one you gave a shout-out to on-air? Ah, no wonder you were cheesing on-air. . . ."

Tanika bit the inside of her lip. "That obvious? Yeah. Well. That's over with."

"He's mad about the Colin thing?" Sara took a sip of her cocktail.

"I've tried to tell him it's a lie. A total fabrication. But he won't return my calls or texts. So here I am with a broken heart and broken glasses."

"Don't take no for an answer, girl," said Sara. "Tenacity is kind of your thing." She raised her glass. "I'm learning from the best."

Tanika laughed, clinking her glass against Sara's. "You're right about that."

"By the way, I loved the glasses. You looked so fly with them."

Tanika smiled sadly. "I thought so too."

CHAPTER 39

Gideon had managed to evade the paparazzi for a few days by parking in the back of the building and entering his practice through the back door. Eventually, just like Jackie had promised, the hordes of photographers left. They were no longer interested in trying to get a picture of him.

Otherwise, the week had been quiet. Gideon's regular patients had their visits; he took comfort in their laughter and smiles as he performed exams and answered questions. He also began filling out paperwork for Vision Without Borders, much to Celeste's dismay.

"You are just running away," she chastised. "Lauren wouldn't want you running away from your problems."

"That's where you're wrong," Gideon countered. "I think Lauren gave me a sign, clearly pointing in this direction. This is going to be good for me."

"And the practice? Your patients? Your house?"

Gideon smiled, putting his hands on Celeste's slumped shoulders. "CeCe. I'm going to take care of everything. Don't worry about a thing. It'll only be for six months. A sabbatical."

"Six months, Gid! Oh, you've totally lost it. I should tell Jackie's tiny self to come scare some sense into you."

"Sis, don't worry," Gideon gave Celeste a quick kiss on the cheek. "Jackie knows she can't talk me out of it. Trust me, she's tried."

Celeste chuckled. "She's a little thing, but she sure is mean, isn't she?"

"Like an angry Chihuahua," agreed Gideon.

Celeste gasped dramatically, clutching pretend pearls around her neck. "Are you calling your cousin a bitch?"

"No," Gideon laughed. "She's just tiny-but-mighty. Her bark is worse than her bite. That's not true. Her veneers are pretty sharp."

The front door chimed, and Gideon and Celeste both looked up. Gideon froze, unable to move as Tanika stepped through the door.

"Time to face the music," mumbled Celeste under her breath as she made her way toward the back. "Call if you need me."

"Hi." Tanika stepped forward. "I'm just here as a patient. That's all."

Gideon stared at Tanika. He took in her full lips, brown skin, wide-set eyes, and black hair streaked with silver. It was as if he was memorizing the landscape of her face for the last time. "How can I help you, Ms. Ryan?"

Tanika winced at his formality. She pulled out the broken pair of glasses from her purse. "I broke my glasses. Had a little incident in Vegas."

Gideon's eyes fell to Tanika's hands, eyes wide in disbelief. "What happened?"

"They slipped out of my pocket, and I stepped on them when we . . ." Tanika's voice trailed off, her eyes avoiding Gideon's. "Anyway, I'd appreciate if you could fix them."

Gideon reached out for the glasses, his fingers accidentally grazing Tanika's. Despite his anger, a jolt of electricity pulsed through him at the brief touch. He took a deep breath, trying to hold onto his professional demeanor. "They are pretty banged up. We'll see what Tony can do to fix them, but I don't know. Let me check with Celeste to see if we have these frames in stock."

"Like I said the first time, those were one of a kind," called Celeste, who had clearly been eavesdropping from the break room. "And no guarantees on fixing them! But we do have some similar frames."

Gideon gave a slight smile. "There you have it. Since Tony is full-time now, he can get a pair ready for you in an hour, same prescription. How have you been getting along since?"

"A really janky pair of readers from Walgreens," chuckled Tanika uncomfortably. "Not the flyest. The teleprompter is kind of fuzzy, and I can't drive well in those. I'm afraid the next time I'm behind the wheel, it won't be a fire hydrant I hit."

Gideon felt a smile forming, imagining Tanika bumbling around in off-brand readers, but suddenly stopped. He had to remind himself that he was mad. He was hurt. She didn't deserve the affection he felt for her. "Celeste will take care of you." He turned to go to his office but felt a hand on his elbow.

"Gid, please," whispered Tanika. "Just let me explain myself."

He turned to face her. Soft worry lines creased her forehead. He moved his arm out of her grasp but softened his tone. "You have ten minutes. I have other patients to see."

Tanika followed Gideon into his office and closed the door behind them. He sat at his desk while she opted to stand. He looked at his watch. "Nine minutes."

"I know that Colin being in my room looked bad, but I assure you, for the millionth time, nothing happened."

Gideon felt his jaw tighten and stick like a round screw in a square hole. "You've got to understand what that was like for me. You were standing there in a robe, and he was drunk, all over you."

"He was drunk, yes, trying to convince me to pretend-date him, to keep the press interested in us. It was his team's idea. I don't want him!"

"Was it his team's idea to have him come to your room?"

Tanika rubbed her hands together. "I don't know."

"So, they didn't know you had a man?" Gideon spoke with confidence, but he was full of doubt. *Are you her man?* They had never discussed exclusivity, not really. But as an adult, he didn't think it was necessary to go through with formalities. Were they supposed to define the relationship like a couple of teenagers?

"I . . . I told Colin I was involved with someone. Yes."

Gideon blew out a breath, straightening the sleeves of his white coat. "I appreciate the honesty."

"So, can we please get back on track? I miss you, Gid. So much." Tanika moved closer, sitting on the edge of the desk. Gideon's eyes moved down to her thighs, and he had to adjust himself in his seat. She reached out for his hand. He stilled as she ran her thumb across his knuckles. He wanted to intertwine his fingers with hers, pull her down onto his lap and kiss her. Stroke the sides of her face, skin smooth as chocolate silk, and slip his hand under her skirt. He wanted to make her come until she said his name. That was the apology he wanted. The one he deserved. The one he craved but shouldn't.

Gideon moved his focus back to Tanika's face. Her eyes were pleading, but he shook his head. "There's no getting back on track. This just isn't going to work."

"Gid, please. We can fix this." Tanika reached out toward him, and he pulled away. "I'd never hurt you. I'd never break that promise." Tanika's voice was unrecognizable, breaking apart at the seams.

"Ten minutes are up," said Gideon, standing from his desk, walking out of his office. Tanika quickly caught up to him, grabbing him by the hand again. He allowed her to touch him, the warmth of her palm pulsing all the way through him.

"Gideon, please," Tanika begged, her voice cracking. "You came to see me in Vegas for a reason. It's the same reason I didn't go along with some ridiculous PR farce. You love me, and I love you."

Gideon turned, facing Tanika as she stood in the middle of the lobby. Patients watched, a soap opera playing for them in real time.

Gideon swallowed, trying not to lose his resolve. *She loves me?* He couldn't cause a scene. He didn't need any more attention on him.

"Ms. Ryan, your new glasses will be ready shortly. Celeste, send back my next patient please."

Gideon gave Tanika a final look before heading into the exam room.

CHAPTER 40

"Hmm," said Bronwyn, tilting her head to get a better look at Tanika. "I don't know if I like them."

Mya rolled her eyes. "Girl, they literally look like the last pair she had."

Jackie had picked Forza for their monthly gathering; it was a chic Italian spot in West Midtown with an exceptional patio. The weather was finally warming up, so it wasn't totally unbearable to sit outside without a jacket or coat on.

Tanika looked in her compact mirror, adjusting her glasses. "They're okay, but they don't feel the same at all."

"Are you still seeing those things we talked about?" Bronwyn leaned in closer.

"No," Tanika answered flatly. She'd been adjusting to her new glasses for nearly three weeks, which was the same amount of time that'd passed without hearing from Gideon. With the new glasses, there'd been no strange, tingling feelings. No auras above folks' heads. The magic was over. Or maybe it had never been real in the first place.

Mya picked up a forkful of carbonara. "I think you were seeing things because you were stressed. That's all."

"Clearly, you're not in touch with your spiritual side," chided Bronwyn as she picked up a breadstick.

"Girl, I go to church faithfully and tithe. Just because I don't pray to a tree don't mean I'm not spiritual." Mya clearly thought Bronwyn's spiritual practices were no match for Jesus.

"I'm sensing some tension here," said Bronwyn, looking sideways at Mya. "Speaking of tension, Tanika, have you heard from Gideon? That whole Colin debacle was awful."

Tanika shook her head. "No. And I don't know if should contact him."

"Why not? The rumor has seemed to die down."

Mya giggled. "Especially since Colin has been spotted out with a certain young television starlet from that very emo show."

"Right. I say you talk to him." Bronwyn nudged Jackie. "What say you, Jacqueline? He's your cousin."

Jackie jumped, startled by Bronwyn's elbow in her side. "What?"

Jackie had been suspiciously quiet during lunch, checking her phone every five minutes and stuffing her face with pasta as if to avoid talking. Mya raised a brow. "Jackie, you've been awfully quiet. What's up?"

Jackie slurped up the last of her bucatini, then finally put down her fork. "I'm not getting in the middle of my best friend and my cousin's bullshit. Which, for the record, is bullshit. Did I say it was some bullshit?"

"Oh, so you *do* have an opinion?" laughed Bronwyn.

"It's okay," Tanika said. "Jackie doesn't have to say a word. Gideon and I already talked. Well, I apologized. I *think* he accepted the apology. But we are done."

"Did he say you were done?" asked Bronwyn. Jackie and Mya looked up from their plates, turning their attention to Tanika, who fiddled with her ravioli.

"I haven't heard from him in weeks. He's obviously done with me. He was so cold the last time we saw each other."

"Well, I think that man ain't through with you," said Mya. "He'll at least circle back around for another taste of that booty." Mya did a body roll in her chair, breaking the tension for everyone, even Tanika.

"I have to agree," said Bronwyn, taking a sip of her prosecco. "I consulted my tarot cards before our lunch, and they confirmed that the window to a reunion is still open. There was something really nice between y'all."

Mya pointed her fork. "I agree. Tanika was much more relaxed when she was getting dick on the regular."

Tanika coughed, nearly choking on her martini. "What the hell, Mya! You act like I was a tyrant when I was celibate."

"I'm not saying you were a tyrant. More like wound tight."

"Tense," chimed in Bronwyn.

"Uptight," added Jackie.

"Okay!" Tanika raised her hands in defeat. "I get it. I was a mess."

"Once you started getting some, I had to order a lot less pencils," laughed Mya.

"So," Bronwyn chuckled, playfully throwing a cocktail napkin at Mya. "Tanika? Are you just going to let Gideon get away?"

Tanika bit her trembling lip. "Even though I love him, I think I have to let him go."

"He's leaving!" yelled Jackie.

The other women turned and looked at Jackie, who'd dropped her head into her hands.

"What the hell are you talking about?" asked Tanika.

Jackie lifted her head, letting out a deep breath. "He's packing his bags. I don't want to say anything else. Y'all need to talk this shit out. Before it's too late."

Tanika looked at Mya. Before she could ask, Mya was pulling out her tablet. "I can move some production meetings around. Actually, I'll reschedule the rest for tomorrow."

Jackie looked at her watch. "You can get to East Lake in about forty minutes. He's at the office. Go."

"I called you a car. You don't look like you should drive," Mya said.

Tanika guzzled the last of her martini, slamming the glass on the table. "Good. I'll go see him." She shook her head, trying to build up the confidence. But her shaking hand on the table told the truth.

Jackie, Bronwyn, and Mya piled their hands on top of Tanika's.

"Be honest," said Bronwyn, giving Tanika a reassuring wink.

"Be brave," said Jackie, trying her best not to cry.

"Girl, tell that man you are in love with him," said Mya with a wide smile. "I like a relaxed boss."

Tanika's eyes were brimming with tears. She was glad she had lash extensions instead of mascara this week. "You all are the best. I love you."

"Uh-huh!" said Jackie. "Save all the mushy stuff for Gid. Okay? Now, go! I'll square up the bill."

Tanika grabbed her purse and headed out of the restaurant.

Thanks to a snarling traffic jam on I-20, she made it to East Lake by 2:00 p.m. She tried the front door at Miles Optometry, but it was locked. Gideon usually saw his last patient out by 4:00, but Jackie had insisted he'd be here. Tanika rang the bell, then knocked on the front door. Again. She rang and knocked five more times before Gideon finally appeared.

Here goes nothing.

CHAPTER 41

Gideon opened the door and stood staring at Tanika. She was blinking at him as if he were a stranger.

"Yes?"

Tanika took a breath. "You've been ignoring my calls. Leaving my texts on read. And when I asked Jackie what was going on, she said I needed to see you. I took a chance and came here. Can I come in?"

Gideon leaned against the doorframe for a moment, needing something to hold him up. Then he moved aside, allowing her to pass. The office was dimly lit, the sole source of light coming from his office. He turned his back to Tanika and headed there. He didn't invite her to follow, but she did anyway.

Tanika looked around. Gideon saw what she saw: Several cardboard boxes were packed or halfway full, papers neatly filed and stacked inside. And Gideon wasn't in his usual white coat or slacks. He had on sweatpants, an NCA&T hoodie, and sneakers. *Not even my fly ones.*

"Are you spring cleaning?" she asked.

"No," Gideon sighed.

Tanika sat on the edge of his desk. She wore a simple black dress, pumps, and her new glasses. Given the attire, he figured she'd come straight from the studio. Her shapely legs nearly distracted him, but he forced himself to keep organizing. "What do you want, Tanika?"

"I wanted to see how you're doing." Tanika bit the corner of her lip. "That's a lie. I know you're fine. I wanted to know what's really going on with us. And I want us to be—"

Gideon put the file he was holding in a banker's box and sat on the opposite end of the desk. "Tanika, I'm not a guy who likes a ton of attention. It's one thing to shout me out on-air, and trust me, I'm super grateful for the business. It's another thing to be part of a fake love triangle with one of the world's most famous race car drivers. You turned my life into a zoo. I had cameras showing up at my job. At my home. I'm not built for this life. I'm a freaking optometrist for god's sake."

Tanika reached for Gideon's hand, but he pulled back. He tried not to notice the look of hurt that flashed across her face. "Gideon, trust me when I say I didn't want that either."

"He was there, in your hotel room. . . ." Gideon said softly, his voice trailing off as his mind flashed pictures of that night.

"I told you; nothing was going on. What will it take for you to believe me?" Tanika's voice cracked.

"The thing is," Gideon began, "I believed you. I still do. And I accept your apology. I'm just not cut out for dating someone like you."

"Someone like me? What does that mean?"

"You're the sun, Tanika. A bright, gorgeous star that pulls everyone into her orbit. Trust me, I understand Colin's attraction. You're surrounded by multimillion-dollar athletes all day long. You can have any man you want. I felt like I'd hit the jackpot. Somehow, you chose me. But I was kidding myself thinking I could date you like a normal guy. I don't fit in your world."

"A normal guy? My world? What are you talking about!" Tears flooded Tanika's eyes. "Gid, you dummy, you *are* my world. I love you."

"I love you too." Gideon met her gaze for a long moment. The tears in her eyes were unbearable, but he pressed on. She deserved to hear this from him, and to know he meant it. "I really do. But—"

"But what?"

Gideon lowered his eyes. "But I need a break from all of this."

"Does *all of this* include me?"

Gideon nodded. "Yes. I need a break from everything. From my life. Just for a while. I need to clear my head."

Tanika nodded to the pile of boxes. "So, is that what the boxes are for? You're moving? Closing the practice?"

Gideon ran a hand down his face, scratching his fuller, nearly snow-white beard. The stress of the past months had changed him, inside and out. "Yes and no. No, I'm not closing the practice. But yes—I'm leaving the country."

Tanika's eyes widened. "Leaving the country? I've ruined your life so badly that you need to go to another country?"

"Hold on. Don't give yourself that much credit." Gideon gave a wry smile at Tanika's attempt at a joke, though she wasn't entirely wrong. "I do want to get some perspective on what's happened between us. I think I just need a break for myself too. To do something that'll get my mind off things and be good for my soul. Something I've always promised Lauren I'd do. So, I'm heading to Belize to do Vision Without Borders to provide vision care across Central America."

Tanika nodded her head. "That's great. Truly. Glad you're knocking something off your bucket list. I'm happy for you."

Gideon moved closer to Tanika. "I have an optometry school friend who's going to handle things for the time I'm away, so I'm clearing some space in the office for him. And of course, Celeste will keep the ship running smoothly."

"How long will you be gone?" Tanika's voice sounded shaky and small. *She's scared*, Gideon realized. Hearing the fear in her voice shattered his resolve to give her as few details as possible. He didn't want her worrying about things that didn't involve her. That wasn't fair. They'd shared so much with each other over the past few months. There was no reason to be secretive now. Whether he liked it or not, Tanika was part of his world. She didn't deserve to be left in the dark.

He reached for her hand. "I'll be gone for six months."

"Six months? Seriously?" Her eyes filled with more tears.

"Yes. Six months. Then I'll be back, and—"

Tanika's head dropped and her shoulders shook as she cried into her hand. Gideon pulled a tissue from the box on his desk and went to wipe her tears. Tanika shook his hand away. "Don't."

"Tanika. . . ."

"I can't be away from you for six months. I won't!"

Gideon blew out a breath, rubbing his bald head. "I'm going. I'm sorry. It's already settled."

Tanika stood. "And you weren't going to tell me? So, what if I hadn't shown up this afternoon? Would you have just snuck out of the city like a thief in the night? Don't you think that's cowardly?"

Gideon felt his temple throb and his pulse quicken. "A coward? You have a lot of nerve calling me a coward, Tanika. Given recent circumstances, I think I've handled things with a lot of grace."

Tanika shook her head. "But now you're just running away! Running when things get hard."

"Tanika, you aren't listening. This isn't my life! Tabloids and jealousy and rumors. . . ."

"Well, what do you want your life to be? Crying over Lauren? Not living? Being miserable? Being alone?"

"Don't!" Gideon's words were a stern warning, which Tanika heeded. He stood to move around her, but she grabbed his arm. They stood staring at each other for what seemed like eons, until she moved closer. She pressed her forehead to his and breathed him in.

"Gideon, please. Don't go," she whispered softly.

Gideon swallowed, then licked his lips, trying to compose himself. "Baby, it's all settled."

"Don't," she whimpered as she pressed her lips against his, barely moving. She breathed warmly across Gideon's lips. "Don't make me miss you so much it hurts."

"Nik," Gideon breathed, his fingers finding the hem of her dress, already fisting it and moving it up her thighs. He was angry. He was hurting. Yet more than anything, he wanted this woman like a thirsty man wanted water. He wanted to feel her walls close in all around him, wanted her to suffocate him with her screams. Wanted to taste her moans and bottle them up for eternity.

They said nothing more, their breathing erratic and staccato as Gideon pushed Tanika's dress up around her waist. He pawed at the front of her panties, which were already soaked.

"You and this greedy, needy pussy," Gideon groaned as he hooked a finger between her panties and flesh, moving them to the side until he found her hot, slick, wet opening. "I missed her." He plunged in two fingers at once, not giving Tanika time to ease into it. She opened her stance wider for him, clearly welcoming the intrusion.

Gideon pumped inside of her, and she ground against his fingers, coating his hand with her juices until she moaned. He wouldn't give her the satisfaction of a quick orgasm. He needed her to feel him. To feel his pain, his hurt, his longing, his devotion, his turmoil.

He turned Tanika around to face his desk, pushing pens and papers out of the way, positioning her so that her back arched toward him and her breasts spilled out of the top of her dress and pressed onto the cold wood. Tanika, without a word, reached to pull down her panties, exposing her glistening pussy and plump, round ass. Gideon spit into his hand, mixing his wetness and hers, took out his dick from his sweatpants, and stroked until he was nice and hard. He eased into Tanika, then slammed his pelvis against her, over and over. The sound was so obscene, so unlike anything he'd experienced with her, that Gideon felt outside of his body. He didn't know who or where he was.

All he knew was that he wanted Tanika to feel him, to feel this fuck for as long as he was gone. He wanted to implant himself in her memories, just like she had done to him.

Tanika clawed at his desk, moaning, screaming words that were barely coherent. Gideon couldn't respond as he watched himself go in and out of her, her ass slapping against his pelvis and a string of wetness pooling onto the floor. He loved her—god, he loved her—but he hated everything about how she'd made him feel. Hurt. Angry.

Discarded. Vulnerable. Ridiculous. He pulled Tanika by the hair, his other hand on her throat, gently applying pressure.

"You're gonna miss this dick," he groaned. "Are you gonna miss it? Say it."

"No," Tanika panted, almost breathless. "I'll miss *you*." As she turned her head slightly to look at him, he could see tears beginning to stream down her face, a sign that she was on the precipice of an orgasm. "I love you."

"I love you too, princess," Gideon grunted, his lips curving into a smile against her neck. "Now come for me."

Tanika lifted a knee up onto the desk and Gideon angled his dick right into the spot where he knew she wanted him. She cried out, and he slapped her ass with his hand. "Take it," he commanded. She did, meeting him stroke for stroke until her body nearly collapsed. Once Gideon met his own threshold, he released his cum, hot and deep inside Tanika's pulsating pussy.

The two of them didn't move for a minute, wanting to savor the moment. Finally, Gideon's dick slipped out as it returned to its resting state. He tucked himself back into his sweatpants and Tanika pulled up her panties and pulled down her dress. Neither bothered to reach for a towel or tissue. Gideon wanted to keep a part of Tanika on his body for as long as he could. He wondered if she felt that way too.

Tanika turned toward Gideon. "When do you leave?"

"Next week. Thursday."

Tanika's lips trembled, but she took a deep breath, straightening her shoulders. "Okay. Maybe when you get back . . ." Her voice trailed off. Gideon was glad she hadn't finished the sentence.

"Maybe." Gideon's voice broke, fractured by a sense of impossibility. "We'll see."

Tanika kissed his cheek, her lips lingering there for longer than usual. "Safe travels," she said, holding tightly to the strap of her purse.

"Thanks."

Gideon watched Tanika turn the corner out of his office. The front door chimed like a death knell, signaling her departure.

CHAPTER 42

Tanika looked at her calendar. It was Tuesday. Thursday was looming, a shadow in the corner of every thought. Her mind played and replayed her last encounter with Gideon, making love to him in his office, saying goodbye. She couldn't stop trying to piece together where and how their brand-new relationship had collapsed. If she was being honest, there had been some cracks that she chose to ignore—things they had both needed to heal from to be the best versions of themselves for each other. *Maybe time apart will be good for us.* Tanika tried telling that to the ache in her chest, to the clenching muscles in her stomach every time she thought of Gideon. It was absolutely no use. She missed him. These past few months, he'd been a safe place to land. Now, he'd be gone. He wouldn't be a car ride or quick flight away. They'd be separated, many miles away—for a long, long time.

"Tanika," asked Mya. "You okay girl? Do you need a coffee? A shot? I know you're nervous about your meeting with the board."

Oh. The board meeting. Tanika had nearly forgotten. Tanner had requested her presence without saying much else, and she wasn't sure what to expect. She didn't know whether it was budget cuts or a program change or leadership coming down on her after the Colin fiasco. But it didn't seem like good news. She'd just added it to the massive jumble of nerves she was already dealing with. She took out a chewable antacid tablet, throwing it in her mouth. "I'm good. Let's just get this over with."

She put on her blazer, adjusting the collar, and eased her feet back into her pumps. Mya strode behind her, down the hallway and onto the elevator.

"Whatever this is," Mya said, her voice a little too calm, like she was trying to be cool for the both of them, "just know you're a damn good reporter. And any network would snatch you up."

"You're damn right I am," said Tanika with a nod.

"And you're a great friend and mentor. I've learned so much."

Tanika turned to Mya. "Mya, you are the little sister I wish I had. That is never going to change, no matter what happens. Okay?" She put an arm around her and squeezed.

Mya sniffed, wiping her nose on the sleeve of her cardigan. "I know. I just pray my next boss isn't an asshole."

"Oh, hold up, I'm not giving you up as an assistant. I'm taking you with me in the divorce, kid. Now, dry those crocodile tears messing up your Fenty foundation, and remember that I haven't been fired. Yet."

Mya and Tanika laughed until the elevator opened to the executive suites. They made their way to the board room with confident strides. Tanika held her head up high. If she was about to be sacked, she might as well take it like a boss.

In the boardroom, the full board was present, including Tanner Dobbs. Tanika took a seat at the table while Mya sat in the corner, trying to tame her nervousness by pretending to take notes on her tablet.

Tanner welcomed Tanika with a nod and a tight smile. "Tanika, so glad you could come. I know you're busy right now, with the football draft and combine coverage coming up soon. This shouldn't take long."

"Sure thing, Tanner." Tanika returned his smile, then shot a look at Mya, who was nervously scratching her neck. Tanika tried to silently signal to her to stop it before she scratched herself raw, but to no avail.

Nadia Greene, daughter of the founder of WWSN, cleared her throat from the opposite end of the long table. "Well," she began, "your interview series on Colin Bello, despite that madhouse of rumors started by that trash rag, is garnering major award buzz. A possible Emmy is what we're hearing."

"Seriously? Wow, that's amazing." Tanika's shoulders relaxed, and she glanced at Mya, who finally stopped scratching. Did they call her up here to congratulate her? That would be a first.

"It is," said Nadia. "We couldn't be happier. Which is why we have an offer for you."

Tanika leaned in, trying not to appear too eager. "Okay, I'm listening."

Nadia nodded toward Tanner, prompting him to jump in. "Well, I ran your name past the board regarding the VP of Programming position. Tanika, we are *all* enthusiastic about you taking the helm. Over the years, you've proven that you're more than capable. You've delivered original, thought-provoking pieces, and I know you'll bring that visionary flare to the wider range of sports here at WWSN. I know you'll take us to the next level. Congratulations, Tanika."

The board began to clap, and then one after another, they pushed back their chairs and stood. *A promotion and a standing ovation?* Tanika's heart was beating so fast, she had to take a few breaths to compose herself. "I'd be honored," she finally said. She paused, looking at the happy faces of the board. "But with a couple of conditions."

The board hummed with confusion, some members taking their seats, some still standing, one exec whispering loudly, "What did she say?"

"Go on," encouraged Nadia.

It was now or never. Tanika had their attention, and she wasn't going to squander it, even if it could cost her the job. "Well, with me moving to the VP position, my spots at *Thursday Night Football* and *Football Center* will open. I'd like you to rehire Sara Taylor."

A surprised murmur moved through the room.

"Tanika, she is suing us and Ross. This would be a PR nightmare. And a legal mess," said Donald Ellis, the network's head of legal.

"Or," Tanika countered, "a redemptive arc. People love an underdog. I think Sara, with the right mentorship, could be a great reporter. Ross manipulated her and then threw her out there to the wolves with absolutely no preparation. That's not her fault. I've been in touch with her, as a friend. And she's working on her craft. Taking it seriously. In terms of the lawsuit, my guess is that she'll accept an olive branch if you extend it. And when people, especially women, see that you stand with Sara, I can see that working to your advantage with the numbers. I'm willing to take her under my wing. As VP of Programming, I'll need to have input on hires and promotions, and I'd like that input to start here. Trust me, I think this will be great."

Board members whispered amongst themselves. For a moment, Tanika thought she'd made a mistake. But Nadia leaned forward, her head cocked to the side. "Interesting. Well, if she's willing to drop the lawsuit against us, we will consider rehiring Sara. Is there anything else?"

Tanika cleared her throat. "Yes. I want to add gymnastics coverage to our regular programming. Sara is perfect for that, and it's an untapped market that our competitors seem to be neglecting. It shouldn't just be relegated to Olympic coverage. I want room to be creative if I take this role. To think outside the box. For example, we are in a great position to introduce a reality TV show. We could center it around a sport that needs more exposure, like lacrosse, or even rodeo." Tanika didn't care for Ray-Lee McQueen, but she'd seen firsthand what the drama of rodeo could do for the network.

Tanner tapped a pencil against his chin. "You know, I ran similar suggestions by Ross in the past, and he'd shot them down. I say, why not? I'm the one making the decisions now. And with your leadership, this could work." He gave Tanika a slight smile. "I'm on board."

"Thank you," Tanika said with a genuine smile as she rose, extending her hand for various board members to shake. "I'll need my team to review the offer, of course. But I'm really looking forward to bringing original, thought-provoking programming to WWSN."

"We will be in touch with the details," said Tanner. "I can't wait to see what you do, Tanika."

Tanika nodded, hanging back as she watched Tanner and the rest of the board file out.

Mya stood in the doorway, waiting, then gave Tanika the sign that everyone was out of earshot. She pulled the heavy boardroom door closed and pushed the button to lower the blinds. Alone in the boardroom, they let out a collective squeal so shrill they could have cracked the glass.

"This is so damn dope! VP of Programming," said Mya. "I wonder if I'll get my own fancy office."

Tanika had so much energy built up inside her after that meeting, she was ready to blow. "I know! I've got to call Gi—" Tanika stopped herself before she could say his name. It was on the tip of her tongue, weighing heavily like a tongue depressor. "I mean, the girls. I've got to call Jackie and Bronwyn." She turned away to hide the embarrassment she felt for thinking of him at this moment when she should feel nothing but happy. But then, perhaps there was a reason Gideon was on her mind. For the past few months, he'd been part of some of the happiest, joyful moments of her life. He would have been excited for her. Why shouldn't she share her joy with him?

He's not thinking about me. He's thinking about . . .

"Actually, Mya, can you do me a favor? You think we can start a fundraiser? Post it on my social media and website?"

Mya looked up from her tablet. "Sure. For what?"

"For Vision Without Borders. I want to raise funds in honor of Lauren Miles."

"Lauren *who?*" Mya looked confused for a moment, but then it dawned on her. "Ooh. Doc's late wife. That is really sweet, Tanika. I'll set it up. No problem."

Tanika smiled. "Thanks. Maybe I can get the network behind it as well."

"You know Tanner would appreciate any good PR right now. I'll run it by him."

Tanika opened the boardroom door, her heart overwhelmed by all that had happened in the last hour—hell, in the last *year*. She needed to take a deep breath and regroup. "Come on, chick," she said to Mya. "Let's chill, get a coffee, and refocus. We have a lot of work to do."

CHAPTER 43

Celeste hovered anxiously as Gideon organized files in his office. "I should put you over my knee and spank you."

Gideon looked up from his bureau, giving Celeste a sly grin. "If you do, I may like it."

Celeste rolled her eyes. "That's not what I mean, and you know it."

"For the last time, I'm not calling it off, CeCe. I need to do this." Gideon put the files down on his desk, lifting his eyes to the worried face of his sister-in-law. "For Lauren."

"Using my dead sister as an excuse for running away from your problems is a sorry one. I admit I was a little upset with Tanika when you first got home from Vegas, but I believe her. I saw how she looked when she came in here last week. The girl was torn up about it, G."

Gideon leaned against the bureau and rubbed his beard. "It's not an excuse, and I'm not running away. I'm intentionally closing a chapter on my life with Lauren." He'd wrestled with the idea a lot lately. He wanted to make this trip meaningful, do all the things that he and Lauren had planned to do with the organization. He wanted to let Lauren go, like she herself—when she'd appeared in his dream—had asked him to. It would be his final act of service on her behalf. But what was next? He wasn't sure if that could be rekindling things with Tanika. Not so soon. He needed time. "Once things die down, maybe I'll consider dating again."

"Dating in general, or dating Tanika?"

Gideon shrugged. "Both. Maybe."

"Gid," sighed Celeste. "For the last time, why throw away a beautiful connection?"

Did I throw it away? Gideon swallowed, a poor attempt at stopping his chest from aching. "Maybe I'm just a fool."

Celeste walked over to Gideon, pulling him into a hug. "You're a fool in love. That's all." She pulled away from him, looking into his eyes. "If taking this trip is what you need, then so be it. Just know I'm here for you."

Gideon held Celeste tight. "CeCe, I don't deserve you."

Celeste laughed into his shoulder, then pushed him away. "Oh, I know it. But who else is going to keep it real with you at times like this? Besides, I made a promise to my sister to look after you, and I'm keeping it. I'm going to keep this place running just like Lauren would while you're gone."

"Thanks, sis. Just don't give my boy Jeremy a hard time. He's doing me a solid looking after my patients while I'm gone. I'm trying to convince him to be a partner in the practice."

Celeste folded her arms across her broad chest. "Of course I'll be giving him a hard time. I wouldn't be me if I didn't."

"Of course not. Just don't run him away."

"Well, before *you* run away, I thought I'd let you know I had Tony fix Tanika's glasses. The man works wonders. They are as good as new."

Gideon frowned. "I thought you said they couldn't be fixed."

"I said Tony wasn't *certain* they could be fixed. I didn't say it was impossible. The man is a miracle worker. Gid, I'm giving you an excuse to go see this woman before you leave for Brazil tomorrow."

"Belize, Cee. I'm going to Belize," Gideon laughed.

"Belize. Brazil. All I know is that it ain't close, and you have to get on a plane, and then another plane. And . . ." Celeste paused, tears welling up in her eyes. Gideon was taken aback. The last time he'd seen Celeste cry was at Lauren's funeral. She blinked rapidly. "I'm going to miss my brother so much."

Gideon pulled Celeste in for another hug, this time allowing his own tears to fall as well. "I'll miss you too, sis."

"Don't be a fool," Celeste whispered, her voice hoarse. "Don't wait until it's too late to be happy." She pulled back. "If you change your mind, the glasses are in the top drawer of my desk."

Celeste quickly wiped her tears, then hurried back to the front desk.

Gideon wiped his own tears and finished readying the office for Jeremy, emptying his desk completely. He paused when he came across Lauren's photo again, the one from their last vacation in Saint Lucia, with the conch shell to her ear. He stared at it more closely and couldn't believe what he saw. Something he hadn't noticed in all those years. In her hair was an artificial band of flowers—including several large white magnolias.

Well, I'll be damned.

Gideon felt his cell phone buzz in his pocket, indicating that he had a voice message. *Odd. I hadn't heard the phone ringing.* When he looked at the missed call log, only one number appeared: Tanika's. Cradling Lauren's photo under his arm, he pressed the voicemail and listened.

Hi. I'm glad I got the voicemail, because if you answered, I'd probably chicken out and hang up. Anyway, I just wanted to say this before you're miles away. You're going to think this is wild, but since we've been together, I've experienced some interesting things. Let's just say, new glasses didn't just give me sight, they made life a lot clearer for me. I'd lost sight of what was important to me. One of those things was love. I was afraid to love you because of my own issues and yours, but I realize maybe that was for nothing. Somehow, I think you know what I'm talking about. Maybe you've felt like something, or someone, was pushing us together. Literally, every single sign was telling me yes. Yes to you. Yes to us. We're meant to be. Like, predestination. Damn, here I go sounding like Bronwyn. Again, it sounds wild, but one day I'll have the words to explain it all. Look at me, the former reporter lost for words. Oh yeah, and I got the VP job so . . . yay me! Anyway, be safe. I hope . . . never mind. This is getting too long. Shit. Bye.

Gideon slipped his phone back into his pocket, trying to process the message. He looked at the photo of Lauren again and thought about all the strange coincidences and seemingly otherworldly things that had happened since meeting Tanika. *Was this predestined?* Maybe she was right. Perhaps *someone* was pushing them together. Helping them to write a new chapter in their lives. Maybe she still was. . . .

He took some bubble wrap, wrapping the photo of Lauren carefully and placing it in the box he'd marked "Memories." Everything in the box, he realized now, had to do with Lauren. Just like his house, his office had become a mini shrine to their life together, the practice they'd started, and the love they'd shared. He was ready to leave the pieces of broken promises and dead-end possibilities behind—to start a new adventure. This trip was for Gideon. Some memories may have been tucked away in a box, but they would always be in his heart.

We are doing this thing, babe. Gideon kissed the top of the memory box before taping it up and tucking it under his arm, carrying it to his car along with the rest of his things.

CHAPTER 44

T anika had been vomiting all morning. Mya was worried. She'd bought every antacid and anti-nausea medication that she could at the drug store.

"You sure you're okay? Should I have bought a pregnancy test too?"

Mya laughed, but Tanika cut a sharp look in her direction as she hovered over the wastebasket. "I'm not pregnant. Just sick to my stomach."

The reason she was sick was because it was Thursday. Soon, Gideon would be gone—two thousand miles away, to another country. The probability of seeing him again was slim. He'd made it perfectly clear there wouldn't be any reconciliation—when it came to Gid, *maybe* and *we'll see* often meant *no way*. Tanika was doing what she could to manage the breakup rationally. She'd already had Mya find her a new optometrist. And Tanika was already getting her excuses ready, reasons to miss Jackie's cookouts and parties once Gideon was back in town. As much as she loved Jackie's parties, her heart wouldn't be able to take seeing him again.

What Tanika didn't tell Mya was that she'd already taken a pregnancy test that morning. It was negative. When she woke up sick, her mind had flashed to the last time she'd had sex with Gideon.

They'd been completely reckless and carnal, but she wasn't sorry. It was what they'd both needed in the moment. It had been a goodbye.

If she was honest with herself, she was a little disappointed she wasn't pregnant. Having Gideon's baby would have been a beautiful surprise. A bittersweet parting gift. Tanika shook her head, swiftly popping the bubble of that idea. She was VP of Programming. With a new job came new responsibilities, and she wasn't sure where a baby would fit in that plan.

Mya rubbed Tanika's back. "Well, are you at least able to stand up straight to head down to the studio? We are doing a little test run with Key-Juan, Jacob, and Sara for the revamped *Football Center*. You have about twenty minutes to pull it together."

Tanika stood, grabbing a napkin and dabbing her sweating brow. "Yeah. I'm good. Maybe it's just nerves. Let me get some Listerine, and I'll be okay."

Mya nodded, leaving the office in search of Listerine and gum. Tanika sat back down and took some deep breaths, looking around her new office. She smiled. All her hard work had paid off. The plaque on her door read *Tanika Ryan, Vice President of Programming*. Her full name, her full title. Ross had been fired from WWSN, terminated without a payout. Sara had dropped her suit against the network and had accepted the offer to return to WWSN. Tanika's new paycheck was larger than she'd ever dreamed, and she felt ready to step away from the cameras and into leadership. As the highest-paid Black woman in sports broadcasting, she was in an excellent position to open doors for other women and people of color in her field. On a personal level, she was finally at peace with her aging body, thankful for her health and strength. She fully embraced her graying hair, wrinkles, and glasses. She'd also made peace with her father, realizing that their relationship would never be that of a typical father and daughter. She was okay with that.

So why was she still unhappy?

She looked at her phone, full of group chat messages.

JACKIE: Good luck today, boss chick! You're going to be amazing.

BRONWYN: 👍 You've got this, bestie!

JACKIE: Focus on today. Nothing else!

BRONWYN: If he comes back to you, he's meant for you. Let the gods do their job.

JACKIE: Didn't we agree not to talk about Gid? You just had to bring him up.

BRONWYN: I guarantee Tanika is already thinking about him. I'm just saying.

Tanika smiled. Her friends knew her too well. Bronwyn was right; she was already thinking about Gideon, even though she shouldn't have been. Today was a big day for her. Every bit of her focus should have been on working her magic.

JACKIE: 😑 Anyway, good luck! Drinks at 5Church on me after work.

BRONWYN: I'm on a juice cleanse, Jack.

JACKIE: Then order gin and juice. Duh!

Tanika scrolled from the group chat to her last message from Gideon. He hadn't responded to the rambling voicemail she'd left. She hadn't expected him to. She wanted to text him, to see if he'd made it safely to Belize. She wanted to tell him that today was her first day as VP and she was nervous. More than anything, she wanted to tell him that she loved and missed him. None of that mattered, however, because he didn't want to hear from her. She'd made his life miserable, which she regretted most of all. He was right; he hadn't asked to be thrown into the limelight. She certainly hadn't asked for that paparazzi madness either. They both deserved better. Once she'd found out Fred Livingston and his PR team at Lou Reddy Racing were behind the rumors, Tanika had had Jackie call and threaten to sue. They'd issued a weak public apology, stating that *someone* in their camp had leaked false information and would be terminated. For now, that was good enough. But the damage to her relationship was done.

After freshening up, Tanika made it down to the studio floor to see the new setup with Key-Juan, Jacob, and Sara. Sara was relaxed and prepared, getting along well with the guys. Tanika gave Sara a thumbs-up, and Sara gave her a genuine, warm grin.

"Looking good," said Tanner, joining Tanika on the floor. "I didn't quite believe you when you said you could convince Sara to work with us, but you did."

Tanika nodded. "She's doing great. I'm glad I could pass the torch to someone so eager to learn. We had a mini football camp last weekend to get her up to speed." Passing two decades of knowledge to Sara had been a lot of work, but it was worth it.

"And the pilot episode of her web series on the US gymnastics team is playing well with our focus groups. We're projecting viral numbers when this thing launches. You were right. She knows her stuff. Good eye, Tanika. Can't wait to see what programming you have for us next." Tanner gave Tanika a quick pat on the shoulder before turning to address the production team.

Tanika pressed a button on her headset, turning on her mic so she could be heard in the production control booth. "Hey Danny, can you make sure they adjust the lights on Sara before we go live? She looks washed out."

"Got you, boss," said Danny. "Or should I call you *jefa*?"

Tanika snorted. "Please don't call me either, dude. Tanika is fine."
Danny laughed. "Copy that."

Mya rushed in, a little winded. "Sorry," she said, sidling up to
Tanika with her iPad in hand. "Anything I miss?"

Tanika couldn't hide her annoyance. "You rushed me down here,
and when I turn around, you are nowhere to be seen. What was so
pressing that it cut into my time?"

"I was just . . ." Mya swallowed nervously. "I was making sure
your notes about postproduction meetings were relayed to the crew.
That's all."

Tanika looked at Mya, confused. The girl was totally frazzled.
Postproduction notes weren't that deep. She put a reassuring hand
on Mya's shoulder. "Chill. We will get the hang of things. Okay?"

"Yeah. You're right. I'm just nervous. I probably should have had
some of your antacids." Mya put a hand on her belly.

Tanika pulled out a roll of chewable antacid tabs from her suit
jacket pocket. "Pop two in your mouth. You'll feel better."

Mya chewed, looking at her watch. "Thanks. Did you want to
do a run-through again? I think we have an update regarding the
possible trade with New England."

Looking over her notes, Tanika agreed, "Yeah, let's run it again. I
know Chris is handling the day-to-day as EP, but I want us to get it
right. Make sure everyone has their notes." She pressed the earpiece in
her ear. "Danny, can you pull up that piece on New England again?"

Tanika waited a few seconds and heard nothing from the production booth. "Danny?"

Instead of Danny's reply, she heard music. *What is happening?*
She recognized the opening chords to *Maggie May* by Rod Stewart.
And the song wasn't in her earpiece, it was playing throughout the
entire studio. Tanika froze.

"Magpie," said a voice in her ear. "You there?"

Tanika's pulse raced. Her heart thumped against her chest. She
held the microphone so close to her mouth she thought that she was
going to swallow it. "Gideon?"

"Come to the booth, princess."

Tanika looked at Mya, who had a sly smile on her face. "Did you set this up?"

Mya lifted Tanika's headset off her head—careful not to snag it on her curls—and took the notebook out of her hand. She nodded toward the production booth. "Better get up there . . . *princess.*"

Tanika nearly ran up the steps to the production booth. She was grateful today was the day she'd decided to wear her VaporMax instead of heels that might have slowed her down. Inside, she found Danny at the control board and Gideon standing nearby, a bouquet of assorted roses resting in his arms.

"What . . . what are you doing here? I thought you were on a plane." Tanika moved toward Gideon, suddenly shy. He met her halfway, pressing a kiss to her cheek.

"Well, I couldn't leave without wishing you good luck on your first day as VP."

Tanika smelled the roses, setting them on the table. Her hands were shaking entirely too much to hold them. Sensing her nervousness, Danny chimed in. "I'll go give these to Mya to put in water and let you two have some privacy." Danny grabbed the flowers and left Tanika and Gideon alone.

"I thought you didn't want to see me again," Tanika said, her voice hoarse with emotion.

"I got your voicemail." Gideon moved closer, taking Tanika's hands. He rubbed his thumb across Tanika's knuckles, lifting her hand to his lips. "I lied when I said I didn't want to see you, and I'm so sorry. That was ego talking. I was hurt and trying to save face. I love you, Tanika Magnolia Ryan."

Tanika's chest rose, her breathing attempting to keep pace with her racing heart. "I love you too. But I—"

"No," Gideon interrupted. "Let me talk. I was scared to move on, to close that last chapter in my life. I thought the entire Colin thing—and my bugged-out reaction—was evidence that I wasn't ready or that we weren't right together. But that wasn't true. You're right. Something or someone has been pushing us together. As much as we try to fight it, we can't ignore . . . what did you call it? Predestination. This is meant to be. I know I messed up, but I want to fix this."

"I messed up too. That whole fight about the guest room, the bed, that was my fault, my insecurity," Tanika began. Gideon waved a hand.

"Not entirely. You were right; I was keeping you close but not letting you in. I was holding on to memories so tightly, I was not allowing myself to make new ones. Mother Mary's psychic reading was right too. I've been in mourning too long. It's time to live. And part of living is loving again. Fully. And I do love you."

Tanika attempted to smile, as Gideon wiped tears from her cheeks. "So, are you not going to Belize?"

"I booked a later flight. I'm going. I gave them my word. But I want you to understand what this means to me. It's about finding closure and starting fresh."

"Six months seems like forever." Tanika wondered what had happened to her old self, the one that would never have been this vulnerable with a man. She'd said goodbye to that woman the moment she knew she was in love. And she wasn't ready to be without Gideon for that long.

"I'll have cell service. You can WhatsApp me. I'll have internet. We'll talk every day, I promise. If you want, you can fly down. I'd love that. All I ask is that when I get back, you give me another chance. I want us to be together."

Tanika nibbled at her bottom lip. "Are you sure?"

Gideon pressed his thumb against Tanika's lip, freeing it from her teeth's clasp. "As sure as the air I breathe, I know I need you. I'm going to come home to you. Please give me—give us—another chance."

Tanika pressed her forehead against Gideon's, inhaling his familiar cinnamony, woodsy smell. *He smells like the perfect autumn day.* She tried to think clearly. "But what about my new job? What if I get busy and can't get the time off to visit—"

Gideon pressed his lips against Tanika's, quieting her. "We'll figure it out. Right now, I need to kiss my woman goodbye. Just until the next time I see her."

"I guess we better make it damn good."

Gideon hoisted Tanika up and propped her against the audio mixing console, pressing his hands against her thighs. "Of all the days you wanna wear pants," growled Gideon in Tanika's ear. "I'm trying to see that tattoo, Magpie."

"I'm sorry I'm impeding your easy access." Tanika groaned as Gideon's lips hit the sensitive spot on her neck.

Gideon nibbled her ear, kissing her temple, then her forehead. "That's okay. But you'll have to send nudes while I'm away. Just you and your glasses. Speaking of which." Gideon reached into his pocket and pulled out a glasses case. "These are for you."

Confused, Tanika took the case and opened it. She would have recognized those frames anywhere. "I thought Celeste said my glasses couldn't be fixed?"

"Nah. She was pissed at you, but Tony worked some magic. May I?" Gideon slipped off Tanika's glasses, replacing them with her fixed pair. He stared at her for a few seconds. "Beautiful."

His warm green aura was bright as ever. Tanika had missed it, welcoming it back like an old friend.

She felt a blush warm her face. "Thank you."

Gideon pulled her chin upward, looking intensely into her eyes. "Nik, I see you. Every beautifully flawed, imperfect perfection about you takes up space in my heart. I see all of you."

"Is that another optometrist pun?"

"Not this time." Gideon pulled Tanika to him, kissing her deeply. When she moaned, he gripped her ass, tracing his tongue inside her mouth, sucking her bottom lip as if it was his last taste of home. "I love you."

"I love you too," Tanika said, kissing Gideon back with everything she had.

They heard a commotion down on the studio floor and looked down, seeing the entire floor cheering and whistling. Key-Juan, Jacob, and Sara were exchanging high fives. Danny was whistling. Mya, Tanner, the interns, the crew, and the rest of the production staff were clapping.

Tanika looked down at the flashing light on the console. "Oh shit, I've been sitting on the intercom. Think they heard everything?"

When Mya yelled, "YES!" she got her answer.

"I'll be back down in five," Tanika said into the intercom before she turned it off. "How embarrassing."

"Could be worse," Gideon shrugged. "Like caught-in-a-robe-with-a-drunk-hotshot-level embarrassing."

Tanika shot him a look. "Too soon."

Gideon rubbed his bald head. "My bad. Seriously though, I'm glad I didn't try anything else with you while the whole crew was listening." Tanika pouted, sticking her lips out like a disappointed child, and Gideon laughed as he lifted her off the console. "Trust me, I wanted to. I'm very backed up after all these weeks."

He pulled her by the waist, pressing his hard, muscular chest into hers. "I've got to go, or I'll miss my flight."

Tanika nodded, close to tears again. When had she turned into such a sappy person? "Okay."

Gideon kissed her, and then, again, his hand gently tugging at her curls with every kiss. "Six months will fly by before you know it."

Tanika smiled against his lips. "I hope so, Dr. Miles."

"Trust me," Gideon pressed his lips against Tanika's, then kissed her nose, fogging her glasses just slightly. "I know so, princess. Predestination, remember?"

EPILOGUE

"**W**ho the hell fed PeeWee a hot dog? PeeWee is on a strict pescatarian diet!" Jackie yelled over the music, hoisting her beloved furry baby in her arms. "I'm going to kill you all!"

Because the summer heat wave had been brutal, Jackie's end-of-summer cookout was now a beginning-of-fall cookout. Nevertheless, her place was packed. The crowd included athletes she represented, their entourages, Jackie's family, and most of all, her friends. Tanika and Bronwyn were trying to learn the latest line dance craze from Mya and were all but ready to give up when Sara came over with a bottle of champagne in one hand and several flutes in the other.

"I think we need to be drunk to learn this dance," Sara said, distributing the glasses.

"Thanks, Sara." Tanika smiled. "Because surely someone had to be drunk to come up with these steps. What happened to the regular ol' electric slide?"

"Ugh, that's so boring!" Mya said. "Y'all old people get on my nerves."

"Who's old?" Bronwyn and Tanika demanded, nearly in unison.

Sara put her hands on her narrow hips for greater emphasis. "I am actually Gen Z, for your information. I will let it be known that, just a few minutes ago, some young rookie MLB player was trying to get my number."

"Actually, that's a good look," Mya said approvingly. "MLB money lasts way longer than any other sport."

"That is true," said Jackie, setting PeeWee down to let him go to his air-conditioned doghouse. "But please don't date my clients, Sara. I'm starting to like you, and I'd hate to have to make you sign an ironclad NDA."

Sara threw up her hands. "I don't want a man. Just a booty call."

"Speaking of booty and boos," said Bronwyn, trying and failing at a smooth transition to a new topic, "Tanika, how is Gideon? He should be home soon, right?"

Tanika felt herself light up at the thought. "Two more days. I'm so excited. I really missed him."

Jackie rolled her eyes. "Bitch, please. You've been flying down to Belize every chance you could get."

Tanika felt a flush move up her neck, all the way to the top of her box braids. "True. But I still miss him. Those trips were really about volunteering, not being all sexy. I mean, we got it in when we could. . . ."

"Ugh! Still don't wanna hear about y'all boning." Jackie reached for a rum punch, downing it in record time. Bronwyn elbowed her gently in the side, then gestured for Tanika to continue.

"Anyway," laughed Tanika. "With the money we raised with our WWSN fundraiser in Lauren's honor, Vision Without Borders was able to do a lot in Central America. It was so cool seeing Gid give back. He made kids and elderly people so happy, giving them glasses and medication for their eyes. It was beautiful. He was in his element. We are going to try and get back there at least once a year."

Sara grabbed a slider from a passing tray. "I can't imagine you getting down and dirty. Your manicure is too pristine for that, girl."

"No way. Um, if anyone is prissy here, it's you, Sara," Tanika teased.

"Speaking of down and dirty, I think I see Tommy Lawrence. He was dodging my questions about his offseason negotiations. I'm going to hit him up. Excuse me." Sara finished her last bite of slider, wiped her hands, stole a look in her compact, and went to hunt down a story. Tanika smiled. Watching Sara made her extremely proud. Sara had come a long way as a reporter in the last six months, listening to her intuition and taking the initiative to get the job done. The board had been impressed by Tanika's programming, and her decision to fight for her former rival had paid off. Ratings were through the roof in all areas, including Sara's gymnastics coverage.

Tanika turned her attention back to her girls. "So, what's good? Can we get the DJ to play some hits from our era so we can dance? Stuff I can understand the lyrics to?"

"I'm on it," said Jackie, who paused and then frowned, looking past Bronwyn and Tanika. "On second thought, get Mya to do it. I see a snake whose head I need to cut off."

Tanika, Mya, and Bronwyn followed Jackie's gaze, turning their attention to a very tall, fine piece of almond-colored mancandy. It was Antonio Steele, Jackie's rival sports agent. They watched as barely 5'2 Jackie marched across the lawn and laid into the guy, pointing her freshly manicured finger into his linen-clad chest, about to tear him a new asshole. He must have been a sadist because he was just standing there, smiling and taking the abuse.

Mya quirked a brow. "You know, from here it looks like they are about to have really hot hate sex."

Bronwyn laughed. "No way. Not after that guy tried to steal her client, PJ Dawson, last year. She hates Antonio Steele."

Tanika's eyes nearly popped out of her head. "Is that what happened between them? Jackie has been mum about it."

Bronwyn lowered her voice. "She didn't want to tell you, given your whole VP of the network thing. You could have run with it."

"I'm really offended by that," said Tanika in faux shock. "But she's not lying, I would have scooped that story. Enough about that; c'mon, y'all. Let's dance."

Mya moved toward the DJ booth, calling over her shoulder. "I'm going to tell the DJ to play some music you all can throw a hip joint out on."

Tanika scowled. "I'm not that damn old!" The truth was, her knees *had* been aching lately, but Mya didn't need to know that. She could still drop down and get her eagle on. She just might need help getting back up.

Bronwyn picked up an attention-starved PeeWee, who was circling her ankles. "Count me out. I'm going to look for some healthy food for him. These people are giving this baby animal products. A damn shame. Let me find Kenny." She nuzzled PeeWee against her chest, tucking him underneath her long locs as she hurried away.

What the heck had gotten into everyone? "Fine! I'll dance alone," Tanika called out to no one, as she bobbed her head to the tunes. She closed her eyes, letting the late autumn sun warm her face as she twirled in her yellow sundress and Gucci sneakers. As the DJ began to spin a remixed house version of "Baby I'm Scared of You" by Womack & Womack, Tanika felt someone move way too close to her, uninvited breath warming her ear. She froze, prepared to knee this creep in the groin. But then she heard a familiar voice.

"You look too damn good to be dancing all alone, princess."

Tanika turned, throwing her arms around Gideon, squeezing him so tight for so long, she was probably cutting off his air supply. "Gideon! What are you doing here? I thought I was meeting you at the airport two days from now?"

"I caught an earlier flight." Gideon kissed Tanika's lips and smiled. "Just got in. I swung by the house, dropped off my suitcase, and freshened up. And now I'm here. I wanted to surprise you, baby."

"Aww." Tanika put her arms around Gideon, pulling him into her gentle sway. "That's sweet. But I know the real reason you're here is for Jackie's baked beans."

Gideon threw his head back in laughter. "Damn, you know me too well. That's true. The beans are banging."

"No, Mya told me no one says *banging* anymore. They say *bussin'*."

"Well, the beans are bussin'." Gideon pushed up his glasses on his nose. "Nah, that didn't sound right coming from me."

Jackie ran up to Tanika and Gideon, throwing her arms around their conjoined waists. "Gid! You're here! I thought you'd be here closer to the end. Let me guess, my world-famous beans got you here early."

"Exactly." Tanika chuckled. She looked at Gideon and Jackie, who were giving each other weird looks. "Wait a minute. You knew he'd be here? What's going on? Is there something else on the menu I didn't know about?"

Jackie was still looking at Gideon as she answered. "Actually, there is. Hold on a second."

Tanika watched as Jackie made her way to the DJ booth on stage, asking him to turn down the music and give her the microphone.

Jackie smoothed her denim jumpsuit, tapping the mic a few times to get everyone's attention before speaking. "Hey y'all! Thanks for coming to my annual backyard jam. I appreciate all my clients, family, and friends who made it out. Including Uncle Roydell who is trying to hoard all the Hennessy White. I see you, Unk! You ain't slick."

Everyone broke out into laughter. Tanika felt Gideon's palm getting sweaty in hers. "Are you alright? I know it's a big change in temperature from Belize."

He gave Tanika a weak smile, then a wink. "I'm good, princess. Trust me."

Jackie continued. "Anyway, I hope you all have a drink in your hand because I want to give a toast. I don't normally do this, but I feel like it's only right. I want to toast my cousin, Dr. Gideon Miles, who just returned home from six months in Central America with Vision Without Borders, which was able to provide vision care to thousands of people who otherwise would be without. I'd also like to toast my best friend and his girl, Tanika Ryan, who, along with the efforts of WWSN, raised over a million dollars for the cause—in a campaign that honored the late Lauren Miles. So, I want to raise a glass on behalf of my cousin and my bestie, and to the memory of Lauren Miles!"

Glasses clanked all around them. Gideon raised Tanika's hand to his lips and pressed a kiss to it. He mouthed a *thank-you* to Jackie, and she simply nodded. Tanika thought the music would come back on, but Jackie pointed the mic in Gideon's direction. "I'm turning it over to my cousin now. He has some words he wants to say."

Gideon walked up to the stage, taking the mic from Jackie and giving her a hug. A little grayer and tanner than six months ago, Gideon looked mouth-watering on stage in his olive green shirt, khaki slacks, and classic court sneakers. He cleared his throat and took a deep breath. "I want to thank my cousin Jack for all the kind words. Giving to others and being of service was my late wife's love language. Working with Vision Without Borders these past months was the ultimate way to honor the memory of Lauren and begin a new chapter in my life."

Tanika watched, eyes wide, as Gideon walked off stage and stood in front of her. He took her hand and looked into her eyes, still speaking into the mic. "When I first saw you, two years ago, right here in Jackie's backyard, I knew I wanted to get to know you. But as you know, I wasn't ready. This past year has been a whirlwind, some moments wilder than others. I know now that I'm ready for the woman you are—feisty, funny, driven, fine as hell, with a dope sneaker game, but also kind, caring, and selfless. I am more than ready to spend the rest of my life with you."

At that moment, Mya ran over with a large rectangular box and handed it to Gideon as he handed her the mic. The box was covered in fancy metallic paper, the lid wrapped in gold, and the bottom wrapped in silver. Tanika looked around, and everyone had their phones out. She felt sweat beading on her forehead as she watched Gideon drop to one knee.

"Tanika Magnolia Ryan. My Magpie. Princess, will you marry me?" Gideon opened the box. There was no ring inside, but Tanika screamed in delight.

"Oh my god! Are those the Travis Scott Jordan 1s?" Tanika was jumping up and down, beyond giddy, forgetting the crowd. "How the hell did you get them?"

"Our boy got them for me." Gideon nodded over toward Eric, who was in the crowd with Keke, all smiles. "But before you get too excited about the shoes, I need an answer, babe."

Tanika wiped the tears from her eyes, careful not to knock her glasses from her face. She needed to see this moment clearly.

"Yes, Gideon! Oh my god! Now please, get up," she laughed, pulling Gideon up by the hand and kissing him. Everyone was snapping photos and cheering. Her girls were close by, squealing their heads off.

Jackie was crying, squeezing PeeWee nearly to death. "Oh my god. Keeping this secret this long was killing me."

Bronwyn, one hand affectionately on Kenny's (*thankfully*) clothed behind, nodded. "It sure was. I had to make an excuse to walk away from you, Nik, so I didn't give anything away. I just love an unconventional proposal."

Celeste pushed her way through the crowd, giving Tanika the biggest of hugs. "I am so happy for the both of you. Thank you for making my brother so happy."

Tanika looked between all the women in her Boss Chick Village, which now included Celeste and Sara. Each one of them was wiping away their own tears. "I cannot believe you all knew about this. I love you ladies so much."

"Yeah, for months, girl." Mya laughed. "I had to go pick up the shoes for Gideon because he was still in Belize."

"And I hope you can forgive me—I broke into your office and stole that ring you've been looking for—the cheap CZ one you sometimes wear on your left hand to fend off the men at happy hour. Had to get your ring size," said Sara, coming up to hug her.

Tanika looked at Gideon, confused. "Ring size?"

"Look inside the right shoe," he whispered.

Tanika opened the box and slipped her hand inside the right sneaker. She felt something at the toe and pulled out a light green Van Cleef & Arpels ring box. She opened it and gasped.

"Oh girl, he got money," Sara said under her breath, earning a swift elbow in the ribs from Mya.

Gideon took the classic solitaire ring from Tanika and slid it onto her left hand. "Listen, I know jewelry isn't your thing, but I wouldn't feel right not getting my fiancée an engagement ring."

Tanika laughed, tears spilling from her eyes. "Trust me, the Travis Scotts were enough."

"Baby, it's never enough when it comes to you," said Gideon, pulling Tanika into a long kiss. Once they let go of each other, Gideon gave her a serious look. "Also, don't get mad at me, but I called your father."

Tanika was genuinely shocked. "You did? Why?" Apart from a few check-ins about his health, she hadn't spoken with Walt in months. It was better for her peace of mind. Her therapist called it setting boundaries. Tanika called it self-care.

Gideon sighed. "I wouldn't have felt right with him finding out in the media that his daughter was getting married. I called to introduce myself. I didn't ask for it, but he gave his blessing anyway. He told me to tell you he's proud of you." Gideon lowered his voice so that only Tanika could hear him. "He should have told you that a long, long time ago."

"I'm not mad, but you didn't have to do that. I know he's not an easy man to talk to."

"I guess I'm still a touch old-fashioned. And I thought he should hear how much I love his daughter."

Tanika put her hands up to his beard, her fingers running through his silver strands. "Want to get out of here? I made sure Jackie put some beans away for you before the crowd smashed them."

"Yeah, that's cool. Besides, we still have some shopping that we need to do."

Tanika wasn't sure she could handle any more surprises. "Shopping for what? Babe, I think a gorgeous ring and these priceless sneakers are enough."

"A new life with my new fiancée wouldn't be complete without a new bed for our bedroom." Gideon smiled, kissing Tanika on the cheek. "What do you think, baby?"

As she looked from her handsome fiancé to the happy crowd of partygoers, Tanika swore she saw the profile of the woman who looked just like Lauren, the one who had helped her pick out glasses all those months ago. But before Tanika could find the words to tell Gideon what she saw—*the woman in white, who is maybe, probably, the ghost of your first wife, the same ghost who's been orchestrating our relationship*—the woman was gone. Tanika blinked, focusing her eyes back on Gideon, who was all smiles underneath a forest green glow. This time, the glow was provided by a party light hovering above his head, just as the sun was setting.

Tanika squeezed Gideon's hand as the DJ played the opening chords of "Before I Let Go" by Maze featuring Frankie Beverly. Immediately, her friends were running to the dance floor to hit the electric slide. She watched for a few minutes, taking in the joy on their faces and the laughter in the air. Finally, Tanika turned to Gideon.

"I'd like that."

ACKNOWLEDGMENTS

None of this would be possible without God, from which all blessings and creativity flow. To God be the Glory.

To Elaina Ellis and Amber Flame at Generous Press. Thank you for taking a chance on me and pouring love and care into this novel. As editors, you respected my voice, humor, and point of view. I appreciate everything and am excited to find a home for my brand of romance.

To my agent, Keisha Mennefee. Thank you for being in my corner and pushing me to try something new. You are one of my biggest cheerleaders. Thank you for thinking this "book about glasses" wasn't so far-fetched after all.

To the readers, especially Black women. You keep me going and inspired. I hope that everything I write allows you to see yourselves. These are your love stories. I celebrate you. I am so thankful for spaces such as TikTok, Instagram, and Twitter for bringing you to me. Thank you to all the book clubs and bookish spaces that have embraced me and my writing. You bring me joy.

To my writing communities, Inclusive Romance Project and Wordmakers. You are a fabulous and talented group of writers who have always had my back. No idea is too wild or ridiculous. Thank you for supporting me and inspiring me to soar higher and dream bigger.

To the independent bookstores, especially Black-owned stores. Thank you for supporting me and carrying my books, exposing my work and voice to a vast number of new readers. For that, I am forever grateful.

To my writer besties, Lily Flowers, Miss J, M. L. Eaden, and Terri Ley. Thank you for always being a chat or text away and saving me from myself. You keep me sane. You are the best beta readers that I could ever ask for.

To my podcast partner, Yakini. We've been rocking for over twenty years. Thank you for being along for the ride that has been this writing thing.

To my bestie, Candace. I love you more than words can say. Thank you for always talking me off the ledge.

To my vast network of extended family and friends. Cousins and sorority sisters. Aunts and Uncles. In-laws and Outlaws (lol). Coworkers and college buddies. Thank you for your support. Always. Special love to my cousins Derrick and Keosha, owners of Wildlyfe clothing brand for helping me with the sneaker stuff. I still am quite clueless when it comes to the sneaker game, but you all got me together.

To my Daddy, Ronald. Thank you for answering all my stock car questions. If you hadn't dragged me to races as a kid, part of this book wouldn't have come to be. I love you.

To my daughter, Teagan. You still aren't old enough to read Mommy's books, but when you are old enough to read them, I hope that you'll be proud of me.

Finally, to my husband, Jay. I could write a million book boyfriends, but none would compare to you. You are my rock, my love. Thank you for your love, support, endless cups of coffee, snacks, superior hugs, and forehead kisses. I couldn't ask for a better person to call my own. Just like I said in our vows, you're the best character in the novel of my life.

ABOUT THE AUTHOR

Tati Richardson is cofounder of the *Romance in Colour* podcast. Her debut novel, *The Build Up,* was picked as an Amazon Editors' Best Book of 2023 and a Booklist Top Romance of 2023. An Apple Books Writer to Watch, Tati lives in the Atlanta suburbs with her husband and daughter. She collects red lipstick, Wonder Woman memorabilia, and unique eyewear.

Tati is represented by Keisha Mennefee at Honey Magnolia Media. Learn more at www.tatiannarichardson.com.

COMING SOON FROM
TATI RICHARDSON

Jacqueline "Jackie" Miles, a no-nonsense sports agent, is shaken when a secret from her past threatens to disrupt her carefully curated existence. Antonio Steele, her rival and former lover, re-enters her life under unexpected circumstances, igniting old passions and new conflicts. When Jackie mysteriously loses her voice, she must learn to communicate in new ways. Can she maintain her professional edge and reconcile her feelings for Antonio, despite being struck speechless?

Find out in Jackie and Antonio's story, Book Two in the Boss Chick Village series. Follow Generous Press for a title reveal and more details.

ABOUT
Generous Press

Generous Press publishes lush, high-caliber romance fiction by brilliant BIPOC, LGBTQIA+, and disabled authors. We tell finely crafted, poetic, cinematic, messy, weird, hilarious, and swoon-worthy love stories—romance with a generous twist.

Titles by Generous Press include:

Someplace Generous
An Inclusive Romance Anthology
edited by ELAINA ELLIS and AMBER FLAME

Losing Sight
by TATI RICHARDSON

Forthcoming

Nearly Roadkill
by KATE BORNSTEIN and CAITLIN SULLIVAN

A radically inclusive imprint at Row House Publishing, Generous Press is built on joy and the conviction that all people should be cherished and free. Learn more at www.generous.press.